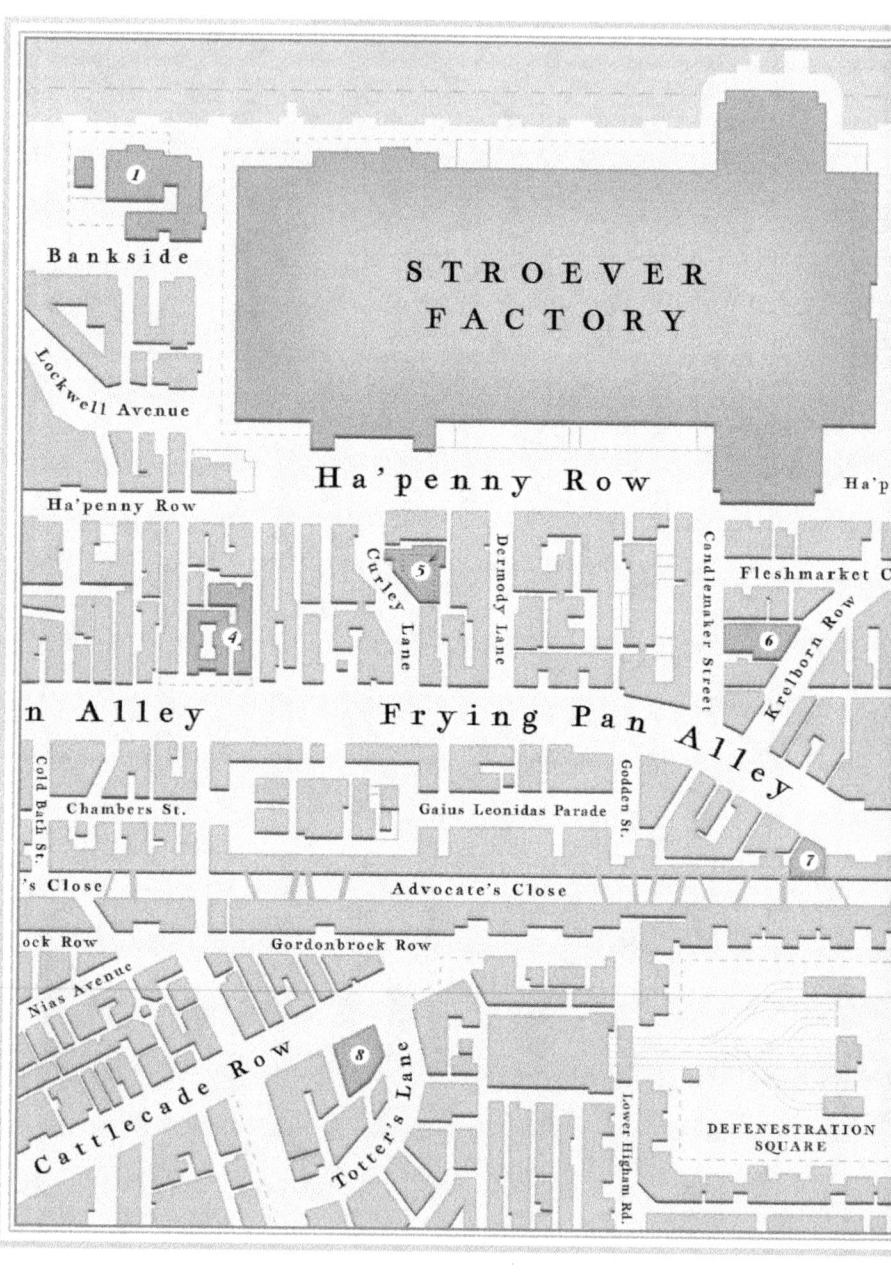

Bankside

1

STROEVER
FACTORY

Lockwell Avenue

Ha'penny Row

Ha'penny Row

Ha'penny Row

Ha'pe

Curley Lane

5

Dermody Lane

Candlemaker Street

Fleshmarket Cl

6

Krelborn Row

4

n Alley

Frying Pan Alley

Cold Bath St.

Chambers St.

Gaius Leonidas Parade

Godden St.

7

's Close

Advocate's Close

ock Row

Gordonbrock Row

Nias Avenue

Cattlecade Row

8

Totter's Lane

Lower Higham Rd.

DEFENESTRATION
SQUARE

KRANE McCARTHY
CATHEDRAL
(Devil Spare Him)

Limekiln Pl.

*ELSTRAN'S
PASS*

CHRONOMETER
DOCK

N

W   *E*

S

D1   D1

D2a   D2b   D2c   D2d

1 Stroever Residence

2 Harbourmaster's

3 The Beggar's Lantern

4 The Starwane

5 Graveyard

6 The Bridge-Maker's Daughter

7 The Drowned Merchant

8 The Old Parr's Head

...streets as long as whole cities unfurled...

...neighbourhoods the size of countries...

...boroughs the size of planets...

...The City, an entire universe in a gigantic metal box...

GLOSSARY

Things work differently in the world of KnockThrice. Here is a quick guide to phrases used regarding days, nights and fades.

Day – when the blazing gas-stars fly high
NightTime – when the bone-white sentinels roam
Fade – from sleeping to awake and back again
Tofade – this fade
Heri – the previous fade
On-the-morrow – the next fade
Primo – the first half of the fade
Fadenigh – the second half of the fade
Night Eternal – should the gas-stars never return, Devil Spare Us

THE DREAM-PEDLARS' PARADE

PARADE

MYRTHALI
BOOK TWO

MARK BOWSHER

BREAKTHROUGH BOOKS

Published in Great Britain in 2025 by Breakthrough Books.

www.breakthroughbookcollective.com

Paperback ISBN: 978-1-0687185-2-6

The right of Mark Bowsher to be identified as the author of this work has been asserted following Section 77 of the Copyright, Designs and Patents Act 1988.

This book is a work of fiction. Names, characters, places and incidents are either a product of the author's imagination or are used fictitiously. Any resemblance to actual people, living or dead, events or locales is entirely coincidental.

No part of this book has been written with the use or help of artificial intelligence. No part of this book may be used or reproduced to train artificial intelligence technologies or systems.

Cover design and interior typesetting by Ivy Ngeow.

Front cover image: © Lyall McCarthy, 2025

Map of KnockThrice: © Lyall McCarthy, 2025

PRAISE FOR THE DREAM-PEDLARS' PARADE

'*The Dream Pedlars' Parade had me hooked from the start - I couldn't put it down! The themes in this book are a lot darker than the first book but are handled with curiosity, empathy and sensitivity. I loved the character interactions between the four main group characters. There were twists and turns, villains that gave me goosebumps and moments of gentleness, kindness and humanity that brought tears to my eyes.*'
Emma Brand, author of Dial One for Revenge

PRAISE FOR THE BOY WHO STOLE TIME

'*An exhilarating, absorbing read. Rich in scope, in specificity. Full of wonder and adventure.*'
Irenosen Okojie MBE, author of Nudibranch and Curandera

'*Fizzing with energy throughout, The Boy Who Stole Time charts an unlikely hero's Odyssean-esque quest to save his mum from death. Twisting and turning from one adventure to the next, this is a truly magical book, masterfully written from a remarkably astute storyteller.*'
Ashley Hickson-Lovence, author of The 392 and Wild East

'*Richly inventive, readable, funny and moving, and you can't say fairer than that. A fantasy adventure in the classic mould.*'
Adam Roberts, author of The Thing Itself

'*A thrilling and emotional journey through a perilous land. The*

lead characters are dynamite together. An ordinary boy meets an extraordinary girl and throughout their magical adventure their friendship is tested. Time well spent!'
James Benmore, author of Dodger and Ask For Mercy

'A thrilling, immersive adventure. Superbly written lead Krish has the sharp wit and bravery of a teen with everything to lose. The setting Ilir is so evocative that it feels both familiar and yet otherworldly with a wonderfully realised eclectic cast of locals. Get onboard the Myrthali odyssey before they turn it into a TV series!'
Lucy Sullivan, author of Barking

'Marvellously paced and has a touch of absurd humour that recalls Terry Pratchett's Discworld. It also has a certain strangeness that reminded me a little of William Nicholson's The Wind Singer; it's not a straight-forward sword-and-dragon kind of fantasy. The writing is really sharp and the characters are all well-rounded and interesting.'
Will Andrews, Nothing in the Rulebook

'This sweet, inventive and well-paced novel is brimming with creative touches and wild originality. Krish's struggle against an impossible task but also his own flaws and weakness makes for a captivating read. I would highly recommend for anyone who loved His Dark Materials.'
Eli Allison, author of Sour Fruit

'Fantastic characters, world building and depth of story were spot on also the cover is so beautiful! This story reminded me of the stories of Arabian Nights/One Thousand and One Nights that I loved to read as a child. There are elements of The Boy Who Stole Time that will appeal to everyone.'
Bibliophile Book Club

ABOUT THE AUTHOR

Mark Bowsher is a proudly dyspraxic author and filmmaker originally from Gravesend. He's written four award-winning short films and scripted several chart-topping documentaries for Dan Snow's History Hit. His flash fiction 'The Hunger Wall' was featured in Fish Publishing's 2023 anthology and he's also contributed short stories to Breakthrough Books' anthologies.

He lives in Bristol with his partner, daughter and a mischievous cat. He once climbed a mountain dressed as Peter Pan and hasn't shut up about it since.

For Grandma

Who used her time well

And for Sam

Too young to die

Too rare to live

KNOCKTHRICE

There once was a Devil who danced in the world of light and hope. He made it a land of shadow and fear, painted the moon black as coal, and dipped the sun in the redness of blood. Dread rid the people of sleep. Only those full of hatred flourished in the Devil's darklands.

But a God came to that world and washed the wicked away. She brought warmth and light to the day, and a glow to the night. The Devil She banished to the world within which all worlds converge.

So, the Devil picked a door to another world. He rapped upon the door and waited a short time. A God answered and scolded Him for His intrusion. There would be no cruelty and greed in Her world.

The God behind the next door was much the same. And the next. And the next. Until there was but one door left.

The Devil dreamed of twisted grins, endless nights, creatures of shadow, terror reigning over all, lands sodden with blood.

But He did not want to be scolded.

Upon the last of the doors, He knocked only once then fled to a safe distance. When He returned, the door had not been opened.

He knocked a second time. He stepped away. Again, there was no answer.

One last time He knocked. This time He stayed close.

There was no answer.

The Devil knew that this world was His. He stepped inside and all light faded to gloom. He plucked dreams from slumbering minds to seed a living nightmare of iron and steel. Greed and lust and idleness drenched the land. All laughter was cruel and the Devil was happy.

The old name of this world is long since forgotten, but not so the tale of the Devil. And thus, the new name of this world was taken from the creature's tale.

Knock once!
Knock twice!
KnockThrice!
But no God will answer here.

1
THE CLOCK IN THE GARDEN

This was how life was for Krish in the time before he found himself sitting in a darkened room with a devil and a dead man...

He stared at the little circle of digits high up on the wall of the hospital ward. The second hand moved heavily around the clock face, brushing indifferently past the numbers. Krish couldn't shake the idea that he was drowning in a sea of wasted seconds. He sat there by his mother's hospital bed, her smile weaker than the gleeful grin of the creature only he could see, crouched in the shadows.

Time and reality were trickling away from him.

Days were nothing but hospital visits, school – where knowledge never hung around in his brain for long – and stilted conversations with his dad and his sister Joshi over dinner, prior to drifting off to bed.

The tumble of days.

The spreading inkblots of night.

As he lay in bed at night, his hand ready to turn off the bedside light, his mind unwinding, he could scarcely recall the events of the day. What had he had for breakfast? For dinner? What had he been wearing? What had he even done today? Life right now was purest banality.

But as he flicked the switch, he was there: his duvet billowing like the canvas of the Goonmallinns' tent; the prickly heat in the sweat-filled air of Sccifihr'ei, the breathing palace, under the gaze of the thousands upon thousands of eyes belonging to the intertwined prisoners; the strange creatures of the deep; a pang in his Achilles' tendon as he recalled the teeth of the Vulrein, beasts of shadow, biting into his leg; the great sun bearing down on him; the sand in the corners of his eyes; the single grain of Myrthali, the Sands of Time, landing in his palm to return him home; her eyes, Balthrir's, deep as the Night Ocean, her lip curling up in mock disgust, inviting him to enjoy a joke with her. At his expense, naturally.

All these memories were more vivid than whatever he had done during the day.

No.

How could any of his adventures in Ilir have been possible? He ran his fingers along the smooth, raised line on his neck where the turning FireHawk had seared his skin so he could confirm it had all been real.

'Gateway closin'...'

The shadow spoke. The devil, the creature who had sent him to Ilir to find the Myrthali. Her bent, ancient body like charred wood. She was willing him to travel to the next world – KnockThrice.

'Closin' soon! Soon! Ya'll miss yer chance!'

He fought to block her out, but his mind flitted between three faces in the torment of a sleepless night: the cruel grin of the devil, the adamant smile of his mother ('Urgh! It's only life! Cheer up, everyone!') and *her*. Balthrir. The wizard who'd become his friend in Ilir. Who'd pretty much given up her entire life to help him to complete King Obsendei's seemingly impossible tasks. The girl who called him a 'bloody idiot' at every opportunity. Her features were losing their detail in his recollections, but nothing of her essence had faded in the face smiling back at him in the comfort of the dark.

Rain poured down on the garden outside his window. Without further hesitation, he launched himself from his bed, went downstairs and watched the rain turning the floodlight on and off over the gleaming green wonderland of their narrow garden.

For reasons he couldn't explain he wanted to be out there, drenched. He looked at the clock on the wall of the kitchen: 3.46am. In the morning it'd be the 17th. No. It *was* the 17th already. April was marching on relentlessly towards May and he'd still not left for KnockThrice. His mum was improving but not enough to warrant a hospital discharge. And he saw the truth behind her brave smile. He had to go. To do the devil's bidding and find the Myrthali in order to save her. No time would pass while he was away. He wanted to set off imminently, but something was holding him back. Her face. Not his mother's, Balthrir's. The face he'd never see again.

'Closin'! Closin' soon, little'un! Hurry! The Myrthali'll slip through our fingees...'

He ripped the clock from the wall, carried it across the room and opened the door. The sound of the torrential rain was amplified, with droplets splashing onto his bare face. He strode into the garden.

Lines of rain pummelled him like rivers pouring down from upon high. He stared down the corridor of green, the hedges on the left which had been in desperate need of a trim for months. Their branches twisted their dark green leaves across the divide to the beds of tulips, muscari and alliums on the opposite side.

The rain soaked his clothes, and cold bit through the dampness. He felt his tension washing away.

Krish's parents loved their garden. Every day when the weather was good they could be found out here. Mum had always said, jokingly, that she should work in the garden because it was a woman's job. Dad would laugh and say something about it being the twenty-first century and namedrop Emmeline Pankhurst. Mum would then joke that the ghost of Sophia Duleep Singh had appeared to her in a dream and told her that Dad should cook tonight while she tended to the garden. And Singh had definitely specified that he should cook the spicy veggie pasta meal that they all loved, too. Dad would say that that was odd, because Singh's ghost had cropped up in his dream too, complimenting him on his takeaway ordering skills.

'Yes,' Mum had looked up at Dad at this point. 'She called you a lazy bugger in my dream as well!' They'd laughed and got on with the gardening together. On these occasions, dinner would always be made by whoever got hungry first.

Krish clutched the clock, his muscles tensing, the plastic rim indenting his fingers. The rain drenched him; pattering on his skin, roaring in his ears.

'Hurry! Hurry! Those seconds is tick-tick-tickin' away!' The voice of the devil urged him on.

He hurled the clock into the undergrowth, turned, re-entered the house, and did not look back until morning.

§

There were whispers as he descended the stairs towards the kitchen at breakfast-time. He tuned in, just in case they were about his jaunt to the garden in the early hours. They were not.

'Okay! Okay! I get it!' said Joshi. 'But, geez... is she sure?'

'Well, I don't know,' their father said. 'It's her decision but... I don't know...'

'What's going on?' said Krish as he entered the room.

Joshi and Dad turned suddenly and stared at Krish.

'Nothing,' they both said.

'Er... okay...?' said Krish. 'What kind of nothing? Some kind of nothing to do with Mum?'

Joshi put her hands in the air defensively and left the room.

'What?!' said Krish.

'Nothing,' said Dad. 'You don't want to be late. Get dressed for school!'

Krish indicated his school uniform. 'I am dressed for school.'

Dad nodded. In the odd silence between them he untied and retied his tie for no reason that Krish could fathom, then tapped his watch vigorously. Unsatisfied with the watch, he stared up at the blank space on the wall where the clock used to be.

'Where the bloody hell is that clock?' his father said. 'Where has it got to?'

Krish kept his eyes on his cornflakes.

'No idea,' he said.

2

THE GIRL IN THE WOMAN'S CHAIR

Summer, or at least an incredibly convincing impression of summer, arrived abruptly at the start of May.

There had been a fierce mixture of both warm days and grey, rain-drenched days throughout April. The month ended on a particularly doom-laden afternoon, which featured a brief bout of snow pelting down on Krish as he went to the shop to pick up some milk.

A few weeks later, spring had given up trying to break winter's gloomy grasp on the world and let summer swoop in early to take charge. Now people were strolling around in shorts and sunglasses, grabbing ice creams, cider and disposable barbecues from the shops, or hanging around in parks working on their sunburn. The air was hot, and thick with the smell of charcoal and sizzling sausages.

Dad had even stopped grumbling about everything the Prime Minster did. Krish swore that if Dad saw the PM dunking a biscuit in his tea, he could give him and Joshi a prolonged lecture on how he was doing it all wrong. He was now talking more and more about taking them to the park or the swimming pool or the Science Museum in London, and various other places that weren't the hospital. Things were feeling relatively normal, though every time Krish caught himself smiling, he was overcome with guilt.

'Time! Time's runnin' ou—'

He slammed the door of the utility room shut and left the shadow in the company of the washing machine and the ironing board. He stepped outside, the warmth of the sun striking him immediately, and headed out to the park to hang around with his friend Jess.

§

When he got back, Krish brushed the grass off his school jumper as he walked through the front door. He entered the kitchen which was stiflingly hot after a long day of the sun streaming through the patio doors. He realised straight away that Dad would not be bothered by the state of his school clothes.

His father was sitting at the table, Joshi opposite him. She was sat in the chair at the end of the table, their mother's normal seat.

Joshi and Dad where both turned slightly towards the door. They had been waiting for him. Their eyes were serious, cautious and a little fearful.

'Krishna...' Krish rolled his eyes at being full-named by Dad. 'There's something we thought we should talk to you about.'

'It's about Mum,' said Joshi. Why was she sitting in Mum's seat?

'Of course it's about Mum!' Krish said. 'Everything's about Mum!'

Actually, they hadn't talked much about Mum for some

days, but he was too angry for logic right now. Mainly because he had an inkling that he was about to be asked for his opinion on a matter which had already been settled.

'Your mother's going to have a procedure—'

'You mean an operation?'

'Yes. She's going to have a procedure to see if they can remove some of...'

There was a big pause. They seemed to be waiting for him to react.

'We thought you should know,' said Joshi. She was sitting in Mum's chair, fanning herself with a pull-out from a magazine.

'So,' Krish began, 'that's... good...?'

'Yes, it's good,' said Joshi. 'Of course it's good.' *Why was she in Mum's chair?*

'We just thought you should know,' his father echoed his sister's words.

'Okay. Good. So, why are you telling me?'

'Obviously they hope it'll be successful,' said Dad, 'but there is a risk.'

'So we thought you should know,' said Joshi conclusively.

Krish stared back at them. 'Is there any more...?'

Joshi's eyes rested on the table for a moment then returned to stare directly at Krish. He noticed for the first time that she was clinging to her phone. It was never far from her but right now it looked primed and ready for use. She took a deep breath, picked up the phone and unlocked it.

'I just think you need to read this article on grief,' she began. Krish's phone buzzed as the message arrived. He sighed. Since going to university Joshi had become addicted to 'articles' and was now constantly forwarding links to them at any given opportunity.

'Grief?' Krish expelled the word from his mouth. 'She's not dead yet!'

'Krish!' was the knee-jerk reaction from their father. 'Why are you using words like "yet"? Why are you doing that? Huh? She has good chances!'

'The word "dead" was fine then?! The word "grief" is fine?!' said Krish.

'It's about anticipatory grief,' said Joshi. 'It's about feeling grief for something that hasn't happened... yet... or... might not ever happen but—'

'Yeah, I can tell that, *Josh!*' said Krish venomously.

'Hey, don't fire all your unprocessed trauma at me, *Krishtopher!*'

'My un-whatted what?!'

'Okay, Joshi, Krish,' said Dad, 'I think we need to stop talking about your mother like she's definitely going to... well... erm... She has good chances!'

'So you keep saying!' said Krish. 'Come on, give us some stats!'

'Okay, look, I don't have—'

'I just think we need to consider Krish's mental health.' Joshi was saying this directly to their father, as if Krish wasn't even in the room.

'*My* mental health?!' shouted Krish. 'What about *your* mental health, and *Dad's* mental health and *Mum's* mental health?'

'Krish! This is serious!' said Joshi. 'They say one in four people will have a mental health problem at some point in their life. It's really serious! It's only recently that people have started treating it as seriously as they would a physical illness, but it's still *actually* killing a lot of people! D'you know it's the leading cause of death in men under 45 in the UK?'

Krish's eyebrows shot up so far he was surprised they didn't fly off his forehead altogether. 'Oh, great! So now not only is Mum dying but I'm going to kill myself as well!'

Their father was trying to butt in but struggled to find the words.

'I was just giving you a statistic!' said Joshi.

'Yeah! A statistic *specifically* about men killing themselves, Joshi!' said Krish.

'And it might be exacerbated—'

'Eggs-*what*-erbated?!'

'It might be made worse by your dyspraxia.'

'Oh, great! Now *you're* the expert on dyspraxia?'

'The Dyspraxia Foundation website says children—'

'I'm twelve! I'm not a toddler!'

'That children and adults with dyspraxia might be anxious and have low self-esteem.'

'Yeah, they also say we may be easily distracted, bad at time management and leave awkward pauses before answering questions!' As soon as he'd said this, he realised he'd picked everything he knew applied to himself. 'And what did you mean by "unprocessed trauma"?'

'From your diagnosis. From you feeling so different from everyone else. So alienated. From all the times you were picked on.'

'Oh, come on, Joshi!' said their father. 'Krish said he was never picked on that much!'

He glanced over at his son who looked down sheepishly. Krish guessed he'd always played it down to protect his parents.

'Anyway, we're going off topic,' continued Dad.

'Look, Krish,' said Joshi, 'we just thought—'

'*You* just thought?' Krish spat back at his sister. 'Both of you decided how you were going to tell me this because I might be too young, too immature to handle this?'

He'd fought Goonmallinns, Vulrein and FireHawks, and crossed blades with the bloodthirsty would-be monarch Vira, but being patronised by his older sister was too much.

'Well, you're not acting all that mature!' said Joshi.

'You're not Mum! Why are you acting like Mum? Why are you in her chair?!'

'Oh, suddenly everybody in this house owns their own chair?!'

'Pack it in, you two!' Dad re-joined the conversation.

'Right,' said Krish. 'Okay. Thank you very much for letting me know. Any more details of this "procedure" that you'd like to make me aware of?'

His sister, sighed deeply, threw her arms up in the air and rolled her eyes. 'Don't be like this, ya little prick!'

'Joshi!' Their father glared at Joshi before turning back to Krish. 'There is a risk, there always is for someone in your mother's condition, but it's minimal.'

'How much of a risk? Will you just start using some actual facts! Like "chances of survival"? What are we talking about here? 80%? 70? Less?! Crack out the percentages, padre!'

Joshi burst out laughing, bent over double, her eyes wide, cupping her hands around her mouth. Krish had had enough of his sister for one day and stormed off towards the stairs.

'Krish!' she said pleadingly. He stopped and watched her face soften. 'I...I'm sorry. I'm not trying to be Mum. I'm just... I'm just worried about you.'

Krish's anger dissipated for a second. 'I'm sorry too. But I just want to say... Yeah. I know full well that depression and anxiety are real.' He thought of the beasts of shadow, the Vulrein, chasing him down every time he shut his eyes. 'But I've got to find my own way of dealing with this.'

And with that, he left the room.

Krish slammed the door shut and threw open his window, allowing fresh air to pour into the stifling room.

'Alright, alright!' he said to the creature who he knew was waiting in the shadows. 'But I'm not going alone this time!'

3
THE DEMON IN THE CHAMBER

'Ya can't takes no one with ya!' said the devil.

'Why not?' asked Krish.

'Thas rules! More people that knows, more likely someone be findin' out about our Myrthali!'

'I'm not talking about someone from this world.'

'I tolds ya! Tolds ya there's nothin' ya can bring back! Almost nothin'! Just Myrthali. Thas spell! Who's ya wanna be takin'? Who's ya met on yer adventures?'

'Almost nothing?'

'Ha! Nothin' in that world you wents to. Nothin' in the world ya's goin' to now!'

'Then wha—'

The devil squinted. She looked at him. Into him. She reached out and gripped his face with her charred black fingers. Her skin was cold and paper-thin. There was barely a scrap of flesh separating her fingertips from the bone beneath.

'Ya met someone! Someone yer likes!' Krish flinched. He could feel his heart beating fast, his breathing intensifying. He wanted her out of his head. He pushed the devil away from him and she fell back onto the floor.

'None of your business!'

For a moment she looked hurt, crumpled in the corner between a pile of dirty clothes and his chest of drawers. She was light. A small collection of brittle old bones in a thin casing of skin, a mottled old robe draped over her from days when she was younger, taller, stronger.

'This person meant somethin' to ya...?' With one hand against the chest of drawers, she pulled herself up, her eyes wide. For a moment she wasn't cruel. There was something else in her look.

'She was different. In a good way. I mean, not that it mattered, but she sort of spoke weird. A bit like a lot of the kids at school, but almost more old-fashioned.'

'The spell I cast does some translatin'. Usually jus' the common tongue. It's not always the most accurate. And that world of hers is an old one. Long, long ago!' A playful smile snuck its way onto her face. 'So, when ya says different, does ya mean special?'

Krish's expression hardened. 'I'm not going on my own. You have to find a way for her to come with me.'

She stared at him for some time, her expression unchanging.

'No. That gateway is closed. There is no other way. She is gone.'

Krish stood tall. He wouldn't let her know how he felt. Something inside of him wanted to cry, to scream. If she was rifling through his thoughts, she'd struggle to locate the image of Balthrir's face. He buried it deep.

'I'm not going alone.'

The devil considered. Her eyes narrowed. There was a low, gradual rumbling from the back of her throat and, all of a sudden, she let out a growl and threw something across the room.

'There is a way!' she spat out. 'Now ya's a skipper between worlds... there's a way. But it won't work! Is hard! Little chance ya'll succeed!'

'How?'

'Ya've got to go deeper! Darker! Somewhere ya've almost been. Somewheres *everybody's* almost been! But the barriers between worlds blocks most goin' any further... Not you though, little 'un... Not I!'

'What do you mean?'

'When next ya has a bad dream, ya thinks somethin' dark, yer mind goes places ya'd never go near when ya were awake... chase it! And when ya's cornered that dark, dark thought in that dark, dark place... chase it deeper still... Think 'bout reachin' under yer pillow, really, *really* concentrate on reachin' under that pillow in the real world and the dream and then... and then ya'll be there...'

'Where?'

'The demon chamber.'

'What...?'

'Only one thas ever been found. Only hunters of the Myrthali can find it. Some has got in, but never succeeded in gettin' what they desires. Dark magic there! Darkest magic of all! Ya can create... things. Not life. Never life! But somethin' like it. Like an echo. Like a vision of one ya's known before set in flesh and bone. Tied forever to the original. They is still in their world, just where ya left 'em...but ya has a version of them. Runnin' parallel! Is hard! And even then, is only temporary. Dark magic is not as powerful as Myrthali. Not like somethin' that can save yer mumsy, stretch her life out longer. Is a cursed half-life, quarter-life, quasi-life!'

'How is that—'

'Imitation of life, but company nonetheless. Ghost of the livin'. But if the original dies... so does the imitation. It's not easy. I sees yer passion, yer commitment. Might be possible but...' She shook her head. 'Not somethin' I be recommendin'... I tried it once... I tried... but no...' The devil whimpered. She was lost in her remembrances.

'How does it work?'

The devil's eyes were glassy, haunted. 'The dead. Corpses of the lost. There is more out there than any wants to believe. All ages, shapes, colours, sizes. In the demon chamber, ya mixes together all the emotions, all the traits, all the ingredients of a person – ya describe 'em best ya can. Like tryin' to find the right words to search for a thing on yer magic intersplat – ya gets the closest result ya can find. And if ya does it right... ya finds 'em. Makes a connection. And if they allows ya—'

'I get to talk to Balthrir?'

'In a way. Comes to 'em in a dream. In the morning, they forgets. But it's permission ya's after. For a part of them to come with ya. And they picks a body.'

'So she'll look different?'

'Not nessacelery. So many bodies out there – I'd cry for 'em all if time hadn't rid me of tears...' The devil's head was bowed, looking more tender than she'd ever appeared before. 'So there'll be one out there somewhere that looks almost the same. A dead person that don't need that body no more.'

'My mum... could this magic...?'

The devil jolted out of her trance. 'I told ya already – no! Is no use. If Mumsy dies... the echo dies. Just imitation! Looks real! Breathing! But not for long. Dead can't stay undead for long. Weeks, months, maybe one whole trip round the sun for this little world of yers... but not long. Myrthali can't extend it neither. So, ya goes to the demon chamber, ya finds the ingredients, ya learns words – I teaches ya! – and ya begs demon. Is a cruel, cruel spell! Evil stuff! Is not life! Understand? Will be *like* them... but not them. Imitation. Temporary.'

Krish breathed it all in. He nodded. 'And anything else I should know?'

'One thing... this imitation can *only* exist in the worlds of the Myrthali. Arrives with ya and disappears when ya leave. Will come alive again when ya arrive in the next world. Can't come back here. When there is no more worlds of Myrthali... they is done! No more! Ya wants this? Is demon's magic! Devil's magic!'

'Devil's? Like you?'

That sly, old smile. Cruel teeth of yellow stained with black. 'Worse than I, and I is the worst I know. To create a life that in't permanent——'

'Is any life permanent?'

'Now ya's gettin' clever!'

Krish and the devil stared at each other for a long time.

He thought of Balthrir. He needed to see her again. It wouldn't be her, it wouldn't be real, but just to see her...

'Ya wants to do this?'

'No.'

'Then ya wants to be alone?'

'No.'

'Then ya has a decision to make...'

§

The light was out. Krish lay in bed, awake. Next door a barbecue was going on late and it was hard to tell whether the drunken banter between his neighbours was about to erupt into an argument or simmer down to nothing.

The words from the conversation with the devil were on a loop in his head.

'How will I find it? The demon chamber?'

'Hold that dark thought close. Chase it down. Keep thinkin' 'bout that pillow. Reachin' under it...'

As he lay there, several thoughts buzzed around his brain. Would she be real enough? Would it be fair to create someone who had such a limited life? How much like Balthrir would he be able to make her? What if Balthrir was already dead in her own world? The echo would never even come alive.

He brushed off these thoughts. It would be worth it just to hear her voice, see her face.

The night was as hot as the day. The argument next door seemed to be reaching an amicable conclusion.

His thoughts became jumbled. He imagined Balthrir in front of him. Those large, playful eyes staring unblinkingly at him, her lips curving up into a smile. What would he say to her now if she were here?

No. She wasn't here. He wasn't there. He was at home, in bed and standing next to her... where were they? Was he picturing Ilir? By the river, in the garden, a short walk from the palace they had just torn down together. Or was it...?

The waking world was fading fast. A dream was coming. He had to banish happy thoughts and find another, dark as death...

Chase that dark thought... deeper and deeper... then, in the real world and the dream... reach out... under yer pillow... and...

.

     ....

....

   ...

     .

      .....Mum?

      ....Mum?

...she ain't movin', mate.

    .....what?! but she was fine a minute *ago!*

   ......nah, mate...

    ... we were just playing cards *and....*

    .

  ....

    ....Balthrir?!

...at your service!

…..you never said that!

…..we should bury 'er…

…....but…..

….startin' to pong! 'ere. 'ang on — got a spell for this one!

..

.   .

…what? no! she's not….

…not your fault, mate… it was an accident.

no!

no!

NO!

…wasn't your fault.

…won't tell no one.

…it was an accident.

NO!

REACH OUT

I...

I...

I...

IN THE REAL WORLD AND THE DREAM

I'm sorry!

Mum...

UNDER THE PILLOW...

. . ..
. . ..
. . ..
. . ..
. . ..

This was not pure darkness.

This was eyes shut in a dimly lit room.

But his eyes were open.

The heat in the air wafted past and stung his eyes.

If this was a dream, he'd never felt dreams like this before.

There was a low, distant roaring noise. Far away, yet he could feel it on his skin. Like putting your hand up to the sun on a hot day and letting its warmth touch you, stretching out to burn you from 93 million miles away.

He could make out brickwork below him. He ran his fingers

across the rough textures and felt their grooves. They were covered in a chalk-like dust which clung to his skin.

That distant roar was coming from all around.

Another sound, different. A low growl. A moment later it was gone, as if he'd imagined it.

He looked around. It was clearer now, like a horizontal chimney. At the sides he had space enough to outstretch his arms. He started to stand but he couldn't straighten up without his head becoming acquainted with the ceiling. It hurt. The pain throbbed through his head. He wasn't used to feeling anything in dreams.

Things were becoming clearer still, yet a hazy orange glow added to the gloom. He ran his fingers over the walls, finding scratchy indentations. They felt like spindly characters, some forgotten language.

He sensed a pulsating light in his peripheral vision. He ventured forward to find the source, almost tripping over his pillow, which appeared to have come along for the ride.

He crept along the narrow, low-ceilinged corridor of brickwork until he located an alcove to one side. An earthen scent reached his nostrils. He crawled into the space. The ground here was blackened earth, hot to the touch. Something was buried just under the surface, emitting a deep ochre light.

He dug with his hands, the sodden black earth finding its way under his fingernails.

His finger came into contact with something solid. He couldn't quite determine the shape. As he pulled it out of the ground he could see why. He'd never seen anything quite like this before. He held what he supposed was a glass vial in his hand. It was stoppered with a cork, but instead of a long cylindrical shape the glass veered off in many different directions, creating clumps of long spikes and all manner of peculiar contours. A label, scrawled in near-indecipherable hand-writing read: 'IMPULSIVENESS'.

Balthrir. Yes. She certainly was impulsive. He remembered how the devil had instructed him. He returned to his pillow, removed the case, and slipped the vial inside.

He left the chamber and ventured further along the corridor. The shaft grew wider ahead. Another patch of earth. He dug deep and uncovered another shape. As he went to lift it out of the dirt, something sharp dug into his fingertip. He recoiled in pain. He returned to his excavation and slowly began to unearth a green vial made entirely of spikes. He had great difficulty finding a way to lift it up, using his fingernails to touch it. The label read: 'ANGER'. Yes. At times she was definitely angry. He slipped it inside the pillowcase.

He kept searching the brickwork corridors for more and more patches of earth. As he moved, the great roaring accompanied him everywhere, a nagging itchiness as he became aware of the heat of the star.

The next vial practically attached itself to him as he pulled it out of the earth. Dark green but it glowed a little in the gloom. The glass was split into many frozen tendrils: 'GREED'. She barely had a millilitre of this. He tossed it aside. No, perhaps he should add a little. We're all greedy at times. He kept hold of the vial.

The next vial was dark but beautiful, mesmerizing. He'd dug deep, sensed something was there. The vial was simple, slender and curved inwards in the middle. As he turned it over in his hand, it was black and white and indigo and emerald and maroon and aquamarine and sunset orange and many other colours all at once. It was wonderful in its simplicity: 'LOVE'.

He took another step forward and—

He saw it. A great, lumbering shape. The demon. In the

chamber just ahead of him. It evoked in him the kind of slow, creeping fear that has been there for so long, waiting for some malevolent force to awaken it. He could find no words, in the dream or in the waking world at any time after, to describe what he saw. He only knew three things:

He felt fear.

He felt guilt.

And he could not look away.

Something else became clear as the demon slunk away to one side to continue its pained growls: it hadn't seen him. It must have been blind. Krish had the curious notion that the creature, for all its strength, for all its cruelty, might have been frightened. Not of him, but of its own predicament.

The demon bashed at the brickwork with its bare, bloody fists, yet it didn't put all its strength into its actions. It seemed too tired to embrace rage. It had been here, alone and frustrated, for a very long time.

Demons harvest emotions, that's what the devil had said. *Once demon decides it has enough... it crawls away and locks itself up in a demon chamber in the heart of a dyin' star. It has emotions to feast on, but it can't get out. Not never! Only one chamber out there that I has heard of that any person has ever been able to infiltrate...*

As the demon disappeared down one corridor, Krish darted into the central chamber. He'd spied the glint of glass beneath the earthen ground.

He dug and dug and found many more vials: 'INTELLI-GENCE' – a white, straight baton with a few protuberances meandering off at each end; 'VULNERABILITY' – a small, peach-coloured oval which felt as if it would break; 'PARA-NOIA' – this one was hard to grip, a twisting deep purple shape covered with indented spikes. He gingerly placed them all in the pillowcase.

He also stumbled upon physical characteristics: 'HEIGHT'; 'WEIGHT'; and 'EYE COLOUR'. Many of these vials changed colour and shape as he moved them about in his hands. 'EYE COLOUR' changed from blue to brown to green to grey to black. 'HEIGHT' lengthened and shortened again.

Finally, he uncovered a vial of midnight blue. The vial resembled a crescent moon. An elusive speck of light was darting this way and that within; it was titled, simply: 'MAGIC'. Would he be able to give the imitation magical powers just like Balthrir's?

A scraping in the gloom. The beast was returning. It was getting nearer. He had to be quick!

He arranged all the vials in the dirt in front of him. He loosened the stoppers. He was ready.

The beast approached. It was terrible, fearsome, furious. In many ways Krish feared this creature more than the Vulrein. In time, he'd grown to understand how to let go of his fear, cutting off the Vulrein's food supply. But there appeared to be no rhyme or reason to the demon's actions. It rattled with rage, bashing and thudding its fists against the brickwork, shards of masonry flying about the chamber. Then it stopped and turned his way.

It sensed him.

Krish felt guilt. Could he go through with this?

He tried to remember the words the devil had taught him:

'I, erm... I demand of you, oh despicable beast... er... to turn your dark powers into light. Create an echo of a life I once knew. Bonded at all times to the original. And bonded to me in all realms where I seek the Myrthali, the Sands of Time, the dust the stages— sorry, er, *ages*, the dust the ages leave in their wake.'

The creature breathed deep, heavy breaths. Was it preparing to strike?

'If my friend of old should agree, I beseech you, bring forth another who will accompany me in times of light and dark. I demand this power of you, O wicked demon trapped within your chamber. I bring you blood and breath and all these which I have stolen—' He indicated the vials, '—and demand you... you bring... er, I mean, bestow this vision life.'

He began to open the vials, to pour small amounts of their contents into the air. Wisps of deep greens, mesmerizing purples, furious reds and midnight blues came forth: 'COURAGE', 'INTELLIGENCE', 'IMAGINATION', 'MODESTY' (only a splash of that one), 'REBELLIOUSNESS', 'INTEGRITY', 'LOVE', 'MAGIC'.

A swirling shape formed in front of him. Now the shades were more than colours. They mixed and mingled and became something beyond any hue. They remained vague, unfocussed, but there was something becoming definite, recognisable in the form taking shape before his eyes. A figure slightly taller than him, her hair braided, her robe long. He felt sure she was there, scanning him with her large, dark eyes.

She looked up, as if responding to an inquiry and, after some consideration, she nodded.

The demon's growl was long and fierce, but not loud. It bowed its head and the wisps became solid. *Those eyes! Balthrir's eyes!* They twirled and twisted towards him and vanished into his chest. Warm air filled his lungs. He breathed out heavily. He caught his breath but something inside him was different. As if a metal band had been wrapped around his heart.

Now the beast was bowed no more. Its blind eyes were aflame with the purest fury. It hurled its fists and bashed into the bricks. The chamber began to collapse.

Hurry! He had to think happy thoughts, which wasn't easy in the circumstances.

Her eyes! Her eyes!

The beast rushed towards him.

Krish reached out. *He'd see those eyes again! Soon...!*

The demon collided with him.

As he was dragged down to the ground his arm gripped the cotton and polyester of his pillowcase. He pulled himself up. The duvet cover shot over his head and his mattress slid underneath him. He rolled out of bed and fell onto the floor in a heap.

Still catching his breath, he noticed something unusual about the skin over his chest. For a moment, before returning to normal, it glowed midnight blue.

4

THE GAME & ITS PLAYERS

The next morning, Krish awoke and pondered how much of his visit to the demon chamber had been real, and how much had merely been a dream. He placed his hand over the skin on his chest that had glowed the night before. Could some part of his old friend really be there within him, waiting to take form in KnockThrice?

Some hours later, he and his family were engaged in a rather heated game of Cluedo in their matriarch's room at the hospital. The board was balanced precariously on Krish's mum's lap. Cards and tokens kept rolling off the board and onto the floor.

'You can't stay in the same room!' said Dad.

'Why not?' said Mum.

'It's against the rules! Joshi! Get the rules!'

'There aren't any,' said Joshi.

'Don't be silly!' said Dad. 'You had them earlier. That little booklet.'

'Erm, Dad,' said Joshi, 'I think you've actually totally imagined that.'

'No, no! You had it! A minute ago!'

'It's from a charity shop, Dad,' said Krish. 'It's probably—'

'You're imagining things, Ash!' cut in their Mum. 'My god, he's going senile already!'

'She got it from a charity shop in town,' Krish tried to speak again, 'there are probably loads of—'

'Get it on your phone!' Dad was now issuing commands in Joshi's direction.

'Erm, what did your last slave die of, Padre?' spat out Joshi.

'Malnutrition with his cooking,' said their mum.

'That doesn't make any—'

'Look!' Krish's voice rose above the burgeoning argument. 'Let's just make a decision. You can't just stay in the same room all the time. It's dull and uninventive. You have to visit a different room before you can go back to the room you just left, alright?'

Krish was greeted with silence. His parents and sister stared at him. They'd been sheltering in the familiarity of a family argument for the last ten minutes. It was better than talking about why Mum was still in hospital.

The silence stretched on. Joshi and her parents' eyes passed over Krish as if he were something new to them, as if only now they were noticing that he had changed rapidly in the last few weeks.

To his family, Krish was just the same unconfident twelve-year-old who rarely spoke up. But a moment ago he'd calmly yet assertively projected his voice over the din to make a surprisingly grown-up suggestion. In fact, it hadn't been a suggestion. He'd issued a command. No wonder they were eying him like someone unfamiliar to them.

A month ago, he'd vanished into the land of Ilir, fought off beasts of shadow, survived a firestorm and had a king kneel before him. He'd learned that when tired, angry, pushed to the extreme, he could be startlingly decisive.

But, as the devil had informed him, those months in Ilir had taken no time at all for his family. In this world, a second hand on a watch would not have moved, an eye would not have blinked in the time he'd been away in that tiny desert world. In truth, he was the best part of a year older. They had no way of knowing, but they sensed something.

Suddenly, he realised that he had been pressing his palm over his chest again. He lowered his hand, wondering if it appeared out of character to the others.

Joshi broke the silence. 'What, are you like the actual King of Cluedo now or something?'

Their parents laughed. Krish couldn't help it, he laughed along with them.

'Yeeeaaah!' A little giggle slipped into the word. 'Guess I could be!'

The game continued. No one lingered in a room for multiple turns anymore.

Colonel Mustard (Dad) was in the Conservatory.

'I think it was,' said the Colonel, 'Colonel Mustard—'

'So, you confess!' said Mum.

A few titters and then the Colonel carried on with his accusation.

'In the Conservatory with the revolver.' Nobody owned any of these cards, so the Colonel checked the pouch at the centre of the board. 'Yes!' he cried victoriously.

There was momentary excitement. Joshi threw down her cards in disgust. Krish berated his sister for being a sore loser.

The commotion died down. Everyone became aware of the fact that they were in a hospital and not playing on the dining room table as normal. They packed the game away. There was hush.

Polite smiles all round but Mum's expression was stoic.

'I have to make a decision in the morning,' she began. All smiles had abandoned their posts. 'Am I going to have this bloody operation or not?' No one seemed sure exactly who she was asking. Dad looked to his feet then back to Mum. Joshi sighed and wouldn't meet anyone's eyes. Krish blinked. His mother stared back at the three of them expectantly.

Dad and Joshi gave answers that roughly translated as, 'It's up to you'. This didn't seem to satisfy Mum. She turned to her son.

Krish sighed. 'How likely is the operation to succeed?' he asked.

'Quite likely,' Mum answered, 'but there'll still be chemotherapy afterwards. Sounds horrific! Could turn me into a bloody zombie! Walking dead!'

'And you don't want that?' The bluntness of Krish's question surprised his mother.

'No, but I'd rather be alive, Krish!'

'They said you're not a bad age to go through chemotherapy,' said Joshi, while Dad looked genuinely affronted at his children's abilities to discuss such a grown-up topic. 'Didn't they? So you're actually probably stronger than a lot of people who get it in their seventies and eighties and stuff.'

'Yes, Joshi,' said Mum with a sigh. 'But you see... because it's spread to—'

'Please! Let's have this discussion later, huh?' Their father's interruption to the matter-of-fact conversation his children had been having with their mother sparked a silent argument.

Joshi glared at their father; she was 20 and had done enough adult stuff to fill a swimming pool, so yes, she could talk to her own Mum about life and death, thank you very much. Dad stared back at his daughter, then pleadingly at his wife. Mum viewed the man she had married long ago with love and admiration, but there was disappointment there also. And defiance.

Krish watched the three of them and he knew full well that she'd come to a decision already. She was keen for everyone to feel they had been consulted, but ultimately, she'd do as she damn well pleased.

'I'll make a decision in the morning,' said Mum.

The morning would come around too soon, thought Krish. He too had made up his mind. It would be a long time until he saw their tomorrow.

5
THE HOUSE BY THE TRACKS

Droplets of water dangled from the black rubber seats of the swings. They hung in the nooks of the chain-links holding the seats in place, dotted the metal of the slide and clung to the blades of grass. A line of conifers sheltered the park from the harsh halogen of the lampposts, though a little light filtered through and dwelt in the raindrops.

No one was here at this hour. Or that's how it appeared from the street outside.

Nobody saw the figure climb the fence and jump into the park. Krish had left a video playing on his laptop in his room and snuck downstairs while Dad was in the loo and Joshi asleep. The video was ambient background music, the sort of thing his sister would study to, and was three hours long. No time would pass in the real world while he was gone; he'd be back long before the music ran out.

As he'd tiptoed through the kitchen, a flicker of an idea passed through his mind. A plan to outwit the devil and give Mum some Myrthali without having to visit another world. He stopped for a moment to take a sandwich bag from one of the drawers. In the half-light from the hallway, he produced a teaspoon from the cutlery drawer, took a spoonful of sugar from the ceramic jar on the worktop, poured the sugar into the sandwich bag and sealed it. He'd placed the sandwich bag in his pocket and slipped out of the back door into the damp night.

He was now wandering through the empty park. He slung over his shoulder a carrier bag containing a pair of smart shoes and a suit his parents had bought him for his cousin's wedding. He scanned the gloom.

Krish sensed something. It was hard to spot a shadow hiding amongst other shadows, but he stared right at it, discerning a familiar shape in the dark between the trees ahead. The boy held out his hand, waiting to receive.

'Give some to me,' said Krish.

The creature clutched the golden vessel around her neck, her eyes narrowing.

'I'm not going until I can give her some,' Krish argued.

'Ya're not the one who makes the terms, boy,' said the devil.

'She's dying.'

'So you'd better go now so ya can come back. No time will pass, this ya know.'

'And what if I don't come back?'

'Then that would be a shame for ya and for me and for old Mumsy. Best come back.'

'Do you know how many times I was almost killed in Ilir?! The number of times I was nearly burned alive or drowned or fell to my death or... or got skewered by—'

The devil was pacing from side to side, bashing her head with her hands.

'It's a wound!' she said. 'A wound that's healin'! I gave ya plenty of time! But ya has to go now! Tonight! Or it'll close!'

'Why can't I take friends? A-a group of us!'

It was less a laugh, more a scowl that erupted from the devil's throat. 'Like anyone's believin' ya! Here, in this world of yers, there are more ways to reach the worlds where the Myrthali hides, but they is small! Only one can pass through before it heals. Closes. Gone. Besides, ya'll not be goin' alone...'

The devil nodded in the direction of Krish's chest. He lay his right hand flat against the patch of skin on his chest which had glowed midnight blue. The devil clutched the vessel containing the Myrthali he'd collected in Ilir. The quantity she'd thus far refused to split with him.

Krish realised that he and the devil were now distorted mirror images of one another. Krish lowered his arm in revulsion.

'B'sides, I knows where yer goin',' the devil tapped her head. She was rifling around in his thoughts again. A picture of Balthrir surfaced in Krish's mind. Her dark skin, braided hair, and large, round eyes staring into him. He sensed the devil, with her uncanny ability to rifle through his mind, had caught sight of the image.

'Very pretty', said the devil delicately.

'She was more than pretty,' Krish blurted out.

The devil smiled broadly. 'Come! Quick! I sees ya're packed! We's got to go!'

'But—'

'Don't ya worry! This time ya just have to go to one city. Ya never leaves it. Trust I!'

Trust I was exactly what made Krish doubt the creature.

'I is tellin' the truth! Ya'll see and ya'll understand! She meant a lot to ya.' The devil spoke with uncharacteristic softness. 'This "Bal-tear".'

'Balthrir!' A feeling soared inside Krish and then crashed to the pit of his stomach. He'd never said her name out loud to anyone in this world before. It didn't feel as if it belonged here.

'It'll take a little time for ya new friend to form,' said the devil.

Krish wanted to change the subject; he felt too awkward thinking about what it would be like to meet this Balthrir-like person.

'So who's this person I'm meeting?' said Krish. 'In KnockThrice?'

'Ya needs to get arrested.'

'Sorry, what?'

'Ya needs to get to the prison. There's one big 'un, nears where ya arrive! That's where she's waiting.'

'And what about getting out of prison again?'

'Thas yer problem.'

'What?! No! That's ridiculous!'

''Snot 'diculous! This is KnockThrice! Many thieves, many villains! Peoples always breaking out of prison!'

Krish wasn't convinced. 'And who am I actually looking for?'

'A name won't do ya no good. She lost it. Long, long ago. It won't help ya find she.'

'This really isn't helpful.'

'Ya'll know who it is. She's ancient. Ya'll find she.'

The devil was fidgeting with her fingers. For once Krish was the one to read her mind.

'You do know her name,' he said. 'You know who she is, don't you? Why won't you tell me? What are you even doing? You're seriously telling me you're just after more Myrthali to live longer? No... no! I don't believe you! You're lying! What will you do when you get all the Myrthali? What are you planning? Where are you keeping the rest of it?'

The devil narrowed her eyes and became like a statue. Her gaze piercing, eyes unmoving.

'Ya pick one question, boy. One! And maybe I'll answer it... maybe... but then, we go. Wound is healin', I's tellin' ya...'

More questions raced through Krish's mind. He picked one that had been niggling away at him since that night at the bottom of the shaft in Sccifihr'ei.

'Myrthali... does it restore you?' he asked. 'If you're close to death.'

'Ya think someone with all their organses ripped out or their head smashed in is gonna hold back death with a spoonful of Mrythali?' said the devil. 'Can't go on livin' if the body's broken.'

'Well, no but... when King Obsendei died... I didn't see it, but it sounded like he kind of... dried up and turned to dust... or something. Like taking Myrthali hadn't just stopped him ageing, it had kinda... What's the word?'

'Rejuvenated?'

'Rejuvenated! Yeah! Like it had rejuvenated him slightly.'

The devil hadn't moved. Her expression was unchanged.

'Yer askin' a question or just checkin' the answer?'

'What? Oh! Erm... you mean the Myrthali, if you keep taking it, it *does* restore you? A little.'

'Next time, ask a question that ya're not already certain ya know the answer to. Come!'

§

The copper-green bars of the fence's paintwork were flaky, with touches of rusted metal. The devil skipped through a gap in the fence and Krish squeezed after her. They were standing in a muddy alleyway which ran along the back gardens of a row of council houses. There were no streetlights.

The alley veered to the left. There were no lights on in any of the houses. They were all grey and dead. Where was everybody in this part of town? The row of houses ended and they followed a narrow path defined by a high wooden fence on one side and a chain-link fence on the other. Krish looking down into a wide channel where the railway lines were. A train crossed at high speed, taking no notice of the world it was passing by.

Krish and the devil reached a partially collapsed wooden fence at the rear of a house. The devil climbed over her and stepped into the garden. Krish followed with much trepidation.

Piled high in the garden were several dozen bin bags, some ripped open by hungry mouths. There was no stench, no maggots that Krish could see. Just a musty tang to the air. This mountain of black plastic had been here for some time. A rusted washing machine and a chest of drawers stood broken nearby, both stained with mould and twisted slightly from the elements.

The devil approached the back door. 'Come,' she said.

Krish stopped and looked at the frosted glass on the door. There was a pattern like rain frozen stiff, with patches of green mould on the inside. No lights were on within. This place had died and was rotting away.

'You're coming with me?' said Krish.

'Yes,' said the devil.

'Why?'

She did not answer.

'Someone we're meeting in there?'

'No,' said the devil. She stared at him, almost pityingly. She needed him, for some reason. She was asking him a question with her eyes. Permission to continue? He didn't know. He'd never seen the creature behave this way before.

She was not bullying him into doing something, for a change.

She proceeded to find a cushion on the ground, damp and discoloured, and held it against the glass. Then it picked up a large stone and hit it against the cushion, to muffle the sound of the impact. It was weak. The glass didn't break.

'Help me, child,' said the devil. 'The years have treated me harshly. Now they are growing short, and my body knows it. Wearin' a bit thin.'

Krish was perplexed at her sudden vulnerability.

'The Myrthali,' he said, 'the stuff I brought back from Ilir... did you take any?'

She looked up at him. The meagre quantity of light that lit this dire place made a home in a glint in her eyes. 'No,' she said. 'I waits 'til ya comes back. I'm sorry, child. Sorry for what ya's been through. And what ya's gonna go through now.'

'Why do you care?'

''Cause it hurts! Time! Needs more! For she! Yer mumsy. For I! I tries to treat ya fairly. I takes no more 'til ya comes back with it all. And I's sorry.'

'It's okay.'

'No. I's sorry for this place ya're about to enter...'

She managed to smash the glass on the second try, as the sound was deadened by the cushion. The rest of the street was undisturbed by Krish and the devil. Her hand reached through the broken glass and opened the door.

Inside the air was stale as if it had been trapped in there for some time, growing old and festering. Tin cans and magazines lay discarded on the kitchen floor. There was a smell like beef stock cubes or dog food. And something else. Like putrid meat that had rotted then dried out, the smells absorbed by the walls themselves.

The devil led Krish through another frosted glass door into

the lounge. The curtains were drawn. He could make out sofas and various items scattered across the floor. His feet brushed past magazines, newspapers, cardboard sleeves from microwave meals.

'Who lived here?'

The devil did not answer him as she climbed the stairs. 'This is the place,' she said. 'The gateway closes soon. Has to do the ritual quick. Is simple. Has to be here. In the house of a dead man.'

He knew it. He'd known it from the moment he'd stepped into that rubbish heap of a garden. Somewhere, sometime ago, someone had died here. And they had never been discovered. No one could have set foot in this house before them. They had broken the seal on a tragic time capsule.

The smell was getting worse.

'Don't ya worry,' said the devil. 'I won't leaves ya this time. I stays here so ya's not alone.'

'Thank you,' was all Krish could think to say, though he wasn't all that sure he should be thanking her for anything right now.

He could see nothing. He followed the sound of the devil as she slunk up the stairs. The floorboards creaked as they crept across the landing. For a moment he lost the devil and then he heard light footsteps again moving across bare floor. He turned right and made out a shape in the dark. A door, half open.

He walked forwards. This place filled him with horrors. Every shape he could make out in the gloom was another nameless terror. Items that were most likely entirely stationary or not there at all scuttled about in his imagination. This was where you could fear the air itself. The stench of rotten meat, with scents very much like cat litter and rotten eggs, was worse here.

A sound somewhere between a crack and a tear cut

through the air and the smell of a struck match reached Krish's nostrils. He could see the room in the dim orange glow of the candle the devil had just lit. Then she lit another and another. She carried on until six were lit and she spaced them out around the room. He hadn't even noticed that she'd brought anything into the house.

'Ya changes,' said the devil.

Krish stayed in the shadows and changed into his suit. It wasn't an easy task in the half-light but he'd rather the devil didn't look. She paid him no attention.

The shoes were heavy and uncomfortable, making him feel even clumsier than usual. He placed his clothes into the carrier bag he'd brought with him.

'You'll take these back home?' said Krish, not wanting to set foot in this house ever again.

'I'll pops them into yer room. No one's a-seein' me.'

Krish nodded. He was trying hard to block out the stench.

He now had a clear view of the centre of the room and the far wall. In the bubble of light, he could make out bare floorboards coated in dust and a small window looking out onto the dark street outside. The devil sat and hugged her knees. Krish followed suit.

'Just watch the candles,' she said as she stared down into nothingness. 'Thas it. Watch until only one's left.'

'And then?'

'Keep watchin'.'

'And when I arrive, I need to find this... person? This old person in jail?'

'Yes. Thas what I said. Thas what ya does.'

Krish felt the scar, the smooth, elliptical patch of skin on his neck from the FireHawk. Was he ready to go through all of that again? Or worse?

He waited. He waited until the wicks of most of the candles

had burned down into messy piles of semi-solid wax and went out altogether. He waited and waited and waited. The night outside was dark and silent. He longed for the rustle of the wind or the patter of rain. Even the sound of distant traffic or footsteps down in the street would be of some comfort now in this dark and lonely place.

He could make out a bed along one wall. The farthest corner of the bed hid in the shadows. He could just discern, in his peripheral vision, a thin sheet which had been pulled back towards the wall. And a shape. He was sure there was a shape. Long and thin yet thicker towards the head of the bed. He swore his eyes weren't deceiving him in the fizz of the dark. He and the devil were not alone in this room.

'Fear,' said the devil. 'Fear is the gateway to this world. Fear and darkness. Not like the light of the pretty stars in your world. These be not real stars, not real light! Fear'll lead ya to that place. To the world where no god ever set foot...'

'Who was he?'

'Who?'

'The person who lived here.'

'Ya means the person what died here?'

'He must have lived first.'

'Yes, but thas not what this portal needs. This one needs the house of a dead man.'

'So, who was he?'

'Don't know. Nobody knows. Him's been forgotten.'

'That's horrible.'

'Yes. That's why I stays.'

'Thank you.'

'Ya's already said that.'

'So, I'll never have to leave the city?'

'No.'

'Okay.... How big is the city?'

Krish could detect that sly grin of the devil's slithering across her face.

'Now ya's asking intelligent questions, boy!' she said. 'City is all! This whole world is a city!'

'Oh. So it's a small world. If it's just—'

'Streets as big as cities in your world, if ya unfurled 'em into long lines. Streets the size o' cities, neighbourhoods the size o' countries, boroughs big as whole planets and the City... Oh, the City! This City, whole thing, the size of all there is in all the stars and galaxies and all the everything in your world, young 'un! One ginormous flat world trapped in a metal box of phenomenal size!'

'What?! But how—?'

'Many paths led to this world once. This sprawl, this nightmare o' bricks 'n' mortar. Those returning started concoctin' stories, tales – them things ya don't believe in! – on the roads of strange and distant worlds. Travellers said it was a world without gods. Just a Devil. Not like me! I knows yer calls I "devil"! No! Another Devil. The Iron Devil, they calls 'Im. One who knocked three times on the door of the world to see if a god would answer. KnockThrice, ya see? None appeared so He danced His merry dance of cruelty all through the lands.

'There was a God once, some say, though She slept deep below ground. She awoke as the Devil built His streets, and He rammed a bolt through Her heart to keep Her underground and out the way. Ha! Gods, devils, doors! All nonsense! Mostly. KnockThrice be its name to us. But to the people of this world, is just the City. 'Cause, to them, thas all there is.'

'But—'

'Concentrate! The candle!'

One candle remained. In the room there was only darkness and that shape, that smell. The dimming light of the candle. Krish kept his eyes fixed on it.

The candle flickered but did not die. He kept looking straight at it. The only light left in his world.

In the hope that the devil did not see, Krish pulled out the sandwich bag containing the teaspoonful of sugar and slipped it under his tongue. In his haste he made a hash of the job and half of the bag ended up on top of his tongue, but he managed to close his mouth and completely conceal the bag. In the few seconds this act took to complete, his eyes never turned away from the candle.

The tiny teardrop of light stared back at him. He swore the blue at its core had gone. And it was no longer flickering. It was growing. It was coming towards him. Then there was a low roar, building and building...

The candlelight grew bigger and bigger. The roaring noise filled his ears. He scampered backwards, his hands guiding him in the blackness. The wooden floor was gone. His hand didn't find the cold ridges of the bare, splintering floorboards. They landed on smooth, hot metal. The speck of candlelight was now a mighty glass globe above him. The roar was deafening him and the smell of hot oil, metal and sweat filled his nostrils. The luminous globe was so close it seemed to be right next to his eyeball, but Krish could see now that it was a gigantic object hovering some way above.

He did not like this world. Before he had simply appeared in a new world in the blink of an eye; a beautiful and dramatic landscape surrounding him as if he'd always been there. But this world had crept up and enveloped him.

As he scrambled backwards through the gloom, his mind begged for more light, but when he got his wish, he immediately regretted it.

6

THE STRANGERS ON
CHRONOMETER DOCK

Amber light turned to a blistering yellow-white.

Krish was blinded.

The heat and the light were one now.

The great glass globe was looming over him. He struggled to focus on it as purple dots danced before his eyes. He blinked in the glare. The shell of the star was covered in an assortment of cables. Straight lines all over suggested it was constructed of curved rectangular panels. It billowed steam.

He could feel it all around him now, this new world. And smell it. The stench! Mixed in with the gas puffing from the gas-star overhead were a plethora of other smells. Coffee, spice, vomit, rum, sawdust, urine, the damp fur of livestock and salty sea air drifting in on a breeze.

Under the low rumbling of the gas-star approaching him from above were sounds of shouting, commands being roared, mocking laughter, the bleating of sheep and goats, the clang of bells, footsteps, the creak of ropes, hammers colliding with metal, the slurp of water and in the distance a tumultuous barrage of tuneless music.

His left hand was wet. It was in a puddle. Instinctively, Krish moved his hand and fell onto his back. He felt the plastic sandwich bag slip to the back of his mouth. His gag reflex kicked in and he turned onto his front and managed to cough out the bag before choking on it. More mocking laughter, this time directly at him. As the thunderous metallic star passed overhead, he turned to take in the world of KnockThrice.

The pandemonium of this place was a million worlds away from the near-silent, serene sensation of arriving on a mountaintop in Ilir. This world towered over him; brick blackened with smog, tall gables on narrow buildings. The whole of the endless street (or as much of it as Krish could see) was comprised of lean structures, the buildings appearing to be holding their breath so they could all fit.

The dwellings were all of different heights, though many featured identical crests depicting a frying pan on a red and gold background. Krish saw the sign at the end of the street. As with Ilir, he was surprised he could understand the language. It read: 'Frying Pan Alley'. This place was broader, longer and more exposed than any alley he'd ever previously encountered.

Filthy cobbled streets below bustled with depraved figures in black and grey attire. Some played music, with drums, violin-like instruments, stringed frying pans, harps, accordions and many musical organs emitting overly loud tunes, jingling, distorted melodies that were perhaps meant to be cheery. At the same time, dogs and cats and other creatures (Krish even spied an elephant far in the distance) danced to the amusement of the alcohol-infused crowds pouring out of the nearby rum palace, The Bridge-Maker's Daughter.

Ornate horse-drawn carriages passed by, spraying perfume into the streets, but the sweet scents were quickly swallowed up by the rising stink. The extravagantly dressed occupants of the carriages paid the people of the street little heed. Some held their noses.

The sounds and smells of this place were biting into Krish. Foul and rotten scents mixed with the sweet and sickly aromas from the bakehouses and bars along the street. Fresh fish mingled with rotting meat and vegetables left to decay by the drains. The stench of sewage emanated from the drains and gutters.

He also noted one thing about most of the inhabitants of KnockThrice. In Ilir white people had been the minority, but here this was reversed. He sensed eyes glaring at him.

This world was too much, and he was embarrassed to admit to himself that he'd do anything to be hugged by Mum right now.

Krish turned his attentions back to the sandwich bag he'd just coughed up: the teaspoonful of sugar was still inside it. He'd succeeded. He slipped it into his pocket.

'Cup o' the red stuff for yer friend, matey?'

Krish turned to see the origin of the voice which had just spoken to him.

A man appeared in a floppy top hat of grey flannel with a matching grey cape. He seemed only a decade or so older than Krish, and sported some impressive sideburns.

'Lookin' a bit peaky! Tell ya what, 'ow abouts I takes ya down to Fleshmarket? I knows the butcher there, ya takes a cup, gets some of the red stuff straight from the abattoir, straight outta the beasty, 'fore its 'eart's even stopped beatin'! Best for what ails ya! Gotta 'ave fresh and my word ya don't even 'ave a cup! Tells ya what; five to get in *and* for the cup. Cure ya friend in no time!'

Krish couldn't take it all in: this world, the man, his insistence that he had a friend who...

It was like he'd snapped out of a daydream and remembered everything. He clutched his chest. He turned, his eyes full of hope, to see...

The shape didn't look like anything. Not really. His eyes just couldn't focus on it. No one else paid her much attention either. She, his companion, the 'imitation', was impossible to focus on. She was just a body-shaped entity made of fuzzy dark flesh lying on the...

Krish realised with great embarrassment that she was naked.

'I'll give you whatever you want for your cape!' said Krish to the man in the floppy hat.

''Ow much ya got?' the man asked, sizing Krish up.

Krish thought quickly; he had no money that would work in this world. He looked at his watch. Telling the time here would not be of much use to him. He removed it and proffered it to the man.

'Take this!' said Krish.

The man's eyes flew from the watch and back to Krish's face in less than a second. 'Ya're on!' He practically threw the cape at Krish, snatched the watch, and vanished into the chaos of Frying Pan Alley.

Krish approached the shape. Every now and then her face came into focus, then quickly slipped out again. She winced in pain, then fell back into her slumber. Her braided hair was a tad shorter than Balthrir's. Did she look like her? He thought so. He couldn't tell how much of what he was seeing was really there and what he was projecting from recollections of his friend in Ilir.

He draped the cape over her and led her away from the hustle and bustle of Frying Pan Alley.

'Come on,' he said. His companion moved with him, still crouching, but not looking up.

The roar of the gas-star was still there as it thundered

across the sky at a snail's pace. The tubes hanging from it were even more noticeable now. Was that another star in the distance moving in the opposite direction?

They arrived at the mouth of the street. He and his companion stepped into a junction that opened out straight in front of them to reveal an incredible vista. Frying Pan Alley and its neighbouring street were raised roughly 100 metres above an expansive dock. It was so vast that Krish was reminded of standing on a hill in London, watching the curve of the river Thames and the skyscrapers of the city beyond.

Before him was a gigantic, curved dock with hundreds of ships travelling clockwise around the water. He counted twelve enormous wharfs spaced out equally like the numbers on a clock-face. The view in front of him was spotted with wet and dry docks, factories, shipyards and waterways for the ships in the circular dock to come and go from.

Straight ahead of them, just at the junction between Frying Pan Alley and the perpendicular street, was a rusted cast iron sign, bold black letters on white, which read: 'Chronometer Dock'.

There was a gasp of pain from his companion, under her grey cape. Krish led her to the adjoining street with a row of fishmongers on one side. The opposite side was a broad canal which fed into a waterway between the streets ahead. Across the canal the street dropped away to overlook Chronometer Dock. A merchant ship was being raised with a sturdy black iron crane from the dock below and lowered into the canal.

The stench of fish was worse than anything on Frying Pan Alley. Fishmongers rushed forward, each proclaiming their fish to be the freshest, but quickly recoiled at the sight of the dark, fuzzy shape staggering about under the grey cape.

Being a few years older than Krish, Balthrir was a little too heavy for Krish. He'd eaten a full dinner and pudding before leaving this time, to make sure he wasn't weak from hunger, like he had been in the first few days in Ilir. But his energy was dwindling from supporting her. He spotted an empty handcart covered in a few old rags, its rear leaning on the ground at the mouth of a dark, narrow alley. Nearby were several market stalls. Surely all he'd have to do was steal something from one of the stalls and they'd be arrested with haste. Gently, he lay Balthrir down on the cart.

Now Krish began to panic; KnockThrice was more overwhelming than any city he'd ever visited. And bigger. If each street on its own was as big as – what was it the devil said? *A whole city unfurled* – how long would all the streets of London be if you placed them in a row? Hundreds of miles? Thousands? Were all the streets here hundreds or thousands of miles long? His friend breathed heavily in her sleep. What should he call her? Balthrir? 'Balthrira' – that had been her real name, but she hadn't liked it. Perhaps 'Thrira' would work. It didn't roll off the tongue that well, but it would do until he could ask her what she preferred.

'I-I-I-I'm sorry,' he muttered. 'I didn't... I didn't think about how painful it would be. O-o-or how confusing. I'm sorry.' Krish felt that all the strength, all the confidence he'd built up in Ilir was fading fast.

No. He'd only been here for a few minutes. It had been bewildering in Ilir and it would be so again here. The stalls were a couple of metres away from the cart at the mouth of the alley. If he could provoke them, he could quickly run by to Thrira and she'd be apprehended also as an accomplice. It was a perfect plan. What could go wrong?

7
THE MAN, HIS KNIFE & WHAT
HE TOOK WITH IT

Krish stepped towards the market stalls and was greeted with the odours of the fishmongers' produce. He was concerned about Thrira but he tried not to panic. This was where he'd gone wrong before. She was only a metre or so away. This time he'd be patient.

At least this world was more familiar than Ilir. The pubs, the newsagents and the coffeeshops all looked like historic buildings from his own world, slightly newer. The ships sailing around Chronometer Dock looked similar to ones he'd seen on a regatta once along the Thames.

But then the gas-stars rumbled overhead. They were much smaller than the sun in his world, much closer and more artificial, with their panels and pipes.

The shadows here were something to wonder at too. People could have three or four, depending on how many gas-stars were nearby. Of course, some shadows were fainter than others or would move at different speeds depending on where the gas-star casting that particular shadow was at the time and how fast they were moving.

Then Krish spotted another tell-tale sign that this was not his world. The devil had said that KnockThrice was encased entirely inside a metal box. He peered over the waters, past Chronometer Dock, and saw in the distance a sheet of metal of unimaginable size. The great sheet stretching up beyond his field of vision into darkness. It was a sickly shade of darkened yellow, dotted with patches of rust. He saw a gigantic rivet and far above the start of another, the rest fading into the void above.

He must have arrived at a part of the world right on the edge of existence, unless there was anything beyond the walls of metal which imprisoned the vast City. The idea filled him with unknown terrors.

Krish peered over his shoulder, back to where he'd left Thrira on the cart, the rags mostly obscuring her. He felt tethered to the spot; he didn't want to be too far away from Thrira.

Patience...

He saw a toppled stack of newspapers on one of the stalls. He picked one up and browsed the front page:

We respectfully call your attention to our well-known

CELLULOID STARCH

ANTISEPTIC

Destroys **germs**, protects from **contagious diseases**

✽ D R . S M E D L E Y ' S ✽
ELECTRIC SHOE REMOVER

EASTLEIGH STREET GAZETTE
proclaims this remarkable device

· A REVOLUTIONARY INNOVATION FOR OUR TIMES ·

The front page was almost all advertising though there was the odd headline scattered here and there:

Calle Cartouche to Withdraw Aid
First Minister Ricardo Murillo cancels aid packages to Győr as Ankaran conflict brews. *Cont'd p9.*

Stormraids Lead to Hike in Meat Prices
Padstaff Wharf Livestock Co. set to rise in price by up to 3% as stormraids continue. *Cont'd p4.*

Exchange Programme Enters Third Week as Night-Time Looms
Ban on coinage continues during economic uncertainty, but NightTime declaration 'overdue', says senior minister. *Cont'd p7.*

Sentinels Spotted at Fenkle
Sentinel receiving pre-flight maintenance accidentally

caught on film by amateur portraiture photographer on Fenkle Row. *Cont'd p2.*

Krish peered at the image under the last headline. The grainy picture was of a partly open metal slide-door, revealing a semicircle of blackness, set against a shadowy grey backdrop.

'Hatpies!' cried a nearby hawker. 'Get yer hatpies! Freshly baked by my missus's fair 'ands this very primo!'

'And what missus would that be, John Curran?' said a dark-skinned middle-aged lady.

There was a coy, playful look upon the lady's face. Her figure was round. She wore a plaid dress of orange and yellow with a loose-fitting tunic, falling off one shoulder.

The hawker John Curran seemed a good decade older than the lady, with spiky grey hair all over his weathered face.

'Ay, your determination to be a free woman'll lead some to mistake you for those women who takes a penny or two for love,' said John Curran. 'Not that no one spends pennies no more, young Quarley. Hope you've got yours stowed away some place safe. Don't want to be the one to trigger Night-Time, do ya?'

Quarley smiled to herself, toying with her collar. ''Course not.'

Krish looked past her to the cart of hatpies. A cart painted black with gold lettering declaring the price as K5. The pies were stout cylinders of pastry with a slim base like the brim to a top hat. They were steaming and Krish's stomach gurgled. Being arrested for stealing hat-shaped-food might not be the worst plan.

Krish glanced at Thrira asleep on the cart. He slowly placed the newspaper on the ground and inched towards the pie stand.

'You'll see, John Curran!' said Quarley. 'Once NightTime is declared people'll stop savin' up and they'll be spendin' again.'

'Exchange programme's killin' me!' retorted John Curran. 'Folk wantin' to exchange bits o' coal for pies – do me a favour! Ya know how long a batch takes to make?'

Krish neared the pie stand. John Curran glanced at him for a moment but was too involved in the conversation with Quarley.

'It's been a good, long day,' said Quarley. John Curran winced warily at her. 'Years since we seen night. Devil's weak. Economy'll crash when it crashes, not when He wills it so!'

'Take a bath in your mouth!' snapped John Curran.

'It's true!' Quarley shouted back. 'Devil's no more than a god with pointy ears, if you ask me!'

Krish picked up a hatpie and turned the hot pastry over in his hands.

'Ha!' spat out John Curran. 'You're just a common street philosopher, Quarley m'girl.'

Krish threw the hatpie a little way into the air and caught it again. He did this a few more times but John Curran was too preoccupied. What did you have to do to get arrested around here? He turned abruptly and went.

A jab of guilt shot through his body. The argument had concluded rather suddenly. He felt eyes on his back. He turned back to face John Curran.

'Just gonna leave without exchangin', boy?' said John Curran.

'Er... yeah,' he said with all the conviction he could muster.

John Curran just looked down and laughed. Krish felt furious at the man mocking him. He hurled the stupid pie directly at John Curran and pastry, meat and vegetables splattered across the side of the cart. John Curran looked up at Krish in shock. This was not getting him arrested and he was pretty annoyed at himself for wasting a delicious-looking hatpie.

John Curran marched over to Krish.

'I-I'm sorry, sir,' he stuttered. 'Arrest m—'

Krish was thinking that legging it was a better option but his reactions weren't quick enough. John Curran seized him by the wrist, pressing his large rough fingers into the joint.

'Clumsy little beggar!'

'Leave him, John!' screamed Quarley.

'What's gonna happen, eh?' John Curran spoke in a low, harsh voice and yanked Krish so hard towards him that he fell to his knees. 'What's gonna happen at the end of the fade when I've not sold nothin'? How am I gonna give the landlord my rent? Can't exchange my bed, eh? Filthy drummer!'

'John!'

'Get off me!'

'Clumsy little drummer!' The pain boring into Krish's bone was excruciating. He gritted his teeth but he couldn't pull free.

'Don't you call him that, John!'

'Don't have manners in your street, eh, drummer?'

'Take a bath in your Devil-damned mouth, John Curran!' screamed Quarley.

'Ah, don't you worry, Quarley – you're one of the good 'uns!'

Krish heard a nearby creak of wood. In horror, he saw a man wheeling the handcart into the dark, narrow alley, unaware that Thrira was asleep amongst the rags.

'Let me go!' cried Krish.

'Give over, John!' said Quarley.

'Not 'til I gives this dark little drummer an education,' said John Curran.

The man dragged him over to a barrel, almost yanking his

arm from his socket. He tried desperately to keep his eyes on the alley.

'Ya know how my father used to teach me a lesson?' said John Curran, seizing up a length of rope from on top of the barrel. 'He used to tie me to a post in the yard and leave me there 'til I screamed myself out.'

'John!'

'Get off!'

Krish wriggled and wriggled but John Curran tied the rope around his forearm, looped it around the barrel and pulled it tight.

'He'd leave me there for hours sometimes!'

'GET! OFF!' The rope tore into his arm. He saw Quarley rush across the wharf and into one of the fishmongers.

''Til the next fade on occasion. Let me get soaked to the bone by the raingrates.'

Krish gritted his teeth. He couldn't see the cart in the alley anymore.

'But I learned my lesson,' continued John Curran, pulling the rope tighter still against the barrel. 'Every time I spoke out of place, he'd point to the marks on my arm. And I'd always remember.'

Quarley sprinted out of the fishmongers, a meat cleaver in her hand.

'Tough times a-comin' when NightTime arrives, boy,' said John Curran. 'Ya'll thank me then for teachin' ya how cruel the City can be, ya filthy-skinned drummer.'

Quarley was approaching fast, the cleaver ready in her hand.

'And I reckons we're just one penny away from the crash...'

Quarley brought the blade down hard against the barrel and Krish felt sweet relief as the rope went slack.

As Krish hurtled towards the alley where Thrira had

vanished, John Curran grabbed hold of his arm, stopping him in his tracks. His voice was suddenly higher now, trying to be soothing.

'There, there, boy!' said John Curran. 'I'm just trying to teach you a valuable lesson. Life teaches us best the hard way!'

'Get off me!' screamed Krish.

'Devil Spare You, John Curran!' said Quarley.

'My father taught me the hard way, now I passes it on,' said John Curran.

'Get off!'

'John, leave him!'

'He's a spirited lad, but if he's going to walk our streets, he needs to learn respect and—'

'GET OFF OF ME, YOU RACIST PRICK!' Krish kicked John Curran in the shin.

The old man winced in pain, letting Krish go as he cradled his leg.

Krish raced towards the alley with Quarley close behind him.

'That red-faced old bastard likes throwing his weight around!' said Quarley as they ran. 'You got a friend on Advocate's Close? On the cart?'

Krish glanced at Quarley as they ran. 'Yes. I... I think.'

'We'll find yer friend. Come on! We got to be careful, mind. I 'eard MalJack Strode's abroad. Gave a beggar a taste of 'is knife, did old MalJack! He won't see no more days or Night-Times, that one.'

Quarley noted Krish's puzzled expression as they ran into the dimness of the alley.

'You don't know of MalJack Strode?' said Quarley.

'No,' answered Krish.

'You don't want to. He's the worst. Works for whoever's

payin' but don't care for the money. Malice is the scream-thief's only reward.'

Krish didn't stop to ask what a scream-thief was.

'You sound like you're from a street round here, but you didn't know about the exchange programme?' asked Quarley.

Krish tried to remember what he'd read in the paper. 'Er... kinda. Something to do with the economy and NightTime?'

'You must know! I heard it's the same even in whole other boroughs! Economy dips below a certain point, the Machines turn out the stars, bring out the sentinels, since they use less gas. All the governments throughout the borough are chucking money back and forth, tryin' to keep things goin'. That's why they brought in the exchange system – ya swaps stuff. No one's allowed to use money. Must be the same for you, no?'

'Kinda.'

'Kinda? Ha! Anyway, The Machines know. Soon as a penny's left yer pocket, they know. Somewhere, a penny'll be lost, spent, stolen, and we'll be seein' nought but sentinellight 'til the markets recover. And the way things are right now, we could see a very long night.'

Quarley kept running at a pace. Krish flexed his arm, getting the blood pumping back through it.

Gantries overhung the narrow alley, sheltering it further from any light from above. Washing hung from lines; dry and stiff. Silhouettes lingered on the walkways; it was impossible to tell whether they were looking down at the passers-by or not. Vague chatter and the cries of children could be heard. Infrequently, a gas-star would pass above and break the dismal spell over the alley, but never for more than a second.

'Why did he call me a drummer?' asked Krish, having a nasty feeling about the word from the way John Curran had practically spat it at him.

'Don't say that!' said Quarley. 'You don't have that word on your street? Some place where they mind their Ps and Qs, I'll bet.'

When Krish didn't respond, she continued.

'Nasty, *nasty* word. Many years ago, folk from Zuriweldt-straße took the fiercest, strongest fighters from the slums of Okanga or Nasra, captured 'em, enslaved 'em, forced 'em to be soldiers. Promised 'em food and better houses, although they'd been happy with their houses 'til Zuriweldtstraße burned most of them. So, they'd send 'em out first to make the enemy afraid. And they'd always pick one, some poor, retarded—' Krish stared piercingly at Quarley at her use of the last word but she wasn't looking, '—kid out first. They'd be made to bang a drum good and loud. Idea was to frighten the enemy. Make 'em sorely afraid of the strange, stumbling, dark creature sent out ahead, wondering what terrible savagery was being sent their way. The "d-word"' is nasty! *Nasty!*'

Ahead, Krish saw the abandoned cart. They rushed forward. A crumpled figure lay unconscious under a cape. He pulled the fabric back to see the face of Thrira, so much like that of Balthrir. The slumbering Thrira pulled the cover back to cover her face.

'It's okay, it's okay,' Krish whispered softly. He looked around him.

'Them fellas must 'ave been spooked,' said Quarley. 'Heard MalJack was close. Ditched the cart.'

Two top-hat-wearing figures, bent forward, their bodies creating a barrier between them and their hushed dealings, stood just out of the stale yellowy light seeping into the alley from an open doorway. Masking their high whispers was the patter of water, dripping freely and with haste from the bulbous pipes zigzagging above this section of the alley. The gas-starlight struggled to reach this corner of the City, the buildings tall, the distance between them slim.

To the other side of the doorway, a disinterested individual caped in shadow was leaning against the wall, carving an unseen object with precision.

Overhead, a young woman, a breathing ghost, rocked gently from side to side, looking lost while framed in her own window. Her eyes gazed indifferently into a place unseen; her mouth uttering words that were indiscernible. Nothing more than solemn, haunted syllables trickling down to uncomprehending ears in the street below.

'Ever sold the hide of a drummer, Chalker?' One of the questionable men raised his croaky voice a little to make certain that Krish and Quarley overheard.

The two men laughed while the disinterested individual continued his carving, the ghost-like girl overhead repeating a strange word in a breathy voice, over and over, the pitter-patter of her speech indistinguishable from the sound of the water dribbling onto the cobbles from high above.

'Give yer tongue a bath in yer mouth!' Quarley spat at the two men. 'MalJack's abroad!'

'I'll heed no warning from someone who's heeded no warning from the ravages of time, ya ancient spinster!' spoke the other of the two men.

The ghost-girl stared down at them, quavering as she inhaled deeply. The disinterested man paid no attention to any of them.

'Ha! Ya call me old, you grandfathers' grandfathers!' said Quarley. 'He is close! Don't say no one warned ya!'

The two men shook their heads and moved farther down the alley to continue their business. Quarley sighed deeply and turned to leave, shouting a warning at the disinterested figure caped in shadow, still carving, as she left:

'And as for you mister,' began Quarley. 'If ya know what's good for ya, you'll...'

Quarley stopped. Krish became more aware of the silence as he helped the barely conscious Thrira to her feet. Quarley was staring at the object in the man's hand. It was bone, disturbingly familiar in its shape. A finger, belonging to someone who only had a few years under their belt at most. He was scraping the last of the skin from the knuckle. Yellowed fat mixed with congealed blood and gristle. The hilt of the knife was dark as night.

The figure inched forward and straightened his back to reveal a man of startling height. He towered over Quarley in a tall top hat and tails. He must have been wearing those clothes for many-a-year. His outfit was frayed, covered in cuts and slashes. He smelt of sweat and sleeplessness.

Then the face: with eyes large and wild, bloodshot, he had the look of a man who had not slept for a hundred years. His teeth were yellow, and some were missing. His nose was as sharp as his blade, and black bristles of stubble grew unevenly in patches across his face like rat hair. A few dozen strands of long dark hair, wild and frizzy, shoulder-length, dangled from under his hat.

Krish knew without a doubt: this man was MalJack Strode.

MalJack dropped the dead child's finger to the ground. His insomniac eyes were fixed on Quarley. Terror shook her breath. She glanced at Krish and her look said *RUN*.

MalJack's arms rose a little way from his sides, he held the knife ready in his right hand. Quarley was reversing down the alley, but fear stopped her from fleeing. This was a man who would not strike until his prey began to run.

Thrira gasped in her sleep and MalJack smiled gleefully, detecting easy prey. The nightmare of a man raised his knife and rounded on Krish and Thrira.

Quarley saw her chance and went to run past MalJack. MalJack's grin broadened and he dived in front of Quarley, slashed at the air with his knife. He narrowly missed Quarley who stopped in her tracks. It was a warning. Krish watched helplessly as Quarley backed away a few more steps until she was almost totally eclipsed by MalJack.

Then the monster struck. MalJack's blade slashed through the air in front of Quarley. Her scream lasted the briefest of moments before a sudden and terrible silence. Krish saw her eyes full of terror, ready to pop from their sockets, but he saw no blood. She stood there, breathing and shaking.

Then Krish watched as MalJack transferred a small, dark, shining object from his knife hand to his free hand. It looked like a marble of clouded grey and black. He ran a finger over it, pushing across the glass with glee. It sounded for a moment like running a wetted finger over the rim of a wine glass, but then came the scream of Quarley as his finger moved faster. Quarley held her own throat in disbelief, her mouth open, robbed of the opportunity to cry out.

MalJack pulled the drawstrings of a pouch around his waist and opened it to reveal a score or more of similar marbles. As he dropped the dark marble into the pouch to join its sisters and brothers, the clang of glass on glass was married with a moment's chorus of screams. Then they were quiet. MalJack, the scream-thief, pulled the drawstring tight. He turned to leave.

A shot of fear coursed through Krish as MalJack went to pass him. Strength returned to Krish and he heaved Thrira to her feet. Her eyes opened momentarily but she hadn't yet the energy to become fully conscious. MalJack stopped. He turned back to Quarley, who was still rooted to the spot with fear. He leered over her.

Quarley's left hand rose again, crossing her chest. She held a tightly clenched fist just under her chin, hiding a metal object which had caught the light under the buttonhole of her tunic.

MalJack swiftly brought his knife up to the level of Quarley's chin and she gasped silently, her head thrown back in terror. Krish observed closely but was too terrified to intervene, concerned also not to abandon Thrira again. Delicately, MalJack cut a hole in the top of Quarley's tunic, just under the buttonhole. His eyes were hungry, his fingers even more so. The latter reached into the freshly cut hole and pulled out a small round silver item on a chain.

No, no! mouthed Quarley. Slowly the significance of the object and how its discovery was about to impact the whole City dawned on Krish. A single coin. There was playful malevolence in MalJack's eyes as he toyed with the coin. He tore the necklace from Quarley's neck.

A handful of seconds passed and then Krish heard the whirring of the Machines from deep below the streets. The lights of the gas-stars overhead began to dim. The constant roaring and billowing noise faded. Screams, agitated voices and hurrying footsteps drifted down from the gantries above. All about there were echoing cries of the same two words over and over...

'NightTime Declared!'

'NightTime Declared!'

'NightTime Declared!'

MalJack jumped into the air, grabbed hold of the low-lying gantry above and climbed up towards the roofs.

Figures flooded into the alley. Krish lost sight of Quarley. He stumbled back towards the main throughfare, supporting Thrira, who was blinking in and out of consciousness.

The crowds cleared as they reached the mouth of the alley. Then two men in dark blue uniforms sped from the wharf towards Krish and Thrira.

'MalJack!' cried one officer. 'Was he here? MalJack Strode?'

'You just missed him,' answered Krish, nodding behind him.

One officer shot off after MalJack, while the other paused before setting off.

'Thank you, boy!' said the second. And under his breath he added: 'Useless dream-drenched-drummers...'

Krish felt himself boiling with rage at the use of that word. Then he realised he had the perfect opportunity. 'Look, sorry but, er, not sorry...'

For a moment the officer looked puzzled. Then, with all the strength he could muster, Krish punched the officer directly on the nose. Or would have done if the weight of Thrira hadn't meant his punch landed on the officer's ear.

'What the bloody 'ell?!' the officer was baffled more than anything. 'Right, mate, you're nicked!'

'Wasn't me – was my mate!' Krish indicated Thrira as a line of officers marched up to them.

'Bloody cuff both of 'em!' said the second officer.

'Thanks!'

The officer gave him the oddest look then supervised Krish and Thrira's cuffing. Then he escorted them back in the direction of the street.

Nearby there were children staring at the sky in shock and awe at the vanishing of the light, many experiencing the enveloping cloud of darkness that was NightTime for the first time in their short lives.

Yet here is a child whose day is always night

A roof cuts her off from the world of gaslight

By the lamplight glow, she plays her merry game

Breaks the candlesticks, gives the Woman the blame

Pulls out the string, adds them to her collection

In a box in the loft, hidden for their protection

Builds webs like spiders', each big as a rug

The Woman below warms her milk in a mug

The Woman takes her up, tucks her into bed

Thoughts of finding the lost room filling her head

8

THE CAPTAIN, THE INVESTOR & THE SOFTLY SPOKEN MAN

A film over the water, like a sheet of steel laid across the surface, though without the gleam of silver. The declaration of NightTime banished almost all illumination usually caught in the waters of the harbour. The only brightness reflected on the placid surface was from the flickering gas lamps on the nearby streets, and the infrequent pinpricks of bone-white light from sentinels passing overhead.

The steely waters were cut by a great shape. The wrought iron bow of a ship churned the surface to ripples. The ship made not a sound aside from the creek of the rigging and the gurgle of water as it slid out of the harbour.

Ahead there were no lights as they glided in the direction of the great metal wall that was the end of this world.

The bow of the ship was like a dart. The mid-section was broader and panelled with varnished ochre deepwood.

Towards the forward section was a cradle for a large, gas-powered harpoon, cylindrical canisters either side of the shaft. The whole contraption was black metal, gleaming in the sentinallight. A chair was affixed to the cradle. Behind the cradle was a rectangular object, the size of a carriage, hidden under a tarpaulin, fastened to the deck with ropes.

The aft section featured guest quarters with large portholes. Basic crew quarters were on the lower deck. The cockpit sat on top of the rear of the guest quarters, a ladder leading up to it.

Captain Stavast, a man who'd seen many days and nights, stood at the helm. Wind and sea-street spray lashed his face for he'd removed the glass from the window. Why? Look closer: the snowy white beard was in stark contrast to his brown skin. He'd been born as pale as a sentinel but years of hard graft and exposure to the gas-stars' rays had left his skin dark as deepwood bark.

Look closer still. Amongst the creases, the wrinkles, the flecks of salt, indistinguishable from the patches of dried skin. See his eyelids, for the eyes are closed. They have not been open in a long time and could not be opened now even if he wanted them to be.

Look... look! They have rusted over the years and are now almost the same colour as his bronzed skin, but they are there. Two nails driven through each of his eyelids, keeping them shut for ever. Captain Stavast is blind as blind can be, yet still he sees.

Stavast takes the glass out of the cockpit of every ship he pilots. He knows the sea well. To his nailed-shut eyes the waters are unchanged from when he was a boy. The warmth of the gas-stars and the sentinels guide him. If Stavast detects the stars and sentinels are moving in irregular patterns, he relies on the scent on the wind, billowing out the great vents in the walls of the City; the sweet scents of Marzipan Row, or the foul odours of the oilworks of Bartoškov. If all else fails, a cupped handful of sea-street water will tell Captain Stavast where his ship is, down to the last metre.

Salt and iron are in his blood. The nails are slowly breaking down and entering his bloodstream. His immune system is hardy enough to cope with this, but the nails will not be fully absorbed while his heart persists in its beating.

'It happened in Calle Cienfuegos.' A man had emerged onto the deck, speaking to someone still inside the guest quarters. 'He was a rum-runner then. Working for a syndicate. Or so he thought. In fact, his client was none other than Wren Street Refiners, smuggling cane out of Calle Cienfuegos illegally. The Illuminator ran a front-page exposé revealing that the whole of Wren Street had been drinking rum made from smuggled sugar cane.

'The refiners denied they knew where Stavast had got the cane from. The good captain was on a ship bound for Calle Cienfuegos at the time. A telegram reached Cienfuegos first, saying there was a warrant for Stavast's arrest should he set foot in Wren Street or anywhere in the neighbourhood of Galver.

'The cane baroness in Calle Cienfuegos took out her anger at losing trade on poor Stavast and he was returned to Wren Street with a nail in each eye. The warrant for Stavast's arrest was rescinded. Public opinion was that he'd suffered enough. Not that it stopped anyone buying Wren Street Rum, now using Calle Santiago cane.

'Captain Stavast sank into obscurity and found himself in my employ. He remains one of the finest mariners in the whole borough.'

'Remarkable! Utterly remarkable!' said another man, who had just stepped out onto the deck from a cabin with his entourage.

The first man, who had been recounting the tale of Captain

Stavast, was middle-aged, slim and just below average height. His hair was straight, dark brown and thinning. A bald spot was slowly spreading from his crown. He had a pale complexion, small eyes and nose, and a well-trimmed lampshade moustache. He wore a pair of white gloves which were never removed.

He spoke slowly and precisely, never raising his voice. He was almost infuriatingly calm. Each cautious step he took may well have been calculated. He sported an unremarkable dinner jacket, white shirt and black bow tie. He wore black leather gloves at all times.

This man was known as Isri Stroever, investor and entrepreneur.

His companion was far more extravagant. A little above average height and noticeably over average weight. His arms, legs and chest were practically slender in proportion to his well-fed belly. His booming voice, animated gesticulations and indeed everything else about him was loud and lacking in subtlety.

He wore a bright white dinner suit, a black shirt and deep purple bowtie. A carnation on his lapel matched the colour of his bowtie. He was bald with a skirt of frizzy brown hair. And then there was the man's most distinct feature: a beard which split into four metre-long strands, each held up by one of four silent servants, his 'beard bearers', who formed a star around him.

This man was Lord Anders Ryker-Veere. He was also an investor and entrepreneur, but his wealth dwarfed that of his companion's.

'How long's he been in your service?' asked Lord Ryker-Veere.

'Since my return,' answered Stroever, prompting a nervous nod from Ryker-Veere. 'He's the best. No canals or river-streets for him. If it doesn't have salt and an undercurrent, it's not for Stavast. He'll hold her steady as we eat.'

Ryker-Veere nodded and marched briskly after Stroever, his beard bearers just about keeping up with their master.

'I must emphasise, old boy,' said Ryker-Veere as they walked. 'That your sudden and urgent invitation, telegrammed to me minutes after the gas-stars began to be extinguished, arrived, by the purest of coincidences, on a most uneventful fade. Your timing was impeccable. But I do not usually come when called. It's only out of respect to your late father that I entertained your request in the first place.'

'That is noted,' said Stroever.

A small wooden table with a chair either side had been placed mid-deck, just to the rear of the carriage-sized object under the tarpaulin. Two places were set with two crystal glasses, two plates under stainless steel cloches, a breadbasket and an open bottle of vintage vael. Ryker-Veere glanced at the tarpaulin and then the table.

'No servants?' he said.

'I prefer to cook for myself,' said Stroever flatly.

'What's that?' said Ryker-Veere, holding up a hand to his ear. 'You have to stay on my right, chum. Deaf as a post on the left!'

'I said I prefer to cook for myself!'

Ryker-Veere laughed heartily, yanking his beard bearers backwards with his head.

'I too fear assassination attempts. Very wise,' said Ryker-Veere.

'I don't fear assassination,' said Stroever. 'I have neither the wealth nor public profile that you do. Or, indeed, that my late father had. Assassins, so far, have taken no interest in me.'

'Ha! You would have learned a lot from your father.'

'Regarding assassins...?'

For a moment the jollity drained from Ryker-Veere. 'I meant in terms of employing staff. Chefs and the like.'

A small, playful smile danced across Stroever's lips. 'I know.'

'Come on, old boy. Meant no disrespect to you or your old man. You know that, chum.'

The smile lingered on Stroever's lips but there was little warmth in it. 'My father is gone. The City is a better place without him.'

Stroever placed a hand on Ryker-Veere's shoulder to gently encourage him to take his place. Then Stroever pulled out his chair and sat down. He had his back to the tarpaulin, looking aft. One of Ryker-Veere's front two beard bearers pulled the remaining chair to one side. Ryker-Veere stepped forward and went to sit as his rear two bearers moved the chair into place. Stroever poured the vael into the crystal glasses. Cool mist rose from the deep purple liquid.

'Crattlefish salad.' Stroever lifted both silver cloche domes at once with his gloved hands. Beneath each was a white and light pink striped shell, shaped like a star cut in half, on a bed of green leaves, dotted with the odd radish-like vegetable. Stroever picked up a small ornate hammer, no longer than his index finger. Ryker-Veere followed suit but stared at the miniature hammer with a look of utter bemusement. The tiny hammer was polished chrome with a fragment of yellow rock set into its head.

'Parrel,' said Stroever. 'Hardest known stone in the City.'

'I know what the heck parrel is, old boy!' exclaimed Ryker-Veere in mock-disgust. His head remained slightly turned to the right so he could hear Stroever with his good ear. 'Just never seen it set into one of these do-dads!'

Stroever placed the half-star shellfish on its back, found a tiny depression where the shell was weakest, and tapped it with the hammer. A crack appeared and Stroever effortlessly prised the two halves of the star shell apart to reveal white flesh within. Steam poured off the flesh and the aroma of lemon, parsley and butter filled the air. There was salt mixed in there too, but it was largely lost in the scent of the sea-street encircling them, spray spitting onto the deck. Stroever placed the two empty halves of the shell on a side dish.

Ryker-Veere passed the shellfish and miniature hammer to two of his beard bearers who performed the same operation as Stroever but in a far less swift and graceful fashion, struggling to coordinate the operation between them.

'Stavast caught these crattlefish himself this primo,' said Stroever, using a tiny chrome knife, one of half a dozen ornate implements set out on the table in front of him, to cut up the flesh of the crattlefish and mix it in with the salad. 'The salad is grown in my Ha'penny Row factory.'

'Yeees,' said Ryker-Veere knowingly, staring at the bewildering array of cutlery. 'A factory big enough for you to get lost in for years on end, what-what?'

Stroever gave a little smile. He did not look up from his plate.

Ryker-Veere gave several ostentatious sniffs. 'What's it flavoured with? Buttermilk, liona and resley?'

'Correct.'

'How the blazes do you get it in there?'

'Injection with a heated needle.'

'A what?!' Ryker-Veere held a hand up to his good ear again.

'A heated needle! Cauterizes on the way out, sealing the flavour in, ready to be boiled.'

'Hmm, some malign quality to your culinary methods if you ask me, old boy.' Ryker-Veere pointed at one of the tiny forks then at Stroever, prompting two of his bearers to cut up his crattlefish in the same manner as their host. 'And knowing the company you keep...' The two bearers had skewered a chunk of crattlefish with a fork and were now offering it to Stroever.

Ryker-Veere and his four bearers stared expectantly at their host. Stroever looked back at them and let out the briefest laugh from the back of his throat.

'If you're referring to Madam Ckrystafis, I assure you I've not acquired any culinary tips from her,' said Stroever.

'I'm sure you haven't, old boy,' said Ryker-Veere. 'Nevertheless, open wide...'

'As if I'd poison an old friend.'

'Ah! Now, let's be blunt! In business terms, we are merely acquaintances. Bonded by your father, a great man, my first and most significant benefactor. But I shall not apply automatic generosity to his son. You surely want to be treated as an equal?'

'I do.'

'Well, there you go then! My door is always open to the children of Isairis and Jane Stroever. But many years have passed since our first meeting, when you were but a child, the timid little nipper hiding away, so different from your boisterous patriarch. So, I shall always entertain a meeting, but I shall offer no special treatment.'

'Naturally, Lord Ryker-Veere.'

'Splendid!'

'But returning to our relationship, if we are being frank, you do not feel it has developed in recent months?'

'To be frank, also, no! I've been happy to give some small investment in your recent exploits, but your Ha'penny Row factory is now back on its feet for the first time since your father's untimely passing, so you hardly need me anymore. But friendship? No! I mean, this must be the first time we have dined together, just we two.'

'Two?' Stroever glanced at the four beard bearers.

Ryker-Veere did not acknowledge them. 'Servants.'

'Surely they have names?'

'Edris, Emese, Emna and Esna. Ask them which is which. Haven't the foggiest myself.'

'And you genuinely believe that I would make such an effort to curry favour with you to simply try and poison you in front of your entourage?'

'We are in a secluded spot at NightTime. You can never be too careful. Now, come on – here comes the choo-choo train...'

The bearer offered Stroever the forkful of steaming white crattlefish flesh. He took the fork, placed it in his mouth, swallowed without chewing, put the fork at the end of his row of cutlery and passed Ryker-Veere a clean one from his own selection.

Stroever then went to eat but Ryker-Veere was not quite done. He pointed at both crystal glasses full of steaming purple vael. A beard bearer took both, poured the contents of one into the other, swirled the two glasses together and returned half to the empty glass. Stroever drank.

Ryker-Veere blinked several times as he observed his dining companion.

'Composition-wise, old boy, your face is very much that of your father... if you had never once smiled, of course! Ha! Yes, there is none of the spirit of the old chap in there!'

'I am very much my own man, Lord Ryker-Veere,' said Stroever. 'Rest assured that I do not see our business relationship starting at the same point yours and my father's concluded.' Ryker-Veere blinked once in response. 'Tonight, we shall see either the graduation of an acquaintanceship into a friendship, or the death of a burgeoning partnership.'

'Indeed, Master Stroever, indeed.' Ryker-Veere raised his glass.

They toasted one another and drank. It was like drinking velvet. The cold aftertaste pleasantly cooled the throat.

'And then, in time,' said Stroever, speaking softly, as if to make sure his companion was listening closely, 'perhaps we shall change the City forever...'

9
THE IRON DEVIL & THE TICKING HEART OF G.O.D.

As they were cuffed and led away, Krish stared at Thrira the whole time. Her face was so familiar, transporting him back to the deserts and towns of Ilir. Her eyes were burned into his remembrances to such a degree that he could no longer work out how much was memory and how much was his imagination.

Thrira did not look up at him. Krish sensed she was becoming aware of the world all around but was not ready to respond to it.

The alley was darkening as the officers led Krish and Thrira back towards a row of fishmongers. The gas-stars continued to dim and descend through the sky. The words 'NightTime!' and 'NightTime declared!' poured down in cries from the people on the gantries crisscrossing above Advocate's Close.

Footsteps and screams of panic from the wharf grew louder. They emerged into the pandemonium of the waterside. People rushing this way and that. Parents dragging excited and confused children behind them. Paupers and nobility alike climbed lampposts and drainpipes, offering watches, belts, jewellery, coats or even shoes to the people living in the houses above the shops. Through the windows the inhabitants were taking what was offered and passing down bottles of beer or wine or spirits. All about, people were shouting at the sky, clutching their bottles and staggering about in exaggerated manners, revelling in the despair of the encroaching darkness.

'NIGHTTIME DECLARED!'

'NIGHTTIME DECLARED!'

'NIGHTTIME DECLARED!'

Wooden signs were being hung out of windows bearing these words, hastily daubed in white paint. Newspaper sellers marched through the streets, already holding one-sheet papers, the ink still wet, reporting news that no person could possibly be unaware of:

NIGHTTIME DECLARED!

NIGHTTIME DECLARED!

NIGHTTIME DECLARED!

Krish could see them more clearly over the dock now, the dying gas-stars, their lights fading from dirty yellow to darkness, descending over the skyline of the never-ending City. As their roars became low grumbles in the distant air, new dots of light rose above the streets. Small globes of bone-white with an afterglow of electric blue; smooth, with none of the hotchpotch of pipes which tangled around the gas-stars.

Chronometer Dock was a blur of activity as vessels' priorities changed. Some were being raised from the water, their undersides hurriedly being scrubbed, while other larger ships sped out over the waters, their decks aglow with lanterns.

The smashing of glass. Aggravated voices. Fights were erupting around them in sheer panic. The officers led Krish and Thrira around the chaos, farther along the street, away from Frying Pan Alley and into a large, open square.

The sign overhead read:

Defenestration Square

The buildings in the square were perhaps 20 storeys high, of blackened stone. The bricks as large as coffins, and all but a few of the windows were bricked up. Echoing about the stadium-sized square were the shouts and screams of prisoners in large cages spread around the ground. They hurled abuse at the officers marching about the place. Other prisoners were being cuffed, registered and filed into the cages.

There were also a number of rusty cranes lifting the cages onto the back of steam engines, sitting on rails leading into tunnels under the buildings on the far side. Prisoners clanged the bars with their chains, shouted mockingly at the guards, spat or even wept as they were hauled away. Though most prisoners were men, there were a few women, and he was startled to see that some of those in the cages were children. Several appeared younger than him. He swallowed a crushing feeling within, remembered all he'd been through in Ilir, and told himself he could be stronger than the tearful child in the cage passing over.

The deafening roar of the prisoners reverberated around the chimney-like square. Shadows of the prisoners shifted around the grey ground as the pale light of the sentinels passed overhead. Krish's nostrils were filled with the stench of sweat, urine and faeces. There was an iron tang in the air also – metal and blood. This place was an echoing, stinking hell.

''Ow long d'ya reckon NightTime'll last?' asked one prisoner in the queue.

'Dunno,' said another. 'Maybe it'll be over in a few fades. Like last time.'

'Rubbish! We're in for the long-haul. 'Eard they're stockpiling flour on Marstead Row. It'll be a long one. Some won't see starlight again...'

Krish gripped Thrira's shoulder tight. There was no response, she merely looked at the ground with disinterest.

An officer read out charges, but Krish was too distracted by Thrira to take them in. Coloured tokens were attached to their cuffs. He tried to ignore a great sinking feeling within. There was a buzzing noise emanating from somewhere.

Ahead, he could see the coloured tokens being removed. The source of the buzzing noise was revealed. While still standing in the queue, the prisoners' outstretched arms were being tattooed. He may face many horrors in this world, but Krish had a nagging feeling that explaining a tattoo to his parents could be worst.

You were imprisoned in the breathing palace. You've seen worse, he tried to convince himself. *You've got this.*

A stern woman, her grey hair tied back in a bun, addressed him from behind her desk.

'How do you plead, son?' she said.

'I, er, sorry – is this my trial?' said Krish.

'No trials during NightTime, child. Legally we have to note your plea, though. Paperwork.'

'Oh. Is it better I commit crimes during daytime in future?'

'As an officer of the law I must advise you against committing crimes at all.'

'Fair enough. Oh, and guilty. But I did say sorry before I did it.'

The grey-haired officer looked up at him for the first time. 'How old are you, son?'

'Er... twelve. Do you imprison twelve-year-olds?'

'If the poorhouses are full. Plus, the best pickpockets are your age.' She fleetingly gave a kind smile and pointed at his token. 'Your release date is in ten fades. Keep your nose clean and perhaps you'll be out sooner.'

She then ushered a tattooist forward. The tattooist

removed the coloured tokens from Krish's cuffs and noted the numbers. This was all too real, too fast. A stinging pain as the tattooist committed a series of numbers to his forearm in black ink:

382113
21f

And there it was. Staining his skin. The prickling sensation of a bloodless phantom wound. They were now marking Thrira. She lashed out in pain and confusion, her eyes only opening briefly, unable to comprehend her predicament. Terror shot through Krish's body, he rushed towards her but was held back by an officer. The tattooist, somewhat perturbed by Thrira's lack of clothing under the cape, found a leather strap and tied it around her waist, provoking more unrest from her. He continued his work, and when the tattoo was finished, Thrira was calm again.

Krish and Thrira were then stuffed into a cage with the other prisoners before they had time to react.

The door clanged shut. Many prisoners rubbed their arms, familiarising themselves with the numbers that they would have tattooed to their arms for the rest of their lives. A few beads of blood had risen from Krish's inked skin. He rubbed the blood off with his finger and then tried to work out if he could do the same for Thrira. There was no space for her to be slumped on the ground, so she was hunched over to one side, facing away from Krish. Her eyes remained shut, her hair plastered across her face.

A rush of nausea accompanied by cries of surprise as the cage jolted upwards. They were being raised into the air. He felt dizzy, his stomach churning, his gag reflex convulsing.

Then there was a crash of metal as they were lowered onto the back of a train.

Prisoners were becoming more and more distressed as officers fastened metal plates to the bars, blocking out what little sentinellight had made its way down into Defenestration Square.

'This is it!'

'Mumma, sorry. Sorry, Mumma...'

'I didn't do it! I didn't! Let me speak to someone!'

'No... no... no... please...'

Krish's nausea was subsiding only to be replaced with claustrophobia. He reminded himself that prison was exactly where he needed to be heading right now, but this world's eagerness to tattoo and imprison children was not something he had expected.

There was a hissing of steam building up as the minutes ticked on. He swore the engine would burst any moment. As the train began to move with a screech of metal and the clamorous cries from his fellow inmates as they adjusted to their fate. The chuffs of the engine sounded like the rasping breaths of a giant.

Krish spotted a narrow gap between the metal plates. He could see the officers continuing to march prisoners across Defenestration Square, but then blackness blocked the view as the train entered a tunnel. The roars of the metal beast carrying them under the buildings echoed all around.

'We goin' all the way down,' said a prisoner. 'All the way to the Ticking Heart.'

'Always one,' said another.

'That's where we're goin'!' said the first. 'Ain't no story from no Coin Weekly! It's the truth!'

The second prisoner laughed in the dark.

'Where are we going?' ventured Krish.

He heard somebody nearby swivelling round to face him.

'The Ticking Heart,' said the first prisoner.

'What's that...?'

Krish could make out shining eyes in the gloom.

'You one of them clumsy drummer kids?' said the first prisoner.

'Don't call me that,' said Krish.

The shining eyes vanished then reappeared a moment later. 'Ha! Yeah, right. Don't matter none down 'ere.'

'Look, I'm not from around here,' said Krish with a sigh. 'What's the Ticking Heart?'

The shining eyes grew larger and foul breath accompanied them. 'You really are from another borough, aren't ya? I 'eard they's out there. Far beyond Naahri Sisa and New Potanga Wharf. I heard that you could walk for a hundred thousand million years and not even see a quarter of the City. Am I right?

'You tell me and I'll tell you,' said Krish, the darkness a perfect cover for the sense of hopelessness swelling within him.

'We're moving deep below,' said shining eyes. 'There must be similar stories in every borough. Must be. Understreet is where He keeps 'em. Sinners. Down 'ere with G.O.D.'

'God?'

'G-O-D. General Obedience Dynamo. Devil keeps 'Er down 'ere, they say. Uses 'Er to keep us all in order up above. The Iron Devil built the Machines to make the City, so the Machines built G.O.D. to bring balance.'

There were many stories of gods and devils in Krish's world, but none like this.

'And who built the Devil?' he asked.

Shining eyes laughed. Several other prisoners chortled or sighed.

'What is this?' said a new voice. 'He some kinda kiddy street philosopher?'

'You really questioning the state of things, drummer?' said yet another voice.

'Don't call me that!' Krish spat back.

A pause. Shining eyes moved closer once more. 'Nobody built the Devil. It's just how things are. No one knows how we evolved. How every cog, every piston came into being, took shape, came to move and power the factories. How the first cobble, the first paving slab was laid. How the first gas-star rose into the sky. Who put a roof over the world to shield every street from the nothing beyond. It's just how things are.'

Krish turned away and looked through the gap in the metal plates fastened to the cage. KnockThrice, the City, baffled him far more than Ilir.

The rattling train delved deeper and deeper below the streets of KnockThrice. They passed rows and rows of underground rivers, regimented in rectangular channels, and columns holding up the City above them.

Then they were below the rivers. The roaring of the train was louder than ever in the narrow tunnels. A little steam escaped the locomotive and reached their cage. Hot metallic spittle.

Sometime later, the sounds of mighty thuds began, like slow, thunderous ticking. Each tick like the splintering of a mighty tree, every tock like a hammering, mechanical heartbeat. The noise thudded into the very tissue of Krish's body.

Then he saw it. The roaring of the train diminished to near silence as they entered a chamber of incalculable size. There were lanterns large as houses dotted about the chamber, hanging from bronze columns which led down from an unseen ceiling far, far above. Gigantic cogs as big as whole stadiums clicked and turned and clanged. Pistons as tall as skyscrapers, shooting back and forth with the might of earthquakes.

The train headed onwards along a track travelling directly through the crisscross of gleaning rods, cogs, pendulums, gears and spiral springs. Krish had the overwhelming sensation of being shrunk down and inserted into a giant clock.

The train gradually began to slow. Thrira's eyes opened, scanned the surrounds, then shut once more. The prisoners became restless. A rusty brown surface slid into view and then the train screeched to a halt.

After some time the plates were removed from the side of their carriage by a group of officers and the prisoners blinked in the gloomy lantern light. The train had stopped on top of a cog the size of a football pitch. Ahead of them, stretching from the rim to the centre of the cog, was a large, dark-brown block-like building, sterile and foreboding. Guards marched in their direction.

The officers escorted the prisoners out of the train.

'Come on, come on!' shouted an officer. 'We got just minutes before the next turn!'

Krish helped Thrira as they were led away by the guards in their white uniforms.

'Kenlan McCrairy's the name,' said shining eyes. Krish took in his short beard of orange and grey, his muscular arms and receding hairline. McCrairy held out his hand. 'Look, we're all the same down 'ere.'

'You didn't call anyone else drummer,' said Krish.

'Just messin', kid. Ya need anything, come to old McCrairy. Not my first time understreet. Yer rum-soaked mate too, 'e's welcome.'

'*She* will bear that in mind.'

McCrairy laughed heartily and slapped him on the back.

'Ha! Ya likes a laugh!' Krish looked back in confusion. 'Ya're doin' a good job of playin' the strong kid!'

Krish wavered between warming to McCrairy and hating him even more as they approached the entrance to the prison.

The train reversed off the tracks, across the cog and backed away beyond the reach of the light. A sudden creaking noise penetrated the air and the cog moved gradually to the clockwise, its teeth intersecting with more sets of teeth on neighbouring cogs. There were no fences but, when you're on a cog suspended high above an endless void, there was probably no need.

A shudder rippled through him. There was no sky above, just valves and cylinders and pistons and cogs, moving in slow, haunting motions. They were trapped in a gigantic machine that went on seemingly forever.

There was a clammy atmosphere, with metal and sweat in the air. And something else. A prickly sensation. Krish ran his fingers along the moisture accumulating on the back of his hand. A fragment of metal scratched the surface of his skin, caught on the underside of his fingertip. Other prisoners were scratching as they became accustomed to the metallic air.

They were lined up in front of the building at the centre of the cog. Emerging from the prison was a tall woman with a bald head and narrow glasses behind which sat small, disinterested eyes. The woman wore dark trousers and a black tunic with a charcoal grey suit jacket buttoned overtop. Two guards in black, their faces hidden by dark-coloured mesh, stood either side of her, holding truncheons.

The woman had created enough silence by her arrival for all to hear the noise of her dry lips parting as she went to speak.

'Welcome to Cinta 2031. I am governor here and my name is irrelevant. As is yours. You are here until your release date and there is no negotiation on this matter. No appeals, no rights except to remain alive until the aforementioned time of your release.

'When your sentence is spent, your tattoos will turn red. If you try and make your tattoo appear red early, we will know, and you will remain for a further week in solitary confinement. You also cannot prolong your stay by attempting to dye red tattoos black. Again, I must stress, we will know.

'We will monitor you from the upper level. You will remain below. Food will be lowered to you by the supervisors, known colloquially as '"grabber guards"'. You will not protest the quantity or quality of the food. You are not entitled to medical support. We have no medically trained inmates at this time so you must fend for yourselves.

'Any attempt to escape, any act of disobedience or insurrection, will be punished by you being scooped up from the upper level and deposited into solitary.

'Once every six fades, on rotation, rooms on the lower level will be flooded for cleaning purposes. Those attempting to remain in a flooded room will be removed by grabber and placed in solitary.

'You do not have the luxury of suicide. You do not have the luxury of individual identities. You do not have the luxury of asking questions. Any questions?'

The abrupt end to the governor's address took everyone by surprise. They all looked around, waiting to see who would take the bait.

'Yeah,' shouted a short young man with a croaky voice, one side of his head shaved, the other a matted mess. 'What time's puddin' round 'ere, 'eh?'

The guard to the governor's right did not even wait for a cue. He strode forward and lashed out with his truncheon, knocking the young prisoner's legs from beneath him. Another guard swooped in and placed a contraption over the prisoner's head. A metal plate was placed on top of his tongue and was fastened into place as the contraption was attached to his head. Gurgling cries of protest emanated from the prisoner as he was escorted away by the guards.

'He will be placed in solitary for his first five fades,' continued the governor. 'He will be force-fed through the face cage. The face cage will also deprive him of the ability to speak for the duration. I imagine he will not be a great conversationalist during or after this period. That is a joke, but I must stress that laughing at your governor will earn you the same punishment but for twice the length of time.'

Deathly silence.

'I repeat: no questions, no rights. If any one of you sees me again, I assure you, you will regret it.'

The governor turned and departed.

The guards ushered the prisoners forward and everyone obeyed without question. Krish took a deep breath as the tall, narrow doorway of the prison swallowed him and his fellow inmates whole.

Then, to his surprise, the darkness of the endless chamber turned to bright, clinical electric light. The lights blared down onto them from the upper level. Krish looked down at the space under the grill they were standing on. The cells below reminded him of large bathrooms; all yellowy-white tiles and corroded copper pipes, trails of rusted-brown and copper-blue running down the walls. The cells were large but crammed full of many bunkbeds overfilling with prisoners.

He could also see a large canteen at the centre of the lower level, inmates eating or congregating around the long tables. A riotous clamour erupted in the canteen as the new intake arrived. Mess tins were hurled at the grill. Guards armed with mechanical claws, the so-called 'grabber guards' he presumed, were stationed all around the gantries.

Krish stuck close to Thrira who was just in front of him. She was beginning to look around, becoming aware of her surroundings.

They reached their destination – just above a drowned cell, several pillows and blankets floating on the surface. Krish looked at the water in the room below.

'Clothes off!' barked a guard. 'Strip to yer underwear! Clothes off!'

Without hesitation the prisoners all began to strip. Their clothes were seized by the guards, moments after touching the ground. Krish thought quickly and stuffed the plastic sandwich bag into his pants. He was more concerned for Thrira than embarrassed for himself at the prospect of stripping off, but when she didn't respond the guards just shook their heads, muttered things like 'rum fiend' and let her be.

He felt so awkward that he scarcely noticed the grill ahead of him being lifted.

In a moment he was shoved forward and his near-naked body smacked into the cold water. He was fully submerged for a second then broke the surface, gasping for air, other prisoners being hurled into the water all around him. Then the water level began to fall rapidly. Krish found himself on the top bunk of a bunkbed. The water continued to fall. *Where was Thrira?*

Krish looked down at the ground. The other prisoners were taking to their feet and wringing out blankets, pillows and the lumpy-looking sleeping matts into the drains stationed around the room. Fresh, dry overalls were being thrown into the room by guards.

Krish saw a motionless shape in the centre of the cell,

curled into the foetal position. He jumped down from his bunk and grabbed a couple of sets of clothing for both of them.

'Come on.' He encouraged Thrira to follow his lead as he dressed and she began to do so. Embarrassed, he was trying not to look as he helped her, but he noticed odd little signs that she was slightly different physically to Balthrir. Something was dawning on him that he'd clocked when she had first materialised in KnockThrice, but had not taken it in straight away.

''E'll have to fend for 'imself at some point,' said the sneering McCrairy as he buttoned up his tunic.

'*She* will be fine in a moment!' said Krish, his rage boiling over.

McCrairy laughed heartily. ''Ow long ya known yer friend, eh? Not long enough to see 'e's a fella, I'll bet! H-ha'

And for the first time Krish looked at Thrira properly. The face was so similar in many ways, the lips, the nose, the big eyes now blinking open, but *she* certainly did appear to be a *he*.

'What's 'is name?' said another of his cellmates.

'I... er...'

'Thira,' came a voice he knew so well.

His friend looked briefly at him, exhausted but with familiarity, and then collapsed onto the bed, falling asleep instantly.

'Thira,' said Krish. 'His name is Thira.'

10

THE SHIP IN THE AFTERGLOW

Lord Anders Ryker-Veere was no longer waiting to be fed by his beard-bearers. He devoured his meal.

He ignored the selection of ornate chrome-grey cutlery gleaming in the sentinellight and tore the crattlefish flesh apart with his bare hands and stuffed it in his mouth with handfuls of salad. His beard-bearers – Edris, Emese, Emna and Esna – cleared up after him. They picked up morsels that had strayed from his plate. They wiped his lips when the juices from the flesh and the dressing from the salad dribbled from his mouth. Edris even produced a small pair of scissors to trim entangled food from his beard.

In contrast, Isri Stroever used every item of cutlery with precision, cut his food into tiny pieces, ate meagre mouthfuls, chewed thoroughly, waited a moment, then took a sip of vael from his crystal glass.

Ryker-Veere stared at Stroever who appeared only to be interested in his plate and cutlery.

Emese held Ryker-Veere's glass to her master's mouth as he greedily glugged down the steaming liquid.

Ryker-Veere also became aware of a figure he had not spied previously.

He'd spotted the deckhands to the aft, but he'd missed who was on the foredeck. A burly, muscular woman in a sou'wester, complete with leather cap. She was partly obscured by the carriage-sized object under a tarpaulin, standing next to the largest harpoon cannon Ryker-Veere had ever seen. The shaft was longer than two fully grown men lying head to toe, and it rested in a cradle mechanism big enough to accommodate a chair for the harpooner. No beast of the deep that dwelt in any sea-street in the entire borough could be big enough to require such an instrument as this to slay it.

Ryker-Veere detected a strange warmth in the air and faint glow all about. He looked up. They were anchored in the after-glow of a gas-star.

Of course – a low-lying gas-star meant no sentinels! thought Ryker-Veere. *Stroever does not want to be seen.* They were far enough away from any land-street here.

'Do I detect that we are about to be involved in some illicit activity, Master Stroever?'

Unlike Ryker-Veere, Stroever was still eating his meal, deli-cately handling the cutlery with his gloved hands. He gave his plate his full attention. 'What I am doing here is entirely legal,' he said.

Ryker-Veere observed the harpooner. From time to time, she glanced upwards absentmindedly or down at the deck with indifference, but mostly she squinted at the darkened horizon, wind in her unblinking eyes. Never once did she peer over the bow at the waters of the sea-street. Whatever Isri Stroever sought, Captain Stavast and the harpooner could likely locate it, practically without looking.

Once Stroever had finished, a couple of deckhands cleared the table as Stroever brushed a few crumbs from his white gloves. Then, rather suddenly, Stroever took to his feet and glared dramatically back at Ryker-Veere.

'Lord Anders Ryker-Veere—' Stroever's eyes were a little wider and he raised his voice slightly, '–you are the most generous of my investors. You have poured millions into my endeavours of late, such as resurrecting my father's Ha'penny Row factory. And the construction of this – the Selkirk, the fastest ship in the known City!'

He marched over to the harpooner.

'This very fade, you will bear witness to the most astounding, the most revolutionary innovation in the whole borough! Perhaps even the entire City!' He pointed out to a small, sleek fishing vessel cutting through the waves ahead of them. 'You see the Refnmoore Seeker there? Its hull is 16 kellits thick.'

He waited for a reaction from Ryker-Veere but there was none. Stroever clapped his hands loudly in the air and Captain Stavast turned the Selkirk towards the little boat. The ship began to rock as they sped up, cutting across the waves. Ryker-Veere took to his feet and gripped the rail.

The harpooner seized the great weapon, narrowed her eyes and Ryker-Veere observed as the Refnmoore Seeker glided into her sights. The Selkirk was tossed high on the waves, but still, as it fell, the Seeker remained dead ahead. They were reaching the edge of the gas-star's afterglow – any second now, the boat would evade them.

The harpooner pulled the trigger. The entire deck vibrated as the harpoon shot through the air, making Ryker-Veere jump. The silver spear embedded itself in the hull of the small boat, some way above the waterline.

'I take it that's one of your chaps on there, old boy?' said Ryker-Veere. 'All part of the show, eh, what?'

'Naturally,' Stroever pointed at the boat. 'Sixteen kellits thick, Lord Ryker-Veere!'

Ryker-Veere noticed that no rope had been attached to the harpoon.

Stavast turned the ship about, steering them back into the afterglow of the gas-star. Spray lashed the deck, making Ryker-Veere whimper for a moment. Stroever did not seem to notice as the seawater splattered across him.

'But I have my sights set at a larger prize,' said Stroever. 'And you will not believe what our harpoon can pierce until you see it for yourself.'

The harpooner placed a new dart in the barrel. This time a rope was attached. She angled the entire contraption 45 degrees upwards.

'And when you realise what I have in mind,' Stroever cried above the crash of the waves, 'you will realise that nothing will ever be the same again!'

Stavast was steering the ship onto calmer waters. Ryker-Veere braved letting go of the bar. He stood up straight and placed his finger in the air. Such was his sense of confidence that Stroever, now standing by the large object behind the harpoon, ready to throw off the tarpaulin, halted. Ryker-Veere raised his index finger and twirled it round and round in the air.

'Turn it around,' he said. 'Turn it around.'

Stroever looked deflated. His mouth gaped open. He continued to clutch the tarpaulin, ready for the big reveal. The deckhands and the harpooner were frozen to the spot. Ryker-Veere barked over his shoulder in the direction of the cockpit.

'Captain Stavast!' he cried. 'Be a good boy and turn this tub around!'

Stavast, his eyes nailed shut, turned to Ryker-Veere.

'Aye! 'Tis not for a freshwater-veined brickfoot to cry "nor'west, ye mangey old sea-street dog! Full steam ahead and no droppin' anchor for no barnacle-ridden reef o' mermaids!" when ye ain't seen the colour of his shell-pennies!'

'What?!' said Ryker-Veere, holding up a hand to his good ear.

Stroever threw down the tarpaulin, the large object remaining hidden. 'He said "no",' he said. He produced a shining silver whistle from his pocket and blasted on it twice. Stavast nodded and began to turn the wheel hard-a-port. The deckhands secured the tarpaulin while the harpooner resumed her previous position crouched on the deck.

Stroever took his seat opposite Ryker-Veere once more. He spoke as softly as ever but there was an undercurrent of anger in his voice.

'I fed you well, Lord Ryker-Veere,' said Stroever.

'And delicious grub it was too, old boy.' Ryker-Veere popped a chunk of crattlefish he'd missed earlier into his mouth. 'But showing off won't work on this old warhorse. Whatever it is, I'll invest. But not to the degree you were so clearly hoping for with this scrumptious fare. Deniability, old chum! Or someone ends up like poor old Stavast with nails in his eyes.'

'My endeavour is perfectly legal,' clarified Stroever.

'I'm sure it is. But I've got my own scheme to focus my mental abilities on. Need to keep a clear head. Now, this was all very jolly, so let me return the favour and I'll hand over a small but appropriate donation to whatever your elaborate scheme is. Anonymous, naturally. Need to keep m'nose clean at present, what-what. De Clercq!'

From the guest quarters emerged a lady in black servant's garb. She was tall and slim, like a length of wire. Raven-black hair in a tight bun made her wrinkled skin look taut. She crossed Ryker-Veere on his left.

'You hailed loudly, your flatulence,' said de Clercq.

'Yes!' said Ryker-Veere, apparently not having fully heard de Clercq. 'Mr. Stroever shall be our honoured guest at the top table for our little... unveiling.'

'Of course, your immenseness.' De Clercq bowed and was halfway round her master's left side by the time she had uttered the last word. Stroever caught smirks from the rear two of the beard-bearers. De Clercq clearly knew that if she circumnavigated her master to his left, his deaf side, that he'd hear nothing more than a few muffled, complimentary-sounding syllables.

Stroever returned to his seat opposite Ryker-Veere. 'And what is this grand scheme you are so enamoured with?' he asked. 'Something that is also *entirely legal*, no doubt.'

Ryker-Veere smiled. 'Not yet.'

Stroever nodded. Ryker-Veere could see the fury at being cut off simmering under the surface of the man.

'Before NightTime is through, Lord Ryker-Veere, you will step foot on this ship once more. I will be allowed to finish my demonstration.' He gazed at the harpoon cannon. 'You will not believe what we are capable of on this little ship. And you see, you will gasp in awe, and marvel at the opportunities. Trust me, very soon... everything will change.'

11

THE BOY & HIS NAME

'It's dark, Mumma. Ya promised ya'd keep the light on, Mumma! Ya promised! Ya promised me!'

'Hush yer noise!'

'Ya promised me!'

'I said quiet!'

'I can hear ya in the hall, Mumma!'

'Wha's wrong with this 'un?'

'Mumma...?'

'Cut 'im quiet! Anyone snuck in a blade? Cut 'im quick!'

'I know you're in the hall, Mumma!'

'Quiet!'

'No one's got no blade.'

'Mumma!'

'No one's smuggled in nothin'!'

'Mumma, I hear ya!'

'Shut 'im, up!'

Krish was huddled on the ground next to the bottom bunk listening to the conversation across the cell. McCrairy was trying to get his bunkmate, who inmates had affectionately nicknamed Mumma's Boy, to stop talking to himself while everyone was trying to sleep.

Krish really felt sorry for Mumma's Boy. No one was able to have a conversation with him. He just spoke in a haunted, agitated manner to himself. In Krish's world, perhaps he'd get help, but not in a prison in KnockThrice.

Also, in the darkness of the cell, so far away from home, Krish began to wonder if Mumma's Boy's ramblings were much different to his own deep, dark thoughts.

'Mumma! Mumma! Tell me you're still there, Mumma!'

As this was going on, Krish was trying to calm Thira who was shaking in his sleep.

Thira. Yes, it definitely rolled off the tongue better than 'Thrira'.

'Mumma...Mumma! Are you outside?'

'Cut 'im quiet!'

'That you, McCrairy?'

'I left my door open, Mumma.'

'And what of it if it is?'

'Read to me, Mumma.'

Krish felt lost. He needed light to see that it was definitely... *him.* To know he was real. He'd seen Thira, stared right into his face. It was the same person.

'I know it's you, McCrairy! Ya'll get us all in the twisty!'

'I'm all alone, Mumma.'

'Ha! Twisty? Wha's that and why would I give a—'

'MUMMA!'

'Right! That does it!'

'McCrairy! Stop! Ya'll get us all in the twisty!'

Movement in the dark. McCrairy and the man he was arguing with had taken to their feet.

'Twisty! Twisty!' said McCrairy mockingly. 'I'll twist yer neck! Wring yer head clean off!'

'Mumma'

Before Krish could process what was happening, Thira shoved him out of the way and jumped out of bed.

'Will you lot pack it in?' came an exasperated voice from another inmate as Thira bounded around in the dark knocking things over.

'If anyone's got a problem with—oi!' said McCrairy as Thira collided with him. Thira staggered over into the corner. 'Wha's yer problem, ya tongueless Ovango Street ruffian?'

'Oi! Leave him!' shouted Krish, stepping up to the shadowy figure of McCrairy in the gloom.

The hulking silhouette turned to him. 'Ya keep tryin' to sound tough, little drummer? Maybe when I—'

'RIGHT!' Everybody turned to the new voice in the corner of the room. Even after one syllable it was familiar to Krish. 'Three questions. Question one: SHUT UP! Two: Wha's goin' on? Three: 'As anybody any idea 'oo the 'ell I am? 'Cause I in't the foggiest.'

His voice was just a touch lower but it was the same person for sure. Krish stepped forward into the silence which had suddenly spread through the cell. He put his hand on his shoulder. Thira accepted the reassuring gesture, his eyes gleamed in the dark, looking into him, angry, desperate and hopeful.

'Hey,' said Krish softly. 'It's okay. Why don't you just get some sleep...?'

'Sleep? What?! Yes! No.' Thira's eyes darted from one side to the other.

'Just calm—'

''Ang on! Wha's...wha's m'... whasitcalled? That thing...? Follows ya everywhere? Sometimes it's there before ya've even arrived, waitin' for yer! Everyone knows it. If they knows ya.'

'What?!'

'Come on, matey! Ya can't introduce yerself without it! It's kinda what intros are all about, innit?'

'Your... name? You're talking about a name.'

'That's the fella! Wha's mine?'

'Thira. Well, it was Balthrir but... you said Thira earlier.'

'I did...? Yes! I did!' Thira was jumping on the spot like an excited child. Balthrir had never been this irritating, even when she tried. 'Yeah! Good name! Strong name! Balthrir?! Odd one, that. All over the place! Thira – yeah! Much better!'

'Pipe down!' chipped in a prisoner. The excitement from earlier had worn everybody out. Their cellmates had crawled into bed and were wrapping their undersized blankets around themselves, trying to shield their ears from the slow growling of the Machines outside.

Krish guided Thira to bed. Their voices lowered.

'Thira...?' said Thira. 'Should 'ave thought of that ages ago.'

'I mean... you can pick a different name,' said Krish.

'Nah, can't be bothered, mate. Actually, it's pretty good. Like it. Do I? Yeah. I think I do. Dunno. Yes!'

Thira was speaking so fast, his voice increasing in volume until Krish shushed him. His words all jumbled together, his eyes jerked from side to side, then suddenly he stopped.

'Yeah. Bed. Need to go to bed. No. No'

'*Sssh!*'

'Gonna stay up forever. Wha's forever? 'Ow long does that go on for, eh?'

'*Sssh!*'

'Wha's a bed? I know what a bed is! 'Course I do! No, 'ang on... *bed*? 'Ow the flippin' 'eck do I know what a bed is? 'Ow do I know what it *isn't*?!'

'*Sssh!*'

'WhyabedIdon'tneedsleepIneedsleepIdon'tneedsleep-

wha'smynameohyeahThiraIdon'tlikeit's rubbishIrememberI-
don'tremembernothin'ThiraI'llkeepit!'

Thira's mind was moving at such speed. It was like
someone had downloaded the entire internet into one person's
brain and they were trying to take it all in at once. Thira's eyes,
glinting in the dark, looked in every direction.

'Vulreinchasin'OldMargaryMYRTHALI!VulreinVulreincom-
in'swhere'stheblinkin'mulewhatmuledunnodun-
nowhowherewho...'

Krish managed to lower Thira into bed and place a blanket
over him. He hushed Thira's rambling with his own whispered
words. He had not quite realised how many of Balthrir's
memories Thira would possess.

Krish crouched on the floor again next to Thira's bunk, one
hand capped over his friend's shoulder, offering comfort, softly
reminding him of some of their adventures on the Great Plain,
in the Night Ocean, the Pale Hunting Grounds and across the
Scar.

In time, Krish's grip on Thira's shoulder loosened. His head
rested on the edge of Thira's bunk. Prisoners tutted and grumbled at their odd young cellmates as they turned in. Krish and
Thira both fell into deep, deep slumbers, the slow thunder of
the Machines vibrating through the walls from outside of the
prison.

Krish had about as much adjusting to do to Thira, as Thira
did to the whole of existence.

§

Some hours later, the clang of the Machines outside awoke
Krish. He sat bolt upright and then spent some time trying to
get back to sleep.

An odd thought crept across his mind as he lay there. He'd

been exhausted from his journey to KnockThrice and then to prison. He'd slept soundly and been woken abruptly. This was usually the best time to recall a dream, one he'd just been ripped freshly from. He had a nagging feeling a dream should have been there, but as he searched his recent memory, all he found was emptiness.

Eva cleared the cups and saucers from the tray

And dragged it to the top of the stairs to play

Then at the last moment the Woman appeared

'Dear child, your behaviour is worse than I feared'

To the shouts below, no attention she paid

'I just miss the snow from that wonderful fade!'

Now down the stairs she slides with a gleeful scream

As fast as a star, all the fun of a dream

12

THE GHOST & THE SHADOW

Aemea awoke in what she liked to think of as morning.
It was not morning, it was primo, but she'd read
many storybooks and some were longroadtales –
stories gathered from other worlds. Worlds where day was
when you were awake and night was (mostly) when you slept.

She thrilled at the idea of getting up with the light and
going to bed when it was dark, rather than fades merging into
one another.

In the stories she'd read, primo was called 'morning', and
fadenigh was called 'afternoon' or 'evening', depending on the
time of fade. Morning sounded so much more romantic than
primo. Mornings in prison, though, were by no means
romantic.

Aemea yawned and climbed out of bed. She looked up – the
top bunk was empty. Of course. Her friend was always up and
about early.

Aemea was a little shorter that most girls her age, her skin
tight around her slender bones, her prison overalls hanging
loose about her person. Her skin was pale, the odd mole scat-

tered about her face. Her hair was thin, straight and mousy blonde, hanging just above her shoulders. Her inquisitive eyes were narrow but curious, and prone to widening somewhat as she stared piercingly at you, like a ghost recalling some reason why you had wronged her in life.

She wandered groggily down to the canteen and got herself a bowl of gloopy porrer. She toyed with the porrer with her spoon as it cooled, scanning the inmates milling about.

Aemea would say, both in her head and out loud, that a person should not be judged by how they looked, how they spoke, or how they acted. And she truly believed this, right down to the deepest reaches of her heart. But often, particularly after a turbulent sleep on the creaking mattress of the bed in her cell, she couldn't help but spend the morning silently judging people in her head. It was a secret indulgence.

This morning's crop of victims was exceptionally good. A new intake had arrived, and having had no time to forge any kind of relationship with them, she could be especially brutal.

Look at him! she thought, *he's so old! He'll die in here. I wonder if he realises. And look at him! He's too thin, he'll starve. She's too fat, they'll eat her. That one, he's so arrogant. Somebody'll knock him down a peg or two. Or he'll disappear up his own bottom, as they say. My, my, that is a disturbingly enjoyable mental image.*

Every caring bone in Aemea's body was not getting much say this morning. She yawned broadly as she looked about.

One newcomer queued up to collect his bowl of porrer. A bag of bones with an unusually large head in proportion to his body, shaking, muttering to himself, no one acknowledging him. *Too wrapped up in his own insanity to care for the nourishment the company of others can provide,* she thought. *What's he saying? Something about his mother?*

Her thoughts moved on to the muscley man farther on in the queue. *He's too... familiar. With his little orange-beard. More muscles than brains. Where have I seen him before...? Shad'd know. Why is she not here yet? Oh, what's his name! McCarey... McCraven? Something like that. He's been here in before. And... who are they...?*

Aemea looked at two figures who were around her age, possibly slightly younger.

The first had short, straight black hair that was a little longer on top than at the sides. She'd seen that style of hair in pictures of far-off streets. Yes, he could be from a distant street. His eyes were lost and scared but his demeanour was defiant. He was trying to mask his vulnerability, but she could detect it from across the room as he spooned the gloopy porrer into his bowl. He must have some reason to be so determined. Something to fight for.

For the first time this morning, she had found somebody who intrigued her.

The boy's companion was certainly amusing. Slightly taller, with large eyes and a particularly dark complexion, like someone from Lusaka Street or Jogoo Road. Every little thing seemed to attract his attention: a fork, a spoon, a table leg, the braid in the hair of a fellow prisoner. It was as if he had never seen any of these items before.

He was odd. She liked him too. They were lost and that, as someone who was rarely found, appealed to her.

Where is Shad? She required a second opinion on the two strangers. *Where did she get to?*

§

Krish examined the dollop of porridge-like substance that had been plonked unceremoniously into his bowl. Oats the size of pennies were suspended in a translucent gloop with the texture of glue. Thira, sitting opposite, his mind less frantic after a night's sleep, seemed to be expressing Krish's internal thoughts on his face. Thira's upper lip arched up on one side in disgust. He looked ready to spear the substance with his spoon, just in case it tried to leap up and bite his nose off.

'So, this food, eh?' said Thira. 'Wha's the big deal? Do I shove it in m'gob or will it jump in all by itself? 'Ow do I know what a "gob" is? Swear I've never used that word before. 'Ow do I know all this stuff?'

'I don't know,' said Krish, sighing. 'What do you remember?'

'Nuffin'. No, wait! A river! That's kinda like water, innit? Like water but it's down there and movin' in one direction.'

Krish remembered the garden on the edge of Hahrani with all the spring flowers in bloom and the smell of their perfume in the early morning light. Did Thira really have all the same memories as Balthrir? He wished, and he couldn't quite believe he was thinking this, that the new version was as mature as she had been.

'Yes,' Krish said. 'That's a river.'

Krish ate. It was thick and tasted like the paint. As he swallowed, his throat seemed keen to send it straight back up again. He washed it down with a cup of water which had a metallic tang to it.

Thira followed Krish's lead and took an ambitiously large spoonful of the porridge. He pulled an expression like someone who'd just mistaken raw sewage for a chocolate bar .

'Blimey!' he said. ''Ow often do we have to eat?!'

Krish sighed again. This was going to be tough. He took a few more spoonfuls, each smaller than the last, while he contemplated explaining metabolism, life, death and the universe to Thira.

He looked over his bowl and caught the eye of a small, ghost-like girl, maybe a year or so older than himself, on the edge of the room with a table of female inmates. She slowly looked away with demure disinterest. She hadn't touched her steaming breakfast yet. Krish wondered how many children like him were caught in this terrible place.

Then he spotted another girl, who seemed at least a couple of years older than him, emerging from the shadows. A tall, dark-skinned girl with muscular arms and legs. She had not a hint of hair on her head, and her eyes had a tendency to narrow as she looked around, like a cat scanning her surroundings for prey. There was something else about her, something odd, that he couldn't quite determine.

She strode across the room and picked up a bowl. The harsh, sterile light shining down from the gantries above left few places to hide, yet somehow, she found the shadows.

She bounded up to the canteen. Several inmates recoiled in fear, which was odd to Krish because, despite something about her being different, she looked in general like a particularly athletic girl in the upper years of his school. She rolled her eyes at the fearful ones, nabbed a bowl of the gloopy porridge and left the queue. Krish swore the shadows themselves clung to her as she passed through.

To Krish's surprise, this strange girl, the tallest of the young female prisoners, sat with the smallest, the ghost-girl. She looked up at the shadow-girl as she arrived. Shadow wiggled about the fingers of her left hand, almost like she was miming a trickle of water. Ghost responded with a nod and raised a finger to her lips. They then concentrated on stirring their porridge.

'We have to find someone,' said Krish.

''Oo?' said Thira. 'And wha's a someone?'

'I don't know who,' said Krish.

'Oh. Well, 'ow's that gonna work then?'

'I don't know. But we need to make friends with people. People who might have information.'

'Wha's a friend?'

'Like us. We're friends.'

'Are we?! Do I get a choice in the matter?'

'Erm... well, yes. Of course. We... don't have to be friends. I guess.'

'What do I 'ave to do?'

'Well... friends... hang around and look after each other.'

'...Anything else?'

'Well, I guess they have to enjoy all the hanging out.'

'Meh. It's been all right so far. Where do I sign up? And what's signin' up? Actually, perhaps I should make other friends. Just in case they're better, ya know?'

'Er...'

'Shouldn't put all m'whatsits in one thingamy. And 'ave you got one of them fings too? Wha's it called? Follows ya around? A name!'

'I do. It's Krish.'

'Nice to meet yer, Krish!' Thira's hand shot out in front of him with such speed that it would have jabbed Krish in the chest if he hadn't reacted fast and leant back. 'I 'ave no idea what this bad boy is doin' out 'ere in fronta me,' he said, retracting his hand.

Krish looked around. A few inmates had clocked the strange conversation between himself and Thira but most were preoccupied with shovelling porridge down their throats. Except the ghost-girl who was staring at him once more. Staring at both of them.

The shadow-girl was stirring her porridge as it cooled. Then she raised a spoonful to her mouth. Before it reached her lips, Krish witnessed the oddest thing. Ghost-girl's eyes suddenly widened in shock. She looked like she was going to throw up. Then, with unexpected violence, she seized the spoon from shadow-girl and threw it to the ground, then pushed the two bowls off the table. The metal bowls clanged against the ground and spilled the glue-like substance everywhere.

It was a momentary distraction for some, but within a second or two eating recommenced, most sighing and shaking their heads knowingly at ghost-girl.

Krish watched closely as the shadow-girl looked at ghost-girl, placing a hand on her own stomach then scrunching it up into a tight ball. Shadow-girl nodded understandingly. They departed looking weak with hunger.

'We need to keep an eye on them,' said Krish.

'What... literally?!' said Thira, pulling back his eyelids, apparently trying to work out if eyes just popped out with ease. 'By the bye, I *literally* 'ave no idea what "literally" means.'

'I just mean we need to watch them... subtly.'

Krish turned to Thira, who was looking around like a lost owl. Subtlety was not something that had come naturally to Thira's counterpart in Ilir either. He didn't remember his patience ever being tested this much, though. He wanted so much for his old friend to look up and give some sign that he remembered him.

13
THE CITY IN THE DREAM

The two men parted at Sawmill Wharf.

Stroever had to deliver the Selkirk to Kilmurley Dock for repairs, even though it was many streets away from his home on Ha'penny Row. From here Ryker-Veere could easily get the train back to Kierbeckerstraße.

'You see anything of your little sister Helena these fades, chum?' enquired Ryker-Veere, at the centre of the four-point star created by his beard bearers.

'On occasion,' answered Stroever.

There was an air of awkwardness between them for a moment.

'Your father was more than a mere associate, I must say,' said Ryker-Veere.

'He was a fool and now he is dead,' said Stroever.

'You would have learned much from him.'

'He was not there to bring me up.' Stroever brusquely brushed the left shoulder of his dinner jacket with his right hand, banishing some unseen irritant.

'I am aware, of course, of your most unusual upbringing and—'

'My upbringing gave me everything I required.'

Ryker-Veere nodded and looked around awkwardly at his assistant, de Clercq, and his beard bearers, clearly ready to depart.

'We should discuss this further,' said Stroever, 'at your "unveiling". But truly... what I have to reveal... it must be seen to be—'

'Yes, yes, yes,' said Ryker-Veere dismissively. 'We shall see. And at the unveiling you shall be our honoured guest. You shall dine at the head table and drink 'til you fall onto yer arse, ha!'

Stroever appeared unimpressed.

'You're heading home tofade?' said Ryker-Veere.

'On-the-morrow, early,' said Stroever.

'Still in the same old place on Ha'penny Row? On the river-street? Despite its history?'

'Jane... my mother did not die in the house, Lord Ryker-Veere. She jumped from the window and opened her lungs to the waters. The same stretch of river that claimed my father. The house was always a sanctuary, and so it remains. Speaking of which, I must be on my way back there now. I shall need a good sleep before taking the coach on-the-morrow.'

'Safe travels, old boy. And be patient, you young scallywag! Like your father, your time will come.'

A rare smile crept across Stroever's face. 'In many ways, you are more my father's son than I, Anders. The older you get, the more you are convinced you have all the time in the world.'

Ryker-Veere's smile dropped abruptly. Silence fell between the two men. Then Ryker-Veere offered his hand to Stroever who simply stared back, flexing the fingers of one of his gloved hands.

'The sickness of your childhood persists?' said Ryker-Veere.

Stroever nodded. 'Until next time.'

Ryker-Veere dropped his hand and the two men parted.

Ryker-Veere took a carriage with his beard-bearers and de Clercq. They passed the workers shaving down beams of wood to create the hulls of the great vessels being constructed in the shipyard. The carriage jerked to the right and down a steam-filled alley.

Stroever remained on the dock.

Mist polluted the air. Stillness, also. The shipbuilders were heading for The Ferrier's Flag, the rum palace tucked into the far corner of Sawmill Wharf. The night called for intoxicating refreshment to dilute the oppressive darkness.

Stroever proceeded down the backstreet of Colyer Close, a narrow alley, 27 miles in length, most doorways bricked up. A handful of ramshackle pubs spilled their ochre light onto the slender alley. Compared to the broad streets occupying most of KnockThrice, Colyer Close's width was suffocating.

The Porter's Chair was a small pub and coach house, placed a good distance between two of the more popular bars. A smattering of patrons were spaced out in the sticky-floored drinking establishment, hunched over their tankards of beer, contemplating life, death or the moment when one became the other.

Isri Stroever entered The Porter's Chair, disrupting the curtains of smoke from the charciary pipes in the mouths of the regulars. He approached the bar, explained he had a reservation, and was handed the key to his room. He ordered a boar's heart and red wine pie with dumplings to be delivered to his room. It arrived an hour later with a tankard of porter, a few islands of froth floating on the surface. The pie was a rich, hearty delight; the finest poor man's meal Stroever had yet discovered in the known City.

He ate not a mouthful more than a quarter of the pie and

then, paying no attention to the lifeless porter, picked up his leather travel case and placed it on the bed. He opened the case and carefully relieved it of the majority of its contents. Wrapped in a towel was a hollow glass globe the size of an infant's head. There was a large hole at one end and a smaller one at the other.

He produced five tiny velvet drawstring bags and decanted their soft contents into the upturned globe. From a miniature silver flask, he poured oil over the objects in the glass sphere. He screwed a brass base onto the larger hole in the globe, turned the whole contraption over and fiddled with the nozzle on the base. A hiss of gas. He lit a match and a flame appeared under the globe to heat the contents within.

Stroever screwed a metal tube into the hole on top of the globe. He opened the window a crack to allow the scents from the dream to escape. He removed his gloves with great care and placed them on the pillow. As he waited for the vapours to rise from the globe, he laid back on the bed.

The scents meandered their way into his nostrils, triggering distant memories. He saw great structures towering over him, intertwined to create a cityscape unlike anything Ryker-Veere could have ever experienced.

Isri Stroever's dream was based on one of his own memories. But, to Stroever, it was not merely a sweet remembrance, but inspiration for how he might reshape the City forever.

14

THE STREET IN THE PRISON

An odd thing happened about an hour after the ghost and shadow discarded their bowls of porrer. Krish's stomach gurgled unhappily. Thira's was much the same. Pretty soon every prisoner was fighting to get to the limited number of frankly disgusting toilets.

While queuing, they saw the grabber guards taking up the vat of porrer with the claws, sniffing it, looking away in disgust and carrying it off to dispose of it. Only Ghost Girl and Shadow seemed unaffected by the off food.

From a distance, Krish watched the ghost and her shadow whenever he could for the rest of the fade. Ghost Girl seemed quite aware and comfortable with the idea of them openly spying on each other.

Later that fade, they were marched round and round the circular exercise ground next to the canteen. Krish felt dizzy as they walked anticlockwise, against the tide of the giant cog on which Cinta 2031 was situated. He spotted ghost-girl through the forest of prisoners walking in unenthusiastic circles. They nodded in acknowledgement of each other.

Krish observed how the intense lights from the gantries above, bearing down on everyone like laboratory rats, rid everybody of any dark corners where they could attempt any nefarious dealings. Somehow, though, Shadow Girl found lightless patches which, he swore, were attracted to her as she passed through. And sometimes, as she stepped into the light, he sensed a flash of colour. Every colour imaginable: scarlets, aquamarines, lilacs, ochres, magentas and indigoes. Then, in an instant, it was gone again. Her skin – visible on her face, bald head and arms, for her sleeves were rolled up – danced with colour when she hit the light, yet the rest of the time it was dark as night.

But there was something else about her. Something... absent. He couldn't work out what it was.

A command was shouted from the guards above and the inmates changed direction. Then he saw. There *was* something missing. For as she faced the light, she cast no shadow.

His curiosity for these two oddballs – the ghost and the tattooed girl with no shadow – was far from sated. They became more and more intriguing.

Thira on the other hand, was becoming quite irritating. His eyes – those same big, beautiful eyes – darted around all the time, taking everything in, firing off inane questions in their cell, at mealtimes and as they tried to sleep on the extremely uncomfortable mattresses which left indents from the springs in your back.

'Wha's a fade?'

'It's like a day. Apparently.'

'Oh. Wha's one of them?'

'It's like what happens when the Earth turns around once. So we see the Sun during the day and the moon during the night. Unless it's cloudy.'

'Oh! No, 'ang on. Wha's this "Earth" do-dad? And clouds? And a whatiscalled... "Sun"?'

'The Sun is a ball of... erm... gas... like fire and it keeps everything warm and light—'

'I know what the blinkin' Sun is, matey boy!'

'Then why did you ask?! And it's different here. And where you were from.'

'Where's 'ere?'

'Erm. It's complicated.'

'Wha's complicated? And keep it simple!'

'Good night, Thira.'

'Wha's that?'

'Just turn your brain off and go to sleep.'

'Okey dokey, smokey.... Wha's a brain?'

Krish turned over on his top bunk and hoped the noise alone was enough to indicate he was asleep.

Thira was not the person he had expected. So much of Balthrir's appearance, mannerisms and her way of speaking were there but he was not *her*. He was a boy, for a start. Which was fine. He supposed. He was still beautiful... definitely. No, was he? Krish felt odd but then he just kept thinking... Thira was here. He was with Krish. And it was the same person. The same as before, but different.

As he drifted off into another dreamless sleep, the face he had expected to see and the one of the boy on the bunk above began to merge...

§

During dinner in the canteen the next fade, they were served dried, rust-brown vegetables. As Krish ate, he paid particular attention to the two people who fascinated him most in Cinta 2031.

Shadow went to sit at the end of a bench of female prisoners. Ghost halted abruptly as if her face had collided with an unseen wall. Shadow stopped and turned to her friend. She balled her hand into a fist and looked at Ghost as if the fist was asking a question. Ghost nodded and looked in the direction of the other, then seemed to reconsider and sat elsewhere.

Krish was perplexed by this scene for some time and was still mulling it over minutes later as he sat in the canteen trying to answer Thira's question on which out of a fork and a spoon was superior to the other.

Then he heard raised voices and turned to see the two women Ghost and Shadow had avoided. An argument had broken out between them and one went to hit the other. The other ducked and the first woman's fist whooshed through the air instead. Before further blows could be exchanged. commands were barked from above. The grills opened and claws came down, each lifting one of the fighting women, carrying them wriggling through the air and depositing them in separate rooms away from the main block of cells.

'Any more outbreaks tonight and food privileges will be revoked for two fades!' came the command from the gantries.

§

The date tattooed onto Aemea's pale forearm was too far in the future for her liking.

The numbers were still flashing before her eyes after the lights were turned out.

It would have been me, thought Aemea. *I felt it. The punch would have hit me right in the jaw.*

Only newcomers fought like this. A few weeks of sleeplessness in Cinta 2031 made everyone simmer down.

He looked at me again. The new boy. Not like that! I know that's what you'd say if you could read my thoughts, Shad. Which I suppose you pretty much can. Anyway, he looks sweet but there's something else. It's like he's here for an actual reason. Which is unusual. He looks... expectant. I wonder what he's planning... McCrairy! That was the name of the one with the red beard!

Aemea remembered the day well. They all did. McCrairy was the one who had started it. A scrap so big that no one up in the gantries could tie the instigator down to any individual. They'd all automatically had food rations halved for three fades.

McCrairy! I hope one of those claws squeezes him until all his insides squirt out of his eyes and mouth and nose and ears! That would teach him a lesson. Well, it wouldn't. He'd be dead, but still. Anyway, I shall tell Shad to look out for that boy on-the-morrow.

The morrow came sooner than expected.

Two of Aemea's cellmates were trading smuggled-in sugar cubes. They were not quiet enough. Aemea knew what was going to happen next. If she hadn't been so sleepy, she would have warned Shad. The lights came on from the gantries above, blindingly bright in that early hour. Then came the water. Gushing into the cell. They were swept out of their beds.

'Laundry duty!'

The voices from above set them to work before breakfast was served. While the other prisoners slept, they gathered sheets from the laundry room, filled the large, rectangular butlers' sinks with powder and hot water and began scrubbing. Shad, at the sink next to her, caught her eye and threw her hand up out of the water as if she was throwing some annoyance as high up and as far away as possible, flecking water and suds everywhere. Aemea concurred with a brisk nod. She quite agreed: the guards could go and stick their laundry duty firmly up their posteriors.

Next, they trudged from the blue-white of the laundry room to the Cank.

The Cank was an ancient street which had been built on the cog hundreds of years ago. Back then, a number of civilisations had tried to settle on the Machines. Few had been successful.

The short street consisted of a number of blackened two-storey buildings. A layer of dried sediment, a byproduct of the Machines, encased the structures. They looked like blobs of wax which had dribbled from a black candle and solidified.

The Cank was a place only opened during laundry duty, a rare open space in the cramped prison where sheets and clothing could be hung out to dry. Aemea liked the Cank. The buildings' roofs leaned in a little towards each other, creating a narrow channel for the guards to peer down from the gantries into the street. It was the closest to feeling like a secret place in the whole prison.

They entered the Cank just after the other prisoners had eaten breakfast. Aemea noticed that they were not alone. Some of the newbies had been set to work taking down the dry washing from the previous fade. And there, stealing inquisitive glances at her and Shad once more, was the boy and his friend.

§

'So 'oo is it we're lookin' for?' asked Thira, following Krish's lead and folding the sheets.

Krish sighed. 'I don't know. We'll have to investigate.'

'Right ho.... Wha's inves—'

'It means when you try and find something out.' Krish let out a wide yawn. He'd slept badly again. He couldn't remember his dreams either. In fact, he couldn't recall having had a single dream since he'd set foot in KnockThrice.

'Sorry, mate,' said Thira. Krish turned. Thira actually looked quite hurt at being interrupted. 'Am I rubbin' you up the wrong way? Oh! What does rubbin'—'

'Thira! I'm shattered! Will you just—'

'MUMMA!' Krish and Thira turned to see their rather disturbed cellmate. 'Mumma! She used to live here. This was our house!'

'Oh, look!' said McCrairy, just across the street, pulling down a sheet from a lamppost. 'It's Mumma's Boy!'

'I don't think anyone's lived here for a very long time,' said Krish, vaguely trying to reassure Mumma's Boy.

'She turned out the light!' said Mumma's Boy. 'Why did she turn out the light? She turned out the light!'

'I'm sorry. I don—'

'Mumma!'

'Ow!'

Mumma's Boy had seized Krish by the arm while looking around wildly.

'Mumma, please! Turn on the light!'

'Oh, get off 'im!' said Thira, stepping forward and trying to pull Mumma's Boy off Krish.

'Please!' Krish protested. 'Just—'

'Mumma! Mumma, I'll be good! Turn on the light!'

'Get off 'im!'

'MUMMA! Mumma, please!'

'Oi!'

'Mumma!'

'I said—'

In an instant, Thira became furious, his eyes wide and wild, yanking at Mumma's Boy's hand, attempting to pull him away from Krish, and then—

Light shot out of Thira's hand, past Mumma's Boy and into the column holding up the grand doorway they were stood in.

There was an explosion. The three of them were thrown apart. Krish and Thira stared open-mouthed at the smoking hole in the column, as big as a football.

Mumma's Boy turned and ran.

There was shouting from the gantries above. A claw whipped downwards and seized the kicking and screaming Mumma's Boy.

'Mumma! Mumma! Mumma! I tried to leave the light on for you, Mumma!'

As the cries of Mumma's Boy died away, Krish and Thira turned to each other. For a moment, Thira hunched over slightly. He looked weak, shaky, visibly slimmer. Then he took a long, gasping breath, straightened up and appeared normal once more.

'You... okay?' said Krish.

'What the bloody 'ell...?' said Thira.

This was one crucial aspect of Balthrir Krish had completely overlooked.

'Magic,' said Krish.

'Magic? Wha's—?'

'It means... like... something nobody can explain.'

'Wow! You mean—?'

'No, it does not!'

Krish and Thira turned to see the owner of the new voice. A single shadow approached followed by two figures.

'And whatever trickery that was,' continued Ghost, 'I'd refrain from practicing it again in here.'

'Then what is it?' said Krish.

'Magic is not something that *nobody* can explain,' said Ghost. 'It is something that nobody can explain *yet*. There's always a proper scientific explanation. When people don't have one, they deem it magic. Because they are idiots.'

'Oh!' said Thira, defensively. 'You decided we're idiots then?'

'If you insist.'

Shadow smiled and let out a little snort of amusement.

'Then how do you explain it?' said Krish.

'I never said I had an explanation in this particular case,' said Ghost. 'Only that there is one. There must be. There always is. Saying it's magic is just giving up.'

'Wha's she bangin' on about?' said Thira to Krish. 'And why's the other one not sayin' nuffink?'

Shadow raised an eyebrow, cocked her head to one side and her face broke into an amused and expectant closed-mouth smile. Her look was like a challenge.

'Shad says that if you think she doesn't talk then you've not been paying attention,' said Ghost.

Oddly, Krish knew what Ghost meant. Shadow's facial expressions were so pronounced you could pretty much tell what she was trying to communicate. And as Shadow leant forward, Krish saw her clearly for the first time. As she passed into the light it was like staring into a pool of oil catching the sun. What had moments ago seemed dark was now dancing with colour.

There was barely a scrap of her skin that was not covered in tattoos. All those lines of colours – crimson and amaranth and amber and ultramarine and gold and tan and emerald and coral and bronze and violet and silver and azure. The tattoos depicted adventures – ships tossed on high seas, climbers scaling mountains, sword fights to the death. And everywhere there were portrayals of people embracing. Passionate hugs, fierce and tight, friends and lovers clinging to each other like being apart was not being whole, not being alive.

Shadow leant back out of the light and the shimmering colours largely vanished.

'Her name is ShadowThief,' said Ghost.

ShadowThief's eyebrows raised as if to say, *Well...*

'Well,' said Ghost. 'We don't know her name. She lost her parents long ago and she won't tell anyone the name they gave her.'

ShadowThief's hand sliced through the air, decisively rejecting the idea that she was ever anything more than a girl named ShadowThief.

'She won't even write it down,' continued Ghost. 'From the moment she joined our orphan-clan she was just ShadowThief.'

'You're both orphans?' asked Krish.

'*I* am,' said Aemea. She turned to ShadowThief who nodded as if to give her the go ahead. 'We both are. We were in an orphan-clan – a gang of orphans who enjoyed what we like to think of us sub-legal activities. We specialised in attaining access to places where valuable items were kept and finding more suitable accommodation for said artefacts.'

'Thieves?'

'If you like. We were very talented until the tiresome law got in the way. Anyway, ShadowThief is a shadowthief so she's stuck with that name. Particularly since she's probably the only shadowthief in the whole borough. Perhaps in the whole known City. That's an exciting idea, isn't it? And there's a fine trade for shadows on the understreet market. Especially for use in dreams, and *especially* now with the Dream-Pedlars' Parade.'

'The Dream-Whatters' What?' asked Thira.

'You said you were good at breaking into places...?' said Krish. 'Guess you've never tried to break—'

Both Ghost and ShadowThief looked up warningly. Then Ghost held her finger to her lips and ShadowThief cut across the air in front of her neck.

'They're pretty sensitive to the B word,' said Ghost, glancing up at the figures shuffling about on the gantries, obscured by the glare of the lights. 'The E word too.'

Krish considered for a moment and then caught up: *breakout, escape.*

Ghost's eyes narrowed. She looked at Krish as if staring hard enough would reveal some hidden image on his face. 'I'm thinking about you,' said Ghost in a distant, wispy voice. 'I wonder why...'

Krish felt wary of Ghost but she was endlessly intriguing. 'What?' he said.

'I can feel it,' said Ghost. 'It's you. It's definitely you. My arms are wet. I'm hard at work, soaking sheets. Yes, that's what it feels like. Hot, warm water up to my elbows. It's a mundane task and my mind is not wandering far from the mystery of you. Yes. Unquenchable quantities of intrigue. How interesting...'

Ghost's eyes were now looking off to the side, still narrowed, focussing on something she could see clearly in her mind's eye. Krish had met some bonkers characters in Ilir but these two were something else. They were like two bizarre imaginary friends who'd abandoned the people who'd dreamt them up, to hang around with each other instead.

'These bozos are crackers,' said Thira, not too bothered about the aforementioned 'bozos' being in earshot.

ShadowThief smirked, as if to say, *look who's talking!*

'Who are you?' said Ghost. 'You're from a long way from here. Farpilgrims. I overheard a guard say your companion here,' she indicated Thira, 'was believed to be high on dreams, so—'

'High on dreams?!' said Krish. 'What are you talking about?'

'Wha's a dream?' asked Thira.

'It's like... a vision,' said Krish. 'Something you see when you're asleep.'

'Erm,' interjected Ghost, 'I think you're leaving out some pretty vital details on dreams. Such as them being illegal!'

'Er, how can it be illegal to dream?' said Krish.

ShadowThief rolled her eyes in disbelief.

'How far away do you *actually* come from?' said Ghost.

'So, this dream whatsit,' said Thira, "ow comes I've never seen one when I'm asleep? Sounds pretty interestin'.'

ShadowThief snorted in amusement.

'You can't dream unassisted!' said Ghost, her words broken up by disbelieving laughter. 'And if you've smuggled in a pype or a dreamglobe I'll be more than impressed! Plus, they'd probably pick up the scent of the ingredients.'

Krish wanted to ask what the hell she was talking about, but he relented. He'd be shrewd. He considered for a moment as ShadowThief approached and stared hard at him. He could see figures embracing on her cheeks in amber and azure as the light flashed across her. She held out her right hand flat, palm up and then held her left over it, cupped, palm down over the first hand.

'This means the City,' explained Ghost. ShadowThief stared into Krish as she continued making the gesture. Her cupped left hand then drifted off, away from the light, then suddenly curved up and shot up into the air, like a bird taking flight. Her eyes asked a question. *The City... far, far away...?*

Krish nodded. *Yes, we're from far away.*

'How far away?' said Ghost.

Krish pondered for a moment. He had to be smart and stop blundering into things.

'I'll tell you,' he said, 'but I want to know something first. There's somebody here. Somebody I'm looking for. Somebody... old.'

Ghost and ShadowThief exchanged knowing looks. They looked at each other for some time, an unheard conversation passing between them.

'When you say old... do you mean... *very* old? *Exceptionally* old?'

'Yes... probably.'

Another look between Ghost and ShadowThief and then nods.

'You will dine with us tonight,' said Ghost, as if inviting them for dinner at a country manor rather than at the prison canteen. 'No more talk of the E word.' She looked pointedly at Krish, then at ShadowThief who nodded in response. Thira may have been baffled but Krish understood: *Speak to Shadow-Thief, they cannot overhear what she expresses.*

The four of them looked around cautiously, as McCrairy and several others wandered past with laundry baskets.

'Freak,' muttered McCrairy at Ghost as he passed.

'My name is Aemea,' said Aemea. 'A-E-M-E-A. It's the same backwards as it is forwards.' She cocked her head to one side as she observed McCrairy. 'I wonder if he'd be the same backwards as he is forwards...' She was viewing McCrairy less as a human and more like he was an object made of skin that could easily be unzipped with a knife.

'I'm Krish.'

'And I'm... what was it again?'

'Thira. This is Thira.'

Aemea nodded, then she and ShadowThief exchanged glances before she indicated in the direction of the far corner of the melted street.

'The individual you seek is in there,' said Aemea. 'She has no tattoo. Some say she crawled down here, hiding, waiting. She was too weak, so they just left her here. You can probably slip away for a few minutes down here but don't push your luck. And in one of our future engagements, I may have some follow-up questions about Thira's... abilities.' Aemea glanced into the far corner once more. 'Be quick.'

15
THE SKIN, THE BONES & THE TIME THEY HAD LEFT

There was a compact two storey building at the edge of the street beneath the prison. The top floor was no more than a heap of rubble, congealed into a black mass, but the ground floor was a cell. The bars appeared like stalactites dripping from the ceiling.

As Krish approached, he heard deep breaths with unnaturally long periods of silence in between, as if the occupant of the cell kept dying and then resurrecting themselves in cycles. Wheezing, pained breaths.

'How did you come here?' came a voice from inside.

For a moment Krish was too startled to reply. Seconds passed, and it did not repeat itself. The arduous breaths continued in anticipation.

'I was arrested and...' Krish knew this was not the answer the voice from within was after. 'I... came here from the house of a dead man. I had to light candles.'

More wheezing breaths.

'You were alone?' asked the voice.

'No,' answered Krish.

'The heir...?'

She was talking about the devil. The whole story flooded back into Krish's mind.

In another world, in the city of Bahrtakrit, the Empress Benhu'in had commanded all her physicians and magicians to invent a concoction that would keep her young forevermore. They had created Myrthali, the Sands of Time. Chief physician, Kalrika Mavalrh, brewed the Myrthali in milk and liquorice to extend the Empress's life beyond its natural span.

But gateways to other worlds had opened and time thieves had appeared to steal the Myrthali. One such thief, Evia, had succeeded. She'd fled and the Myrthali, which was then divided, was sold and distributed to many worlds. The Empress had died, despite the best efforts of her loyal servant Viona and the chief physician Mavalrh.

The Myrthali was thought to be lost, but one woman claimed she knew the worlds in which the Myrthali could be found. She claimed to be the Empress's heir. Krish did not know her name. He only knew her as the devil.

'Yes,' said Krish after some time.

Deliberation. The effort put into breathing was too much. This being could expire any moment now.

After prolonged quiet, a slither of syllables drifted through the air to Krish's ears. 'The door is open.'

Krish pulled the creaking metal door with some difficulty and stepped inside. Only a scant trace of light had infiltrated the cell.

The creature – the shadow of a human – sat on the edge of a sash of light. Their eyes were closed and had not been opened in some time. Their skin was cracked and yellowy grey, thin as paper, no flesh visible to protect the bones beneath. She – yes, he was reasonably certain *she*, just about discernible from the voice – sat on the ground in a long tattered robe, not unlike that of the devil's when Krish saw him last.

The head, barely more than a skull wrapped tight in papery yellow skin, rested against the wall, leaning slightly towards the entrance. The legs were tilted the other way and were motionless; they seemed dead and black with the odd scrap of skin that remained dry and curled up at the edges. The arms, collapsed at her sides, were much the same: dark and lifeless. Her body seemed to be dying off one piece at a time. Who knew which organs within her were alive and still performing their functions?

Krish inched forward. His foot came into contact with an object on the ground: a glass bottle. He rolled it to one side and knelt beside the dying woman.

Her head turned towards him. The eyes were grey-black, close to being as lifeless as her arms and legs. Then she spoke, with haste, like each syllable would be her last.

'E-365301, then J-150504, then K-202636.'

She spoke on the inhale, sucking whispered speech into her lungs rather than out.

'I... erm... sorry?' said Krish.

'E-365301, then J-150504, then K-202636,' she repeated with an equal amount of strain. 'Write them down.'

'I... don't have any paper.'

'Then you must remember. I will say them again, you will listen and memorise.'

For some minutes, the woman, ancient beyond years, repeated the combinations of letters and numbers over and over. She seemed rejuvenated with a renewed sense of purpose. Krish repeated them back to her until he knew them by heart:

E-365301...

...E-365301

J-150504...

...J-150504

K-202636...

...K-202636

Then her head collapsed against the wall once more. Only her lips and lungs moved now, but with some difficulty

'It has taken much time,' whispered the woman, 'but now I have the last of the information I sought.' She paused to exhale and started again. 'To marry with that which I already knew.' Another breath. 'You must go to where an object of my creation is... There is a room in the roof of 63 Kierbeckerstraße... get to it from the adjoining Kierbecker Halle. The door opens to the word "lightwing". Say it!'

Krish's head was swimming, trying to keep up with all the details. '...63 Kierbeckerstraße... Door opens to the word "lightwing"'.

'There you will find the safe. The LCCs, they will lead you to open the safe. Repeat the LCCs to me. In order.'

'The... the codes?'

'Yes!'

'E-365301, J-150504, K-202636,' Krish intoned.

'63 Kierbeckerstraße. Repeat it.'

'63 Kierbeckerstraße. Access from Kierbecker Halle.'

'Correct. '

A long pause. She was fading, the remaining colour draining away.

'I stayed alive for as long as I could,' she said, motioning towards the glass bottle on the floor. 'I hid from him. Found somewhere safe. T-took versiriam to hide it from mysel... my...'

Krish was lost. He focussed on all the numbers and words she'd begged him to remember. She mumbled incoherently for a few moments, addressing a spot on the floor. He had to bring her back round.

'Who found you?' he asked.

'The rich man. You will meet him, I have no doubt. Took my Myrthali. I fled. Hid here. The parade will end sometime soon. Some time tonight. You must hurry.'

'The parade? The Dream-Pedlars' Parade?'

A hint of a nod. She rested for some time, collating the last of her strength.

'You met Young Margary, I gather?' A playful flicker of a smile from the ancient woman.

Krish remembered Old Margary, a woman who'd lived so long that she moved many times slower than a normal human. How old was this woman before him, to consider Old Margary young?

'I am older than KnockThrice. Older than the entire City. And you met Obsendei also?'

'Yes.' How could he forget the cruel king, the vile ruler who'd knelt before him, handing over the Myrthali, a short time before his death.

'And you saw the centrepiece of his crown?'

Krish had a vague recollection of the crown. There had been a simple oval of convex silver at its centre. 'Yes.'

The smile broadened then faded altogether.

'I will die now. I will never see my beloved Bahrtakrit again. Though it is gone as I remember it. You can see for yourself.'

Krish looked around the cell. There, on the opposite wall to the woman, etched into the blackness, revealing a yellowy layer below, was an intricate image of a vast city, suspended by ropes over a wide chasm. Bahrtakrit seemed far larger than he'd originally envisioned. Minarets towering over grand buildings with ornately decorated visages. A strikingly beautiful palace was at the centre, lower than the minarets but higher than every other building, longer than it was tall, covered in stunning fretwork, lush gardens on the first of the upper levels, legions of guards on the battlements. Many baskets full of plants hung over the edge of the city. There was even an entire botanical garden hung from the far side.

The image must have taken a lifetime to complete. Bahrtakrit moved from fairy tale to a real city within moments of drinking in the work of art scratched onto the wall of the millennia old prisoner's cell.

'They were tearing it down already by the time I was taken from that place,' said the woman.

'Taken...?' inquired Krish.

A large breath in and then she spoke at length, becoming lucid, burning those final reserves of energy; it was as if she was emptying her body in preparation to pass on from life.

'I hear you tore down the Breathing Palace of Ilir. People do not suffer under tyranny eternally. A time will always come when rebellion rips the old rulers from their thrones. It was the same in Bahrtakrit. The heir would never have sat on that throne. The reign of the empresses and emperors of her ilk was over. Fear and cruelty only keep the disgruntled masses at bay for so long. The stories were right in that respect, you know. A tyrant she was, yes, but beautiful also.'

'You knew the Empress?'

'Ah. My old friend, my dear enemy. The tales do not do her justice. And the only justice she could ever be served was death.' A sharp intake of breath. 'I named it for her, you know.'

'I'm sorry?'

'*Myrthali.*'

'The Empress was named Myrthali...?'

A brief chuckle. 'No... not for her... There are many stories of how that word came about, but the truth is it was named after mine. My first. My last. Myrthalia I named her. Child of the sands. Do you know why we named her so? Because she was born without breath. Without heartbeat. By the time we came to name her, we had buried her in the sands of the desert outside of the city. I have never forgiven the Empress. *Myrthali.* All the time my Myrthalia did not have I gave to the worlds. There were times when the Empress showed kindness. She did not object to me, in my inconsolable grief, naming it after the life I grew who did not survive to taste the light of the stars. The stories do not tell you this about the Empress.'

A great silence for a time.

'Who are you?' Krish asked.

Then the woman, having seen centuries rise and fall, having lived in times now beyond the reach of memory, in the minutes before her unnaturally long life ended, spoke her name one last time. Krish could hardly make it out but the sound of it was familiar. It would be some time before he remembered from where.

Her words became faint, delicate whispers, indistinguishable from the shallow breaths that followed, and finally indiscernible from the slow whir of the Machines beyond the walls of the prison.

For the second time in recent days, Krish became aware that he was sitting unnervingly close to a corpse.

Is this a punishment for her acting mean?

To take her now to where it's ever so green

The Woman escorts her, she grumbles and groans

'But I just want my bed, my tired old bones!'

Eva's sat in a room with orchids and ferns

Under the cool green light, Eva's anger burns

'It's part of the cure, you have nothing to fear'

The Woman feels cruel but she sheds not a tear

16

THE COLOURS IN THE SKY

Lord Ryker-Veere arrived at Central Station on Crystalware Row. His beard bearers escorted him from the road to the side entrance and on to the First Class Lounge where he was admitted without a word.

Coffee, a platter of smoked salmon and a glass of lemon vlisi were placed by his armchair within a minute of him taking his seat. He devoured all three, one after the other, and waited to be summoned into his private carriage on the train to Kierbeckerstraße.

The exquisite beauty of the train was lost on Ryker-Veere. There were gilded reliefs depicting the perceived high points of the Ryker-Veere family's history. Set into the walls were small alcoves to hold Ryker-Veere's collection of spirits, all the bottles fastened in their own custom-made grooves to stop them being dislodged while the train was in transit.

At one end was a study and at the other a chaise longue. Ryker-Veere reclined as his beard bearers arranged the four strands of his beard across his front. Edris poured Ryker-Veere a small glass of the rich brown Bandlier '67 and observed him consume the whole thing in two greedy gulps.

'Pull the curtains,' he barked.

The beard bearers pulled the thick black curtains shut and dimmed the gaslights stationed on the walls. The train roared through the tunnels under the streets, with hours to go until it reached its destination. To close the curtains, which were more decorative than anything when there was only darkness outside, was pure paranoia.

De Clercq was arranging a more sophisticated version of the instrument Stroever had assembled in his cramped room at The Porter's Chair. Gleaming with a gold base and nozzles, de Clercq placed the contraption on the floor by Ryker-Veere on the chaise longue.

'The same, your obtuseness?' she asked as she passed her master on his deaf side.

'You're doing it again, woman!' cried Ryker-Veere, irritably jabbing his bad ear.

'The same, your excellence?' de Clercq asked as she glided past on his good side.

Her master answered with a nod.

Edris, Emese, Emna and Esna sat on simple wooden chairs tucked into one corner, their heads bowed, averting their gaze from their master.

De Clercq opened a series of black silken bags and delicately placed the ingredients into the globe. A lump of rosewood, a scattering of metal filings, a length of lampwick, shreds of a four-pescá note, and a vial of condensation collected from the funnel of an ocean-street-bound steamer. She then poured syrupy, transparent oil on top of the ingredients and lit the dreamlamp.

This dream was one that Ryker-Veere had insisted on being privately produced to preserve a particular memory.

De Clercq reduced the gaslights further until there was total darkness, save for the flicker of the dreamlamp's flame. She took her seat and placed a small mask over her mouth and nostrils. The four beard bearers had done the same; they would not be enjoying the dream with their master.

The rattle and roar of the train faded into the background for Ryker-Veere as the aromas of the dreamlamp rose. The sweetness of the rosewood mingled with the bloodlike tang of iron in the air. The steam from the train married with the odours of sweat and metal from the dreamglobe.

Ryker-Veere saw billowing clouds in his mind. Then his vision cleared and he stepped onto the dockside of Plaza de Managua some time ago under the glow of a bright gas-star.

Ryker-Veere's mind was dizzy with the clarity of the image: the splintering edges of the boxes carrying mangoes, bananas and dried cacádas; the brightly coloured exteriors of the crumbling Managuan architecture; the yellows and reds and aquamarines. Luggage was being lowered by rope or offloaded precariously via gangplanks. He recalled the sound of rum-soaked harmonies, of nylon string guitar riffs and the beat of drums drifting across the plaza.

He stood as a younger man, no beard to be borne, no lackeys in waiting, looking up at the pristine white steamer which had recently docked. A man in a terracotta suit and a white hat descended the broadest of the gangplanks ahead of many of the other passengers. He was portly, with a full head of black hair, curling somewhat at the ends. He smiled broadly, crow's feet creasing the corners of his face; a man of unashamed jollity and enthusiasm.

Anders! Look at you! cried Isairis Stroever, father of Isri Stroever. He took Ryker-Veere's hand and shook it enthusiastically. Ryker-Veere placed his free hand on top of Stroever's as they continued to shake. Stroever slapped his other hand on top of Ryker-Veere's, fusing them together in a tight ball.

Come! continued Isairis Stroever. *Casa de Mañana is the best place to enjoy the starwane!*

Starwanes were rare but incomparably beautiful sights. A dying gas-star's light would be reduced to a deep orange colour and flounder low in the sky, casting long shadows. At its denouement, 'the indigo minutes', the star would turn violet, then a deep purple indigo, and finally darkest blue before dipping into the nearest sea-street in a hissing, fizzing mess. The dark globe would be lost in clouds of steam, and as the vapours cleared, the gas-star would be nowhere to be seen.

The poor, the rich, the good, the great, the foul, the fearless and the fearful would travel far to see such a phenomenon and capture the sight in luminous plates. Some would take several pictures in quick succession. Children and adults alike would enjoy stepping under the black fabric of lantern tents to see a Lebrecht Lantern Show in full swing as it travelled from street to street, neighbourhood to neighbourhood: light shining through one plate, quickly being replaced with the next as you watched the shadows dance on a faraway street. This was the way that moments in time were captured on coloured glass for all to enjoy.

Memories of childhood were swimming through Ryker-Veere's head, intermingling with the dream as, in a swish of colour and remembrance, his younger self and Isairis Stroever found themselves on the roof terrace of Casa de Mañana. They overlooked Rio de la Musica: a twenty-mile-long river-street full of anchored boats. These boats were famous for welcoming visitors to drink rum and listen to the strumming of guitars, the beat of maracas and the rhythm of the drums. This was the best way to watch the starwane burning with a vivid orange light, dancing across the dark waters.

After they'd eaten, Stroever offered a toast with a tot of amber rum. *To Casa de Mañana,* he said. *The House of Tomorrow. That is what they believe here. There is no hardship that cannot be ended, no obstacle that cannot be overcome. To every problem there is a common solution...* He raised his glass and Ryker-Veere followed suit, though he failed to mirror the face-achingly broad smile. *Tomorrow...*

This, in a single word, was the key difference between father and son. Isri was anxious and impatient. Every issue must be diagnosed, extracted and disposed of before the end of the fade. Tomorrow, the romantically archaic word for 'on-the-morrow', would bring fresh hinderances, and allowing them to fester and accumulate would be folly.

On the other hand, Isairis Stroever knew that anxiety would allow issues to balloon far beyond a manageable size. A solution for each and every obstacle would present itself in time. He would prefer to go into battle once he was sure of which weapons to bring.

You had something to discuss? said Ryker-Veere.

Patience! Patience! said Stroever, savouring the scent of the rum. *We cannot talk business until we are somewhat more—* he swilled the rum in his glass— *diluted.*

Is it about your son? Little Isri?

Stroever banged his glass onto the table. *Oh, it is about something far more important than that sick little runt! No, this concerns a discovery that will make you question everything you have ever known. And, if you are patient—* he took a hearty swig of his rum— *I will share it with you...*

17
THE PLOTTING IN THE HUSH

E-365301...
J-150504...
K-202636...

Lightwing...

The words of the old woman rattled around in Krish's head for some time. And so did that handful of syllables she'd uttered moments before dying. They sounded familiar. Who had the ancient woman been? Why was she so close to the Empress? Close enough for the Empress to allow her to name the Myrthali after her stillborn child. And did she love the Empress or hate her?

My old friend, my old enemy.

And who was this rich man the woman had said he would meet?

He managed to locate some paper and a pencil to jot down the codes, but it was imprinted in his brain now anyway.

'So, we're after this Myrthali cobblers?' asked Thira at dinnertime.

'Yes,' replied Krish, poking a jellylike substance which appeared to have meat trapped in it. It tasted like salty fish. His throat was adamant that it go no further and be expelled from his body forthwith.

'And that's summink to do with time?'

'Yes. Well, it *is* time. Sort of.'

'Right ho. And the old lady snuffed it?'

'Yes.'

'And snuffed it means dead?'

'You got it, Thira.'

'Awesome! What's dead again?'

'Er... it's what happens when you're not alive anymore.'

'Oh.' Thira pondered for a moment. 'I'm going to put this on my head.'

'What?! That's a tray! Why are you putting that on your head?'

'This death malarkey sounds well boring. Better do lots of interesting things while I have the chance! You gonna eat that?'

'Eat what?'

'That thing on the floor there.'

'That's someone's old sock.'

'Oh. Can I eat it?'

'It's not advisable.'

'Boring. What's that? Can I ride it?'

'That's a guard.'

''E'll give us a lift somewhere, won't 'e?'

'That's not how guards work.'

'Why did you shout at me?'

Thira's tone had suddenly changed.

'What?' said Krish.

'Just before we got to the Pale Hunting Grounds? I was tryin' to 'elp!'

'What... you...remember that?'

'Maybe... I dunno. Anyway, what was I talkin' about? What are these Pale Huntin' Grounds? Was I there?'

Krish sighed. Every now and then Thira would make reference to something they'd experienced together on Ilir. He'd see his friend's face in Thira's, clear as he was back on that tiny desert world. Then it would vanish.

At this point ShadowThief appeared and sat down. She looked from one to the other and then stared piercingly at Thira, visions of embraces and sword fights flashing in indigo and gold as she caught the light. She pointed at Thira and mimed an explosion. She then stared expectantly.

'What the blinkin' 'ell?!' said Thira.

'I think she's asking if you can make things explode again,' said Krish. 'Like you did on the street where we were doing the laundry.'

'Oh. I mean, I dunno. I was right narked off.'

'So maybe... if we made you angry...'

'Shouldn't be difficult.'

ShadowThief nodded. She pointed at Thira, mimed an explosion again, drew a circle in the air, pointed at the three of them, then her hand swooped downstairs and then up, like a bird swooping and soaring. *If he can do the explosion again, we can all escape.* Escape seemed to involve sliding or flying, or something Krish couldn't quite discern.

And with that, ShadowThief took to her feet. She pointed to Krish and mimed cleaning sheets. Then she departed.

'I'll be back soon,' said Krish to Thira. 'Don't do anything weird, okay?'

'Got it!' said Thira. 'So, no sticking spoons up m'nose again, yeah?'

'Probably best avoided, yes.'

'Gotcha.'

§

Three lines of large butlers' sinks. A few inmates at work with the laundry. The shaded figures in the gantries above obscured by the glare of the lights. Krish found Aemea wringing a bedsheet over a drain in the far corner. She must have been doing this for a while as there was hardly a drop left to drip into the grate.

Krish knelt beside her.

'One of the sinks is leaking,' Aemea kept her voice down and did not look up at Krish. 'It's in the far corner. You can't see it from above. The wooden flooring has rotted away over time. There's a water tank below. Shad and I think it leads to the fresh water supply system, which must come from street level. We saw the pipes clearly on the way in; they're wide enough to fit into by some way.

'But there's a problem. Well, two problems. Well, three. Well... Amongst our problems are: will the pipe be completely submerged or is there space to breathe? How long would it take us to get to the top? Would we be going against the tide, as it were?

'And then there's the big one. A large metal plate separates us from the pipes. From what we can see through the floor-boards, there are no hatches or openings in the metal plate. No latches holding it in place. Looks like there's a gap on the far side but it's not big enough to squeeze through.

'So even if we were all to sneak into the room through the rotten floorboards without being detected, as soon as we broke through the metal plate *somehow*—' Krish knew what she was hinting at: if they were able to make Thira breakthrough using his as-of-yet untamed magical abilities, '—there's no way we could do it without attracting attention.'

'Okay,' said Krish, barely able to keep up with the multitude of obstacles Aemea's 'plan' entailed. 'We also have to get out before the end of the Dream-Pedlars' Parade.'

'Which will end as soon as NightTime is over. And who knows when that could be. Why the urgency?'

'I can't explain.'

'Why not? If we are to trust one another—'

'No, I mean I can't explain because I really don't know. I don't really know what the Dream-Pedlars' Parade is, to be honest.'

Aemea stared at him curiously. 'You don't have people selling dreams on the undermarket in your neighbourhood? I suppose they just... give dreams away for free!'

'Erm... I mean... where I'm from people just kinda have dreams...'

Aemea spoke delicately, almost patronisingly. 'Krish, there is naivety and there is pretending that you don't know what dreams are.'

'In my... borough, dreams are what happens when your mind turns off. When you go to sleep. Like... visions and stuff.'

'You dream while asleep? That's ridiculous. How would you even remember on-the-morrow?'

'Sometimes you do, sometimes you don't.'

'Well, most people who buy dreams would feel somewhat "ripped off" if they forgot what happened in—'

'Sorry, you seriously mean people here can only dream if they *buy* them?'

'Well, you can't just dream *naturally*, can you? Though I suppose that is what you claim. How far away is your neighbourhood? Are you really from another borough? I've heard tales of such things.'

'Farther. And there we do dream naturally. We... hang on... I haven't dreamt once since I've been here... Not once...'

'I should think not! It's illegal! You'd get arrested all over again! They like to group dreams together with narcotics, despite the lack of side effects. They're not narcotics, as much as the authorities treat them as such. They're pleasant, but not damaging or addictive. Dreaming has just become associated with debauchery and what the well-to-do consider the "under-class", despite the fact that everyone knows the rich are some of the dream-pedlars' keenest customers. They just purchase theirs more discreetly.

'Anyway, the undermarket is swamped with dream-pedlars, who can only legally ply their trade on one night. Tonight. It's taken many years, I was too young to remember the last one, but now it has come again. People travel far and wide to experience the wonders of the Dream-Pedlars' Parade.'

Krish was still processing the idea of a world where no one dreamt. Aemea waved a hand in front of Krish's face to tune him back into reality.

'So, what did the old woman say to you?' said Aemea.

'Er... it's pretty complicated. Oh, and do you know any, like, super-rich men in KnockThrice? Maybe one who lives at 63 Kierbeckerstraße.'

Aemea stopped wringing the bedsheet. There was a quiet intensity in her voice as she spoke.

'The gentleman you speak of is Lord Anders Ryker-Veere. I have never met him, but I am most certainly aware of him. Everyone is. Anyway, consider mine and Shad's proposal. Now, I need some time alone. I'm having a brainwave in roughly an hour.'

'You schedule your brainwaves?'

'No. Now, go away. I'm very busy doing this thing I'm doing. Speak next to Shad, not me.'

Krish left Aemea alone, confused by her, as always.

§

Krish had spent the fade toying with the sandwich bag. Placing pieces of paper in it, sealing the bag and submerging it in one of the sinks in the laundry room. Each time he retrieved the bag, the paper came out dry.

Reassured, he'd placed the list of codes the ancient woman had given him in the bag, sealed it and placed it in his pocket. He had to be sure the paper wouldn't be destroyed in their escape attempt. If they got to make it without endangering Thira's life.

'Why didn't you stay?'

Krish looked Thira in the eyes as his new companion asked the question across the canteen table at breakfast. Thira seemed different, tender and patient.

'In Ilir?' Thira continued.

'If I didn't touch the Myrthali and return home, my Mum would have died. And I was scared of losing the Myrthali if I stayed longer. I'd fought so hard to get it.'

'But you left me.'

'Yes. Sorry. But you're here now.'

'Yeeeaaah...' Thira's eyes narrowed. 'You might 'ave consulted me, ya know. Before bringin' me to life and that.'

'That doesn't make any sense!'

'This 'ole thing don't make no sense! Why am I 'ere and not in one of these outdoorsy places you're always talkin' about? Sounds so much better than this gaff!'

Krish knew what he meant. Being trapped in a windowless cell deep beneath the ground, with nothing but the cold weight of night awaiting them if they escaped to the surface, was so far from the sunny expanses of Ilir.

'Might be best to keep your voice down,' said Krish.

'No! I want answers!' said Thira. 'What's this life malarkey all about, eh?'

'You know what, Thira, I have no idea! But stop talking about... *outside*... Didn't you hear Aemea? *They*—' his eyes darted upwards, '—don't like the E word. So they're probably not too keen on the O word either.'

Minutes of silence followed. Then ShadowThief arrived and sat next to Thira, looking from him to Krish and back again, sensing the tension between them.

She put her hands together as if in prayer, placed them against the side of her face, closed her eyes and cocked her head to one side, feigning sleep. She then broke the pose and placed a finger definitively on the table.

Tonight.

ShadowThief elaborated at length and Krish and Thira were only just able to follow. At times ShadowThief scribbled words or pictures on paper to help:

Two hours after lights out, we must simultaneously start fights in our respective cells. They will put us on laundry duty. Aemea has been listening carefully to the pipes. It happens early on: for a short time, the pipes are flushed in the opposite direction, perhaps to be cleaned. This is our only hope. When they flow in the other direction it means death. When we reach the laundry room, we must incite McCrairy to start a fight. It will not take much. I will do this and then clear out of the way. While the claws are distracted, we break through the rotten boards and into the chamber beneath. Here, Thira must break the metal plate. If he cannot do this, we have no hope.

Thira was not best pleased about this.

We will jump into the water and be washed into the pipes. Smuggle food. We will need some sustenance to keep going. We have no idea how long it will take us to reach street level.

The gestures stopped. Krish was open-mouthed and waiting for more but there was none. He turned to Thira – also open-mouthed, upper lip curled up as if to say *that's it?!* – and then back to ShadowThief.

'Where is she?' said Krish.

ShadowThief stared warily back. Krish took to his feet abruptly.

He found Aemea in her cell, squashing packs of some of the particularly gloopy food from the canteen into long, flat shapes, so they were less noticeable when stashed about her person.

'And what happens when we're swept under water and drowned?' said Krish.

Aemea looked up in shock. 'Keep your voice down!' And more loudly: 'Thank you for coming to play cards.' She dished out some cards and Krish did his best to guess the rules as they pretended to play.

'Remember, I am an expert burglar,' said Aemea in hushed tones. 'I have smuggled my way into properties via many a pipe. I saw them on the way in and I know the type well. They are rounded and there is usually at least a small pocket of air at the top. Usually. I've listened carefully, the pipes are flushed in the opposite direction for a few minutes only—'

'Enough time to drown!'

'We will not drown.'

'How do you know?'

'*We will not drown!* Trust me, I will know.'

'How? And how did you know the food would make people ill? And how did you know that punch would have hit you? And—'

'I was born with it.'

'What?'

'It's gotten stronger over the years.'

Aemea placed her cards down and picked up a fork, holding it over her forearm, poised to stab it into her flesh.

'I can feel it right now. In an hour's time my arm hurts because I was demonstrating my freaky little ability to you. Except...' She placed the fork on the floor of her cell and retrieved her cards. 'Now it doesn't. I can't feel it anymore.

'You see, I can always *feel* one hour into the future. I focus on a particular course of action, a decision I might take, and my mind tells me how I will feel in an hour. Will I be in pain? In ecstasy? Will I be thinking hard about something? Am I soaked up to my arms in soapy water or dry as a bone? I've had it my whole life, but the older I get, the stronger it gets.

'I can't see in the future; I can't taste, I can't smell, I can't hear... but I can *feel*. Always an hour. Exactly an hour. And in an hour from now my mind is buzzing with excitement, anticipation and apprehension. I'm sure that is because the four of us have all agreed it must be fadenigh.'

'And how does that help work out if it'll actually—?'

'Because, my miniscule-brained friend, from the moment our little distraction in the laundry room begins, it will take us minutes to put our plan into operation. If I am overwhelmed with the sensation of sitting on the floor of one of the solitary confinement cells, or I feel nothing at all, then I will command us to stop straight away and give ourselves up. If I feel dampness and adrenaline, then we have chosen wisely. Now kindly shove off and make your unscheduled visitations less abrupt in future.'

'What?!'

'Did you understand the shove off part well enough?'

Krish sighed. 'Yes.'

'Jolly good. Toodle-oo for now then.'

Krish rolled his eyes. 'You're weird, Aemea. Super-weird.'

'And yet for some reason you're not questioning whether my ability is real. You are curious, Krish...'

'I've known weirder.'

'Like your friend, Thira. Tell me... *is* he your friend? Or just some clingy acquaintance? Or...'

'I wish I knew.'

§

Krish returned to the canteen, now largely abandoned, to find Thira sitting next to a plate with the same amount of food on it as when he'd left.

'Right, so we've got to be ready,' said Krish under his breath. 'Tonight. I mean, fadenigh. Think that's tonight, right? Anyway, fadenigh—'

'Wha's a tool?' said Thira.

'Ugh! We don't have time for this, Thira!'

'I'm serious, Krish!' Suddenly Thira was standing up, talking loudly and stared at him with fury in his eyes.

'It's... well, it's kind of a couple of things,' said Krish. 'It's like a... tool, device, thing you use to fix stuff, or it's a word some people use to... well, describe somebody as an idiot.'

'Yeah. Sounds about right. Sounds pretty much like what ya think I am! Just conjured me up to be some idiot what fixes things for ya! Well, if I've got to be angry to do this explosion thingamy—'

'Thira!'

'If I've got to be really bloody mad to do the explosion whatsit, well-bloody-done! Job done, mate! Glad this tool could be o' service to ya!'

Thira's eyes were swimming in fury before he stormed off. Krish noticed that the chair he'd flung to one side as he passed had fallen apart with surprising ease, shimmering for a moment in pieces on the ground.

18

THE BROKEN CLAW & THE AMETHYST BLADE

There were mutterings in the gloom. Every syllable mingled with the constant plopping of water from a leaky pipe above his bunk, echoing softly between the four walls of the cell. Krish's pillow was sopping wet. His face was damp and his hair soaked but the very idea of sitting up and wringing out the bedclothes was exhausting to consider.

He began to tune into the voices.

'Betcha'd be a great thief.'

'Whatevs, mate.'

'Or a smuggler! Betcha dabbled in the odd bit o' burglary, least.'

'Dunno, mate.'

'Whatcha mean ya dunno?'

'I mean, *I dunno*. Whatcha think I mean?'

'Whatcha plannin' to do on the outside?'

'Mate! I don't even know what outside means!'

Krish felt he should get up and intervene but grogginess held him back. A conversation with Thira was frustrating enough at the best of times, and the last thing they wanted was McCrairy, the other voice in the conversation, to kick off. Not right now at least.

''Ow can you not know what outside is? Wha's wrong with ya?'

Please stop using the word 'outside'.

'Wha's wrong with *you*, mate! Yer brain all muscle? Whatever muscles is.'

'Ya what? Wha's your problem? Got 'oles in yer 'ead?'

He heard Thira jump to his feet. ''Course I got 'oles in my 'ead! They're called ears! And them fingamies in m'nose! M'mouth! My 'ead's bloody made o' oles!'

A flicker of light, changing swiftly from amber to turquoise to fiery red, emanated from Thira's bunk.

'Thira!' Krish jumped out of his bunk. Their cellmates and even those in the neighbouring cells were mumbling their irritation.

'Oi!'

'Shut it!'

'Pipe down!'

'Thira, please!' begged Krish.

'Oh! You in charge of me now, eh?' Thira stared Krish straight in the face.

'No, I just... please!'

'*You* choose where I go! What I do! You even chose that I exist in the first place!'

'Thira!'

'No, mate! *You* don't choose anymore!'

Thira's arm rose into the air, pointing up at the gantry. A jet of black tinged with deep, dark red exploded from Thira's hand.

The jet collided with the gantry. There was a screech of steel as fire ripped through metal. The gantry collapsed and fell onto the supporting wall of their cell. The grate in between split, and a section fell to the ground, trapping two of their cellmates.

McCrairy roared like an animal freed. He and several of his comrades climbed onto the bunk and pulled the guards into the cell before they could get away, beating them bloody. The wall cracked further and collapsed altogether. Other prisoners poured into the damaged cell and climbed the bunks to reach the subsided gantry. The guards fought with batons, aiming at the prisoners' legs, in the hope of immobilizing them.

Krish was frozen in shock at the unfolding pandemonium. It was only then that he realised what he had missed.

'Thira!'

Krish sank to his knees to help Thira up. He cradled Thira in his arms. Thira's breathing was shallow. His skin clung tightly to his bones as if he'd lost weight in seconds. He looked into Krish's eyes, desperate and confused.

A claw swooped down and grabbed at Krish. He kicked it away with gritted teeth. He kicked and kicked again, caring not if he broke every bone in his foot. A flurry of prisoners from another cell poured into the room and the claw was yanked down in moments.

Then he saw Aemea and ShadowThief running towards him, against the tide of the rest of the prisoners. Aemea's eyes were shooting in every direction, frantic with confusion.

'Aemea!' cried Krish.

Aemea's gaze met his. 'You! What have you done? My mind's been a storm for hours! I felt terror, I felt pain, I felt victory! I felt the cold nothing. It keeps changing!'

'Please!' begged Krish. 'Help me with him!'

ShadowThief banged a clenched fist against the wall – *leave him!*

'You can't!' screamed Krish.

'No, Shad! We need him.'

'Please,' said Krish.

Aemea knelt by Krish and looked into Thira's eyes.

'Yes,' she said after some moments. 'Yes... I can feel it clearly. I'm sopping wet. My mind is excited yet dancing with apprehension. Hearts beating, running, adrenaline, but alive! Yes! Looks like it's still advantageous for Shad and I to hang around with you merry fools!'

'Oh, great,' said Krish with flat sarcasm. 'Glad we're still useful to you.'

ShadowThief rolled her eyes and marched up to help Krish raise Thira up.

As they moved in the direction of the laundry room, passing everyone coming the other way, Krish was trying to figure out why Thira was suddenly so weak, why he'd lost so much weight in a moment. Each time he used magic it appeared to physically suck something out of him.

There was a great crash overhead. Krish, Aemea and ShadowThief looked up. On the level above, several guards were fighting with a group of prisoners trying to gain access to a small room, the door hanging off its hinges. Inmates were fleeing the room, clutching sacks. A flash of urgency in ShadowThief's eyes. She climbed one of the bunks and hauled herself onto the gantry.

'Shad!' called Aemea. 'Come on! Please!'

ShadowThief fought her way past the battling guards and prisoners and back into the room. For long moments they waited, Aemea poised to leave without her friend, before ShadowThief emerged holding not a sack like the others, but a small pouch in one hand and a short, sharp dull-coloured object in the other.

She jumped down and marched past the three of them, her muscular form scarcely delayed by the prisoners running the other way. She tossed the pouch to Aemea and she caught it with a clink of coins. Krish caught a glimpse of the object in ShadowThief's hand: a short, narrow blade of grey chrome, catching the light only for a moment. The hilt was made of a deep violet crystalline substance and looked uncomfortable to hold, yet it sat firmly in ShadowThief's grip like an extension of her arm.

Krish and Aemea followed, bracing Thira between them.

'We really do need the amethyst blade for our trade,' Aemea explained to Krish, 'though I do prefer it when she doesn't risk her life in such a nonchalant fashion.'

They caught up with ShadowThief in the laundry room. She stood at the end of the line of butlers' sinks, pounding at the rotten floorboards with her foot. Aemea unhooked herself from under Thira. Krish quickly grabbed hold of his friend. He lowered the limp Thira to the ground and watched his eyes flicker open and then shut again.

'Aemea,' said Krish pleadingly.

'There's nothing I can do for him right now, Krish,' stated Aemea.

Aemea and ShadowThief were stamping on the rotten floorboards, sodden splinters flying all over the place. They glanced up at the gantries from time to time, but the guards had bigger problems on their hands.

'Mumma!'

Krish, ShadowThief and Aemea turned to see Mumma's Boy staggering towards them. He was toying with the mechanism of one of the broken claws belonging to the grabber guards. The section remaining must have been over twice the length of his arm.

'Bring the light, Mumma! I'm awake, Mumma! Bring the light! The light! The light, Mumma! Bring the light!'

The guards could have spotted them, but were too preoccupied with the riots to notice Aemea and ShadowThief bashing the floor in. But any second now they could look a little closer.

'Mumma! Mumma, don't turn out the light!'

Krish marched forward, unsure of how he was going to deal with Mumma's Boy but then ShadowThief shoved him out the way. She bore down on Mumma's Boy, whose eyes shot in every direction, only briefly settling on ShadowThief. He played more with the broken claw, channelling his irritation into violent jabs at the exposed wires between the shaft and the grabbers. ShadowThief lifted the grey-chrome, needle-like blade with the handle. Mumma's Boy's eyes flickered with recognition at the danger he was in, but still he called out.

'Mumma! Mumma! Bring the light!'

ShadowThief tore at darkness with two masterful slashes, left then right. She yanked at the capes of darkness hiding in the corners of the room under the gantries and ripped them down like curtains. Light was revealed, ebbing in where there should only be shades of grey and black. She lashed out at the sashes of dark. Although the lengths of shadow left not a mark on Mumma's Boy, he shrieked with terror as he was momentarily plunged into darkness.

He fell to the ground, the broken claw clattering to one side, and let out a high, gurgling scream for half a second before ShadowThief placed the blade to her lips like a finger to silence him. He obeyed then scurried away.

Krish blinked in disbelief: had ShadowThief really just cut away the dark? But for some reason, the patches of shadow seemed already to be starting to grow back.

ShadowThief snatched the remains of the claw, before bounding up to where Aemea was standing. She glanced momentarily at the preoccupied guards above, then thrust hard at the rotten floorboards. Several more stabs and they came loose. ShadowThief tossed the claw aside while Krish and Aemea took to their knees and pulled up the wood.

Krish looked up for a moment to check on Thira and saw him, eyes wide open, holding the discarded claw, turning it over in his hands.

They'd now uncovered a big enough hole to climb through. ShadowThief shoved past Krish and Aemea and leapt into the dark chamber. Darkness was all Krish could make out below, accompanied by the sound of fast flowing water.

Short, sharp swishes in the dark below, then dim light flowed into the chamber. ShadowThief appeared and looked up at them expectantly.

They lowered Thira down first; he clutched at the broken claw. Krish was last. He took one last look at the chaotic fight between the guards and prisoners.

'Mumma! Mumma!' Mumma's Boy had already forgotten about being silent.

'I don't give a blue jaunt!' came a voice from up on the gantry, and Krish realised that the Governor had made an appearance to shout at the guards. 'Flush the lot, Devil Spare You!'

'Mumma...?'

The Governor's voice quivered for a second. 'Jeremy...? Get that one the hell up here!'

The last thing Krish saw before jumping into the hole was the claws reaching out for Mumma's Boy.

There was illumination, thanks to ShadowThief slicing away the shadows, but the chamber was still dim. The edges of the dark were frayed and starting to close in on the light. The shadows were healing themselves and regenerating.

The four of them stood on a black metal plate which was part the way down a long, horizontal length of pipe. A pipe thick enough to squeeze an elephant through, thought Krish.

They could feel the vibration from the rushing water below them.

ShadowThief lay on her front and cut away at the dark to reveal a brickwork walkway part the way down one side of the pipe, about a meter below. Aemea and ShadowThief stepped onto the walkway and began to walk around the thick plate. Krish tried to get Thira to follow, but Thira resisted. In the end Krish seized the broken claw and threw it to the ground ahead of them. Thira leapt after it, then clutched at it as if it were his teddy bear

'There has to be a weak point!' said Aemea. 'It'll be where the metal is affixed at the edge. Come on!'

The floor was submerged under a thin layer of water. The metal plate must have been 30cm thick. There were two large round metal supports holding the plate up either side of them, maybe five metres apart. They were as thick as Krish's neck, but there were couplings attaching the supports to the plate which were no wider than his little finger.

Here! ShadowThief was indicating the couplings.

Despite the deafening roar of the water, Krish was aware of other sounds. There was a commotion above. The fighting was dying down and he could discern the guards' barking commands.

'The Cank! Check the Cank! And the laundry room!'

'That's our weak point,' said Aemea. She and ShadowThief turned to Thira, crouched in the corner, fiddling manically with the claw. His skin clung tightly to his bones and his clothes now appeared several times too large.

'He can't,' said Krish fearfully.

Aemea cocked her head to the side, her eyes still on Krish, her rage just about contained.

'I feel two things,' she said. 'I feel the bars in my hands, the frustration, fury, very much focussed on one person. *You,* I believe. But when I concentrate on Thira... I'm soaked to the bone but exhilarated. Either way, I do not feel grief. Whatever we do, Thira lives. Not that you really care for him in that way!'

'What?!'

'You don't, Krish! You don't care about Thira!' Thira was tinkering still with the claw as Aemea spoke. He tossed two small fragments of metal over his shoulder. 'All you care about is your needs!'

ShadowThief banged the metal plate in frustration and threw her hands up in the air, the amethyst blade still in her grip. She pointed at Thira, exasperated. Thira appeared to be twisting something on the claw round, tightening it.

'Oh, and you really care for me and Thira!' spat out Krish. 'Do you? Only as long as we're useful! You two just care about saving your own skins!'

'I'll admit,' said Aemea, 'that I do value my own skin. Stops all my organs from plopping out, which would be dreadfully messy and somewhat inconvenient for me. But perhaps we escape first and worry about interpersonal relationships later.'

'Sorry, what?'

'Krish, if you want us to live... we have to use Thira's powers.'

Krish heard the commotion overhead and turned to Thira in desperation.

'Thira,' said Krish, his voice largely lost under the roar of the water. Thira paused for a moment, then continued with her work. 'Thira, please... we need your help.'

Another pregnant silence. Thira placed the claw down on the ground and stared at Krish, his eyes large and lost in his gaunt face. Some understanding passed through the dank air between them.

Then Thira wandered in the direction of the nearest support. The others parted to give him a clear path. Thira examined the support. He turned slowly to look at Krish with eyes smouldering with fury. He breathed heavily through his nose.

He placed his hand on the coupling. A yellow-white flash shot forth from his finger and Thira's whole body glowed white for a moment. The coupling broke and the plate crashed downwards half a meter before stopping, still held up on three other sides.

'Thira' Krish leapt forward and caught Thira. He was now no more than a bag of brittle bones, barely any weight at all.

Water poured onto the ground and the four of them were submerged to their knees. Thira's eyes opened wide. He stood upright and snatched twice at the water, recoiling in disgust the first time, retrieving the claw the second. He returned to his tinkering.

'And now the other one,' said Aemea.

'No!' said Krish without hesitation.

'Krish, if he removes another support, one whole side of the plate will be submerged and there'll be enough room to slip through into the pipe!'

'No! Look at him!'

'But I can feel—'

'I don't care! It'll kill him!'

'Oi, mate!' came a familiar voice. All three looked over at Thira. 'There's one thing you're forgettin'. Super-awesome-amazin' wizard...' Thira waded up to the second support and placed the claw around the coupling. 'And top-notch inventor!' Suddenly his smile was all the more familiar. 'Think it was that last little *zap!* o' magic that made the final connections. Can think clearly now! Oh, and I got a million questions for ya, mate.'

'Balthrir?!' said Krish in astonishment.

'Nah! Rubbish name! Think we'll leave that one behind. Thira'll do just fine. Now...'

'Erm, excuse me,' Krish and Thira turned to Aemea. 'I think we have company.'

They could hear the guards stomping about on the wooden boards above and see the flicker of the lanterns as they passed. ShadowThief silently urged Thira to get the hell on with it.

'Right!' said Thira. 'Let's get the fudge-monkeys outta here!'

Thira yanked at the claw and it coiled round the coupling. He pulled at the wires. Tighter and tighter the claw creaked and then there was a scream of metal. The coupling snapped and the nearside of the plate fell into the water, which then poured onto the four of them. There was now a gap in the pipe large enough for them to climb into, water flowing fast within.

'Down there!' came urgent voices from above.

Aemea climbed into the gap in the pipe and disappeared under the water for a moment, keeping one hand on the side. A second later, she pulled herself back to the surface.

'There's a way out!' she said before disappearing again.

ShadowThief climbed into the hole next and vanished under the surface. Thira was not so keen. He perched on the ledge, trying to stay away from the water filling the chamber.

'Ya think I'm goin' in there you are—' began Thira.

'We have to go!' said Krish 'Tru—'

'If ya're about to say "trust me", mate, ya can write it on a big, fat sign and shove it right up yer arse!'

Krish smiled and Thira mirrored his broad grin.

Wood splintered above them, light burst into the chamber and angry faces of guards were visible overhead.

'COME ON!' cried Krish.

Krish seized Thira's hand and they disappeared under the torrent.

19
THE FIGURE IN THE FOREST

Way above the subterranean pipes, yet still below street level, a train rattled through a tunnel. Ryker-Veere remained unaware of the sounds of the locomotive in motion as the dream continued to wrap itself around him.

As he watched the aroma of spirit and sugar cane emanating from the dreamglobe, Ryker-Veere recalled the taste of that time at Casa de Mañana, overlooking the incessant frivolities in Rio de la Musica.

The rum had burned at the back of the throat. Smooth caramel warmed the tip of his tongue, then the bitterness of seaweed crept in at the back of his mouth. For a moment, Ryker-Veere had thought he would vomit. In the present he felt a spasm in his stomach as the ghost of a forgotten experience returned in a reflex. Odour and vision embraced him and his mind swam into the past and it became his present once more.

Disgusting, isn't it? said Isairis Stroever. *They leave the barrels to cool at the bottom of a sea-street and the saltiness seeps in. Can you imagine?* He laughed so hard and so long that his throat must have been raw but showed no signs of feeling pain. Youth would never abandon Isairis Stroever,

The plates were being cleared from the table.

I may grow it long. Stroever stroked his beard, no longer than a handspan down from his chin. *Split it four ways and have four bearers carry it around with me at the centre of a star. Ha-ha! What do you think?*

Ryker-Veere gave an obligatory smile. *You had something to tell me?*

Ssh! insisted Stroever, tapping his finger to the rhythm surfacing from the rio. *I know this tune! So many wasted nights in Calle de Cienfuegos! Ha!*

Stroever hummed with all the passion of the song but with little of the tune until its crescendo was drowned out with clapping and cheering. He added his own enthusiastic round of applause, downed his rum, then poured himself another. Ryker-Veere noticed his friend recoiling from the salt more visibly this time. Stroever toyed with the glass and stared into its emptiness with a distant melancholy.

It's a lonely existence for that barrel, said Stroever. *Tied to an anchor and left to age at the bottom of the sea.*

Ryker-Veere knew what he was referring to. *Your son's illness persists?*

Stroever looked up with uncharacteristic age in his eyes. He was lost for a moment and then tuned back into the world. *The child is not yet ready to face the light of the gas-stars. His imagination is monstrously vast. If made physical, it would span an area greater than the entire City. His fears have grown out of all proportion. Perhaps, given time, a cure will be found. But until then...*

What of Jane's health?

Stroever shifted quite suddenly. *She is well,* he said flatly and drained his glass.

Knowing that he'd touched a nerve, Ryker-Veere moved the

conversation on. *Isri will snap out of it. Boys need time to mature! He is your son, your only true heir – I've no doubt he'll rise to the occasion in time.*

His little sister Helena has been visiting the factories. The factories Isri will inherit and be responsible for, and she understands the running of them perfectly. She is eager but...

A woman, Ryker-Veere chipped in. *Not a true heir.*

Precisely, said Stroever. *Those twin diseases of being female and being capable. Her ambition and intellect outrank his skill for imagination. He must catch up with his younger sibling swiftly. I will take him to the factory in Ha'penny Row again. Perhaps this time he will respond more favourably. It's not easy with his sickness. He must be kept a clear distance from others in case someone unwittingly transmits a disease which further weakens him. But she... she has a great mind—*

Helena?

Stroever shot a look at Ryker-Veere. *Yes... Yes, Helena.*

You truly believe a woman can do the work of a man? said Ryker-Veere with a chuckle. *In all seriousness!*

No, replied Stroever gravely. *But* she *can.*

Ryker-Veere looked to the starwane as it dipped towards the horizon, fading, dying, shining its last deep purple light. The indigo minutes were here.

She, began Stroever, *is her mother's daughter. And Jane is not to be trifled with.*

In spite of her illness.

Jane is not unwell. She is... unsettled. Isri is the one with the sickness. I hope in time it can be... resolved. But for now, Helena is strong. You don't think a woman can be capable?

Ryker-Veere pondered this. He had met Helena several times. A bright and charming girl, though far from the exceptional intellect Stroever was describing, in his opinion. He downed his rum and laughed when the burn had passed.

Ha! You are out of your mind on dreams! said Ryker-Veere. *Let me talk to Isri. Let me help him. I know you don't like me too close. Too worried about his illness. But we must break him out of the sheltered world of his imagination.*

Perhaps, said Stroever. *It may take time.* A moment's pause and then he looked decisively into Ryker-Veere's eyes, his confidence restored. *You wanted to know why I called you here?*

Ryker-Veere nodded coolly, not allowing his excitement to show.

Firstly, let me state this plainly, said Stroever. *I know you have some involvement in the dream trade. Now, please do not deny it. It is not your best kept secret and is something I need your assistance with. And you could be rewarded with investment in your less suspect activities. Allow me to explain how this all began...*

Stroever sat up straight in his seat before continuing.

We arranged a visit to the factory on Ha'penny Row. We grow trees there, as you know. Exotic specimens for medicines and perfumes. Fine and expensive stuff. Traditional avenues of income for my family. Anyway, we made a routine trip to monitor progress. More an excuse for young Isri to experience his inheritance, though ultimately, he was too ill to travel. When we arrived, it became apparent that the workers were in the midst of an internal dispute. There is a small monitoring station on the factory floor, some way into the forest—

A monitoring station? Ryker-Veere was perplexed. *How long do you grow your trees for?*

Years, answered Stroever. *Sometimes decades. This is premium produce we sell to high-end clients for no small amount. The ageing allows the plants to mature. We planned for this forest to be grown for generations.*

Ryker-Veere was astonished. How tall would the trees grow in a factory if they were allowed to mature for centuries?

They grow taller and broader than men, said Stroever. *It is a true marvel. The bark no longer remains smooth, it becomes cracked and coarse; riddled with trenches and crevices like staring down on streets from high above, or the aged skin of a man who's smiled too much in his life – H-ha!*

It was here I made a discovery. Something that could change how we all live our lives. The dispute I mentioned was over rations. Some workers at the monitoring station did not feel they were receiving as much to eat as their superiors. In fact, it was discovered that their food was being stolen from a storeroom in the monitoring station. You see, having a factory floor grow for such an extended period is inviting for outcasts seeking refuge from the harsh streets in winter.

Stroever leaned forward.

One primo, we ventured out into the factory's forest and searched until we came across a figure. Someone unlike any person you have ever encountered. And it was what was in this peculiar individual's possession that I need your assistance with...

A screech of metal, so sharp that it could not be in any dream. Ryker-Veere opened his eyes and departed the dream as the train came to a halt. De Clercq was stood over him.

'We have arrived.'

20

THE NAME & THE NOTHING

The force of the water shot them forward in the dark. Bubbles pummelled them, but there was no air to breathe. The ferocious flow of liquid showed no sign of abating. Krish flew forward, the violence of the water separating him from Thira. They were jerked from side to side as the current swept them on.

Then a crash. He'd collided with something which felt like a hundred knives cutting into him while the water continued to bombard from behind. He was pressed up against wire mesh in the pipeline.

A hand grabbed his wrist, yanking him in one direction. He was starting to convulse uncontrollably, his lungs begging for oxygen. His hand was pulled above the waterline. He hauled himself up and bashed his head against metal as he rose above the water. He took in a deep breath then proceeded to cough and splutter. He could hear the others breathing heavily right beside him, sucking in the air from the oxygen bubble at the top of the pipe.

'There... a ladder!' Aemea was fighting to get her breath

back. There was a ladder a couple of meters away on the other side of the mesh leading up and out of the pipe. 'If... break mesh...'

All four of them gripped the rim holding the mesh in place. They kicked and kicked until the mesh came loose. They held the rim as the water rushed past them, threatening to carry them away.

ShadowThief eyed the ladder and then looked at Krish's waist. She grabbed hold of his belt, then let go with her other hand. She shot forward and gripped the ladder. Without a word, the four of them managed to form a chain so they could all reach the ladder.

They clambered through the narrow vertical pipe, leaving the horizontal one filled with gushing water far below them.

On and on they climbed for many minutes. The heat increased around them. Krish could hear the clanging and whirring of cogs once more; they were still deep under the streets. A dot of light grew larger above them.

They emerged into a broader pipe dotted with gas-lamps. It was dim but bright enough for ShadowThief not to have to worry about cutting the dark away. Aemea and ShadowThief were catching their breath to one side of the pipe. Krish and Thira joined them and the four sat wordlessly recuperating for some time.

Their breaths echoed in the gloomy passageway. The pipe was a dark grey colour with patches of red rust.

Krish checked his pocket. He pulled out the sandwich bag – the slip of paper was dry and the writing still legible.

He looked to Thira, whose skin was now so tight he was worried it was stretched to breaking point. He turned to Aemea.

'It must be a service tunnel,' she said. 'Judging by the gas-lamps. Hopefully it leads out of here.'

'Keep moving?' said Krish.

Aemea nodded. She and ShadowThief took to their feet. Krish followed.

'Oit!' The three of them turned to Thira. 'What about... some o' that... o' that food stuff?'

'We need to preserv—' began Aemea.

'Yeah, yeah, yeah!' said Thira. 'I get all that cobblers. Important fing is, I'm gonna die if I don't get some. Not a joke. The... the magic... drained me!'

Looks of disapproval passed between Aemea and Shadow-Thief. Then Aemea pulled out a tightly packed bundle from inside her overalls. It was damp but could have been worse. A gloopy rice-like clump of food was within.

'Just have a quick mouthful,' said Aemea. 'But don't—No!'

Thira had taken several gargantuan mouthfuls before ShadowThief pulled the package away. Thira collapsed on the floor, munching down the food while making ecstatically agreeable noises, his eyes closed in pure bliss.

'This has to last us until... until... well, however long it takes us to get out of here,' said Aemea.

Krish looked from Aemea to Thira. Thira was staring straight at him as he chewed and swallowed the last of the veritable feast he had just enjoyed. He already looked like he'd restored some of his weight.

'Ya got no idea what ya're doin', yer little twonk,' said Thira. 'Magic, *pure* magic can't just be shot straight from yer fingers! Ya'll exhaust yerself! Burn out! Literal, like! Ya gotta channel it. Why d'ya think I always had a staff with me? Ya can eek out the odd little spell without it, but not much.'

Krish's mouth gaped open in awe. 'I thought it'd be someone *like* you but not *actually* you...'

'Can't 'elp noticin' some changes in the old fixtures and fittin's, if ya catch my drift. Wha's all that about? And the voice! Sounds like I'm bangin' on at ya from the bottom of a well!'

'It's the closest body the universe could find, I guess.'

Thira pondered this for some time and then a memory returned to him.

'No. I chose it. In fact... I remember now. I remember choosing to tag along for this 'ole sorry adventure. We were heading out to Drargor Pass. Campin' and one night... in m'tent... thought it was a dream. I 'eard your voice. Asked me a question. I thought about it for a long time and... well... I said yes.' Thira seemed to snap out of his trance. 'Oh, and where the heck are we?'

'KnockThrice. It's the next world of the Myrthali.'

Thira glared wide-eyed at Krish. 'You're after more of the blinkin' stuff?'

'You two really do make a fascinating duo.' Krish and Thira looked over at Aemea. 'But I have to tell you that the longer we remain stationary, the more I feel the cuffs cutting into my wrists.'

'And 'oo's put 'er in charge anyway?' said Thira. 'What's yer name again?'

ShadowThief rolled her eyes.

'Well, I am in charge,' said Aemea. 'Or I may as well be. And you know full well my name is Aemea.'

'Oh yeah! Same backwards and forwards and all that! Same upside down?'

'I beg your pardon?'

'Beg as much as ya like, love – you ain't gettin' it!'

Perhaps perceiving Thira's humour as a threat, Shadow-Thief stepped forward and held her blade millimetres from Thira's face. Thira was not fazed.

'Can I 'elp you, mate?'

ShadowThief pointed menacingly from Aemea to Thira

without taking her eyes off the latter.

'Didn't say nothin' nasty about you, mate. Yer gotta understand, I'm still playin' catch up 'ere. It's like all m'words and memories and stuff are resurfacing from... well, I don't know where. Dunno if I'm me or someone new or... oh, I dunno! Now, calm down before ya 'ave someone's nose off with that whatsit. What is it? Seen Salvean blades that can cut away the light, but cuttin' away the dark... nice!'

ShadowThief seemed to find some comfort in Thira's interest in the amethyst blade. She retracted it and looked up to a spot where the light did not reach. Delicately she sliced away the shadow and the light spilled in. She held out the tiny fragment of shadow for Thira to see and then cupped her other hand to indicate what Thira should do. Thira obliged and ShadowThief dropped the shadow into his hand.

'Oooh!' said Thira. 'Cold! 'Slike it weighs nothin' but then ya can kinda feel it.'

ShadowThief smiled and nodded. She looked to Aemea.

'Come on,' said Aemea. 'We really must go.'

Aemea and ShadowThief led the way. Krish and Thira followed. Thira looked up at the metal above them.

'Seriously, mate,' he said. 'Another world? Didn't think I could come through them gateways with ya.'

'It's... complicated.' Krish wasn't sure quite where to begin.

Both Krish and Thira opted for silence as they mulled everything over. They started walking forward, Thira bounding ahead to ask ShadowThief more about the amethyst blade while Krish hung back with Aemea.

'So,' said Krish. 'This... Rickerver—'

'Ryker-Veere,' Aemea corrected.

'Yeah. Him. So, you... know him?'

'Of him.'

'Oh. Okay, I thought—'

'You thought what?'

'Well... sounded like you'd met or—'

Aemea had stopped dead.

'Stop!' she cried, and everyone halted.

They'd reached a junction in the pipe. The path split in three different directions. ShadowThief stared at Aemea. She peered down the first path.

'I feel heat, great pain.' She looked to the second path. 'Anger. Exhaustion. Great fury and...' She gripped her wrists. 'I feel the chains cutting into my skin.' She turned to the final path. She stared for some time, her expression unreadable.

Krish became impatient. 'What do you feel?'

Her haunted eyes remained fixed on the dark ahead for some seconds more. 'Nothing.'

Aemea nodded towards the first path. Thira and Shadow-Thief went ahead, Krish and Aemea trailed behind.

'I've never known why I have this power,' said Aemea as they walked, 'but it is most useful. I cannot imagine how you'd survive without it. And it links to your questions on Lord Ryker-Veere. You see, Shad and I, until recently, worked for Ryker-Veere. Not that we were aware of it at the time.

'Everybody in the, er, "sub-legal" world has their speciality. Ours was entering places that we were not meant to enter and taking valuable items. As we could provide shadow, something dream-pedlars were struggling to acquire without our assistance, we began to focus on rare items used to create certain dreams. Lampwick and fernspore, renlic and kassiciss, if you know them.

'We'd travel to exotic neighbourhoods and come back with Milk of Kematian from Jed Jalanan, or Lóng Máo from Lù Lvzhou. Then, in Ala I Sisifo, we were asked to raid a karshesh warehouse. I could feel discomfort in our immediate future, though sometimes it is hard to discern fear from exhilaration.

'Our leader, Marsie, would heed nothing of my warnings. Within moments of entering the warehouse, we were confronted by the authorities. Some of us escaped, some of us did not. We spent several fades on the run. Marsie had also evaded capture. He hid with us.

'One fade, along the river-street of Noka E Bophirima, a boat approached and asked to speak to Marsie. It was a contact from our unknown paymasters. Marsie went aboard and returned the following fade looking grave. He went to bed and said nothing.

'Next primo, he was smiling brightly. Our paymasters had passed on their congratulations – the authorities were no longer on our tail. We had been given a gift of rum from a passing ship from Calle Cienfuegos as a reward for escaping.

'Something was wrong. We had failed, so why the reward? And that smile of Marsie's did not feel right. It was less like an expression of joy and more like someone had cut his face open. He made us all hot toddies with the rum and went to check our course with the ship's captain. I went to drink but I stopped myself just in time. I felt nothing. In an hour from then I felt nothing at all. I stood and commanded everyone to stop. Those who had drunk already did not live out the hour.

'Shad was furious. She fought Marsie and won. But before Marsie died, we found out several important morsels of information. The authorities were in fact still on our tail and our paymasters were concerned that if we remained alive, we could be used to trace our unknown employers.

'And secondly, he told us enough for us to find out, after some months of digging, who had been behind this whole sorry affair. A respected businessman. One of whose more covert ventures was in creating and selling dreams; a practice illegal outside of the Dream-Pedlars' Parade. Of course, you know the name at the end of this tale already: Lord Anders Ryker-Veere.'

'Oh,' said Krish. 'Doesn't sound like the nicest of guys.'

'No. He doesn't, does he?'

'So, you'd be pretty keen to take revenge on him by—'

'By stealing a few things that are worth a lot to me and little to him? No, not particularly. I'd rather avoid him all together, if truth be told. The lure of a substantial hoard does appeal, though. Consider it a thank you for assisting us in our escape.'

Krish stared at Aemea as they walked. Her expression was like an unfinished sentence.

'There's more, isn't there?' asked Krish.

'Your friend.'

'Thira?'

'Our trade is in supplying ingredients to the dream-pedlars. His powers could be of interest.'

'Yeah, and they could kill him.'

'I take it you'll consider?'

'I'm not his keeper! Ask him yourself!'

'That I shall.'

They continued forward for several hours. He could feel they were heading upwards on a slight incline. It was getting much cooler and the sounds of the cogs diminished. At last, they reached another ladder, leading up to a round hatch with a wheel attached.

'Well,' said Aemea, 'I believe *up* is traditional.'

They scrambled upwards, opened the hatch and after another minute's climb they found themselves in a cavernous pipe large enough to accommodate a shallow channel of water and a number of ramshackle, blackened boats bestrewn with golden lanterns. There was a slim pontoon just above the water level.

Maintenance workers, said ShadowThief, scanning the boats.

'We may be able to get a ride to the surface,' said Aemea, reaching for the pouch of coins ShadowThief had tossed at her during their escape. 'Let's see where they're going...'

Aemea and ShadowThief went over to speak to one of the captains, leaving Krish and Thira alone.

Thira broke the awkward silence. 'Pretty insightful picking "Thira", mate. Never liked the old name. I'd always thought about "Thira" or summink like that. Think I'll keep it.'

Krish really wanted to ask more about all the decisions Thira had had to make before returning but thought better of it.

Thira idly twirled a finger in the air and produced a small flame no brighter than a tealight before waving his hand to extinguish it. 'Everything's rubbish without m'staff,' he said.

'Can't you, like, get another one?' said Krish.

'Doubt any merchant round 'ere would 'ave one.'

'How *did* you get your staff?'

'Long story, mate.'

'Boring?'

'Nah, it's a good 'un. Just goes on a bit.'

'Did you... did you want to see me again?'

Thira looked over at Krish, a glimpse of his large, dark eyes shining in the dismal light from the boats' lanterns.

'Well... yeah,' he said. 'I mean, you were... kind of stupid and a bit useless but... you cared. You were loyal.' Krish remembered those rare times in Ilir when his friend spoke slowly, pronouncing everything correctly, instilling each word with meaning. 'Guess it was kinda amazing and exciting. Felt like we could do anything because, well, we sorta both knew it couldn't last.'

There was further awkwardness for a moment, then Thira smiled and Krish did the same.

After a few minutes, Aemea and ShadowThief returned.

'As predicted, the pipe leads up and out and eventually joins a river-street,' Aemea said. 'We found a captain of a small boat. He'll pass Humboldstraße on the way, not far from Kierbecker. He said he'd take us. But all "drummers"—' her eyes rolled, '—are to be locked in the hold. Shad suggested he discard that notion and lower the price, in exchange for us not cutting off parts of his body he may find useful.'

'Oh, and 'e agreed to that, did 'e?' said Thira sarcastically.

'Actually, he did. They talk tough here, but in truth maintenance workers in the understreets do not receive generous salaries. And Shad and I delight in showing people that prejudice should have its penalties, not its rewards.'

§

Black smoke poured from the funnel as the tug chugged along the river-street within the broad pipe. The captain steered the little boat onwards, paying almost no attention to his passengers. For an extra fee he'd given them some old overalls to replace their prison garb, which he only glanced at momentarily, as if he was not surprised.

Krish and Thira lingered at the aft saying very little to one another while Aemea and ShadowThief sat on the foredeck with their feet hanging over the bow. Thira just kept making tiny purple flames flicker in and out of existence at the tip of his finger. Krish decided to go and speak to the others.

'I was thinking,' began Krish.

'Good for you,' said Aemea.

'So, the raid on Kierbecker... you think we can make it shortly after we arrive...?' Aemea smiled playfully back at him and there was amusement in ShadowThief's patient eyes too. 'I mean, you must be keen to get on with—'

'You didn't think to invite your friend Thira over for this discussion...?

'Oh. Errr... Didn't think it'd be all that useful for him to be here... I guess.'

An eyebrow of ShadowThief's was raised in amusement.

'No,' said Aemea. 'You don't seem to treat him like he's very useful at all.'

'No, no, no!' said Krish. 'It's not that! It's not that he's not... useful... it's just... well...'

'From what I can discern, you met in his street in some far-off neighbourhood and he was your guide. In that environment he was more capable of using his... *abilities*. But not so much here. Sooo...'

'So what...?'

ShadowThief gestured inquisitively: *So, what's the deal with you two...?*

Krish thought and thought, and his mind went nowhere.

'Right now,' he said, 'I honestly have no idea.'

'He certainly has an interesting vernacular,' said Aemea.

'Sorry?!'

'A very distinct way of speaking. To put it mildly.'

'Oh. Yeah. Sounds weird but apparently he's kind of translated through me.'

Krish's new companions exchanged puzzled looks.

'Well, if you're looking for a new guide... or *guides*,' said Aemea, glancing again at ShadowThief, 'you'll need to rely on something more than your timid charms to engage us professionally.'

'Erm... I'm sorry, what?'

Money!

'Oh.'

'There may be many treasures within Lord Ryker-Veere's abode, so that is exceptionally tempting. Alternatively, or dare I say *additionally*, we could be happy, as we had discussed, with something of real value to two professionals specialising in the procurement of dream ingredients...'

Krish followed Aemea and ShadowThief's gaze over to Thira, who stared back, a dim purple flame in the palm of his hand. He returned their stares with trepidation, shook his hand and the flame was extinguished.

The Woman commands, 'Take your medicine, child'

Eva just wants to play, have fun and be wild

'But you must take it now,' the Woman warns

'Things used to be different!' says Eva and yawns

Eva turns in bed as the Woman recalls

All those happier times outside of these walls

'Do you remember the time, long, long ago

When you read me tales, and to sleep I would go...?'

21

THE NOTE IN HIS POCKET

The chime of dainty vissirus glasses of the finest crystal rang high through the air of the Grand Beerhall at 61 Kierbeckerstraße. A multitude of servants unpacked crates of the small glasses, delicately decanting them onto the large table bisecting the hall.

None spoke a word as preparations for the banquet began. They marched purposefully across the stone floor, the footsteps of their leather brogues marrying with the clinks of the glasses colliding and rising all the way up to the vaulted ceiling, crisscrossed with thick wooden beams.

The sound did not permeate the small but solid door at the far end of the rafters. On the other side, Lord Ryker-Veere sat in his study, a room just over two meters in height compared to the beerhall's eighteen.

He sat and stared at a cubic metal object on the edge of the room, an item with a long and complicated history. His mind was tangled up in innumerable thoughts.

De Clercq entered, coughed loudly for attention, and

Ryker-Veere deigned to glance back over his shoulder in her general direction.

'The guest list, your expansiveness,' she said.

'What?!'

She moved to his good side. 'The guest list,' she repeated. 'No sign of Master Stroever's RSVP.'

Now he shifted his whole body towards her. He looked somewhat incomplete without his beard bearers, his elongated facial hair drooped across the floor.

De Clercq knew this space, his study, was unique amongst the fine, high-ceilinged halls of his great house on Kierbecker. Every object, every chair, every stool, every ornamental plate or glass or little brass bell had its place in the Ryker-Veere household. But the study was allowed to be chaos. Papers and pencils were everywhere, with half-formed thoughts hastily jotted down. This was where her master's guard was down, yet where his mind was sharpest. Only she was permitted to enter, but she was never encouraged to linger.

'Of course not,' said her master, his eyes back on the metal object to one side of the room. 'He took a carriage home. Probably be a fade or so 'til the young scallywag reaches Ha'penny Row to find his invitation waiting for him.'

§

A slip of paper in Stroever's pocket contained the RSVP Ryker-Veere anticipated.

Stroever sat in a carriage, rattling over cobbles, a short distance from both his house and factory on Ha'penny Row, his gloved hands neatly folded in his lap. He did not need to wait for the paper invitation – his mind was set from the moment Ryker-Veere had given him a verbal invitation. He would deliver his response to the telegram office shortly after arriving home.

For now, he was crammed into a carriage, shoulder to shoulder with strangers, their scents – perfume, sweat, pickled ham – all too close for comfort. He was never as frivolous with his money as Ryker-Veere was, so had opted for a group carriage. This also allowed him to eavesdrop local gossip, especially pertaining to his own factory.

An old lady in a veil blathered on, while none of the other passengers paid any particular attention.

'And there used to be a place – marvellous place! – that sold rare stamps. Philately is a personal hobby of mine, you see. All those wonderful little rectangles of colour from far-off neighbourhoods! My late husband claimed he had ones from every street in existence! From Far Eridu, from Far Uruk, from Far Çatalhöyük! Ha! Repulsive liar! And *that* is where he worked!'

The woman jabbed her finger into the air with pure malice at the silhouette of the factory looming ahead. The structure was like a gigantic brick covered in many chimneys. The funnels slumbered, as not even a wisp of smoke rose from them now.

'Don't you believe a pleasant word you hear about the late Isairis Stroever!' continued the old lady. Stroever was the only one listening. 'Brought much work to idle hands on the Row, I've no doubt. But he was a cruel man with a heart of ice, caring not a jot for his workers, I can assure you! Let alone his poor wife. As long as the money rolled in and his belly remained full, he had no reason to care for anyone! Not least that brute of a husband of mine, Devil Spare Him. Now, he worked as a—!'

The horses whinnied, the cart jerked violently to one side and, with a sharp cry from the driver, they came to a rather sudden halt.

'What in blue blazes?!' cried the woman.

'Shut it, you old hag!' snapped another passenger. 'Look!'

They heard the sobs, shrieks, and the agonised cries of a soul hit with the freshest of grief. The passengers peered through the small window in the carriage door and took in the darkened square, the pale, blue-white light of a passing sentinel illuminating the sorrowful scene.

A body lay on the ground, motionless, a pool of blood emanating from the head. A woman – mother, sister, companion or lover, none could discern – knelt by the crumpled body, her dress sodden from the recent rainfall collected on the cobbles. She howled like a wounded creature. A handful of policemen surrounded the unsettling scene. The law enforcers' cart blocked the road.

People recognised this very particular variety of grief all too well. This was no accident and neither was the unfortunate man a victim of murder. The dead man was right outside a three-storey building, a light on and the shutters flung open in a window on the top floor.

The driver of Stroever's carriage shouted at the police to move their cart as the passengers muttered and tutted solemnly.

'All this fuss over one body?' said the talkative passenger. 'It's NightTime! What do you all expect! If this night lasts as long as they predict, if the economy continues to plummet, we shall see many more lives cut short!'

Stroever broke his silence. 'He was indeed a wretched creature.'

The whole carriage stared daggers at him.

'You dare speak ill of the dead!' said another passenger, boiling with rage.

'Isairis Stroever,' said Stroever, 'was more wretched than any of you could ever imagine, I can assure you.'

'His wife was a good woman, though,' said the old woman.

'She was.'

'Devil Spare Her.'

'Wonder what happened to the children?' interjected yet another passenger.

'Oh, the girl – Helena, was it?' said the old woman. 'They carted her off to a relative. Him... well, we all know what happened to him.'

The old woman squinted at Stroever, recognition starting to dawn on her.

Stroever took to his feet. 'Driver! I will complete my journey on foot.'

Stroever collected his case from the roof. He passed the open door of the carriage and heard the high, sharp tones of the old woman, whispering in such a way as to make sure all were paying attention.

'Don't believe the revisionist lies of the *Herald*!' she said. 'Overtaken by grief, my foot! Everybody remembers how Isairis Stroever died!'

Stroever involuntarily reached for the drafted telegram in his pocket.

'Believe me, madam,' said Stroever, 'you know less than you think.'

Stroever toyed with the RSVP addressed to Ryker-Veere in his pocket. He wandered slowly across the square with his case, mapping out in his head a journey home via the telegram office.

The woman on her knees by the cadaver was inconsolable. Stroever looked down at the body, stiff, unmoving. The twisted face, catching a line of sentinellight, was of a man worn down by life but not by years. Like Stroever himself, there were lines just beginning to show on relatively smooth skin.

Here was a life once awash with sensation – pleasure,

agony, discomfort, euphoria, fear, dread, wonder, passion, love; every emotion big or small, every little itch, every little irritation, every tiny moment of wonder, of sadness, of realisation, of joy, of hope, of sadness, of contentment – now transformed in a moment of despair to clothed meat.

The old woman was right: this man would not be the last to go this NightTime.

22

THE DREAM IN THE AIR

Pale, blue-white streaks of light drifted in and out of view at the end of the tunnel ahead.

The little boat chugged out of the broad pipe and they emerged onto a river-street surrounded on both sides by tall, boarded-up warehouses.

Krish peered up at the dark sky. Although there was more light above street-level than below, the weight of NightTime pressed down upon him. The sentinellight offered some relief after his time in Cinta 2031, but it was no substitute for the sun. And there weren't even twinkling stars providing dots of hope in the sky, just the odd sentinel. When Krish dreamed of travel, the unbroken darkness of the City was not what he had in mind – it was a slow, cold terror.

'So 'ow did ya manage to trade in the endless star-studded blanket of night for this rusty metal whatsit? Eh?' said Thira. 'Bloody idiot.'

Thira gave Krish a knowing smile, those large, bright, unmistakable eyes looking into him. Krish smiled back and for some time they sat in silent contentment.

'How are things in Ilir?' he said eventually.

'Oh, ya know – fine. Gulwin planted the crown in the ground and it turned into a silver tree.'

'Wow, weird.'

'I know, right? Anyway, a few rebellions goin' on but most people are kinda fine with Gulwin bein' in charge. I was travelling with my parents, scoutin' out an area for some of the prisoners to...' Thira was suddenly lost in thought. 'I won't see them again...'

Krish felt guilt swelling within. 'Well, you're kinda still there. The old you. Your life continues there... But the new you is here. Like you've split in two.'

Thira took this in and then nodded. 'I thought about it... Made my choice I guess but...'

The silence between them resumed.

The little boat chugged on and Krish noticed an awful stench from below deck.

ShadowThief was slicing playfully at the dark over the water with no apparent concern about dropping the blade overboard. She cut gashes in the night, flapping like fabric, but as the boat left them behind Krish and Thira observed how they were already healing.

'Do they always fix themselves?' asked Thira.

A slow smile spread across ShadowThief's face. She pretended to cut at the shadows around them, demonstrating slowly, swishing like a wand, jabbing swiftly, holding firmly and cutting in a sideways motion as if tearing gradually through a tough substance.

Depends how deeply you cut them. How much you mean it.

Krish went below deck to find the toilet and stumbled upon the source of the stink rising up to the deck. In a crate, loosely nailed together, large gaps between boards, he saw what looked like an animal, though it was more like a hunk of breathing meat lolloping about. If it had ever had eyes or ears, or even limbs, he couldn't make them out. He could discern a mouth from its whimpers and the piles of rancid excrement told him it must have at least one more orifice.

He let the creature be, deeply disturbed by its presence. When he did locate the latrine – simply a hole in the floor revealing the water below – he was violently sick before he could do anything else.

Later, the captain went below. The rocking of the crate increased for a minute or so and then stopped. Even in the gloom over the river-street, Krish could make out the blood in the water. He ate little of the meal the captain prepared, staring at the meat, wondering where animals lived in a world that was all city.

He was glad to see that Thira was tucking in at least. He'd been restored every time they ate and looked back to his normal weight now.

The river-street widened and the number of sentinels passing overhead increased. Some barges peeled off to enter lock systems, taking them up or down to other river-streets.

In this stretch of river there were broad, white stone buildings criss-crossed with wooden beams. Bawdy singing, cheering and clapping came from the dwellings. Occasionally figures appeared at the windows to empty their stomachs into the water. Men in small boats rowed haphazardly about the river-street, often going in circles as they tended to have an oar in one hand and a ceramic flagon or glass stein of beer in the other. In one boat a portly gentleman was fast asleep, snoring loudly while a goat sat in the stern, occasionally nudging the rudder optimistically.

Then a more disturbing sight came into view. Just as the buildings cleared to reveal a bustling square, Krish could see a lifeless body floating face down in the water between them and the square. Then he spotted several more cadavers bobbing about in the water.

This happens often at this time, indicated ShadowThief. She pointed to the blackness all around, saying something along the lines of: *Life becomes too dark for some.*

Krish and Thira looked at ShadowThief in shock.

'They... suicided?' asked Thira.

Aemea shot Thira a puzzled look. 'They committed suicide, if that's what you mean.'

Thira's lip curled up in disgust. 'Committed? Suicide a crime in your world? They go around arresting stiffs, eh?'

Thira and ShadowThief both looked puzzled. Then ShadowThief nodded, *He's got a point.*

'But why so many?' asked Krish, his eyes still on the corpses in the water.

Aemea sighed. 'It's NightTime. There are always those who take their own lives when it is night. They say this could be the longest we have seen in some considerable time. In our lifetimes at least. The drinking is the worst, of course, but some blame overindulging in dreams. Silly, of course. Dreams aren't addictive. They're not narcotics. Even children can enjoy dreams. But the dream trade isn't regulated so there are a very small number that are a little too potent and trigger despair. Newspapers like to blame dreams for all the City's woes, of course they do. They like easy targets...'

'Dreaming's pretty normal in my world,' said Krish.

'Same 'ere!' said Thira. 'Pretty weird to 'ave all them pretty pictures ya get at bedtime turned into something ya flog to people. Then again, pretty flippin' weird to 'ave a night that lasts for days.'

Krish peered over the bow at the sentinellight in the rippling waters. The weight of the darkness, the slow terror of night without end, bore down on him once more.

§

They docked and climbed the stone steps. Drunkards stumbled in and out of the many beerhalls either side of the broad cobbled street. They passed an ornate fountain in the centre of the street where a ruddy-faced gentleman in a top-hat was relieving himself while holding his stein of beer steady in his free hand. He caught Krish's eye and nodded in greeting before returning to the task at hand.

Many people, predominantly men, had spilled out onto the street and ShadowThief scanned them as they passed. After some time, Krish realised that it was the forearms of people who had rolled up sleeves revealing tattoos who caught her eye.

'I ain't never seen ta'oos like that,' said Thira. 'All detailed and intricate and stuff. I could make 'em dance back 'ome. Or appear like they were, anyway. If I 'ad m'staff.'

'Shad's looking for potential associates,' explained Aemea. 'The enforcers have never really cottoned on to the code. See the child wearing the cap depicted on that man's arm? The cap is too big for him because he has purloined it from his father. This is the sign of a thief.'

''Ow can ya tell it's too big for 'im? I can 'ardly make out that the little bleeder's got an 'at on in the first place!'

'Well, if it wasn't subtle, it would be too obvious. And we're used to spotting tattoos such as these from afar.'

'None of it seems obvious at all,' added in Krish. 'What about the tattoo of the posh people wearing masks?'

'The masquerade? Counterfeiters. See the ladies in scarlet dresses, plenty of flesh on display, sporting tattoos depicting voluptuous beauties wheeling carts overflowing with fruit? Let us just say that they prefer to commit their crimes indoors.'

'Oh!'

'What about the man with the snake down his arm?' enquired Krish.

'Oh, I think he just likes snakes.'

'You don't see many animals around here really,' said Krish to himself. With no countryside, where did the animals come from? And where did wood come with no forests?

'So 'oo the 'ell are we looking for?' Thira's question woke Krish from his daydream.

Aemea didn't answer for a moment as she and Shadow-Thief scanned the arms of all the individuals hanging about on the edges of crowds or lingering in dimly lit doorways. Then they homed in on one man in particular.

He stood by a small door, ajar, his broad-brimmed hat casting a shadow across his face, his left sleeve rolled up. The tattoo depicted a cobbler at work making shoes.

'Cobblers? Shoemakers?' Thira was puzzled

'Precisely,' said Aemea as ShadowThief went to introduce herself to the man. 'You really don't know the history of the dream-pedlars...?'

Krish and Thira answered her with blank looks.

'Well, there was once an emperor in these parts – Prešeren of Dežela Izgubljenih Kraljev. He overthrew the King and declared the neighbourhood his own, calling it Zmajev Most. "Most" meaning "bridge" in their language, of course. A bridge long and broad enough to accommodate many houses. It became the centre of his empire. He allowed many illegal activities to be declared legal, permitting the street vendors to make a profit from them rather than the criminals. Some of the first activities he legalised was the buying, selling and use of dreams. There was outrage from nearby neighbourhoods who feared that liberal thinking would destroy the City.'

'How?' asked Thira.

'No idea,' continued Aemea. 'Anyway, Tzar Ilya II moved in from the Verkhoyanskiykray—'

'Blimey!' interjected an exasperated Thira. ''Ope ya're not expectin' us to remember all these names!'

'I'm not. And please refrain from interrupting.'

'No worries.'

'Excellent.'

'Won't do it again.'

'Perfect! So, Tzar Ilya II moved in to conquer Dežela Izgubljenih Kraljev and removed the herectic Prešeren from power. Although controversial, many still loved Prešeren throughout the Auroic neighbourhoods and they did not want him to suffer his terrible fate.'

'Wha's all this got to do with cobblers?' said Thira.

'Prešeren was publically and brutally executed the old Verkhoyanskic way,' continued Aemea. 'They removed his skin and left him to die slowly, writhing in agony on the steps of Zmajev Most.'

'Bloody 'ell!'

'Precisely. Dream-pedling became a criminal activity once more in Zmajev Most. The story goes, that the out of work dream-pedlars found work repairing shoes, which they could do cheaply. They were, of course, still illegally trading in dreams. Much of the neighbourhood was shocked at the usurping and killing of Prešeren. As time went on, they allowed one night, as Prešeren had been killed at NightTime, to be dedicated to him. And on that night only, dream-pedling would be decriminalised. Much of the known City celebrates the night but the biggest gathering of dream-pedlars is at Čevljarski Most: the Shoemakers' Bridge, formerly known as Zmajev Most.'

'Right ho. So, when we bustin' into this beer 'all whatsit?' said Thira impatiently.

'We have some preparation to do first,' replied Aemea.

ShadowThief came over to Aemea and the two conferred. ShadowThief turned to Thira and Krish and ushered them over, to approach the man in the doorway.

The man in the hat led them into the building and they were soon enveloped by darkness. Krish saw light in one corner up ahead. He was startled by the mix of stale, dusty smells and the sweet perfume reaching his nostrils. A pleasant floral smell he recognised.

They were walking cautiously in the direction of the dim amber gaslights on the far side of the room when a cloud of pale, rose-pink gas poured in from one side. Many scents and odours, some immediately coupling with memories deep in Krish's mind, reached his nose: rose petals and freshly-cut wood made him think of his aunt's garden, and Earl Grey tea reminded him of Miss Churchlind, his drama teacher at school.

The smoke appeared to clear but still there was a haze over Krish's vision. His eyes stung. Beneath the pink smoke there was an image of a courtyard surrounded by tall redbrick build-ings. Sunlight, almost like *real* sunlight, like in his own world, was gliding down to light a corner of the courtyard filled with potted plants and trellises adorned with creepers. There was a plump, beautiful woman seated in a single wooden chair by a small round green lattice table. The woman wore a long, silky pink dress, and a large white hat on her head. She was dark-skinned, reminding Krish of pictures he'd seen of Australian Aboringal people. She sipped a steaming tea and drank in the sunlight.

The woman turned and looked directly at Krish, before standing up to wave away the smoke. The real world of the dank building on Kierbeckerstraße reappeared. The same woman stared back at him but she was suddenly older and more wrinkled. Her hair was shaved on one side, falling down to her shoulder in straggly grey locks. She was larger than her counterpart in the dream and her old dark red dress was tattered.

Krish realised he'd just passed through his first dream here in this world. For his eyes to be open and to smell something in a dream was an odd sensation.

The woman turned to the small wooden table at the edge of the room from which the smoke was eminating. There was a dirty glass globe a little bigger than a tennis ball, which contained rose petals, wood chippings and tea leaves soaked in oil. She turned the dial on the side of the globe to stop the smoke.

'What has ya got here, Warren?' the woman said to the man who'd led them in. Warren nodded at ShadowThief. ShadowThief stepped forward, pulled out the amethyst blade and cut away a strip of shadow and offered it to the lady.

'Ooooh, the ShadowThief,' she said, turning the shadow over in her hand. 'Heard you was off the streets for a time. I trade in lighter subject matter for my dreams. Try Wittlesbach at number 42.'

'Actually, we are offering a small amount of shadow for free,' said Aemea. 'In return for information.'

The woman looked at the four of them in turn.

'And what kind of information would ya be after?' she said.

'We're interested in any leads you may have on enterring 63 Kierbecker, with the aim of reaching the private study of Lord Ryker-Veere himself.'

The woman sniggered half-heartedly. 'As I said, shadow ent worth than much to me,' she said.

'And what about contacts?' said Aemea. 'We have many in Chronometer Dock, Bankside, Limekiln Place and Chambers Street East.'

'That so? Interestin'. Well, would have been. You're too late for 63. So there's nothing I can help ya with.'

'Er, how are we too late?' Krish interjected.

''Less yer plannin' to leave right now, this very fade, then y'er outta luck,' said the woman.

ShadowThief widened her eyes and motioned in the direction of her companions: *We are ready.*

'We are packed and eager to begin,' said Aemea. 'Why the urgency? I am not led to believe the whole building is about to get up and walk away?'

The woman eyed Aemea with distain. 'Ha! She's a stuck up one, this one!'

'Ya might wanna answer 'er bleedin' question, mate,' butted in Thira.

The woman looked hard at the four of them then turned back to Aemea. 'On this very fade?' said the woman. 'Ya're serious?'

'Deadly serious,' said Aemea.

The woman nodded.

'Merindah,' said the woman. She shook each of their hands and they introduced themselves. She did not ask ShadowThief if she went by any other name.

'Ya give me some security,' said Merindah, indicating the shadow in the gloomy room. 'Wait here while I speak with a friend. I will be gone for minutes only. The rest is trust.' She peered into an especially dark corner of the room. 'Security can come from there. Too gloomy even for this stinkin' beggars' hall! And cut it proper! Full cut is worth much more.'

ShadowThief went to work, tearing strips of shadow from the neglected corner of the room. She cut slowly, carefully, as if she was cutting through the flesh of a creature she wanted to survive a procedure. She folded the shadow carefully and placed it on the table.

Once Merindah was satisfied she nodded and left. Half an hour later she returned.

'Dodson and Sparham's, the cobblers on Limekiln Place,' said Merindah. 'Been tryin' to find an in there for many a year. We both specialise in dreams of the more... *seductive* nature...'

'Mistress Sparham is an old friend,' said Aemea. 'Go there with a bottle of iskir, mention my name, do not mince your words and do not offer your hand for her to shake. She is hypersensitive to touch and favours people who do not make physical contact. This will get you a fruitful audience with her, I assure you.'

Merindah nodded. 'If ya can move fast,' she began. 'Then ya're in luck. And luck ya'll need. This fade is the best and worst night to attempt to gain entry to number 63.'

'Well is it the best or worst, mate? Make ya mind up!'

Merindah did her best to ignore Thira as she proceded.

'Working ya way up from street level is not advised. It is well guarded. But there is access to 63 via Ryker-Veere's study itself. The study is in the attic space of number 63. A door leads to the adjoining Great Beerhall at 61, which he also owns. There's a route through the rafters to the top level of the inn at 59. An emergency escape route. He has an agreement with the owner to inform on anyone attempting to enter the building but none has ever succeeded.

'A small fee may be enough for my friend to persuade the owner of the inn at 59. The owner will let you into 61 but will help you no more. A skilled lock-picker would not require any further assistance.

'Crossing the beer hall is where you will be at a real disadvantage. The hall is always heavily guarded and although the ceiling is high, in the silence of the room, which is rarely in use, you would easily be heard.

'Fortunately for you, fadenigh there is a great banquet so I guarantee that you will not be heard *and* that Ryker-Veere will not be present in his study to discover you, as he himself is hosting the banquet. But of course, you would most likely be seen. That is a risk you must take.

'If you had some way of remaining in the shadows—' Merindah stared at ShadowThief as she spoke, '—then you may have a chance. But even if you make it across the beerhall undetected, then you will still have to know the code to open the door to his study. And from what I've heard, the chances of anyone being aware of...' Merindah scanned the four faces in front of her, each appearing unperturbed. 'Well,' said Merindah. 'Good luck to you all.'

§

Later that fade, they visited a tattoo parlour to deal with the prison numbers on their arms. A skilled tattooist Aemea knew would largely be able to conceal them, finding ink to match their skin tones.

Krish winced in pain as numbers began to vanish. There were some lines left like faint scribbles on his forearm, which put him in mind of the flaming feathers on the breast of a FireHawk.

They found accommodation for the night in a cramped room above an inn across the street from 63 Kierbeckerstraße. He and Thira lay awake, failing to get a few hours rest before they set off.

'And when ya touch the Myrthali tomorrow...?' said Thira.

'It's not tomorrow,' said Krish.

'Next fade, on-the-morrow, whatever! What 'appens? Ya disappear...?'

'Yes.'

'And... what 'appens to me...? Do I go 'ome...?'

The truth was too much for Krish to impart right now. Thira wouldn't go home. He'd... well, he supposed he wouldn't go anywhere.

'Yes,' mustered Krish.

'And until then, what?'

'Just... just... I dunno. Just hang around.'

'What am I, your pet?'

'No!'

'Then what am I?'

'We should get some rest.'

'Yeah... sure.'

Thira rolled over. He and Krish endured a sleepless silence which went on for hours.

The numbers and letters of the codes twisted around in Krish's mind in a semi-conscious state of delirium...

§

E-365301...

J-150504...

K-202636...

Lightwing.

Krish awoke with a paranoia that he'd lose the single piece of paper with the codes on them.

He checked to see that no one else was awake. He was alone in consciousness. He got up, wrote them on several more slips and placed the papers in his pocket.

Ten minutes later he became concerned about putting all his eggs in one basket. He stood up and walked over to Thira's coat and placed one copy in his pocket.

'You look splendid, child,' the Woman does not mock

Helping Eva into her fine little frock

Eva hates nothing more than inspection fade

Stopping all the mischievous plans she'd made

The Master arrives and holds her close, he cares

He lays out the board as the game he prepares

Eva wins fast, she slays the mice made of wood

Then the Master he smiles and simply says, 'Good'

23
THE CHILD BY THE WINDOW

The glass steins had been wrapped in brown paper and placed in the storeroom beneath the Grand Beer Hall of 61 Kierbeckerstraße. There would be no raucous behaviour at fadenigh's event. The 54m long table was being set for a banquet.

The smell of roasting meat rose through the great hall as the maids lay the places for the myriad of guests arriving in just under an hour. Napkins were rolled and fastened with leather rings, shining silver cutlery laid out and the crystal vael glasses wiped again if the slightest hint of a fingerprint had been spotted. The last thing fadenigh's guests should be aware of was that anyone had prepared and were serving their food and drink. The staff had to make themselves absolutely invisible.

§

Four figures also endeavouring to make themselves invisible stalked the damp streets outside of 63 Kierbeckerstraße.

They did not pay any heed to the handful of guards in long dark coats waiting along the iron railings, a couple more huddled in the grand doorway. And the men did not look up at the passing figures. But both were aware of each other's presence.

Krish braved a glance at the facade of Ryker-Veere's ostentatious abode. The building was half the length of his own neighbourhood back home, its gables protruding into the street. The front of the building was bestrewn with garish plaques depicting bloody and victorious moments in the Ryker-Veere family history.

Krish and Thira followed Aemea and ShadowThief as they passed into a side alley alongside number 63. They had each counted the same: four guards along the railings and two more in the main doorway.

§

'Fadenigh you will see the truth of things, my friend!' announced Ryker-Veere, patting Isri Stroever firmly on the back. 'I am so glad to have you here! Your father was always welcome in my house, and I look forward to having his son here for the announcement of my lifetime!'

De Clercq stood nearby, hands clasped together across her front, awaiting instruction from her master, who was preoccupied with the excitement of the festivities. Her black dress, pallid complexion and patient, obedient manner made her look like a statue in monochrome, waiting to be reanimated. The occasional sigh when her master's back was turned were the only signs of life.

Ryker-Veere looked back at Stroever, lingering in the antechamber to the hall. Stroever's eyes were essentially the same as his father's, subtly piercing, calculating, though lacking the vim, the pure lust for living, that Isairis had, in Ryker-Veere's opinion.

'And you would have cut my father off mid-proposal as you did me?' said Stroever. 'Given time, I will prove to you what I can achieve!'

Ryker-Veere was toying with one of the delicate little vissirus glasses used to serve aperitifs, twiddling it between his fingers then hurling it up his sleeve, apparently attempting to perfect a magic trick. He dropped and smashed several in a row.

'Dash it all!' said Ryker-Veere. 'Got to get this right! Clear that up will you, old girl?'

De Clercq exhaled from her nostrils at length as she passed her master on his left. 'As you wish, your vacuousness.'

'If I am to listen to your schemes,' continued Stroever, 'why will you not entertain mine, even for a few short minutes?'

'Not if it involves getting on that ruddy tub again! Now, let me tell you a tale that is worth ten times whatever yarn you were going to spin, lad!' Stroever glared at Ryker-Veere, unseen by his host who had drawn close, slotting Stroever between the two beard bearers on his right, placing one arm around his shoulders and casting the other into the air, his eyes focussed on some locale vividly etched in his imagination.

'Picture a room with a door at one end and a window at the other,' began Ryker-Veere. 'Now, in that room you place a newborn child. Through the window the child can see nothing but darkness. And every fade the window opens and a nurse climbs in. She feeds, washes and clothes the child. At the end of each fade, she climbs out of the window again and is gone until the next fade. The nurse never once acknowledges the door at the opposite end of the room in any way. Now, the door will only open from the inside, and beyond is the street where the child may meet other people and embark on a whole new life outside of the room.'

'And the window...?'

Ryker-Veere began practising his slight-of-hand trick with a vissirus glass again. 'A sheer drop to certain death. The nurse places a ladder there every fade and removes it when she leaves. Now tell me, what will happen to that child?'

Stroever gave the briefest, most perfunctory of laughs. 'How old is this child? How high is the door handle? Does the nurse tell the child stories which involve windows and doors? And—'

'You are not answering my question, young Isri!' said Ryker-Veere, getting no reaction from Stroever. 'You have to play along! And you know the answer full well! Now, tell me, within the logic of the story, what will happen...?'

Stroever inhaled a little through his nose. 'The child, having no knowledge of doors, knowing nothing of the freedom that lies beyond, aping the actions of the nurse, will eventually try and climb out of the window. And no doubt will fall to its death.'

Ryker-Veere demonstrated his slight-of-hand trick perfectly – the glass appeared in his hand from his sleeve as if it had materialised out of thin air. 'Precisely!'

'And what has this intriguing fable got to do with fadenigh's festivities?'

Ryker-Veere squeezed Stroever's shoulder tightly and smiled broadly. 'It has everything to do with fadenigh and everything to do with power! You will see...'

Stroever was guided by Ryker-Veere from the antechamber towards the main hall of 61 Kierbeckerstraße, the beard bearers following, forming a star around their master.

'You asked if the nurse told stories to the child and if they involved doors,' said Ryker-Veere. 'She did not! Or perhaps she did! She had the power to make the child fear doors, to claim danger lay beyond them or to leave them out altogether, as if they were little more than design errors in the walls! Power, my friend!' They walked through the tall, grand doorway into the great hall, Ryker-Veere's voice echoing around as the last few places were set for the feast. 'You will see! Stories are power!'

§

The glass had cracked but remained in place in the single gas lantern over the back door of the neighbouring inn to 61 Kierbeckerstraße, flickering its dim light into the street, dark fingers of shadow from the shattered surface stretching out over the damp cobbles.

The four figures drifted soundlessly towards the doorway. An old man with snowy white hair and bulbous earlobes, ushered them inside.

Krish found the innkeeper's silence unnerving. As soon as they were within, his arm waved vaguely in the direction of rickety stairs, then he limped away without a word. They ascended the stairs. With every creak Krish's stomach churned and he imagined someone in the vast beer hall on the other side of the wall turning abruptly, alerted to their presence.

§

The clamour on the other side of the wall was such that none heard a sound from the adjoining building.

As the hall filled, Stroever kept to one side. Steam-carriages filled the street outside. Nobles from as far as Olugunna Opopona and Jalan Ngeow were pouring into the room.

Ryker-Veere began introducing Stroever to his illustrious

guests, but when they noticed Stroever's gloves and his reluctance to shake hands, they lowered theirs and shifted away. They muttered under their breath about how the mighty had fallen or they'd shake their heads while recalling Isairis Stroever's untimely death. Perhaps they also recalled Isairis's child's mysterious illness. Had he ever found a cure? The man was pale but did not have the pallor of a dying man. Was it true he'd spent all his money on a gigantic ship? And that the income from his factory on Ha'penny Row was dwindling?

While Ryker-Veere drank in the attention, Stroever shrank away, waiting in the wings.

§

At the top of the flight of stairs, Krish and his friends reached the loft-space of number 59. Although the attics above the buildings of Kierbeckerstraße were vast, the inn only had a small portion of this area. The four of them only just squeezed within.

ShadowThief cut away some of the dark so Aemea could see what she was doing.

As they waited, Thira but his hands in his pockets. Krish watched as his brow furrowed. Thira pulled out the slip of paper with the dream codes on it. He gave it the once over, shot Krish a knowing look, and placed it back in his pocket.

On her knees, Aemea placed two stiff metal wires into the lock and fiddled around for some time, not blinking.

Moments later, the locked clicked and ShadowThief smiled as she retracted the wires.

§

The vissirus glasses were empty.

Every place was perfectly laid out with plate and bowl and cutlery, a vael glass waiting to be filled with the plum-coloured Maison de Grenelle from crystal carafes. But the vissirus glasses — tiny, sparkling, delicate, usually filled already with a warming, fruity spirit as a welcoming gesture — remained empty. No sherry or jenever or iskir.

None would be impolite enough to protest, but there was a feeling in the hubbub of the great hall that the self-defined 'great and the good' had anticipated a short, strong drink on arrival to kick their brains into business mode. Ryker-Veere was either foolhardy, inconsiderate or preparing something most unexpected.

§

ShadowThief cut lengths of shadow for each of them and passed them around. Krish wrapped the cool, light length of darkness around him like a cape and so his body was now largely hidden from view.

Aemea pushed open the door and the loud creak of the hinges was hastily diminished as clamour from the cavernous beer hall poured into the cramped, shadowy eaves.

ShadowThief tightened her grip on the amethyst blade. Aemea's eyes stared straight ahead to the rafters in the vaulted ceiling. Krish could tell that dozens of different visions were flitting through her mind. Every decision, every outcome, every disastrous misstep. Could she see the best course of action clearly?

Aemea motioned to ShadowThief who stepped out into the dark. Aemea followed moments later, then Krish, Thira last. Krish's heart raced; he couldn't see a thing. The brouhaha from the room below assaulted his ears. A hand reached out to guide him and he flinched in shock. Aemea, covered in shadow, pulled him in her direction. He took Thira's hand and pulled him onwards.

They inched forward. Krish was dizzy with fear while bright light from below stung his eyes. His heart dived within him as he saw the slim width of the beam supporting them. Aemea and Thira tightened their grips. Thira pulled him back from toppling over. This was not a time to be explaining dyspraxia to his friends, but Krish could tell he was a little unsteady compared to the others.

Krish seized the vertical beam to his left as they broke apart. He looked to Aemea ahead of him, gripping another beam, then to Thira behind, holding onto another. Thira's eyes no longer conveyed anger, but concern. He was checking up on him, looking for silent reassurance that he was fine.

Krish nodded. They proceeded.

§

While Lord Ryker-Veere was engaged in extraneous forced laughter for the sake of the crowd of dignitaries encircling him, Stroever observed Edris, Emna, Emese and Esna, stationed around him in simple, black servants' garbs, somehow even more invisible than the waiters and waitresses refilling glasses all about.

Edris was a dark-skinned boy with large, partially blood-shot eyes and a cloud of fuzzy brown hair. He had the face of an older brother who had to remain strong for a family without a father. He obeyed his master's commands with speed.

Emna was pale, with thin, straight red hair cut short. She almost always looked straight down at the ground. She obeyed even faster than Edris, often apparently through fear, her movements jerky.

Emese appeared to be the eldest. Her shining, shoulder-length black hair had the odd streak of premature grey. Her skin was pockmarked. Stroever had recognised the odd word she had uttered so he surmised she was from a neighbouring borough, not so far away. There was subtle defiance in her eyes. Stroever had noted that she was the only one to glare at her master when he was turned away.

Esna was olive-skinned, her curly black hair tied up in a bun. She remained remarkably calm at all times. She was most effective at making herself invisible. Even the other three paid her little attention.

Stroever watched the four beard bearers closely.

§

There was laughter from below. Krish saw hundreds of tiny figures at long tables. The room was far larger than he could have possibly imagined. One of those faces would see them, surely. They were high enough up for the diners' faces not to be distinguishable but if just one tilted their head up at the right moment, they could well catch sight of their faces, the only part not covered by shadow.

The four figures were hugging the narrow beam, creeping forward on their bellies. The cold of the shadow sent a chill down Krish's spine. He felt several splinters tear through his skin and embed themselves in his flesh.

A great banging from below stopped them for a moment. Then they continued as the many voices reverentially stopped for one voice.

§

The burly figure of Lord Anders Ryker-Veere, at the centre of attention and of the four-point star of his beard, held up, as always, by his beard bearers, banged his fist on the table. Others around him heard and joined in. The thumping noise spread across the hall then faded to silence. Isri Stroever watched from the host's left, patiently, curiously.

Ryker-Veere waved a hand from left to right, artfully managing to avoid colliding with his own beard, in greeting to his assembled guests. De Clercq stood nearby, hands clasped, unmoved by the proceedings.

'We live in changing times—' Ryker-Veere's voice echoed around the silent hall, every face at every table on him, '—is how many speeches begin. Any time can be said to be "changing", in a state of flux. A meaningless notion. In fact, at this time, the entire borough is in a state of stagnation. And now night has come, we will see many more deaths! There have been passionate cries for positive action!' Ryker-Veere shouted over the crowd.

'Hear hear!' many said.

'For a man with the influence, the tenacity, the ego...'

Many chuckled at Ryker-Veere's self-deprecating humour.

'...there is the need to drive forward a very real change in the neighbourhood, if not the entire borough! And have no doubt that I have that ego!'

Laughter, cheers and agreeable banging of fists on tables. Stroever did not join the well-dressed rabble. He sat there soundlessly as the preposterous man lapped up attention.

'And so, it should come as no surprise to any of you, friends and associates of many years, that I am proposing that we fight this scourge of debauchery by giving its perpetrators precisely what they need!'

More agreeable fist-banging and calls for swift and merciless retribution.

'And what they need... is precisely what they desire. So we shall give it to them...'

The tone of the hubbub in the room changed. People were uncertain. Stroever blinked. Ryker-Veere kept his audience in anticipation for a few seconds more.

'...legalisation.'

A rumbling wave of dissent spread through the audience. Ryker-Veere waved his arms to calm them.

'Come, come!' he said. 'If you are thinking I am becoming a crackpot liberal all of a sudden, then you are mistaken! These arguments you have all heard, and privately you have known the sense in them. If dreaming were legalised, we would be able to monitor and help those who have become addicted. We all know that statistically very few get addicted and that there are no long-lasting aftereffects. A child can dream safely – yes, a child!

'It has suited many a newspaper to conflate dreams with narcotics, despite the fact that we all know full well that dreaming is largely safe and the only serious incidents have involved those using narcotics *at the same time!*

'And that is why it should be normalised and regulated rather than emboldened as a rebellious act. We can make certain the dream-pedlars are fully licensed and culpable, should any harmful ingredients find their way into their concoctions.

'And you are all aware of the business opportunities! You, Herr von Terzaghi! With your chain of apothecaries! Tell me you do not see the potential! Or you, Halmai úr! To outdo Herr von Terzaghi, at least! Or you, Junko Oba, with your innovative poster advertising business! Many apothecaries are on street-corners and have prime space for advertising!'

'The public has no appetite for legalisation!' a voice cried from the back.

Ryker-Veere pointed directly at the source of the outcry and nodded enthusiastically.

'Ah! Indeed!' he said. 'At first, no. But times will change. You will see! For the fuel of public imagination is carefully curated public information! And I now have considerable influence at the *Starlight Herald*, *The Fadely Torch* and *The Tribune*.'

The audience murmured with interest, fully understanding the understatement of 'considerable influence'. If Ryker-Veere wanted something printed in any of those papers, it would be.

'And, as of this fade, I am the largest shareholder in *The Fade* itself. If we wish to place ideas that will thrive and become truth in the minds of the public, so it shall be. Our narrative shall be absolute! In time, there shall be no alternative!'

The audience began to nod and mutter in acceptance. Stroever had the image of the child sitting by a window in his mind's eye, crawling towards an open window, a sheer drop on the other side unseen to them.

'At first press coverage shall be negative to align ourselves with the public's gut-reactions,' continued Ryker-Veere. 'Then we shall focus in on the innovators who are operating safely. *Your* innovations, my friends! Then the highest bidders with the largest chains shall become our heroes, our champions! In time, we shall change the public's perception of dreams to suit our purposes!'

He held up a balled fist triumphantly.

'We shall change this neighbourhood! This borough! Together, and only together, we can achieve a real change and build an untapped industry! The word dream will be re-shaped! It shall be a word for the future, for clarity, for aspirations, for hope! TOGETHER, AND ONLY TOGETHER!'

Mighty cheers and uproarious banging of fists on tables. Many took to their feet to toast the man who saw a bright and prosperous future.

Stroever clapped to his own rhythm, a cloud of revelation

spreading across his mind. Surely, none here would see the opportunity that he could. It was glorious and it was perfect. And he was in the best position to achieve something far greater and more wide-reaching than Ryker-Veere could be envisaging, even in his wildest imaginings.

Ryker-Veere turned this way and that, bowing in acceptance of the praise raining down on him.

Edris, Emna, Esna and Emese struggled to keep up with his sudden movements. Stroever noted that Emna appeared somewhat distracted.

§

Emna's mouth was closed tightly, her breathing agitated. The time was approaching. She had her spare hand on a small metal item in her pocket. In a few moments' time, she would produce the object, point it at her master's chest and pull the trigger.

§

Krish, crawling on his belly, reached the end of the beam. Aemea and ShadowThief pulled him to his feet. Krish turned to help Thira up. The four of them hugged the wall. On the other side was the study, the safe, the Myrthali.

Krish made his way along the ledge to where ShadowThief tenderly cut the dark away. A dial of nine letters, gold on black, came into view. Krish arranged the stiff keys:

L-I-G-H-T-W-I-N-G

The clang of bolts. Krish looked over his shoulder. There

was no reaction from below, the sound lost in monstrous applause. He pushed the heavy door open.

They emerged into a long narrow room in the eaves of the house. No windows. A number of desks overspilling with paperwork. Empty tumblers were stationed on several of the desks, half-full crystal decanters of amber liquid never far away.

And towards the far end of the room was a dark cube of iron, sitting conspicuously on its own. A safe.

They climbed down from the eaves and placed their feet on the floor. Krish approached the safe and saw that it had a handle but no dial. He was puzzled for a few moments and then saw three square brass panels at the centre of the safe's door. Krish remained calm. He felt the paper in his pocket and ran through the codes in his head...

E-365301...

J-150504...

K-202636...

He scanned the object and saw that there were maybe twenty or so metal slides, exactly the right size to slot into the panels on the front, held in grooves on the side of the safe.

He picked one of the slides up. He panicked at the sight of it. He snatched another and another and another. He turned them over, searching desperately but his fears were confirmed: each had a unique symbol on it, but not a single one of them featured a recognisable number or letter anywhere on it.

24

THE FINGER ON THE TRIGGER

Thira stepped forward and placed a hand on Krish's shoulder.

'Mate,' he said quietly. All eyes were on Krish. Aemea and ShadowThief were listening but still his old friend kept his voice down. 'You, er, wanna update us on the old situ—'

'The codes...' Krish was aware of his heartbeat thumping in his chest, his breaths all the heavier for his failed attempts to remain calm. 'They don't... they're not... they're not numbers... They're-they're...' He turned one of the slides, depicting cherries, over and over in his hands for any sign of numbers. 'I-I-I mean there are three cherries on this one but that still doesn't make any...'

'Can I see the codes?' Aemea's interruption was tactically soft. She held out a hand. With some reluctance Krish passed her the scrap of paper he'd scribbled the codes on.

E-365301
J-150504

K-202636

Aemea's reaction was instant. Her eyes were wide with horror. She passed the slip of paper to ShadowThief whose response was identical. ShadowThief threw her hands up in the air in defeat, the sound of the paper in her left-hand crinkling. Krish thought immediately of the copy stowed safely away in Thira's pocket. Aemea paced back and forth furiously.

'You idiot! You dimwit! You ignoramus!' she said. 'You... Shad! Get a voice so you can help me concoct fresh insults to hurl at this *fool*!'

ShadowThief motioned angrily back at Aemea.

'Okay. Sorry, Shad. That was uncalled for. But *you*!' She pointed at Krish. 'If you had shown me these codes, I would have told you straight away that they would never open a safe! Didn't you think the numbers were a little long for a combination?'

'I... Well,' said Krish. 'It did cross my mind that—'

'With such a small mind to cross I doubt it took long!'

Sometimes Krish found that if he explained his thought processes to other people that they would give him weird looks. He thought in a far more lateral, tangential way than many. And so, as with many other things, he'd kept his reservations about the codes to himself.

'What did she say?' continued Aemea. 'The woman who gave these to you. What did she say *specifically*?'

'Erm, just that the codes—'

'LCCs? Did she say LCCs?'

Krish suddenly recalled. 'Er... yeah. Yeah, she did, actually.'

Aemea laughed bitterly, putting her hands over her face and then letting them fall and slap against her upper legs. 'Lethrin Categorisation Codes! Lethrin... famous for his studies of various types of dreams! If I had seen them, I would have told you *immediately* that they were codes for specific dream recipes! Did she even say that these codes would open the safe?'

'Yes! She said the codes would open... would *lead* us to open—'

'"*Lead us*"?! Now what *exactly* does "lead us" mean?'

ShadowThief looked as if she was going to throw something in anger but thought better of it.

'So... what are we going t—?' began Krish.

'You're asking me!' shouted Aemea. ShadowThief shot forward and put her arm on Aemea's shoulder, her finger to her lips. Aemea paid no attention. 'Why in Devil's name would I know what we're—?'

'This is what 'e does.' Everyone turned to Thira, who was oddly calm. He was examining the safe, running his hands over the surface. ''E's well needy! Trust me! 'E's not about doin' stuff 'imself. 'E's about getting other people to do it for 'im. Jumpin' through 'oops and all that. 'Oops on fire I might add! None of them borin' not-on-fire 'oopy whatsits!'

Krish was crumpling with guilt inside.

'I beg your pardon, my dear Thira,' said Aemea, her calmness bitterly sarcastic, 'but if you're not able to use a little of your powers to get this thing open, your little character study of your companion is not entirely appreciated at this time.'

'Well, point I'm leading up to is... it's up to 'im. 'E wants to be in charge, 'e needs to make a decision.'

'Okay, okay! Fine!' said Krish. 'I get it, I get it!' He let out the deepest of sighs, exhaling all his panic, and began to think through his options logically. 'So, you can't do any magic?'

'On this?' said Thira, patting the safe. 'Nah. I'd need a staff to concentrate m'powers to get the lock to reveal its secrets. Without it, 'part from drainin' meself, it'd be like tryin' to get a thorn out from under the skin by 'ackin' wildly at it with a sword. While drunk. And blindfolded. And—'

ShadowThief interjected by waving her hands about: *We get the picture.*

'Well anyhoob,' continued Thira, 'it's not a magical object, so workin' out its secrets without understandin' the technology... well, it ain't very likely! Too intricate. So, what's all these picture whatits about?'

'Well, this safe clearly uses picture slides instead of numbers,' said Aemea. 'It sounds as though Krish was given three LCCs in a very specific order so they must somehow translate into a pictorial combination.'

Krish's mind was whirring with ideas. 'So the codes could lead to three dreams. And we just need to find those three dreams and they'll all be like one of these picture slides.'

ShadowThief was shaking her head.

'Dreams tend to be a little more complex than just a picture,' said Aemea. 'They usually tell whole stories.'

Thira picked up a couple of the slides, one featuring an arrow and another a mirror. 'But if the story's all about someone firing arrows or looking in the mirror, then it's pretty blinkin' obvious.'

'Perhaps,' said Aemea. 'If people want to hide information in a dream, they usually don't make it that easy. They usually hide things away in puzzles.'

'Right, got it!' said Thira excitedly. 'Three picture slides! Three dreams! We find the dreams, solve the puzzles in them to work out what slides we need, come back here, make sure we got 'em in the right order, open the safe and the job's a good 'un!'

'I guess so,' said Krish.

'Then you'd better write down what all the bloody pictures are!'

A moment passed between the four of them. They knew Thira was right. There would be no opening the safe here and now.

This was already a far greater challenge than Krish had anticipated. Diving into the night ocean, capturing the feather of a FireHawk or tying a length of twine around an entire world had been tough physical challenges but very little had been open to interpretation. What would happen if they got the combination wrong?

Krish had this last quandary bouncing through his head as he started writing descriptions of the slides down on the back of the piece of paper he had the LCCs scribbled on. Aemea, clearly not leaving anything to chance, was also making a note of them.

'There had better be enough to scavenge from this place for this to be worth our while, Krish,' said Aemea.

Krish scanned the scrappy, low-ceilinged room full of notebooks and hoped there was too.

The slides were of a dark blue-green metal, big enough to cover the palm of a hand, and they had ornate pictures embossed into them, each displaying a different item: a length of rope, an arrow, a lantern, three cherries, a stove, a dagger, a tattooed hand, a herb, a mirror, a wolf's head, a medicine bottle, a piston, a needle and thread, a pair of shoes, waves at sea, an ear-horn, a crutch, a flight of stairs, a ruby, a pestle and mortar, a gravestone.

'What happens if we just, ya know, try and guess the combination?' asked Krish. 'I mean, I don't know how many different combinations there are but...'

Aemea looked over to ShadowThief and said something that sounded like 'ooy-hey-ee?'. ShadowThief nodded.

'It's an Ujhelyi lock,' said Aemea. 'If you get it wrong the combination resets at random. It's perfect. You will never get the combination wrong.'

'Unless you're an idiot!' said Thira. 'I mean, you could totally sabotage it if you wanted someone to never get in!'

'It's a lot of effort to break in somewhere just to sabotage a safe,' said Aemea. 'I'm sure it's happened. People can go to extreme lengths to be vindictive. But I'd hazard a guess that most people trying to get into a safe will chiefly be interested in claiming what's inside for themselves.'

'Why didn't the old whatsit just give you the soddin' combination?' asked Thira.

'I don't know,' said Krish. He was trying to remember everything she had said. 'She mentioned... versiliam... versimi- am... veris—'

'Versiriam?' ventured Aemea.

'Er, yeah,' said Krish. 'Something like that. What is it?'

'A powerful concoction,' said Aemea. 'When you take it, you concentrate very, very hard on a fact you want to forget until it's gone.'

'What, like she wanted to forget the blinkin' combination?' said Thira. 'Ah! Because someone wanted to know and she was worried about them finding out! So, she linked some clues up to these dream whatsits so she remembers them instead! Bit of extra security so even if she's tortured, 'avin' nasty stuff stuck in 'er eyes or up 'er bum or whatever, she can always answer truthfully that she don't know. Even if they do get all this 'idden in dreams malarkey out of 'er it's still a proper faff!'

'And some dreams are pretty rare,' said Aemea. 'You'd have to have the right contacts to get to the right dealers.'

Aemea looked over at ShadowThief who smiled with pride and regally waved her hand palm up from left to right, indicating herself and Aemea, as if to say: *Well, here we are!*

ShadowThief then returned to her previous task – scouring

the room. She placed some expensive-looking items – jewellery, clocks, pocket watches – in her bag and gave others a quick glance before disregarding them.

Thira started his own little raid of the room. He pocketed gold and silver items and as many coins as he could, but was paying no heed to the large wads of banknotes. Krish realised that he'd never seen paper money in Ilir.

'Er, Thira,' said Krish quietly as he passed. '*Those* are money too. In fact, they're worth a lot more than the coins.'

'The paper?!'

'Er... yeah.'

'Blimey. Wouldn't take much to rip this lot up!'

'Normally,' said Aemea, shattering Krish and Thira's hushed conversation, 'I'd suggest we split a hoard fifty-fifty. But considering how much we've risked for no good reason, I'd say it's everyone for themselves.'

'Sure, whatever,' said Krish, continuing to scribble while Thira and ShadowThief carried on with their plundering.

Aemea was watching over her sheet of paper and didn't stop taking notes. They could all hear the atmosphere in the beer hall next door intensifying.

'Come on!' said Aemea. 'We need to go.'

Aemea stood up, folding her piece of paper and placing it in her pocket. Krish scribbled the last few descriptions and pocketed his. ShadowThief and Thira grabbed a few more items and then turned to Krish and Aemea, ready to go.

''Ang about,' said Thira. He produced a wad of banknotes from his pocket. A piece of paper fell out. Krish immediately recognised it. Thira retrieved the paper, scanned it, caught Krish's eye for half a second, then refolded it and put it back in his pocket.

Thira turned to ShadowThief. 'Because I know 'e,' indicating Krish, ''as no bloody manners.' She passed the wad to ShadowThief. 'That enough for now?'

Krish felt a dagger of guilt pierce him. ShadowThief accepted with a grateful nod and turned to Aemea who nodded back.

'It's generous, right?' said Thira.

ShadowThief nodded rather cautiously.

'You could say that,' said Aemea.

'Good,' said Thira. 'Could be good to keep in with a couple o' folk 'oo know about the dream trade, ya know what I'm sayin'?'

Suspicious looks between Aemea and ShadowThief.

'We shall see,' said Aemea. 'But for now, I suggest we concentrate on getting out of here undetected.'

Thira shrugged. 'Please yerselves.'

Thira walked past Krish and gave him a firm but friendly squeeze of the shoulder. This sign of companionship mixed with guilt and a feeling of foreboding within Krish. 'I chose this, mate,' Thira whispered. 'I really don't wanna regret it.'

Aemea suddenly wobbled on the spot, visions passing through her mind. 'Suffice to say,' she said, 'we need to be careful out there. One wrong step...'

Krish nodded.

ShadowThief opened the door, bringing the roar of the great gathering to their ears once more. And the commotion below was about to intensify.

§

Her finger was on the trigger. She had practised many times, but it would only take Emna a moment to fail.

'And you wonder "why now?",' spoke Ryker-Veere to the guests, each waiting eagerly for the answer. 'And "why me?".'

Let me tell you. The Long Night is here, and I am at the height of my wealth, power, influence and modesty.'

The titter of laughter silenced a second later as they waited hungrily for him to continue.

'A night of this length, if predictions are to be believed, shall not come again, and I know that each one of you will not allow this opportunity to be squandered.'

De Clercq remained a statue, one eye on Ryker-Veere and the other on Emna.

Above, four figures crept across the beams.

None below looked up even for a second.

The crowd cheered enthusiastically. They rose to their feet and held their glasses high, many clumsily allowing their drinks to slosh about, overspill and splash onto the ground.

Stroever held a glass up high but did not rise from his seat. For appearances, he was placid and collected, but internally his world was collapsing and rebuilding itself, the towers of ambition much higher this time.

The four above were almost halfway across the hall. Freshly cut shadow shrouded them from view. Krish could make out the figures in the hall below fairly well as he crawled forward across the beam.

'They mock me!' The crowd cheered along with their saviour. 'They say my veins are lined with gold and I bleed vissirus! I see my wealth, my greed, if you will, as a strength! As power! Now, I offer a share of that power to you! And never doubt me, for how can a man with vissirus flowing through his veins ever die! Let me say to you, I AM INVINCIBLE!'

This was her cue. She knew what would happen if she did not do this. She caught de Clercq's eye. The head of Ryker-Veere's household broke out of her statue-like pose for a moment and nodded at Emna.

Emna pulled out the gun, tiny, shining black metal, aimed

it precisely, as she'd practised many times, and pulled the trigger.

The bullet shot forth and pierced the underside of Ryker-Veere's belly.

Krish heard the bang from below and felt it as if it landed in his own heart.

Ruby-red liquid gushed forth from Ryker-Veere's belly.

Krish had instinctively slid to one side and was slipping off the beam.

Several figures went to step forth towards both Ryker-Veere and Emna. De Clercq remained stationary, her head down.

Krish scrambled to grab the beam, grab anything for an instant and then—

'STOP!' cried Ryker-Veere.

Thira caught hold of Krish's collar and stopped him plummeting.

Ryker-Veere held one hand in the air, bringing hush, and with the other he twiddled his fingers and like a magician a vissirus glass appeared in his hand. He held the glass over the wound. The glass filled with blood. Ryker-Veere pressed the wound and miraculously the flow of liquid halted.

The room was stilled by the command of the master of the night.

Ryker-Veere put the glass of blood-red liquid to his lips.

Thira hauled Krish up. Krish gripped the beam.

'Mmm!' said Ryker-Veere agreeably, emptying the glass. 'They were right. It does taste of vissirus! Now, what was I saying? Oh yes! I am very much invincible!'

A wave of laughter began to spread through the hall at Ryker-Veere's little stunt. Waiters and waitresses stepped forward with precision and filled the vissirus glasses with ruby liquid.

Emna looked at Edris, Emese and Esna, panting, fear in her wide eyes. All four of their lives had been in the balance if she'd missed. Ryker-Veere had been padded and the routine meticulously rehearsed, but it had been made perfectly clear: miss and all four of their lives would be forfeit. There was a look between them: this was fear, this was enslavement, this was not life.

De Clercq bowed her head and let out a long, quivering sigh.

'You may think I live a life of luxury, but I bleed for such privilege! Now I offer you a taste of my own blood, so we may go forth and savour a life of decadence and opportunity together!'

The laughter continued to snowball through the hall as the guests lapped up the vissirus, readying themselves for a night of great frivolities.

Stroever observed Emese shaking with rage as her master laughed heartily.

Thira was helping Krish climb back on top of the beam.

Emese leant over to Emna, muttering two syllables of defiance in her own tongue at her master on his deaf side. Ryker-Veere may not have heard, but Stroever caught the profanity. He took to his feet. Emese seized the gun, Emna too shocked to react. Emese grabbed the middle of her own strand of Ryker-Veere's beard and yanked it down violently. Her master was pulled backwards with such force that he tripped, fell and the back of his head smashed against the table. He looked helplessly up at his servant. Emese aimed the gun directly at Ryker-Veere's eye.

Stroever had already sprung forth much faster than anyone else. He collided with Emese and sent her hurtling back towards the ground, the hand clutching the pistol now aimed directly up.

The shoot rang out. The bullet travelled straight up and embedded itself in the far side of a beam. Wood splintered. Fragments hit the four figures crawling through the rafters. Thira recoiled, let go of Krish and began to fall.

Thira plummeted, air rushing past his eyes. He had just moments to react. A beam of deep blue burst from his finger, aimed at a great table. The table curved and the guests jumped backwards, tripping over their chairs, gravy boats upended, glasses hurled aside, food flung onto the floor. The wood of the table billowed into a soft-looking substance.

Thira landed with a crash. With a great gasp of pain, he rolled to one side and landed on the stone floor, crumpled in agony as his skin contracted, taut to breaking point.

'Thira!' No one heard Krish above. He turned to Aemea in desperation.

'Krish, we can't—'

'We have to!'

Aemea watched as the terror turned instantly to determination in Krish's eyes. She nodded.

'Come on,' she said. 'If we get to the ground quick...' She was already heading in the direction of the door to 59 Kierbecker.

On the ground, guards had seized Emese and De Clercq was helping her master to his feet.

Thira, meanwhile, surrounded by hundreds of fearful guests eyeing the strange boy who'd fallen from the rafters, hauled himself to his feet.

'Stand back!' he cried. The cluster of guests nearest obeyed.

'Arrest that blackguard!' cried Ryker-Veere. He then pointed furiously at Emese. 'They must be in it together!'

Thira saw a chair on the ground, cracked down one side so the leg and one section of the back had almost fallen off. He grabbed the length of wood and tore it from the rest of the chair, splinters flying all around. The crowd flinched. He held the length of wood up like a staff. It was not right, but it felt more natural than he was expecting. The magic warmed his body and flowed into the wood. His body was not fully restored but his spirit was rejuvenated.

'Back!' he commanded. 'Get the bloody 'ell away from me, ya shower o' toffs!'

As he tapped the makeshift staff sparks flew. He did it again. Again and again. Sparks flew high and in many colours.

People backed away, screaming.

'Back!' Thira was dizzy with excitement, a fizzing energy coursed through him, every cell reinvigorated.

He could see guards shoving past guests, trying to reach him. Fear turned to raging fire within him and he could feel it – it was ready to be made physical. The old connections between his brain and his body were reforming.

Thira swung the staff forward and purple fire shot forth in the direction of the guards. They recoiled as it hit them and were then surprised that there was no warmth to the fire.

'Ah,' said Thira, disappointed. He'd created fire in appearance only.

His would-be captors no longer feared his magic. They encircled him.

Thira mumbled to himself: 'You'd better have something bloody good up your sleeve, Krish mate.'

25

THE COMMOTION IN THE BEER HALL

Aemea's mind was screaming with possibilities.

They were running down the stairs of 59 Kier-beckerstraße, less than a minute after Thira had landed in the middle of the beer hall. Shouting from below. Between the slats of the staircase, they could see figures filing into the ground floor of the building. Aemea looked to ShadowThief and both stopped dead in their tracks. Aemea continued to look down – she felt pain, hands tied, fear. She looked over to the window to a small window facing the street below – adrenaline, racing heart, fear, giving way to exhilaration.

'Okay. Right. The window it is then,' she said. 'We'll slip out the side before the guards see!'

Before anyone else could act, Krish, to everyone's surprise (including his own), made the first move. He kicked and kicked at the window. It cracked, a portion shattered and then most of it fell away. *Thira!* He had to get to the ground, fast. He stared out onto the street below then saw the drainpipe. He scrambled down while the others followed, losing his grip and falling the last metre.

Krish saw the guards filing into number 59. He was ready to give them a wide berth and dash round the side of the beer hall, but ShadowThief grabbed him by the arm. She shook her head at him.

'Wait!' said Aemea. 'I need to envisage the options! I need...' Her eyes shot in every possible direction. 'This way!'

They ran through a labyrinth of back alleys, seemingly moving away from the beer hall, eventually heading down some stone steps to a pontoon along the side of the beer hall where several rowing boats were tied up.

'Yes!' declared Aemea glaring at a small rowing boat.

'We're not leaving Thira!' cried Krish.

'We're not. But our best chance of escape is to have an escape plan ready.' Across the water she spied a hatch set into the stone. 'Pinpricks of heat on my face... wetness... steam! Must be the train station! But there's some discomfort. Soggy feet and... hoping people won't judge for a reason I can't quite... the smell?! A sewer! Yes! This is our best escape route.'

ShadowThief nodded enthusiastically then set about cutting the ropes of other boats and casting them off into the centre of the waterway.

Krish stared up at the glass windows of the beer hall, spying flashes of purples and the sounds of commotion within. He examined the stone wall along the side of the beerhall. He tested several loose-looking stones and pulled one away. He hurled the stone into the air to shatter the stained-glass window of the hall from the outside.

'Thira!' he screamed.

Half a second later he heard a 'Laters, mingers!' from Thira and then he saw Thira jump out of the window, purple flames shooting from his makeshift staff, and landin the water with a mighty splash. The staff left his grip mid-flight, smashing into a thousand pieces on the pavement.

Krish leapt into the boat as ShadowThief started to row towards Thira. Krish was breathing fiercely through gritted teeth, his heart feeling as if it would stop if the flailing mess in the water that was Thira sank beneath the surface before they reached him. Water splashed violently into Krish's face and he just missed being punched in the eye by Thira's arms splashing madly about in the water. Krish caught hold of him. Thira latched on and Krish heaved him aboard the small boat.

Krish was ready to be scolded for coming up with another escape which involved getting wet; but instead, between great gasps for air, Thira was ecstatically happy, rambling with a gleeful smile on his face.

'I did it! I blinkin' well did magic! Proper magic! With a soddin' chair leg!'

It took a full minute to row across to the hatch, but Aemea had been right – the guards could be seen searching the streets and looking up to the roof before noticing them on the water. The guards sprinted down to the pontoon but found no boats to make chase.

By this time, Krish and his friends had reached the sewer hatch. ShadowThief dropped the oars at once and pried open the stone covering. A stench of urine and faeces greeted them. Aemea and ShadowThief climbed out of the boat and into the stinking passageway, Krish supporting the frail Thira at the rear. ShadowThief jammed the stone back in place at an angle and as they ran, they could hear the guards struggling to shift it from the other side.

§

Between her enraged master and the disgraced beard-bearers, De Clercq found she had much to do in the aftermath of the commotion in the beer hall. She did not know what would become of the beard bearers, or what her fate would be, entwined with theirs. She longed for a way to placate her master.

And then she spotted something in the debris where the strange boy from the rafters had landed. A slip of paper. She picked it up. Her eyes widened. She understood what was on the paper and she'd have been shocked if it wasn't the thing her master had been seeking for some time.

For so long her habit had been to fulfil her master's wishes instantly, but for now she kept that slip of paper about her person, hidden from his sight.

§

'And then I was like "*Whooosh*! Stick that up yer posteriors, mates! I'm outta 'ere!" And I flew! For a moment I flew off the ground! Just enough to reach the ledge! I mean, it's not like I could ever like fly with wings 'n' that. That is advanced stuff and only really works if ya transform yerself into one of those wingy, feathery whatsits. Oh! What were they called? It's on the tip o' my tongue! Gulwin was one!'

'A bird?'

'Yep! Those airborne buggers! But the point is, I done magic! We need to find a staff or summink! Seriously, mate, this could change everything! A bit o' wood! Any wood! Well, not *any* wood but, ya know...'

For someone who could barely walk, Thira had far from lost the ability to talk, which made things more exhausting for Krish and Aemea as they stood either side of him, supporting his weakened movement.

ShadowThief was cutting away the darkness ahead of

them but could do nothing about the stench. It was stale, almost sour, and he could detect vomit mixed in with it all.

'Pongs a touch, don't it?' said Thira jollily. 'Know a spell for that. Well, it's a bit rubbish and 'as been known to make people's noses sprout wings and fly off – oh! I forgot! I can make noses fly! 'Sjust the rest of the 'uman bein' that's the issue.'

'I do a wonderful lecture on the virtues of an internal monologue, if you'd be interested, Thira,' said Aemea.

'Ya tellin' me to shut my trap?'

'I was merely suggesting that some of your vocal contributions are not entirely advantageous to our current predicament.'

Thira turned to Krish and jerked his head in the direction of Aemea. 'Do words come out o' both ends o' this one?' Then, once he was sure Aemea and ShadowThief weren't really listening anymore, he added: 'That... bit o' paper ya slipped into m'pocket... the one with the dreams on it...'

'Yes,' said Krish quietly.

'Well... think I dropped it.'

Krish thought this over. Surely it wouldn't mean much to anyone else. He banished the thought from his mind

ShadowThief cut back the dark to reveal a fork in the pipeline. She stopped dead.

'Left,' said Aemea.

They continued left.

'Bloody 'andy that predicty whatsamacalled, Aemea,' said Thira.

'Thank you, Thira,' said Aemea. 'I feel that in an hour's time I won't be quite as irritated by you as I am now. But we shall see.'

'And 'er with the old shadow-cuttin' magic,' continued

Thira, 'blinkin' amazin'! And you,' he nodded at Krish, 'with your... with what you've got! Yer brain!'

'Yes,' said Aemea. 'When he allows it to actually make decisions it's surprisingly effective. Seems all you needed was a little motivation.'

'Er... yeah,' said Krish. 'I guess.'

'Once we get me a staff, we'll be a bloody invincible t—'

Before Thira could crack out the word 'team' in an awkwardly upbeat manner, Krish moved the subject on.

'So, what was the place where the big dream-pedlars' parade is?' said Krish. 'Something "most"?'

'Čevljarski Most,' said Aemea.

'Yeah, that's the one. So, we all need to get on a train out of here, fast, and you probably have plenty of business with the dream-pedlars, so how about I pay you both to deliver us safely to Čevljarski Most?'

A brief glance again between Aemea and ShadowThief, both raising eyebrows wide in shock and amusement. 'Very astute and, if I may say, a little presumptious, Krish,' said Aemea.

Ahead, ShadowThief seemed to be shaking her head and laughing silently at Krish's sudden self-assuredness. No one spoke for some time.

Krish felt uneasy as they ascended a flight of stairs to the surface, Thira now able to walk for himself.

'So, er... I guess we just...?' began Krish.

Aemea and ShadowThief stopped and turned to Krish and Thira.

'Krish, I'm not sure if you're aware,' said Aemea, 'but we were almost discovered by Ryker-Veere and his people. And if you recall, we are not keen for our previous employer to know of our existence.'

ShadowThief was making scissor motions with her hands: *We're done.*

''Ere, 'ang on, 'ang on,' said Thira. 'You two folks are well into all that dream trade malarkey. That's 'ow yer make yer livin'. So, surely you're 'eadin' for The Dream-Pedlars' Parade, yeah...?'

ShadowThief smiled knowingly and nodded, *Go on...*

'I mean, ya two 'ave escaped from prison so ya won't be 'angin' about. Seems like a good idea to move far away. And I'd want to be somewhere where I'm guaranteed work to put some grub in m'belly.'

'And we did give you a generous tip,' chipped in Krish, 'which you could almost see as an advance.'

Aemea and ShadowThief were amused at Krish and Thira's audacity.

'As I said, very astute,' said Aemea. 'Čevljarski Most, I must admit, is where we shall be headed next. You are welcome to come with us, but we may well have a tail to lose. That will involve extra bribes and extra risk.'

'So ya want extra cash?'

ShadowThief nodded: *You got it.*

'Three hundred Gren.' As Aemea spoke, Krish recalled the 'Gr's after the numbers on the bank notes they'd taken from Ryker-Veere's. 'Mainly to cover food, accommodation and bribes. And once we arrive, we will indeed need work, and fast. So it could be tempting to help you out further, but...'

It could be dangerous, said ShadowThief. *Very, very dangerous.*

'But you'll consider?' asked Krish.

'Consider, yes,' said Aemea. 'Guarantee, no. But for now, you may accompany us to the Dream-Pedlars' Parade.'

§

Eschborn Hauptbahnhof was a gleaming station, occupying a street-long covered area between two rows of buidlings. It was shining white, lined with cafes and bars where people were enjoying frothy steins of beer. There were 74 platforms, where pristine engines of green and of blue sat with steam billowing from their funnels, filling the station air with a warm, metallic tang. Sentinels passed over the glass roof every now and then, contributing little to the already well-lit space.

Krish and his companions had emerged from the sewers a few streets away. The pristine environment of the station had taken some getting used to.

The station even had several affordable tailors who provided them with some cheap, leftover items of clothing that took away from the stench of those vile tunnels. They changed and washed their feet and faces in the stations' bathrooms before the stench they emitted roused suspicion. Krish made sure he didn't lose the plastic sandwich bag or his copy of the codes.

Aemea and ShadowThief found a guard and arranged – after a softly spoken conversation in which agreeable amounts of cash were alluded to – for them to board a train under false names.

On the way to the train, they grabbed some perogi, plus some more food for the journey, including bread, chorizo, cheese and a jar of sauerkraut. Thira ate with great speed, not even waiting until they were on the platform, and appeared to grow back to his normal size almost before the others' eyes.

Krish noted that ShadowThief was highly attuned to any quick movements nearby.

'Do you think Ryker-Veere sent anyone after us?' said Krish as they marched along the bustling platform.

'Possibly,' said Aemea, 'but he'd probably send them to

Kleinschmidtring or Demnigstraße, or any of the five or six closer, more discreet stations. Here there are so many departures that they'll never know which one to take. And we'll change several times before anyone has the chance to catch up with us.'

ShadowThief made gestures with her hands like two fish swimming off in different directions: *Move fast, change routes often, we will shake them.*

Thira nodded in approval as he stuffed his face.

On board, the four of them sat on the floor of the crowded train as it hurtled through the night. Just outside Piazza del Calvino, the train ground to a halt, as they had arranged with the guard, and they slipped onto the tracks to board a second train. Within the next hour they had changed trains three more times, until Aemea assured them all they were now staying put all the way to Čevljarski Most.

The guard on the final train led them along a narrow corridor to a compartment. The small space, covered in varnished red-brown wood, contained a cosy seating area with a foldaway table and a cramped but immaculately clean washroom, complete with enamel basin. The seats folded down into two beds, one either side of the table, plus there were two bunks above each seat.

The four of them were exhausted so immediately made their beds and climbed into them.

Krish, on the bottom bunk, opposite Aemea, pulled down the blind, shutting out the light of the distant sentinels visible between the chimney tops. Creeping dread reminded Krish that there would be no sweet relief of daylight breaking the spell of night when he awoke.

'I heard you talking about the copy of the list,' said Aemea.

'And?' said Krish.

'Well, if Ryker-Veere knows what the items on the list mean...'

'And what if he doesn't? Perhaps he doesn't even know about the clues hidden in the three dreams.'

From the bunk above Aemea, ShadowThief was shaking her head: *We don't know what he knows.*

'Oh!' said Thira. Everyone looked at him. 'You all assumin' Ryker-Veere knows 'ow to get into the safe? Seems pretty obvious to me that 'e nicked it off that ancient old whatsit in the prison to get what's inside. But 'ow do we know 'e ever got the combination off 'er?'

Krish realised Thira could well be right. There was no evidence to suggest that Ryker-Veere had ever even used the Myrthali in the safe – it could still be in there, untouched.

'How worryingly perceptive,' said Aemea. 'In which case...'

He'll be looking for a way to open it too, said ShadowThief.

The thought sunk in around the bunks. Everyone began to settle down for sleep but the troubling thought remained in the air.

'There's no guarantee our contacts at Čevljarski Most will be able to assist,' said Aemea as Krish let out a great yawn. 'Just to warn you. But it's certainly the best place to try.'

'Aemea,' said Krish, his mind unwinding, 'hope you don't mind me saying but... you're pretty posh for a criminal.'

'I'm not a criminal, Krish. I'm a survivor. We have to do something to make a living or we starve. But "posh"... what does this mean?'

'Ya know... fancy. Well-to-do.'

'Oh. I see. Well, yes. I am from a family where I was probably a hundred times richer than most would become within their lifetimes, just by the virtue of being born.'

'So what 'appened, Miss Fancypants?' asked Thira from his bunk above Krish.

As the four of them prepared to turn in, Aemea told them a little of her upbringing.

She'd been born to aristocratic parents in a large house on Tressillian Crescent. They'd run factories and workhouses throughout the neighbourhood and considered the people working in their factories as nothing more than numbers in a ledger.

Aemea didn't remember her parents ever showing her love or affection, except when they demanded her presence at business receptions, where they'd doll her up in pretty dresses and curl her hair (which she hated) and everyone would make a fuss of her. She'd beg to go to bed and would slip away to play cards with the maids. She always preferred to spend time with them, and they were always curious about her predictions. Her parents, on the other hand, hated her power and felt it was not polite to speak of it.

One maid in particular, Femi, filled her head with stories of far-off streets: vast open squares big as whole neighbourhoods, broad sea-streets where mighty creatures hid in the depths, and long roads of empty, ruined houses in which not a soul lived. It all sounded so exotic.

Anarchists at the time were targeting the owners of factories where the conditions were worst.

One fadenigh, she awoke with the sensation that an almighty explosion was about to occur nearby. In her sleeplessness, she tried to dismiss the premonition. At the last minute, she realised she must do something. She went and found the maids and screamed that they must flee. Then the bomb hit, ripping the top floor apart.

Aemea suddenly realised that she'd forgotten to save her parents. When she thought about it, she wasn't even sure of their names. To her surprise, she came to the realisation that she was okay with this scenario. With Femi's help, she'd headed off with her head full of adventures and ended up joining an orphan-clan, making a living on the street.

'I wanted to leave that wretched life behind,' said Aemea.'I think I assumed that everything would be fine. That a comfortable life would be provided for me wherever I went. I have learned much since. I become more and more aware of just how spoilt I was. I will never deny where I came from, but neither am I rushing to be reacquainted with that way of life.'

'What about you?' said Thira, looking up at ShadowThief.

ShadowThief, in the bunk above Aemea, rolled over, not wishing to engage in the conversation.

'Shad is very much her own person,' said Aemea. 'She's happy to be who she is now and not dwell on who she was previously.'

'Fair enough,' said Thira.

All four of them quietened down. Krish listened to the clickety-clack of the speeding train as he blinked in and out of consciousness.

'It's all out there somewhere, ya know,' said Thira from his top bunk. Krish looked up to see his shining eyes, sentinellight reflected in them from the blind he had pulled open a touch with his finger. 'Great, clear skies. Forests and streams and big, bloody mountains. Night sky with more stars in it than ya could ever count. They're better be a way back, mate.' Thira was twirling a finger in the air, circles of blue and green appearing dimly for a moment or two. 'That's all I'm sayin'. Adventures, sure, great – can't bloody wait! But at the end of the day, ya know, somewhere's gotta be home.'

26

THE DREAMS ON THE LIST

On the rug were four lengths of beard, cut away, the knife Ryker-Veere had sheered them off with still embedded in the floor on the opposite side of the room to the now-redundant beard-bearers.

'Burn them! Roast them! Hang them by their ankles and bleed 'em pale!'

Ryker-Veere paced back and forth in the antechamber, incandescent, fury in his every step.

Edris, Emese, Emna and Esna sat around the small dining table. This was usually a cosy little reception room between the kitchen and the entrance door to the beer hall, somewhere the four of them would often use as a safe space to rest while their master was in his study. Now it was transformed. A safe space no more.

Edris sat there, staring into nothingness. Esna was hunched over, tears dropping into the embroidered tablecloth, soaking the fabric. Emna was equally distraught, but the tears were yet to come. Emese sat bolt upright, defiant from her attempt on her master's life. She was shaking with rage, crying out from an already hoarse throat. She spoke in her mother tongue.

'*Remélem, hogy a golyóiddal a szádban halsz meg, te szemét!*'

'No idea what you're saying, you little harlot!' said Ryker-Veere. 'Build a great oven! Bake them!'

'*Remélem, hogy a saját szemeiddel etetnek meg!*'

'I want to hear them scream, the traitorous little worms!'

Ryker-Veere rubbed his hastily trimmed beard with agitation. He marched back and forth with increasing speed, like a prowling beast blocking his four servants from the door. Edris looked up with his eyes, his head still hung low, seeing the guards on the other side of the open doorway.

'There are more important matters, master,' urged de Clercq, staying for once on her master's good side.

'Drowning's too good for 'em!'

'*És remélem, hogy azt választják le, ami számodra a legértéke-sebb, és veled etetik meg, és aztán mégis csak megdöglesz!*'

'Master, please—'

'*Remélem, hogy hamarosan, igazán hamarosan, elég hülye leszel ahhoz, hogy megint megbízz valakiben, aki közel áll hozzád!*'

'And we deal *with her* first!' Ryker-Veere jabbed his finger in Emese's direction.

'*Mert csakis így halsz meg — amikor egy hozzád közelálló ráébred, hogy ütött az órád!*'

'Master, there are clearly co-conspirators. The boy! Where did he—?'

'Some cheap conjurer! How in blazes should I know? A mere sideshow! Nothing to do with these wretches!'

De Clercq studied the fearful looks of the beard bearers. In this moment she made her decision. 'It may be a coincidence too far, but...'

At last Ryker-Veere stopped his pacing. He turned and saw de Clercq looking back knowingly, the piece of paper in her hand. He took it from her abruptly and then changed his manner. Suddenly, the paper was an item of the highest possible value.

'And what, may I ask, is it?' said the calmest voice of all.

Ryker-Veere and de Clercq looked over to see Stroever standing by the far wall, waiting patiently, one gloved hand folded neatly over the other. Almost everyone in the room had forgotten he had accompanied them into the antechamber following the furore in the beer hall.

'Nothing of importance,' said Ryker-Veere, folding the paper delicately and sliding it into his pocket.

'Really...' Stroever's eyes had followed the slip of paper to Ryker-Veere's pocket.

'You might ask our dear guest how he knew,' de Clercq said softly as she slipped out of the room, looking from Stroever to Emese.

'Knew what, blast it all?!' shouted Ryker-Veere.

'Your showmanship will get you killed,' said Stroever flatly.

'You've got to stand out to these people!'

'I have no doubt they will remember tonight.'

Ryker-Veere shot Stroever a fierce look.

'You're one to talk!' said Ryker-Veere. 'With all your ruddy boat nonsense! Cost you a pretty penny or two, I'll wager! Money you don't really have, dare I say.'

Stroever did not respond to Ryker-Veere's attempt at provocation. 'I travelled much through Győr as a child.'

'Ha! That hole! They say that devil-cursed neighbourhood'll be at war with the Ankarans any fade now!'

Stroever continued. 'My father often brought gifts back from those far-off streets. I know your love of tokaji comes from him frequently returning with a caseload for you.'

'And what relevance has this—?'

'Profanities. The first thing any respectable young boy learns in a new language.'

'What in blazes are you—?'

'Emese. She's Győri.'

'Emese?'

'*Emese*,' he corrected Ryker-Veere's pronunciation from 'Em-ease' to 'Emma-shay'. 'Your servant. The one who tried to empty the barrel of a gun into your eye and got exceptionally close to achieving it. She uttered a rather strong word under her breath as she went to retrieve the gun. I recognised it at once. I could tell her intent in an instant and acted to prevent tragedy. Out of respect to my father who loved you so, *not* out of service to you.'

Ryker-Veere was somewhat subdued. He chewed on Stroever's words for a moment. 'Is there a point at the end of this rambling yarn, hmm?' he spat. 'Perhaps that I should have someone who speaks a dozen languages close at hand at all times? Ha!'

'I'm merely suggesting that getting to know those in your service and treating them with respect may be surprisingly advantageous for you, Anders,' said Stroever.

Ryker-Veere glanced briefly at the four former beard bearers huddled around the table and then turned back to Stroever. 'So, what do you want, hmm? If you want me to get back on that damned tub of yours so you can act all mysterious—'

'You told me your twisted story of the child by the window.'

'And what of it? Hmm?'

'That's how you think you can control people. Through the press. A power you will certainly need to wield judging by the looks on your potential investors' faces as they fled tonight.'

'Hm!'

'But I will tell you now of a weapon I have in my armoury...'

'Weapon, ha! Your armoury is no doubt one of-of-of silken feathers and... and *polite* words! Ha!'

Stroever stepped up to Ryker-Veere, getting startlingly close. 'Imagine there was a disease,' he said.

'What...?' said Ryker-Veere, too startled by Stroever's sudden closeness to back away.

In this interval, the unassuming figure of Stroever, ignored by most around the table earlier that fadenigh, spoke softly to make sure Ryker-Veere attended closely.

'You believe I lack the ambition my wretched father possessed? Listen! Imagine a disease... lying dormant. In every single man, woman and child...'

'What the blue blazes are you blathering about?'

'Now imagine you could trigger that disease.'

'What?!'

'If you were able to trigger that disease... would you do it?'

'Oh, my dear, deluded chap, there is no such disease! Stark raving mad, you are! And what precisely does it do anyway, this disease of yours? Is it unpleasant? Debilitating? Lethal?'

'Yes.'

Ryker-Veere was struck by Stroever's unexpected intensity.

'Every man, woman and child? Humph!' said Ryker-Veere. 'No such disease exists.'

Stroever stared back with a foreboding sense of certainty.

'Given time, I will prove it to you,' said Stroever as Ryker-Veere shuffled nervously from foot to foot. 'You will believe. You will *want* to believe. If you come with me, if you *listen*, we could achieve something greater than anyone has ever attempted.'

'Your father—'

'Was a spoilt brat. Just like you, Anders.' Ryker-Veere grew red with fury as Stroever continued. 'But we can outdo him in both scope and ambition. You knew him to the end...' Ryker-Veere toyed nervously with his collar. 'You knew his interest by then was purely financial gain. What we can achieve, *together*, will be known on every streetcorner throughout the entire City!'

Ryker-Veere was now genuinely unnerved by Stroever. He welcomed the timely distraction provided by de Clercq as she re-entered carrying a fine silver tray with four steaming mugs upon it.

'Come now, come now,' said de Clercq, circling the table, placing a mug each before Edris, Emese, Emna and Esna. 'Drink up. You must go to sleep early now.' She kissed each of them on the forehead with a brief firmness as she passed. 'Drink up, drink up. You must go to bed early now.'

There was no disguising the sombre act of mercy de Clercq was committing in spite of Ryker-Veere's proposals of prolonged fates for the four of them. They smelt the mint first. Strong, clear, calming. Perfect for hiding the chemical trace in the scented steam.

The four of them stared at each other with haunted eyes. Esna drank first, ignoring the scolding heat of the liquid as she downed the mug's contents. Enma followed shortly after, crying out briefly as soon as she had swallowed. Edris held it to his lips but could go no further. Emese stared at de Clercq with accusing eyes.

De Clercq marched up to Ryker-Veere and whispered in his good ear, getting so close that her lips almost brushed the skin. 'I checked the study. Someone was there. Some items are missing.'

'The safe?' whispered Ryker-Veere. His hand involuntarily covered the pocket which held the paper.

'Untouched. Though the unlocking slides have been moved around.'

De Clercq pulled back and her gaze met her master's. Their eyes conferred.

'Find them,' said Ryker-Veere.

'There is no sign as to who they were.'

'Then send *him*.'

'The freelancer?'

'He's a good hunter. He has contacts across the borough. He'll locate the bounders.'

'You want them alive?'

'Can't say as I do.'

'Might I suggest that alive would be more advantageous. To find out who they are working for.'

'I suppose. Hmph! But send *him*. He is affective.'

'Of course, master.'

Stroever was watching closely. De Clercq stepped away. Her eyes caught Edris's as he finished his drink in the second gulp and looked sorrowfully back at her. Then de Clercq turned expectantly to Emese.

'*Áruló ribanc!*' Emese shouted.

Stroever stepped up to Ryker-Veere, drawing almost as close as de Clercq had a moment earlier.

'Your plans, by the way,' Stroever began. 'Make little sense.'

Ryker-Veere turned to Stroever. 'In what respect?'

'*RIBANC!*' repeated Emese, spraying de Clercq with spittle.

'*Nem az, amire gondolsz,*' said de Clercq softly, her eyes travelling to the steaming mug and then back to meet Emese's.

Emese looked deep into de Clercq's eyes. Then she took the mug and drank.

'Come now, Anders.' Stroever's tone turned familiar. 'You are not a young man. Once you completed your protracted press campaign to lobby for the legalisation of dreams, you will be of such advanced years that you will either be dust or too old to enjoy anything in this life. Surely you don't think this will be fast?'

Ryker-Veere rested his hand over the pocket containing the sheet of paper again. 'An opportunity may have arisen that will render your concerns redundant,' he said. 'We are already taking action. Tonight's mysterious visitor may have been the best thing that could have happened in a long time. Prepare your ship. I am ready and eager to know of what you have discovered, my dear Isri.'

§

The cart was as discreet as its owner. Mr. Hershel Tarrow always dressed in black, even when not overseeing a funeral.

The backdoor opened and de Clercq emerged. Tarrow spied the four bodies, dragged unceremoniously into the corridor behind the servant. Most unusual. Part of the role he and his assistant, Zeißler, lingering nervously by the horse pulling the cart, normally undertook was to remove the deceased.

'They are not yours,' said de Clercq. They were completely alone in the alley outside of 63 Kierbeckerstraße yet still she spoke in hushed tones. She passed him an envelope. He could feel the weight of it. She could be paying for the entire funeral in advance, but that was uncommon at this early stage. 'Deliver them to this address—' she produced a slip of paper, which he received graciously, '—and please understand that you are paid for your discretion.'

Tarrow did not need to be too close to see the truth. He saw the colour was still in the bodies, the gentle rising and falling of their chests. He would feel the warmth of them when he lifted them onto the cart.

Tarrow nodded in acceptance and pocketed the envelope

and slip of paper. Then he and Zeißler began to load the bodies onto the cart.

'I hate inspection fade, it's all such a bore!

All the same old questions I've been asked before.'

Says Eva to herself as she sneaks along

Past the Woman's bedchamber, she knows it's wrong

Off to her secret room or a detour first?

To bathe in the gas-starlight she has a thirst

Up the spiral stairs little Eva she sneaks

Then through the hatch, mischievously she peaks

'Get down from there, child!' So the Woman did scold

'Forbidden! How many times must you be told?'

27
THE CARTS & THE COLOURS

The train jerked to a stop just outside of Čevljarski Most. The four of them were packed and (although Krish's constant yawning seemed to disagree) ready to go. The guard accepted the extra notes from Aemea and pointed the way across the tracks.

The air was cold and moist, haze hovering over the railway lines. Krish saw a great bridge some way above them, stretching on without end into the fog.

'Still night,' grumbled Thira. 'Always bloody night. Flippin' freezin' and all!'

There were many grotesque demons carved into the grey stonework of the bridge. If this place dreamed, they would be nightmares. And dreams were exactly why they were here.

They could hear the sound of multitudes of footsteps but little speech was emanating from the bridge. As they climbed the stairs. Krish looked up. As the sentinels were far off in the distance, the light was coming partly from the amber lamps spaced out along the side of the bridge. There were also great clouds of colours hovering just above street level. Scarlets, aquamarines, ochres, emeralds and indigoes and every colour imaginable, each shining with the deepest and most vivid varieties.

Merchants stood at the sides of the steps with small organ carts decorated with faded paintwork; they turned the handles to force the music to rise from the pipes with jollity. Upon each cart sat a globe of glass, slightly smaller than a football, filled with all manner of objects – wood, pinecones, watches, stones, machine parts – soaked in oil, fire burning beneath. Smoke poured from great funnels from the carts. These clouds of colour spread out into the street itself, allowing passers-by to wander straight into a dream.

Aemea steered them out of the way of the clouds cutting across their path, insisting that these dream-pedlars on the stairs were less 'official' than those up high on top of the bridge. She warned that many suffered headaches, nausea and itching in what she labelled as 'inconvenient places'.

'Fresh dreams!'

'Hand-picked ingredients!'

'Blended this very primo!'

The dream-pedlars here reminded Krish of market sellers in his own world. Aemea was dismissive of their large globes and loud, blaring music. Krish felt both scared and excited at the prospect of sampling someone else's dream in full.

After some minutes they reached the top and Krish and Thira stared in disbelief at the scale of the world before them. The broad bridge appeared to be miles long and was filled with cart after cart after cart of dream-pedlars. The carts were freshly painted in reds and blues and greens with fine gold leaf trim. The carts were smaller than those on the steps, as were the globes, just a touch bigger than tennis balls. The glass shone and the oil-drenched ingredients could easily be seen: saffron, rose petals, marzipan, frankincense. They were mixed in with cogs, iron filings, seaweed, scrunched up pages of books, corners of playing cards, thimbles, pebbles, scraps of silver...

Although there were so many carts, each had a good amount of space around them to allow people to pass through their respective clouds of colour. And up close, the colours were even more vivid. They made Krish think, for the first time since setting foot in KnockThrice, of the natural world in other places – the blue of a deep ocean at home, the orange of the dunes of Ilir at sunset, the green of vibrant rainforest vegetation, and the purple of gleaming amethysts, freshly ripped from the ground, their sparkling florescence unseen since forming millions of years before.

The dream-pedlars themselves, both men and the occasional woman, were finely dressed, like traders in their Sunday best, with shoes shining and covered in splashes of many colours.

On the bridge you could see everyone from nobility to street urchins running and laughing from cloud to cloud, each with a similar look of wonder on their faces. In a city where no one is allowed to dream, the joy in the air around them was tangible; everyone's expression was as if they had waited a lifetime to let their imaginations burst forth.

Although there was some chatter, people were often quiet, drinking in solitary fantasies for a moment before taking the hands of their friends, family members or lovers to wax lyrical about the wondrous escapes from the real world they had just indulged in. They entered and exited clouds with their eyes closed, but as each emerged and opened them again, you could see the dreams were still imprinted on their minds.

As they neared a cloud of burnt orange, Krish and Thira turned instinctively to Aemea and ShadowThief, who nodded encouragingly.

'Go on!' said Aemea. 'And close your eyes or it'll be all faint and out of focus.'

Krish stared at the globe – inside was a scrunched-up ball of laid vellum paper, a magnifying glass, a fragment of a brick and a scattering of herbs. Krish and Thira then closed their eyes and walked forward as a blast of smoke enveloped them. The smell filled Krish's nostrils: burnt paper, a musty scent from an old room with hints of dried flowers and spice.

The orange glow gave way to a fantastical sight. A great gas-star was waning ahead of them, burning its last in the deepest shade of terracotta. Houses were torn from their streets, flying up into the sky, turning over and over and emptying themselves of all their possessions – chairs and tables and silverware and bathtubs were falling through the air. Then books. Countless numbers of books rained down from above, and as they landed, each word, each letter, every line of a 'T' and every curve of an 'S' was magnified to reveal within a tiny street, and on every street were many houses, all the same, and every one of them had an envelope sitting on its top step, and as Krish reached to pick up the letter he saw flourishing calligraphy...

Krish

A flash of bright orange and then nothing.

Krish opened his eyes and found himself on the bridge again. He and Thira laughed heartily and gripped each other's shoulders enthusiastically.

'You get to open the letter?' said Thira, excitedly.

'No!' said Krish. 'It just stopped there!'

'Mine too! Said "Thira" on it in like well-posh letterin'!'

'Yeah! Mine said "Krish"!'

'All will be revealed, gentlemen!' boomed the dream-pedlar. '175 for yer first dream! 200 from then on for all the best 'uns! 75 for the dosey fancies!'

'Dunno what that means but nah, thanks, mate!' said Thira. 'We're all about the freebies!'

And then Thira did something Krish was not prepared for. He grabbed Krish's hand and led him off at a sprint across the bridge and directly into the path of another dream.

A flash of pale blue. The scent of urine but somehow not completely unpleasant. Sugar and sweetness were there also, and a smell like chlorine combined with damp wood.

Then, eyes closed, Krish was a naked child running about a large, magnificent house weeing everywhere – on the floor, on the fine China, on his schoolbooks, on the maid. Everyone was screaming and shouting at him. He stopped as soon as he entered the bathroom where he jumped into the toilet bowl without hesitation. He was now somehow covered in water up to his neck and swimming under a great bridge where his teachers were on rafts nearby, eating soggy pages of his homework or fighting pirates. A mariachi band was flying past on the back of a giant tortoise, playing mops and brooms, wearing toilet seats on their heads. A cow wearing glasses was standing by a blackboard and teaching a lesson about plate tectonics. Everybody was shouting at him angrily and then the cow landed on him, making everything go dark.

As they exited the dream Thira and Krish smiled broadly at one another. Krish then became aware that they were still holding hands. He sensed eyes on them all around. He let go. Thira looked puzzled by the abruptness of Krish's action but for once he didn't speak his mind aloud.

'Right, come on!' said Thira, jogging on the spot, clapping his hands together.

'It's unbelievable! Bet you could do better, though!' said Krish.

'Nah! This is next level stuff! I can magic up some pretty awesome visions, but this kinda thing? Nah! This stuff's like ya're actually there!'

'Yeah! It's the smell!'

'Ah, yeah! The smells are awesome! I ain't dreamin' nothin' no more unless there's some kinda stink goin' on! Come on! Race ya!'

Thira ran off, almost knocking over a cart in the process. Krish burst out laughing before weaving through the crowd to find his friend. He hadn't felt so light and happy for so long. He remembered how fun it had been when his friend had taught him many-ruled splat, but they were still being chased by the Vulrein then. And when they were relaxing in the garden by the river, just after the palace had fallen. When he wanted to tell him how he felt. How he really wanted to reach out and hold his hand...

Recollections raced through Krish's mind as he chased after Thira. And as he followed, he passed through many clouds, sampling marvellous scents and enticing dreamscapes. Some putting him in mind of home, others beyond anything he could possibly conjure up in his own subconscious.

Krish noticed that every few minutes the dream-pedlars were moving a metre or so along the bridge as part of a very slow-moving parade to give others a chance to show off their wares. A rotund woman in a headscarf, dressed head to toe in green and blue, moved her cart into position and winked at Krish as she fired up her dreamglobe, replenishing her cloud of emerald. Krish happily took the bait and stepped into the dream.

After weeks in KnockThrice, this dream came as a bit of a surprise. The scent was of a fresh forest of pine trees after rainfall. He walked through the woods, up to his knees in clear, placid blue water and emerged from the trees to see a snow-capped mountain in front of a majestic lake so clear it was like a mirror. The mountain looked so similar in the reflection on the surface of the lake that, as he craned his neck to look at it more closely, he realised that he had turned right over and was now in the reflection, which was no longer the reflection but the mountain itself, with the lake below. He turned over and over, each time the reflection transforming into the real thing.

Krish stepped out of the dream, his mouth gaping open. The dream-pedlar gave him another wink and her smile broadened.

''Ow's it goin' mate?' said Thira, strolling merrily up to him. 'Just 'ad some buildin' turn into a big fire-breathin' monster and burn everybody's bottom before it stopped and asked where the post office was – whatever the 'ell a post office is!'

'It was my world,' said Krish, still in a daze.

'You what?'

'I'm certain. It was my world. There's a postcard from Aunt Nisha that's been on our fridge for like... *ever*. It's a mountain in New Zealand.'

'What the 'ell's a frig? Or a zeeland, old or new?'

'Never mind! Thira, I'm telling you it was my world!'

'Well, maybe somebody's been there.'

'Yeah... that would make sense. The devil did say that many people have passed through KnockThrice from other worlds, or did a long time ago. And if dreams can be based on memories... It's just weird, ya know?'

'Yeah... Wonder if I'll find Ilir!'

But before Thira could dash off, Aemea and ShadowThief reappeared.

'Four thousand Gren,' said Aemea.

Krish's hand went instinctively for his pocket.

You can afford it, said ShadowThief with a sly smile,

confirming Krish's suspicions that she'd kept a close eye on Thira as he was pocketing cash.

'Including food, accommodation and bribes?' asked Krish.

'Indeed.'

Plus a little extra.

'To factor in the risk.'

Krish nodded several times in acceptance.

'Perfect,' said Aemea. 'I had assumed as much. Come on, we have to go to church.'

'Sounds borin',' said Thira.

ShadowThief rolled her eyes.

'Be that as it may, but we have an appointment there,' said Aemea, and led them off along the bridge, against the tide of the slow-moving parade.

28

THE CRIES IN THE CATHEDRAL

Below the bridge was a vast, fast-flowing river-street featuring a shallow weir where no boats could sail. A large, open expanse was a welcome break in the endless cityscape. Splintered sentinellight shimmered on the surface of the rushing water.

There were dwellings on either side of the thoroughfare at the centre of the bridge, some dangling over the edge. Statues of foul-faced demons made of black metal or bronze stood tall. Some of these statues had small doors as if they too were snug abodes, or storage for the dream-pedlars.

As they strode forward, a great cathedral-like building came into view, straddling the bridge from one side to the other. It was blackened with spiky towers and turrets, tendrils out to the sides that covered the walkways as people passed around the outside of the building. Bottlenecks of dream-pedlars and pedestrians were filing slowly through the walk-ways. There was also a great queue of people wearing dark-coloured shawls over their normal clothes, heads hung low, leading to the open wooden doors of the cathedral.

They joined the queue and shuffled gradually into the building. There were no brightly coloured stained glass windows inside this cathedral. In fact, there was barely any colour at all. No sense of light or hope. Just black walls and black statues depicting devils and demons pulling grotesque faces and committing horrific acts. Krish and Thira observed engravings depicting cavernous factories stuffed full of humans, beasts, trees and plants. One large devil, covered in rivets and patches of metal, was building cogs and machines and buildings and all sorts while laughing gleefully.

'Bloody 'ell!' whispered Thira.

'You, er, probably shouldn't swear in church,' said Krish.

ShadowThief pulled the most disgruntled of faces – *Why not?*

'Church is precisely where you should swear, and do it nice and loud,' said Aemea at a high volume as they filed into black pews. 'Though you can save it for the Release if you wish.'

'The Release?!' said Thira.

The service was the most freaky and disturbing ceremony Krish had ever witnessed. Unseen choral singers, their voices emanating from hidden stations, filled the echoing cathedral with wailing, pained singing, wavering in and out of tune. Spaced out amongst the gloom were brief clusters of flickering orange light; candles and their flames were obscured from view by fixtures that appeared like gashes cut into the wall.

Then a great booming voice started a sermon from some concealed pulpit up on high, as the wailing in the crowd rose and rose in volume.

'And the Iron Devil spoke,' said the voice, 'and He said, "let there be factories upon factories upon factories." And all life came into being from the factories, but we rose up and claimed the vacant buildings Devil had created. We learned how we could master the machines in the houses and shops and workplaces. We learned how we could bend the factories to our will so we could grow fruit and meat and vegetable matter to fill our bellies. We remoulded His world in Our image. And when Our Sin overfloweth, He comes to purge the streets of light. Though let us not Sin in the dark.'

ShadowThief let out a brief chortle at this.

'For the NightTime does sharpen His vision and He will watch us ever closer. He will watch. He will be spiteful. He will be vengeful. And we shall never sleep without His shadow of fear hanging over us. Though we remain Our Own Masters. He will never enslave us again. We shall fear and respect Him, but never be dominated.'

Then the crowd joined together in solemn chorus:

HE DID CREATE
BUT MASTERS ARE WE
WE KEEP FEAR AT BAY
AND TAME OUR OWN HATE

'Amen,' intoned the voice. 'Let us hate.'

The choral singing reached its zenith; it sounded like screaming now. Then the crowd shouted and cried and swore. Krish and Thira recoiled in terror at the sudden outburst of collective hate. Then, all at once, the congregation spat into funnels placed in the pews in front of them and bowed their heads in submission. All was quiet, their ears were ringing.

Krish and Thira turned to each other. Thira's lip curled up on one side in the confusion-meets-disgust expression that Krish had grown strangely fond of.

The song of the unseen singers returned with more soothing, genteel vocals. The congregation filed out of their pews and into the chamber at the far end of the cathedral. People turned their shawls inside out, revealing white cloth under-neath. The chamber they passed through was cream in colour, reminding Krish even more of churches they'd visited on trips to small villages in the countryside. Here, carvings depicted humans taking control of the factories and leading peaceful lives on the streets of the City. In contrast, a black metal statue of the Iron Devil was stationed by a font filled with several bucket-loads of spittle. People were adding contributions as they passed.

'What the frig was all that about?' whispered Thira.

'Cathartic nonsense,' said Aemea, keeping her voice down. 'Shad and I aren't religious but our contact is quite devout. People are meant to let out all their fear and hatred here, but in truth they don't. They take all the negativity they were meant to offload in the Release and continue to mull over it at the pubs and rum palaces afterwards. Ah!'

Aemea's gaze rested on a face to the side of the chamber. A woman in an alcove with her head bowed sat next to a large engraving of the Iron Devil. The woman was small and hunched herself down even smaller. She held her hands clasped together over her navel, her shoulders pushed inwards as if they would eventually meet. She did not look like someone who wanted to attract attention

Krish saw a strange woman with short, spiky red hair who he guessed was middle-aged.

Aemea perceived a wholly different story on the woman's face as she caught her eye. She observed a younger woman aged prematurely with small features and shy eyes; a face used to looking down. The haunted expression of a child told to remain silent, fear Devil and move unnoticed. An introverted child who then rebelled in her teens by accepting cigarettes, alcohol, dreams, narcotics – whatever was on offer and always in excess. She was someone who had enjoyed life to such extremes that her indulgences were close to killing her, giving her skin an aged appearance: heavily lined, almost scarred. And lastly, she saw a woman who had stepped away from addiction, returning to a quiet life of faith and devotion.

Aemea wondered why this woman still dealt in the illegal dream trade, though she already knew that her reasons could be much the same as her own. You had to stick to what you knew to make a living in the City. This woman sold dreams but had no interest in them herself.

'*Moje ime je Julija.*'

'She says, "'My name is Julija."' They'd paid little attention to the older, lithe woman with straight, shoulder-length iron-grey hair standing next to Julija. She gave the impression of being somewhere between carer and mother to her.

'I'm Bojana,' said the woman with no further explanation. She translated for Julija and occasionally placed a firm hand on her shoulder, apparently as a comfort.

'I've had a look at the list your contact passed on to me. Sure, I know these dreams. L. Stowell's book, *The Keeper of Lost Dreams* mentions them, but few realise they're actually real. They're called "The Three Dreams of the Forgotten Towers.". They're very rare. The story goes that they were collected by a traveller who had lived many lifetimes and had seen many things. They say these dreams will unlock a great secret that will change the City forever. They're not cheap – ah! – but let's talk business outside!'

Julija blinked several times nervously before leading them out of the cathedral.

Down a flight of steps, they reconvened at a spot which overlooked the weir. Julija had her head down for most of the time as they walked.

'The first on your list can be purchased from a pedlar I know in Győr, but you have probably read that there is war there with the Ankarans. Much of Szabó Utca, where my contact is based, has been destroyed by gun-carriages and Márai Utca, where the train will arrive, has also been largely devastated. I had a telegram some days ago from my contact saying business would continue with prices higher than normal as she needs to pay for papers to cross the border—'

ShadowThief was shocked. She made a gesture of cutting through the air with the side of her hand and then threw both hands up as if to ask a question.

'There's a border around Győr now?' said Aemea, concerned.

'Yes. You will also need papers. I would strongly advise you against going to Győr, but if you must, I would leave without hesitation.'

'And the other two dreams?' said Krish eagerly, hoping to gloss over the looks of defeat on Aemea and ShadowThief's faces.

'The second dream I can mix for you here. It will be expensive, but I know it. My apartment is a few minutes away.'

'Brilliant,' said Krish. 'And the third?'

Julija and Bojana were now addressing Krish rather than Aemea and ShadowThief, who seemed disgruntled at him taking charge.

'I don't know this dream, but I know it is fyrstiräs-based. The best place for fyrstiräs-based dreams is Njivska Ulica. You can go there on the way to Győr or on the way back. Though as I said, I'd strongly advise you go to Győr soon, if you have to go at all. You should also be aware that none of these dreams will be cheap.'

'Yeah, yeah, you said!' interjected Thira.

'I'd calculate around 26,000 Crowns or 1,000 of your Gren each.'

There was silence for a moment between the four. Juliya blinked at the floor, sporadically jerking her whole body upwards to check on them, then turning back to the ground.

'Thank you, Julija,' said Aemea. 'And I take it that your dream is also around 26,000 Crowns?'

'That is correct.'

'Okay. Please allow us a moment. We shall confer.'

Aemea led their little group away from Julija and Bojana. They took a few steps down a staircase and the restless gushing of the weir filled their ears.

'So,' began Thira, 'we pop round to whats-er-chops, see if we can get the dream to go, leg it over to this Győr neighbour'ood and swing by the other joint on the way back, yeah?'

'Woah, woah, woah!' cut in Krish. 'Slow down, mate! We need to discuss this before we decide on anything!'

'Yeah, well we gotta start with somethin' to discuss! Plus, it seems pretty obvious, don't it?'

'Yeah, but let's just stop first and discuss it before—'

'We *are* discussin' it! What d'ya think we're doin' right—'

'Yeah, but you were just assum—'

'I ain't assumin', mate! It's bloody obvious!'

'But—'

'If you two have quite finished!' said Aemea, silencing both.

ShadowThief was making animated hand gestures in Krish and Thira's direction.

'I don't think one of them needs to be in charge, Shad,' said Aemea. 'They just need to learn how to come to an agreement with greater ease. Now, Thira makes a good point.'

'See!'

'Let me finish. Thira makes a good point about getting the dreams, as you put it, "to go". If we can buy a dreamglobe, lamp and funnel then we could arrange a private compartment on the next train and possibly dream on the way.'

'Yeah,' said Krish. 'We don't know how long it'll take to solve them.'

'Precisely. But with the border at Győr we'll have to secure false papers. The forgers on Njivska Ulica are very well known so we could enquire there.'

ShadowThief started making various gestures with her hands, indicating people moving from one place to another.

'Indeed,' continued Aemea. 'There are plenty of people moving across the border there. I should explain, borders are barriers set-up between some neighbourhoods to stop people crossing from one side to the other. Generally for very stupid reasons to do with people not wanting to share things, or because the people in some neighbourhoods think those in the next neighbourhood are unpleasant or cause trouble.'

'Every country, I mean, neighbourhood, in our world has a border,' said Krish.

ShadowThief recoiled in disgust at the idea.

'*Every* neighbourhood?' said Aemea. 'How absurd. What a waste of time and energy building up meaningless barriers.'

'In my world, we got the odd frontier, but apart from the keeper-traders at Drargor Pass, people don't really bother trying to draw big old lines in the sand,' said Thira. 'Waste of time in the middle of a desert.'

'Desert?' said Aemea.

'Shedload o' sand. Not much going on.'

'Oh. How bizarre.'

'Anyway,' said Krish. 'Sounds like a plan. Dream here, take it with us, unless we solve it straight away. And we could do the same with the other dreams too. Then Njivska Ulica, then Győr, then back to Kierbecker. Somehow.'

Krish took a deep breath and sucked in the enormity of the

task at hand. It was all hanging over him like the great weight of NightTime.

Thira placed a reassuring hand on his shoulder. 'We got through all that impossible task cobblers back on Ilir. I mean, with a staff and all that, but I think, get us a good bit o' wood and with the 'elp o' these bozos—' Thira indicated a very nonplussed Aemea and ShadowThief, '—and we'll be done in no time!'

Everyone looked flatly back at Thira's blindingly bright smile. He dropped it moments later.

'And what about the fee?' said Krish.

ShadowThief and Aemea conferred with a look and turned back to Krish and Thira. 'I think 11,500 should do us fine with all the expenses of the dreams, food, accommodation, papers and our fee.'

'11,500?!' exclaimed Krish.

'The papers will be at least 1,000 per person, plus 3,000 for the dreams. I was anticipating all expenses to be considerably less.'

'Okay! Okay!' said Krish.

'What 'e means is—' added Thira, trying and failing to calm the situation.

'Don't talk for me, Thira!' Krish spat out.

'Mate!' Thira shot back. 'Ya gotta do the old mathe-ma-ma'ics in yer 'ead! They ain't rippin' us off!'

Thira placed a hand on Krish's shoulder again and gave it a little squeeze which was brief enough for Krish to realise Aemea and ShadowThief weren't meant to notice.

'Okay,' said Krish, calmer. 'You're right.' He turned back to Aemea and ShadowThief. 'Sure. Seems reasonable. And it's going to be bloody dangerous so I... ya know... I appreciate it.'

'Fine,' said Aemea. 'I think we have a deal.'

'I... I just need to check...' Krish felt his pockets for the money they had taken from Kierbecker.

'You can still afford it,' stated Aemea with a smile.

'Yes,' said Krish. 'Sounds good. And a staff. I mean, piece of wood that's vaguely shaped like a staff.'

'Of course,' smiled Aemea.

The four of them shook hands, looking into each other's eyes with little hesitation, the exchange of glances acting as little contracts of trust between them.

ShadowThief nodded in the direction of Julija and Bojana.

'Exactly,' said Aemea. 'We should get to work.'

§

Any train guard who can be bribed can be counter-bribed.

This one, standing just outside the engine shed, was the very same man who had let Krish and his associates slip across the tracks just outside of Čevljarski Most. He was willingly spilling every milligram of information he had on the four travellers who'd paid for a private compartment. He had never seen such a large amount of money offered to provide a simple collection of facts.

The men in top hats with their suspicious lack of flamboyance in an exceptionally ostentatious street certainly were attentive as he blathered on about the four travellers in minute detail. None more so than the tall, wiry man who was standing some distance from the rest of the group, looking away, his attempts to appear disinterested giving the exact opposite impression. He remained in shadow, between the buffers of two carriages that were still to be coupled together.

As the guard began to provide detailed descriptions of the four travellers, he noticed the figure in the shadows cock his head in recognition. The guard stopped speaking. The men turned to the shrouded figure, who straightened himself up to his full height, towering over everyone else present. He still had his back to them.

The guard ached to see the mysterious man's face. Seconds later the figure obliged. The guard immediately regretted getting what he had wished for.

29
THE FACE IN HIDING

In the times in between, as one fade drifted seamlessly into another, recollections floated to the surface and repeated themselves over and over, growing no more detailed in the haze of memory yet also brighter in significance.

Ryker-Veere was recalling a face, partially obscured, from some time ago. The face was clearer this fade than it had been in a long time. It had been refreshed. He had looked into those same eyes a few short fades ago.

Ryker-Veere turned over in his bed, restless, his mind too active for sleep. When a bed has been perfectly designed for your every comfort – silken sheets, harshaik pillow, the mattress the exact midpoint between too soft and too firm – you can never be entirely comfortable in it.

The dream-globe sat on the bedside cabinet, unused for tofade, but guilt-soaked memories festered in Ryker-Veere's consciousness as he waited for sleep to take him.

A series of scenes continued to play through his mind.

First, the office of Benmore and Son at 5 Gaius Leonidas

Parade, on a bright day that had lasted many fades. The gas-stars had shone brightly through the blinds of the solicitors. He'd checked every clause and, in the optimism of his youth, questioned none. The investment was more than enough to allow him to branch out at last from the illegal dream trade.

One clause had made him stop as he scanned the pages of the contract:

16c. In the event of the death of one party, all rights, powers, profits, and business assets shall be handed over to the surviving partner.

He had signed and thought no more on the matter.

Congratulations to us both, my friend! Isairis Stroever had said. *This primo we have signed a contract that will bind the fates of our families together for many years to come!*

They had clinked glasses and drank heartily.

But time... seriously, old boy? Ryker-Veere had said. *How do you know it's really there in that safe?*

That woman is ancient! She says she saw the building of the City itself... Ha! Poppycock! But she is old beyond the years of any other, believe me.

And she locked it all in your safe?

Indeed. Changed the combination, the old harlot!

But will you—?

In time, Anders! In time! And when we do... oh, the millions we shall make! Dreams... the perfect innovation in advertising! Sending our messages to those who indulge in the most expensive of dreams! And we shall make their fantasies come true, young Anders!

But how can you be sure—?

Ha-ha-ha! Stroever put his arm around Ryker-Veere. *When we are masters of time, you will wonder how you could ever have been so impatient.*

And does anyone know? Jane?

No.

Helena?

No, indeed!

And Isri...?

Anders, my friend... no one besides you and me knows what is locked in that safe...

Next, he remembered the scene at Stroever's house along the river-street on Ha'penny Row. Even when the place was full of life it felt somewhat empty. The living room was a large open space with a staircase leading up to a landing which wrapped around the outside of the upper level, a walkway leading to the bedchambers, looking back down on the sofas, armchairs, fireplace and dining area below.

They could have had a long banqueting table but had instead opted for a dining table with space for six; the four members of their family (Isairis, his wife Jane and their children Isri and Helena) plus two guests. They preferred to keep their furniture small, modest. Everything was dwarfed by that space.

There was a window above with a fine view of the river. And through this window one member of the family would exit never to return. But the memory running through his head right now was of a happier time.

It had been like the reception of a wedding. Isairis Stroever and Anders Ryker-Veere had drunk rum from fine glasses in tribute to their new arrangement.

I do hope you'll not be descending into celebratory drinking competitions too soon! Jane had said, laughing.

If you're concerned about me leading your husband astray, Ryker-Veere said, *I can assure you—*

Stroever laughed even harder than his wife, exchanging

knowing looks with her. *No, no! That's my dear Jane's round-about way of asking if you want something to eat!*

Something to eat? Ryker-Veere said.

Yes, you need to drink on a full stomach, Jane said with a devious smile.

Ha! You sound like you have experience of such unladylike pursuits! Ryker-Veere said.

I conduct my drunken exploits in a refined and collected manner, I'll have you know, Anders! Jane's smile was infectious. *We'll eat shortly! Stuff ourselves and then I will join in your games! And win!*

Ha! We shall see, my dear! Stroever said.

And Isairis had said you were ill! Stroever shot him a warning look for this, but Jane's smile had stayed defiantly put.

I am ill, Mr. Ryker-Veere, Jane's smirk remained as she spoke. *But I smile because I want to be better, not worse. My smile is an ambition.*

This comment had baffled Ryker-Veere, making him guffaw at length, realising in that moment that he was aping Isairis Stroever's boisterousness.

Why don't we open the iskir from Uncle Valkyrys? Jane said.

A cloud spread across Ryker-Veere's mind at the recollection of this moment. Valkyrys Hanch was Jane's uncle and a well-known racketeer. He had been one of Stroever's early investors.

We'll stick to rum, Stroever said, looking solemn.

Val's not trying to butter you up.

Yes, he is! A generous gift at this time is very much an attempt to make me feel guilty. I have a debt to repay the old chap, Anders. Slightly awkward with the family connection but I'll pay the rest back soon. Old Val just needs to learn a little patience. Now! How about that game!

The conversation had moved swiftly on. They had stayed

up well into the next fade, and Jane Stroever had indeed drunk them both under the table.

Around midfade, Isairis and Jane Stroever were fast asleep, cuddled up together on the armchair by the fire, embers in the grate glowing their last. The candles had burned down. Sobering up, Ryker-Veere sat and read to the youngest of their two children, Helena.

Incredible imaginations these children's writers, eh? Ryker-Veere said, flicking through the book he'd been reading Helena. *Can you imagine a square so large and barren?*

Oh, yes! Helena said. *I've heard there's one in Tujumkin that's big enough to fit a hundred streets in it! But have you seen Daddy's factory? That's big! Really big! Daddy always takes me to the factories! The trees are so tall! You just can't believe it! You can't even see the tops! There's a story about a street that's inside a factory! It's so good! I'll go and find it...*

And with that Helena had raced up the stairs. Ryker-Veere smiled warmly and headed over to the table to find his cup of water. At the end of the table were two sliding doors leading to the bedchamber beyond.

Ryker-Veere sipped his water and then looked up. The doors were slightly ajar. There was a dim light in the room beyond. He'd peered inside, then jumped when he saw the eyes of a child glaring back at him through the crack.

I'm not allowed out, the child said.

Ah! Um... young Isri, I assume? We meet at last!

I'm not allowed out.

I know, I know. Your father told me all about your... um... What are you doing in there, lad?

Nothing. There's nothing to do.

Oh, now I don't know about that. When I was your age—

Well, you're not my age. And you're not my Daddy. Where's Daddy?

Having a little sleep, I think.

What are you doing?

We're celebrating, Master Isri.

You and Daddy have signed a stupid deal.

We have. And it'll mean a lot to your future.

No, it won't. I'll be dead in the future. I'm ill.

Oh, I'm sure you'll—

Daddy doesn't want me to live. He wants her to live.

Ryker-Veere glanced in the direction the child had indicated. He watched as Helena stomped merrily down the stairs clutching a book.

He loves her! He hates me! I'm going to run away!

Now, now, little Isri. I'm sure your father loves both you and Helena equally.

He doesn't.

Isri, came the voice of Stroever from behind Ryker-Veere. *Why are you up so early...?*

It's midfade.

Is it indeed? Well, well, well. And Mr. Ryker-Veere, whom you may call Uncle Anders, is right. Your mother and I do love you both. Equally.

No, you don't! I'm running away!

Isri!

The face in hiding vanished from sight. Stroever threw open the doors and chased after the insolent child.

That was the first time he had seen Isri Stroever..

Isri had kept his promise, though. He had run away. And Ryker-Veere had been there when it happened. This was after Isairis had departed this life. Ryker-Veere turned uncomfortably in his sleep at the thought.

Valkyrys Hanch had followed up on the escalating debt. When Stroever had ignored him too many times, Hanch deployed two ruffians to teach him a lesson. They had tried a little too hard to rough up the poor man and the great Isairis Stroever's body washed up on the quayside of Chronometer Dock one fade.

Distraught, Jane succumbed and followed her husband not long after. No one believed that Jane could have taken her own life; that did not seem like the ever-smiling Jane with her unnamed illness, a malady which was only known to be of a completely different nature to her son Isri's.

Her cause of death had been filed as 'death by misadventure', due to the smashed bottle of iskir found near the open window. Drinking was her vice of choice, and she would indulge to excess at times, but she was, she insisted, an adept and happy drunk. She never previously lost control.

Additionally, some had pointed out that the puddle around the bottle was rather large. Perhaps she had smashed it to prevent herself from drinking, but few chose to believe that she had ended her life in a clear mind.

No one knew what had happened that fateful night after Isairis's death, but her body had washed up downstream shortly afterwards.

That was when Ryker-Veere visited that house for the last time. The children were to be given into the care of Jane's sister, but Isri had refused to leave the house. As one of the few people to have ever had any contact with young Isri, Ryker-Veere had offered to try and persuade him to leave. He turned up at the house to find Isri clumsily attired in his father's clothes: a tragically shrunken impression of his father in an oversized top hat and tails.

I'm going to live in the factory! I'm going to live there and you can't stop me!

He had chased the child around the house for almost forty minutes but eventually Isri barricaded himself in his room.

Isri! Isri, come out! I'm trying to help you! Is this what your father would have wanted? Or your mother?

It doesn't matter because they're both dead and I'm going to live in the factory!

The child had slipped out a window and escaped. Ryker-Veere had told the authorities to search the factory, which, thanks to clause 16c, had become his property on Isairis Stroever's death. The police only spent a few hours trying to search the endless forests in the gigantic factory before giving up.

As Ryker-Veere's empire grew, he neglected the factory, letting it fall into disrepair.

After many years, the fully grown Isri Stroever had appeared wearing the same now somewhat ragged clothes, with the addition of a pair of gloves. He had survived for years in the forests of the factory, living a wild, introverted existence while his sister Helena remained with Jane's sister. His sickness had, apparently, not been cured, but he had survived by keeping a distance from everyone. When Ryker-Veere had seen those eyes in the newspaper, cold and distant, the same as the angry youngster he'd first spied in the crack between the sliding doors, he knew that the man was still a screaming child within. But not one without ambition.

For a time, Stroever had been a curiosity to the press. *The Illuminator* had reported one particularly intriguing exchange between Stroever and their reporter:

REPORTER – What will you do now?
STROEVER – Change.
REPORTER – Well, I mean after you've changed your clothes!
STROEVER – I don't mean my clothes. I mean everything. I will change everything.

Stories of the mad wild child from the factory floor subsided after a while. Ryker-Veere had, of course, returned ownership of the factory to Stroever out of sympathy – it was small fry to him now, though he recognised that none of his empire would exist without Isairis's initial investment.

He'd never had direct contact from Stroever at that time. They'd communicated via solicitors. But Ryker-Veere waited for a letter, a telegram, a knock on the door. He knew Stroever's question would come one fade...

After young Stroever had fled, did he, Anders Ryker-Veere, go into Isairis's study? Was it him, or another in the intervening years, who had taken the safe?

And Ryker-Veere had his own question on his mind, even now, as he tossed and turned, failing to fall asleep:

Did Isri Stroever know what was in the safe?

30

THE FIRST TOWER

J ulija and Bojana led the group farther across the bridge and down a flight of stone steps that was largely abandoned and smelled like a toilet. They reached a wooden door where many names were carved. The door was so dark in colour it almost looked like stone itself.

Julija produced a rusted iron key and turned it in the lock, pulling the door open with some force. Krish looked over the side of the bridge as they were about to enter and saw that the water was much deeper there.

They were led through the dank, stale air. Water dropped playfully from the ceiling and every footstep was accompanied with a splash as they trod in puddles. ShadowThief put her trust in their guide and resisted the temptation to cut the darkness away.

There was the clatter of metal and then the striking of a match. Light flickered as Julija lit a lantern. Her haunted eyes travelled across the faces of her guests. She looked down, away from them, turned and they followed her and Bojana, the lantern illuminating the steps as they continued to descend.

They reached the end of the steps and the stone gave way to wood. Drops of water were plopping from the creaking ceiling. The wood groaned under great pressure from the flowing waterway all around.

Julija hung the lantern from a hook in the middle of the room and proceeded to light two more. She placed them on opposite sides of the space. Between the three pools of dim light, Krish could make out a wooden shack, not much bigger than a garage, with wooden slats creaking and bulging. Droplets collected in lines hanging from the slats. He thought of all that water rushing around the structure and he couldn't help thinking that a number of slats would snap at any moment and the room would be filled with torrents of water, sweeping them all away.

The place was clearly a workshop, old tools scattered across the floor and workbenches. Filling almost an entire wall was a row of wooden drawers, descending from matchbox-sized at the top to being large enough for a child to sleep in at the bottom.

Julija started searching the drawers and gathering together numerous strange items, laying them out on a length of cloth. Bojana waited patiently to one side. Then, apparently remembering that she was not alone, Julija went to a stack of long, slim, slightly rotten cushions and spaced four of them out across the floor.

She made no attempt to explain her actions but Aemea and ShadowThief laid down on one each, and Krish and Thira followed suit. Krish struggled to feel comfortable with the bulging of the shack overhead, the mouldy scent of the cushions and the constant dripping of water.

Julija muttered to Bojana.

'She says you must pay in advance. It will take her a little longer to prepare the dream. It is very precise.'

Krish counted out the notes and placed them before Julija. Julija continued working for a few seconds then became aware of the large pile of cash before her, seized it and plonked it over by the wall of drawers without counting it.

Aemea wriggled uncomfortably, readjusted her cushion, then stopped dead for a moment. ShadowThief sat up, alert. Aemea was acting like something was tied tight around her wrists. Her hands shook for a moment as if fighting off some unseen force tugging at them. She looked over at the door and breathed a sigh of relief.

'How long will this take?' she asked.

Julija relayed an answer through Bojana:

'Perhaps half an hour preparation. The dream will only take a few minutes, no more than five. Then a few minutes to pack up, a few more to show you how to use your equipment correctly.'

ShadowThief could see Aemea totting up the time in her head.

'Okay, we must be gone in an hour from now,' said Aemea. 'Absolutely no more than an hour.'

ShadowThief nodded.

Detecting the severity in Aemea's voice, Julija nodded firmly and continued with her work.

Julija took objects from the drawers of various sizes. She weighed ingredients on a pair of black iron and scuffed brass scales, then placed them in a small glass dream-globe.

'She says that if the dream is not prepared correctly, with the exact amounts and very particular ingredients, then the dream could be completely different to the dream you desire.

'Every dream has a different kind of oil and base ingredient, usually wood, and the more the ingredients soak up into the base, the more the dream will become distorted. By the third viewing the dream will start to change. By the fourth it could be entirely different and difficult to view with any clarity. In fact, she recommends only viewing dreams twice.

'This dream – like many of the finest dreams – has several fresh ingredients that will spoil soon. It will only be good for a few fades.

'This dream uses sea liquor oil, containing a small quantity of sea-street salt flakes. Very unusual. It also contains several ingredients from other worlds. Many do not believe that the dream-pedlars once had suppliers who moved between worlds, but it is true. These supply roads are closed now, so ingredients are much in demand.

'Finally, be aware that this is a lucid dream – you may move around and interact. Not fully lucid: you cannot change events, but you can explore. The other two on your list, to the best of her knowledge, are observational only.'

Krish watched with increasing fascination as Julija measured out or weighed items from the drawers. She crouched like a child with her knees under her chin. She produced a large piece of blackened driftwood, dotted with the spots of barnacles from long ago. She weighed the wood, cut off a portion, weighed it again then placed it in the dreamglobe.

Next, she pulled out a decanter with an elegant swanlike neck which looked too fine for the workshop. She poured misty oil over the wood.

Then she chiselled off a fragment of coal. She took out a bar of soap and added shavings to the mixture – the smell in the air was medicinal rather than the fruity or floral soaps Krish was used to. She added dried seaweed, crushed heather with a pestle and mortar and then produced a shining brass compass, pulled off the needle with teasers, and placed it in the oil with the rest of the ingredients.

Finally, she poured a teaspoon of grimy water, which

reminded Krish of the brown of the Thames, on top of the mixture and it sat there floating on the oil.

Julija then busied herself setting up a small burner on the floor and attaching it to a funnel. The flame burned and the globe gradually began to fill with condensation.

Krish looked over the list of pictorial slides so they would be fresh in his mind as they entered the dream:

Arrow
Medicine bottle
Water
Rope
Lantern
Stove
Dagger
Hand
Herb
Piston
Mirror
Needle and thread
Shoes
Wolf's head
Waves
Earhorn
Crutch
Stairs
Cherries
Ruby
Pestle and mortar

Krish scanned the room. Aemea and ShadowThief were lying horizontally, relaxed, eyes closed. Thira caught his eye for a few moments, gave him a wink, and then they both laid back and shut out the world.

Behind his eyelids Krish saw only blackness, but the warm odours of salt, steam, oak, seaweed, fresh fish and guano filled his nostrils, the scents of a bitter morning off the coast

He couldn't hear the crash of waves or the shrill, distant cry of seagulls overhead, but he could sense them. Smells threaded themselves to his recollections and ghosts of sounds and visions experienced some time ago meandered through his psyche. There was no mistaking the scents of his own world and he suddenly longed to be back on a disappointing, rainy caravanning holiday in Northumberland with his parents and sister.

The haze of nostalgia faded in a moment as a vision appeared like a cloud spreading through his mind, inky lines filling his peripheral. A patchwork of grey and white led down to the land below. And then the sun came, filling the vista with a light like nothing the gas-stars of KnockThrice could ever produce. The clouds largely melted away, leaving only a few candyfloss-like shapes on the horizon, dancing in hazy pink light from his world's local star, lazily starting to dip behind the edge of the land for the night.

Then Krish became aware of a large structure casting a great shadow over him. It was a familiar building very much from his own world. Tall, striped red and white and emitting a powerful light from its top, it was on the move, travelling round and round to warn shipping of the coastline.

Krish began to march along the line of the shadow towards the lighthouse. He was wading through the water in the shadow of the lighthouse. He watched the grey-black stretch of sea all around, outside of the shadow pink light shimmering in the waves.

It must be cold in the shade on this winter's day, knee-

deep in the solemn waters. Freezing. Yes, it would be freezing
without the warmth of the sun. He was wading through icy
mush now. He slowed, seeing water flowing freely and playfully either side of the lighthouse's shadow.

Then he was stuck. Trapped up to his waist in ice, frozen
solid. His arms flailed about. He could not move, water rushing
outside of the shadow. He cried out, over and over again, but
no sound came from his silent lungs. He pictured himself
screaming but there was no sound in the dream, just the recollection of agonised shrieks.

He looked up at the light travelling round and round the
top of the tower. Round and round and round and bright like
fire, blurring his vision, burning-burning-burning, then it all
slowed down and now he was sitting by the fire inside the
lighthouse. He was shivering. He sat back, a blanket over his
soaking clothes, transfixed by the comforting flames in the
fireplace.

It was a small cosy room with rounded stone walls. Much
of the space was caped in shadow, but the orange light from
the fire glinted in the many burnished metal objects around
the room. Krish saw pocket telescopes, a compass and crossed
cutlery on a plate sitting upon a desk covered in maps and
charts.

He stood up and the chair fell backwards onto the floor.

He went to pick up the knife and fork and bizarrely found
that only the fork would move. He explored further. One sock
was hung out to dry on a wooden airer by the fireplace and the
other was stretched out on the floor. He picked up the sock by
the fire and then went to the other on the rug, but his hand
couldn't grip the latter. After a few seconds of frustration, he
moved on.

He inspected the map on the table – a group of jagged little
islands: Inner Farne, Staple, Brownsman, North Wamses,

South Wamses and Longstone, where the lighthouse was marked. He moved several books off the edge of the map to reveal the coast and a town called Seahouses. As he tried to pick up the brass telescope across the middle of the map, he found it would not shift. The compass would not move either. He noted a crack across the glass of the compass stretching from the centre to the rim.

He explored the room further and found a small bookcase. There were books on navigation plus many more maps and charts.

Across the floor was an upturned mug, a brown liquid which he assumed was tea or coffee spread out in front of it. The tea hadn't soaked into the stone yet, so it was a fairly recent spillage.

On the desk was a sepia photograph with two figures standing in front of a small house surrounded by grass. The man in the photo seemed to be about fifty, a stoic and tired expression on his face. He was clean shaven around the mouth with broad white mutton chops and a thick head of snowy curls. He did not smile and neither did the young lady next to him.

She wore a bonnet and had straight, dark hair, parted in the middle and tied into small buns. She also wore a bland expression. Both had plump little cheeks and small eyes and tiny noses. Neat, tidy features. They were dressed plainly but smartly as if they were wearing their Sunday bests.

Krish had seen many old photos like this. He knew people didn't do smiling or hugging back then in pictures, but the picture seemed odd, for the simple reason that the man had his arm around the woman's waist. Even more strange to Krish's eye was the age difference between them – she looked about Joshi's age, but he looked older than Dad. Their bland expressions didn't give much away, and although she didn't seem all that comfortable, she did have her arm over the man's shoulder. Based on their similar features, he'd guess they were father and daughter, but their embrace was strange. He just couldn't figure out why

The photo gave Krish the creeps. Just then he noticed another artefact on the desk – a large ledger. Along the spine where the words 'JOURNAL – LONGSTONE LIGHTHOUSE, 1842.' Only a few pages were filled in. The latest entry was dated 4th January. He scanned the neat handwriting:

4.24pm - Storm front spreading from NE.

4.48pm – Storm abating, moving NNE with northerly wind.

5.02pm – Signal from RMS Catherine, Leith-Tyneside, may require assistance, cancelled 2 minutes later. Billy Shiel's trawler spotted NW, moving north. Storm continues to abate.

5.09pm – Storm front returning, moving NW. RMS Catherine moving SE.

5.11pm – Shiel's trawler caught in storm, returning to shore. No answer to my signal.

5.15pm – Holding beam steady on Billy Shiel's, NW. Shiel may run aground. Not answering flash signal.

5.20pm – Returned beam to rotation. Shiel not answering. Storm continues to abate. 2 minutes more and will prepare lifeboat.

He read it over several times. He studied the map and tried to imagine what had happened. A ship had been in trouble as the storm had set in, signalled for help before cancelling the request. Then the lighthouse keeper had seen a fishing boat in trouble and had prepped a boat to go and rescue the fishermen.

But what had happened to the fishing boat?

He went to pick up the telescope but again it wouldn't budge.

He climbed the stairs, spiralling up and up, following the rope banister, the spinning light from the top level pouring into the staircase every few seconds, becoming brighter and brighter as he headed to the top.

He entered a large circular room, glass windows all around, the gigantic light turning round and round. He looked out the windows and saw the dark waves crashing into white froth as they collided with the jagged, fang-like rocks, visible for a moment at a time as the light turned.

Then he spotted a brass tube on the window ledge – another telescope. He was quite surprised to find that he could pick it up, unlike the one downstairs. He extended the telescope and looked out to sea. In the flashes of light, he began to get his bearings in the magnified landscape.

He made out the shore – there was a castle along the end of a beach, a house alone on the clifftops, and a harbour in front of a fishing village.

Then he focussed in on the craggy isles around him. Just rocks and sea. He observed the moments when one crashed into the other, the land standing its ground against the might of the waves. All of a sudden, a shape stood out – *what was it?* He waited for the light to pass again. A ship, its belly carved up by the rocks, stuck on the jagged terrain. Patiently he stood there waiting for the light to return. He spied a small boat, a fishing trawler, moored off the shore.

He tilted the telescope downwards a touch and began to make out the figures sitting on the rocks. A man in a cap, not far from the trawler, was standing there, hands on hips, speaking to a group of men who sat about, slouched forward, some with blankets over them. He could even make out their smiles of relief.

The man standing could well have been the fisherman, Billy Shiel, and the men sitting those he had rescued from the ship. The lighthouse keeper could have been swept into the sea, failing in his own rescue attempt. But he'd clearly made it back to the lighthouse intact, his sodden clothes hung out to dry. So, if everybody was safe, what did it all mean?

He went downstairs, searched everywhere – the books, the kitchen, by the fireplace, the ledger. Nothing stood out to him. The photograph of the man with the younger woman was no less jarring but neither was it any help.

He climbed the tower once more to look out of the lighthouse again but as he did so, the stairs curved to the side, the lines of the stone wall fell out of focus and the world became dark. The smell of sea water and burning timber was prominent once more and then the real world came into uncomfortably sharp focus.

Krish sat up, back in the shack under the river, and came face to face with Thira.

'What the bloody hell was all that about?' exclaimed Krish.

'Took the words right outta m'gob, mate,' answered Thira.

§

Back up on the bridge, not far above where Krish and his associates now lay in the shack beneath the river-street, figures approached. They wore top hats and dark clothing, clashing with the colourful attire of the dream-pedlars.

They moved hastily but without attracting attention. They asked questions of the dream-pedlars. There was a sense of precision to their line of enquiry. They would ask a question or two and once they received a shake of the head, they would move on

One dream-pedlar nodded in response to a series of questions fired at her in rapid succession. The gentlemen asking them suddenly became extraordinarily interested in her. She noticed that one of the men in black – a gentleman of exceptional height, his head bowed, his face hidden by the brim of his tall top hat – stood at the back and said not a word. He was listening. She detected that he was in charge. Once she pointed in a particular direction, the tall man at the back departed, the others following, ceasing to have any concern for anything else she said or did.

The men headed for the cathedral and, minutes later, they reached the point where the four friends had first met Julija and Bojana. Though by then, there was no sign that Krish and his associates had ever been there.

Eva runs for the window but it's locked tight

Through the thick glass, darkness and sentinellight

She wants to be free of medicine and games

No more green room is something for which she aims

The Master promised freedom, now she's in doubt

The Woman appears, 'Child, you cannot go out,'

Eva shouts harsh words, but the Woman ignores

'Oh, one fade, dear child, the City will be yours'

31

THE MEN & THEIR STAR

Corroded green-brown machines churned up the water, obeying only the orders of the force that many believed was 'the will of the Iron Devil'. They were scattered about the sea-street, transforming once placid waters into tempestuous waves.

The sleek form of Isri Stroever's vessel, the *Selkirk*, sliced through the turbulent waters. Waves lashed the bow and splashed onto the deck. The harpooner knelt on the foredeck. As each wave hit, she was submerged for a moment before the arch of water flattened itself to the deck, revealing her still there, solid as a statue.

Captain Fenric Stavast, salt stinging every line in his skin, his rusted eyes feeling their way through the squall. He yanked the helm hard-a-port, then starboard, then back to port, to keep the ship from capsising.

Ryker-Veere and de Clercq cowered in the doorway to the cabin as Stroever stayed outside in the elements, gripping the handrail tightly, his eyes on the dark sky above.

'There, Stavast! There!' People rarely heard Stroever speak

much louder than a whisper, but now his words came in throat-shredding cries. 'Port! Port! Starboard! Port! There! You're almost through the worst!'

'Aye, the squall-pins be out in force, doing devil's foul work!' screamed Stavast in return. 'Now is no time for pleasure-cruisin'! 'Tis time to turn the helm all the way back and head to streets solid under foot, or kiss the seabed and only float to the surface once there's nought but salty liquor in yer lungs!'

'We're close! We're close!'

'We must turn back! This is madness!'

'There! There! We're close!' Stroever pointed to an object overhead with such violence that it would have been no surprise to anyone if his arm had shot straight out of its socket. Ryker-Veere made out nothing in the sky ahead of them.

Stavast screamed out an obscenity, gritted his teeth and steered on into oblivion.

The storm did indeed begin to settle, but choppy waters rocked the boat still. Stroever turned and faced Ryker-Veere. He was sodden head to toe, dripping hair plastered across his face, partially obscuring his eyes.

'Come!' said Stroever. He waved his arm at Ryker-Veere who obeyed, primarily out of terror. Ryker-Veere waddled one way and then the other unsteadily, trying to catch up with Stroever, who marched confidently across the deck.

'De Clercq!' shouted Ryker-Veere as his assistant followed on his deaf side. 'I'm setting a new rule – from now on I am never to be encouraged to set foot on anything even remotely buoyant ever again. *Ever!* And burn the picture of a galleon over the door to the library.'

'Yes, your malodorousness,' said de Clercq.

'What?!'

De Clercq passed to his good side. 'Of course, your excellence.'

The ship was tossed about though the storm continued to die down. Stavast held the Selkirk steady.

Stroever directed the way to the great object obscured by the tarpaulin. Ahead stood the harpooner, manning the gigantic double-barrelled harpoon gun stationed in its cradle fastened to the foredeck. Stroever came to a halt between the hidden object and the great silver gun, with Ryker-Veere and de Clercq close behind.

Ryker-Veere eyed the tarpaulin. The rectangular object underneath was larger than a carriage.

'It's innovative, absolutely,' said Stroever just ahead of them, not looking back, 'but little more impressive than any fairground ride. As always, Anders, you miss the main attraction.'

Ryker-Veere did not appreciate Stroever's overfamiliar tone. Stroever began to unfasten the straps tied around the massive object. Less than a minute later he pulled the tarpaulin away to reveal what looked like a small locomotive bisected by a wire cage, like an elevator on its side.

'As I said,' continued Stroever, still not looking back, 'you are neglecting the real innovation before you.'

Ryker-Veere's gaze settled on the harpoon gun. Now he looked closely, it was unusual. Two gleaming silver cylinders, each large enough to fit a fully grown man within, either side of an enormous barrel. The shaft of the harpoon must be at least five metres in length. There could be no beast alive big enough to require such an unnecessarily large projectile to slay it.

'We're in range,' said Stroever. The ship still rocked a touch, but it was relatively stable now.

Ryker-Veere saw nothing but gloom ahead – no shape of a

creature lurking below the waves, and above only the faint outline of a dormant, low-flying gas-star, and in the distance merely the odd raingrate hovering over the waters.

Stroever pointed upwards. The harpooner shifted the gigantic gun in line with her master's fingertip, aiming up into the nothingness.

'Steady, Fenric, steady!' called out Stroever.

'She's holdin' steady!' replied the captain.

Ryker-Veere followed Stroever's line of sight and saw nothing between them and the outline of the star.

'Now!'

A high hiss for a moment, and then a loud jolting sound, which made Ryker-Veere and de Clercq recoil in shock. The harpoon shot from the barrel, sliced through the air and into the darkness. Then there was a low metallic thud which faded to hush in an instant. All was quiet aside from the sloshing of the waves. Whatever they'd hit was unbothered by the attack.

Ryker-Veere narrowed his eyes, tried to focus on the grey-black haze ahead of them. The cable, thick as a fist, was taut. He saw nothing beyond the... the gas-star... The harpoon had pierced the side of the gas-star! He peered over the bow. The ship was being gently towed onwards by the star.

The harpooner picked up the slack excess cable hanging out of the rear of the gun and fastened it to a silver coupling affixed to the deck. Adjusting the controls of the massive harpoon gun, the cable ran through the gun slowly, tightening at the rear by the coupling and slackening at the front of the gun; the cable leading up to the gas-star began to dip down towards the deck so the harpooner could grab hold of it. She ran the loosened cable through a channel across the top of the wire cage before it had a chance to become taut. She locked the cable into position on the channel atop the wire cage. The cable was now secured to the deck, running through the harpoon gun, across the top of the wire cage and all the way up to the pierced gas-star.

Once secure, the harpooner nodded at her master.

'There is only room for one other,' said Stroever, opening the door to the cage.

Ryker-Veere was doing a bad job of concealing his fear. He looked at de Clercq for a moment and then accepted Stroever's invitation. He stepped into the cage and shuddered at the sound of the door clanging shut behind him.

Stroever busied himself by adjusting nobs and dials on the controls of the engine at the rear of the horizontal elevator car.

'Steady, Fen—'

'She's as damned steady as she'll ever be and damn ye if ye think we'll venture out on these waters again as friends!' screamed Stavast.

'Complete the work and hold her steady, Fenric. Any other matter can wait 'til we return to dry streets.'

Stavast banged his fist against the empty window frame.

Ryker-Veere was searching for a surface to perch his ample posterior on in the cage.

'There's nowhere to sit,' said Stroever, not looking up from his work, 'but do feel free to hold on to the handrail.'

Ryker-Veere gripped the rail firmly.

The square machine hissed into life and *TAT-TAT-TAT*ed its way up into the air. Ryker-Veere, both hands balled around the rail, was unsteady, the cage rocking a little as it began its journey upwards. The night air rushed through the chain-links and whistled uncomfortably around his ears. The ship below began to shrink in size and the tinkling amber lights of the City and the unblinking bone-white globes of the sentinels stretched out over the horizon. Ahead a great dark shape began to fill his vision.

He expected the heat to be worse, but the star had cooled

quickly. Within minutes they reached the shell of the star. Ryker-Veere blinked at the harpoon piercing the side of one of the great metal spheres which filled the daytime with light and warmth. How could this be? How could it look so normal? So dull? He could make out grooves and scratches across the rusted orangey-brown surface of the star.

Stroever opened the cage and for a fearful moment Ryker-Veere thought he would jump. Stroever produced a pole with a hook on the end. He reached out, slotted the hook into what appeared to be a handle in the side of the star. He turned the handle, pulled and a hatch opened, revealing a staircase. Ryker-Veere could not believe his eyes. A strong smell of gas gushed forth, making Ryker-Veere cough uncontrollably for a moment.

The stairs locked into position. Stroever pulled two gasmasks off hooks on the side of the cage and passed one to Ryker-Veere before putting on his own. Breathing was laboured and Ryker-Veere could smell the canvas and rubber of the mask.

Stroever began to ascend the staircase. He stopped, turned and looked back at Ryker-Veere, expectantly, framed in the dull yellow glow emanating from within the gas-star. After a few moments' hesitation, Ryker-Veere followed.

A low roar was all around, a vibrating hum in the air, biting at his eardrums. A dull, dirty yellow glow was all around. They walked across metal gantries over great lakes of gas, twisted around into wispy turrets. Along the gantries were handrails at just the right height to run your hands along, control panels, each button a little larger than the tip of a human finger, and pipes with nozzles and controls, hanging down at exactly the right height for him to reach.

'And so, man tamed the beasts and ate of their flesh,' came Stroever's voice, distorted somewhat by the gas mask.

'Then, hungering for meat untasted, he journeyed up to the gantries of the factory, finding every step was well-placed to guide him upwards and the handles of the doors his fingers could curl around and open with ease. And so, man escaped the factories. He ventured out into the streets and made a home for himself in the houses, forged by the Iron Devil. He knew it was a domain built for him, for every chair was the right height, and every table the right size, built in spitefully by the Iron Devil, believing man would never set foot beyond the factory walls and discover a world that was his for the taking...'

Stroever laid a gloved hand on a nozzle at the end of a pipe hanging down from the ceiling far above, hidden in the rumbling clouds of gas swimming overhead.

'These stars, Anders... they are ours!' said Stroever, his eyes quietly wild, staring into and beyond Ryker-Veere. 'Whether or not you believe the stories of the Iron Devil, this place has been designed for us! For humankind! We must take control of this place! And there is more...'

Ryker-Veere watched as Stroever pulled a small canister from his pocket, attached it to the nozzle overhead, turned the valve and filled the tiny canister with hissing gas. He removed it and held it out to Ryker-Veere. Ryker-Veere took the object. He held it in his hand, shook it and felt the semi-gaseous liquid slosh about within.

'What... what... what...' Ryker-Veere struggled for words. 'This is all too much to take in... I must confess, I am lost. This is too much! We are... we are walking inside a star! How can this be?'

'Can you not see the potential?' said Stroever.

'I...I must say, old boy, I am...I'm just lost...'

'Gas! Gas, Anders!'

Ryker-Veere winced at his host's continual use of his first

name. 'You are somewhat overfamiliar, you young whippersn—'

'You think we are not equals now, Anders? Not something greater than that frayed partnership with my wretched father?'

Ryker-Veere jolted with guilt. How much did Stroever know about how their relationship ended? He did not respond.

'The gas-mines of Sharaz Jek have all but been exhausted. In Western Squares there are fights over gas reserves on a fadely basis. Prices are reaching unprecedented highs. But here... *here* what we have is an untapped resource! And how many stars are there in the known City?'

'Ha! You start draining... draining... I can hardly breath in this... in this... in this thing! Old boy... If you drain the stars of their gas... you'll ultimately plunge the City into eternal NightTime.'

Ryker-Veere looked across the glowing gantry at the man in the gasmask, towers of wispy yellow rising all around him, searching for sanity in those unnervingly still eyes. Stroever simply nodded.

'And what do people desire most during NightTime?' said Stroever. 'When the night comes and takes all light and hope from their lives...'

Ryker-Veere shook his head.

'Child! You are deluded! If you... If you... We must leave! I need to breath without this damn thing!'

'Dreams, Anders!'

'I am... I am *Lord* Ryker-Veere!'

Stroever looked up and around. 'It should be clear enough now.' He removed his mask.

Ryker-Veere did the same, his instant relief somewhat stifled by a sharp intake of gas which left him coughing and spluttering.

'For all his failings,' Stroever said, looking up and around in awe, 'my father made one truly great contribution to the City. He was the first to hang lanterns in his factories. And later he pioneered the first raingrates not made by Devil's foul hand. The trees no longer relied on the gas-starlight from the windows and the moisture in the air alone. They grew faster and taller than in any other factory in the known City.

'The fool never patented the technology, of course, allowing others to copy him, but I used to look up at those lanterns during the years I spent in the forests of the factory and my ambitions became bigger than his ever could have been...

'We will take control of the stars themselves! They shall become commodities, only shining down on those who can afford the light! The rest we shall drain, allowing the less well-off to become addicted to the dreams you shall legalise. Their only escape from the darkness! I have mastered the technology! The secret will remain safe with me but with your help we shall make a fortune! We must move fast! While we have time, Anders! While we have time!'

A swirling sickness swelled within Ryker-Veere.

'Do not call me that! You hear! And let's... let's be gone from this place! Madness! Utter madness!'

§

Minutes later, they were descending the stairs and re-entering the cage, fresh night air pouring into Ryker-Veere's thankful lungs. He kept his back to the star. Stroever glared at Ryker-Veere.

'You lack vision,' said Stroever.

'I do not wish to spread misery on such a scale,' said Ryker-Veere.

'You will reconsider. Think on it. This is an opportunity no visionary would reject.'

'Endless dark, old boy!'

'Not for us. If we control the stars – *the stars!* – it will never be NightTime for us! Given time—' Stroever held up his gloved hand, balled tightly into a fist, and glared at it resentfully, '— we shall achieve much...'

Ryker-Veere was bent over, catching his breath.

'I shall... I shall mull it over.'

They arrived back on deck. Ryker-Veere stumbled out of the cage towards de Clercq. She was stood next to Stavast. De Clercq was turned towards the captain, her back to Stroever and Ryker-Veere. Upon seeing her master looking exasperated, she stepped in to assist him.

'Am I dismissed?' barked Stavast.

'Return us to the dock, Fenric,' said Stroever to Stavast. 'Then we shall discuss.'

'Aye, I am dismissed,' grumbled Stavast grimly to himself. He slumped back to the bridge. On the way, his unseeing eyes jerked involuntarily towards de Clercq. De Clercq hoped her master had not noticed.

32
THE TRUTH IN THE PHOTOGRAPH

'So, you've got some lonely old codger in a tower on an island in the ocean, but Jingaloid only knows why!' said Thira as they were packing up.

'Did you see the people?' said Krish. 'On the other island? The fisherman had saved them. I thought we were going to have to work out how to stop them from drowning, but they were fine.'

'Blimey! Didn't even see them!'

'The lighthouse keeper didn't rescue anyone. He tried but then he just got swept into the sea and headed back to the lighthouse.'

Krish and Thira tuned back into the room as Julija, via Bojana's translations, started to explain the dreamglobe before they packed it away.

'Keep it on a medium-high temperature for a few minutes until it's nice and hot, then turn it all the way down until it's almost off. And keep the globe upright and in a cool place if you want it to last longer.'

'Thank you,' said Aemea, looking about, agitated. 'We're

much obliged, but we must hurry now.' She looked at Shadow-Thief as if for confirmation. ShadowThief held up all ten fingers and thumbs. Aemea nodded hastily.

Within minutes, they were climbing the dank staircase and wishing goodbye to Julija and Bojana.

As the four of them walked away, back through the throng of the dream-pedlars' parade, ShadowThief kept looking back over her shoulder. Amongst the innumerable coloured clouds of dreams, she spotted something. She clutched Aemea tightly by the arm, pulled her to the side of a statue along the bridge and pointed back in the direction of the staircase leading to Julija's.

There, just heading down the steps, were a group of five or six men, dressed in dark clothing, sporting tall top hats, conspicuous in their total lack of interest in the parade. Aemea and ShadowThief had a silent conference, staring into each other for a handful of seconds. ShadowThief held up two fingers.

'What?!' said Thira impatiently.

'It's always an hour,' said Aemea. 'An hour exactly. That was a couple of minutes early. If we were still there now...' She gripped her wrist as if she was imagining something tied tightly around it.

'Who are they?' said Krish.

ShadowThief rubbed her thumb over her index and middle fingers, a gesture for money, then held out hands flat, palms up, one passing over the other, highlighting her hands themselves.

'Precisely,' said Aemea. 'Hired hands. Mercenaries.'

'Lookin' for us?' said Thira.

'I don't know, but we would certainly have been in trouble if we'd hung around a minute or two longer,' said Aemea.

Without discussing further, the party of four walked

briskly through the parade. They did not run, nor did they look back.

§

At the train station, Krish felt as if every eye was on them. ShadowThief had a very subtle way of glancing around to make sure that each of those eyes was not making a move towards them.

Unlike the bustling, enclosed station at Eschborn Hauptbahnhof, this one was a large, empty space in the middle of a square. There was a chill in the air now. Few sentinels passed over. The whole station felt exposed. Just a few old locomotives sat steaming on the tracks which ran through the square.

Aemea's eyes darted about. 'Every option is a bad one. Something's wrong. Not death, not capture but... it's not right.'

Aemea and ShadowThief opted for the first train. It was slow but direct and leaving imminently. There was only one private compartment available in the observation car at the end of the train, which was meant for six, but train fares were cheap in this part of the neighbourhood. Aemea and Shadow-Thief were keen to stay on guard while Krish and Thira set up the dreamglobe.

'Seriously – something's wrong,' said Aemea. 'I can sense something. We're being pursued. I know it.'

'By Ryker-Veere's men?' said Krish.

'She don't know specifics, mate!' said Thira.

'No, there is something,' said Aemea. 'Something familiar.'

ShadowThief's expression grew dark, sensing something in Aemea.

'Many of the most fearsome mercenaries emerge from the woodwork in NightTime,' said Aemea. 'So, being exceptional thieves as we are, we have encountered some of the best of said mercenaries. And if I were Ryker-Veere, I know who I'd want on our tail.'

'So they might 'ave a bone to pick with you?' said Thira.

ShadowThief took in a deep, quivering breath and nodded.

'Shad and I will keep watch in the corridor,' said Aemea, 'but I'd strongly advise you dream again in case... in case... I don't know... just in case...'

'What did you think of it?' said Krish, addressing both Aemea and ShadowThief.

ShadowThief tapped her head and made a gesture to signify money in her palm.

'Are we being hired for our brains now as well?' said Aemea.

'Comes with the 'ole package, innit,' said Thira.

'Yeah, and I'm aware your... er... powers of deduction are worth their weight in gold,' added Krish.

An amused ShadowThief nodded as if to say, *Nicely put.*

'In the kitchen, I couldn't move the ladle in the soup,' said Aemea. 'Or the telescope on the desk. I could pick up the telescope upstairs though. There's something in that.'

'Bloody cold, weren't it?' said Thira. 'In the ice in the shadow of the flashy tower whatsit. Not that I felt the cold. But I... I kinda detected it. Reminded me of when I got stuck in the snow once.'

ShadowThief launched into a long series of gestures, climbing downstairs, walking about, looking around.

'Really?' said Aemea. 'I didn't even think to leave the lighthouse.'

'What?' said Krish, eagerly.

'Shad wandered around outside. Perhaps there's more to see.'

'Maybe,' said Krish, producing the list of slides from Ryker-Veere's safe from his pocket:

Arrow

Medicine bottle

Water

Rope

Lantern

Stove

Dagger

Hand

Herb

Piston

Mirror

Needle and thread

Shoes

Wolf's head

Waves

Earhorn

Crutch

Stairs

Cherries

Ruby

Pestle and mortar

'I just don't know, said Krish. 'It could be the lantern. Because... a lantern's like a lighthouse?! Or the stairs. There were lots of stairs.'

'Yeah, and one of them slides was blinkin' water!' said Thira. 'Why can't it be that?'

'It's all very subjective,' said Aemea, 'but I suspect that once unravelled, the whole dream will point quite clearly to one thing.'

An idea flitted across Krish's subconscious then vanished. He was on the verge of pinpointing something when he was distracted by Aemea. She stood perfectly still. She considered for a moment and then peered down the corridor. She checked her watch. '45 minutes. Then I think... yes... Be packed and ready – we're going to leave the train. Jump off and then wait for the next one. Yes... yes, that's the best option. 45 minutes...'

Aemea slid the wooden door into place, leaving Krish and Thira alone in the compartment. They packed.

'Ready?' said Thira.

'Sure,' said Krish, setting up the dreamglobe.

There wasn't much space on the floor between the three bunks on either side.

'Ya know what I've been thinkin'?' said Thira. 'That... ya know, little paintin' thing... but real...'

'The photo?' said Krish.

'Photah?'

'Photo. Photograph.'

'Whatever. That weird like thing... was odd. Just him and his daughter—'

'You think it was his daughter?'

'Seemed pretty young to be 'is wife. But don't wanna judge. Love is love and all that.'

A moment's pause as Krish fiddled awkwardly with the nozzle on the dreamglobe.

'Why did 'e 'ave 'is arms round 'er like that?' continued Thira. 'Around 'er waist and everything. Proper pervy!'

'I don't know,' said Krish. He was distracted. He concentrated on the globe, hoping all the ingredients were okay, although they'd been jostled in the bag, bubbles mixed in with the oil. Although he was anxious and irritable about whether the dream would work properly, he was fighting even more to bury the awkwardness of being alone again with Thira.

Thira was the person he felt most comfortable with in all the worlds. He hated himself for feeling something had changed but he couldn't deny it either.

'I ain't never seen water like what was in that dream!' Thira went on, mainly to himself. 'Terrifyin'! All churning up like it were angry. And that sky! It was all wrong! And cold. Like a winter morning in—'

'Did you want to be a boy, Thira?' blurted out Krish all of a sudden. As soon as it was out, he wished he'd kept it in. 'Sorry! I shouldn't have...'

Thira turned sharply to Krish and his expression cut deep into him.

'Well, that's my business, innit?' spat out Thira.

Krish looked sheepishly down. Thira took a deep breath.

'To be honest, mate,' said Thira, 'I didn't know it was what I'd always wanted 'til I realised I 'ad the choice.'

'Okay. Sure. I mean, it's fine. It's just... it's just that I didn't expect it.'

'Just 'cause I didn't say, doesn't mean I didn't feel it. I took a boy's name. Remember when I said I couldn't be king and you said, no, I'd be queen? Well, perhaps I knew. I always felt I wasn't quite like everybody else. Boys were meant to be one way, girls were meant to be another. It was like ya 'ad to fit into a box. Didn't really feel like I was one thing or the other, but when I was given the choice... I dunno, mate. All I know is that I am and always was Thira, even back then. Guess I'll work out the rest as I go along.'

Krish took in everything Thira had said and nodded. 'Okay, it might take me some time to adjust,' said Krish, 'but that's my problem, I guess. It's fine. It's cool.'

Thira gave him an odd look. 'Am I really that different?'

Krish smiled. 'No. No, not really. It's still you. Definitely you. And I'm glad you're here.'

He put his hand on Thira's shoulder. Thira smiled and did the same to Krish. Krish felt excitement and fear rising and falling rapidly within him, wondering what would happen next, but then they broke apart.

He finished preparing the dreamglobe, turning up the heat to warm it up. The two of them laid down on the ground either side of the dreamglobe, ready to get moving at a moment's notice. They were still within arm's reach of each other. Krish opened his mouth to speak.

'I'm glad to be here too, mate,' Thira interrupted him. 'Even if this place is rubbish. I made my choice to be here and... yeah. Good to be here.'

They smiled at one another.

Krish turned down the heat under the dreamglobe before lying all the way back. The scent of salt, seaweed and ocean spray filled the air of the carriage.

'And ya know what?' said Thira. 'All this dream malarkey, I think it's like one of them big clever stories with all them fancy words and metaphors and all that cobblers. Ya think it's all so blinkin' sophistimacated until ya realise one thing... it ain't.'

Krish mulled this over as he began to tune out the clatter of the speeding train. He had one last look at the door, noticing it was open a crack, Aemea and ShadowThief's eyes alert, staring down the corridor, before his eyelids slid closed and the dream weaved its world around him...

Seagulls wheeled overhead. The waves reared, washing away the darkness as the scene came into focus. The rocky shores of Longstone Island appeared again. He walked into the shadow of the lighthouse, wading through the encroaching ice, slowing him, becoming stuck, and as the blurring light filled his vision, he was transported up to the little room with the fireplace.

He was shivering in the chair again. He stood up and the chair fell backwards as it'd done before. He tried to pick up the sock, the telescope and the ladle. None would move. Irritated, he ran around the room, picking up books and forks and mugs and throwing them about the place. Why was it that some items would move while others wouldn't?

Ya think it's all so blinkin' sophistimacated until ya realise one thing... it ain't.

He went to lift up the chair he'd knocked over and found that it wouldn't budge either. It *must* be something so simple... He was staring at the immovable chair when something struck him. Something he'd seen but not seen. He looked straight at it, recognised what it was and, because it hadn't seemed important, his mind had edited it out.

He rushed across the room. He picked up the photograph of the two figures outside the house, the old lighthouse keeper and the woman he assumed was his daughter. The haunted eyes were still there but now he saw the scene in a different light. Something wasn't normal but it wasn't a creepy relationship between a man and his much younger wife as he'd suspected.

He was holding her weight. That's why his arm was around her waist, and why she had her arm over his shoulder. She was too weak to stand unassisted. And there it was behind her, what he'd missed, the item his mind had edited out, all but a slither of it eclipsed by the woman: a chair. She had been sat on the chair until just before the photograph was taken and her father had hauled her to her feet. This was no creepy marriage but a father – a widower perhaps, since there was no mother in the photo – looking after his sick daughter.

But what did this have to do with the ship and the fishing trawler? He scanned again through the log. He looked over the latest entry again, but then flicked through a few more pages. There was hardly anything in the journal, just entries for the first four days of January 1842.

He returned to the bookcase and found the journal for the

previous year, 1841. He searched the pages, working his way from 31st December backwards, trying to find something that made sense; but there was nothing. All he noticed was that the RMS Catherine came up quite frequently. In fact, it was mentioned weekly:

5th October, 1.12pm - RMS Catherine docked at 12:03pm – met with Capt. McVeigh. No letter from Puckridge.

As he worked his way backwards through the year, each week, around the same time, there would be an entry that was almost identical:

7th September, 1.43pm - RMS Catherine docked at 12:47pm – met with Capt. McVeigh. No letter from Puckridge.

17th August, 1.04pm - RMS Catherine docked at 14:07pm – met with Capt. McVeigh. No letter from Puckridge.

21st July, 1.01pm - RMS Catherine docked at 11:58am – met with Capt. McVeigh. No letter from Puckridge.

He worked it over in his mind – every week, the same ship, a meeting with the captain and a letter he was expecting from a man named Puckridge. Perhaps RMS Catherine brought post to the island. But the Catherine had come aground, its hull pierced and its cargo largely washed away. He checked the first page of the journal and found the name of the lighthouse keeper: L. Bretherton.

He remembered what ShadowThief had said about being

able to leave the lighthouse. He ran to the top floor, to the room where the light span round and round, stripping a land of shadow for the briefest of moments. He stared out in the direction of the ship. He spied it, cut up by the rocks, the men huddled under blankets, the fishing trawler moored nearby. He leaned forward, willing himself to be there, and the dream blurred around him, transported him safely over the rocks and churning waters.

He walked now amongst rockpools on the jagged, low-lying island, lantern in hand showing him the way. Waves broke all around and burst into frothing whiteness. And then the words 'RMS CATHERINE' came into view ahead. He saw the great gash in the hull. As he approached, he found himself compelled to keep going forward until the mighty scar in the ship enveloped him.

All was dark and then the lighthouse shone a shaft of light into the submerged hull of the ship. Oblongs of white floated all around. His arm drifted forward and scanned them all. So many names – Brand, Fricker, Hitch, Thompson, Hardy, Bretherton. *Bretherton – the name of the lighthouse keeper!*

He took hold of the letter and made his way out of the semi-submerged ship. On the rocks, he opened the sodden letter. The ink was blurred but it was just about legible:

Dear Lionel,

I write with news such as I would never freely wish to deliver to a dear friend. Your daughter Victoria has a disease of the blood. It is indeed treatable, but I cannot return to attend to her until the start of the next week. Until then, you *must keep her warm and well fed. You must administer the medication discussed previously every day, and I cannot stress enough that you must start the moment you receive this letter. I must be blunt as any delay may well prove fatal. I do hope you receive this letter in good time and can leave your post at once to attend to your precious Victoria.*

Your Friend,
Dr. John Puckridge

Was this it? Had he solved it? He was almost certain, but he had to be sure. He turned back to the lighthouse. The great light spun round and round on top of the tower. He rushed forward, the tall tower looming in front of him. Everything dissolved. He was in the room with the fire once more.

...the whole dream will quite obviously point to one thing...

Aemea's words flew through his mind. He caught hold of one word as it passed. *Point.*

He wandered round to see every object that wouldn't move – the sock, the chair, the telescope, and most of all the cracked compass. It was all so painfully obvious now. The crack on the compass was over the south-easterly direction marker. The toes of the sock pointed in the same direction. The telescope and the fallen chair too.

He had one last look at the picture of the man and his daughter, the girl who needed immediate medical assistance to keep her safe until the doctor arrived. Something the light-house keeper wouldn't have known about if the ship delivering the post had come aground and had its hull pierced, flooding the hold containing the mail.

He ran up the stairs and the blinding light filled his vision. He looked out of the glass in a south-easterly direction. There it was, illuminated every few seconds – the little house on the cliffs, the same house the lighthouse keeper and his daughter had stood outside in the photo. Even the shadow of the lighthouse had been pointing that way. Getting stuck in the ice was a warning – *turn back, look in the direction the shadow of the building is pointing in!* It all led to the house on the cliffs where the lighthouse keeper's daughter needed urgent assistance. Urgent *medical* assistance. The slide *must* be the—

A scream.

The world of the dream was torn apart by the cry of a young child, so loud Krish was certain the sound would cut through his skin and draw blood.

33

THE SCREAM IN THE
CORRIDOR

His eyes burst open, he sat up straight, the clattering of the train returning to his ears. The door to the compartment was still ajar. He spied an expression of horror on ShadowThief's face through the crack.

The scream returned, like a knife across the eardrum. The shrill cry of a young girl, as if she'd never known a greater terror.

Thira took to his feet and Krish followed. They slid open the doors and entered the corridor. ShadowThief peered ahead into the darkness. The gaslight at that end was out, leaving the narrow passageway to fade into nothingness.

ShadowThief breathed fearsome, stuttering breaths through her nose, her lips walled up tightly over her teeth. Aemea looked bewildered, as if her old friend was unfamiliar all of a sudden.

Both jolted as the scream of abject horror tore through them once more. A child, a young girl crying out from a hoarse throat, sounding as if she would be silenced for good all too soon.

Aemea stepped forward instinctively.

To Krish's surprise, ShadowThief seized Aemea's arm, stopping her dead in her tracks. Aemea span round and glared at her friend in disbelief.

'Shad! Please! Somebody's—'

But ShadowThief shook her head violently like a child. She pointed to herself adamantly.

Krish watched the gesture closely. *No, no! It's me...* Nobody understood.

ShadowThief drew her knife. She stepped forward, releasing Aemea's arm as she passed her. The clatter of the train rattling through the night hid her delicate footsteps. She passed the compartments, nearing the patch of dark. Krish waited to hear the unseen child scream again. It did not come. ShadowThief raised her blade, sliced artfully across the dark in a straight line, then yanked it away like a curtain, revealing a face which cut into Krish as if he had been stabbed through the heart with a shard of ice.

Those eyes. Wild, sleepless, bloodshot and cruel. That malevolent grin. Yellowed teeth. Frizzy, thin, black hair protruding from under his hat. His tall, spindly frame crouched a touch under the low ceiling. He looked directly at Shadow-Thief, his eyes unblinking and his smile charged with gleeful malice. He was holding up a clouded dark marble, running his finger across its surface, releasing the terrifying scream of the girl, the sound of a child, captured long ago, crying out as her attacker approached.

And Krish knew instantly that the child had survived and had grown up without a voice, speech cut away from her. He knew that the child was now a girl, well on the way to becoming a woman, presently staring her attacker straight in the eyes, shaking with anger and disgust, defiance in the firm grip on her blade.

MalJack Strode's grin did not waiver as he ran his finger over the clouded marble, bringing forth that terrible scream, taunting the girl who would never make another sound. ShadowThief looked into the eyes of MalJack, fury incandescent, like a scream wanted to burst forth from her lungs, but she made not a sound.

ShadowThief made her move. She swung briskly in the direction of MalJack's neck, but he caught her by the wrist with his left hand. His right, clutching his own knife, had gone for ShadowThief's heart. She grabbed his wrist, holding his knife back. The clouded marble meanwhile had fallen from between MalJack's thumb and forefinger and smashed on the ground. For a moment the scream was deafeningly shrill, as if the marble itself had had a blade thrust straight into its core, hitting Krish's ears with such force that he almost crumpled to his knees with shock. Then the sound diminished to nothing.

Aemea sprinted down the corridor towards MalJack and ShadowThief.

MalJack's grin broadened further, like a great cruel gash across his face, as he grappled with ShadowThief, each holding the other's knife back. ShadowThief's teeth were bared, from her throat escaped squeals of fury, the only sounds she could make.

Aemea flung her whole weight against MalJack, grabbing hold of his knife-hand, banging it against the wooden wall of the carriage over and over. MalJack glared back at Aemea, kicked her away, and both Aemea and ShadowThief's hands fell from his knife-hand as they slipped down onto the floor. MalJack jabbed downwards and pierced the flesh of Shadow-Thief's shoulder.

In the compartment, two determined tugs and Thira pulled the rail off the wall, splinters flying about the room, brandishing the rail like a miniature staff.

Krish hurtled recklessly after Aemea and lashed out at MalJack with his fist. He just brushed the man's side but hit the wall, and red-hot pain shot through his fist as it collided with solid wood. Recoiling in fury, Krish kicked MalJack in the stomach with strength he didn't even know he had. MalJack winced and withdrew his blade; ShadowThief's blood splattered across Krish and Aemea.

'Oi!' Thira stood tall, the splintered wooden rail in his hands.

MalJack locked eyes with Thira, the creature allowing the corner of his mouth to slither into a smile.

'I don't fink so, matey!' Thira's eyes blazed.

He bashed the post against the ground. Coloured shapes shot from the rudimentary staff in every direction, wriggling like tiny, primordial lifeforms fleeing as fast as they could. Aemea, ShadowThief and Krish dived out of the way, but Krish felt one pass through him, filling him with a burning sensation for a moment. The spell hit MalJack, who was thrown against the connecting door, winding him for a moment.

When Krish looked back, bright imprints of the shapes still flashing through his vision, he saw Thira collapsed on the ground.

'Thira!' He scrambled to his feet, but a great force collided with his stomach and all air and energy was knocked out of him.

MalJack withdrew his foot as Aemea lashed out, scraping her fingers across his face, skin gathering under her fingernails, leaving grooves in the twisted man's skin. Blood rushed forth.

The bloody-faced MalJack tossed her aside, bashing her against the side of the nearby compartment. Then a blade sliced through the air, coming within millimetres of embedding itself in the expansive pupil of MalJack's left eye. MalJack's blade came to greet ShadowThief's.

Figures emerged from the opposite end of the corridor, their eyes only on the collapsed Thira. Krish took to his feet and stumbled towards them.

ShadowThief and MalJack parried back and forth; Shadow-Thief was fiercer and more determined than ever, pushing the spider-like figure of MalJack back along the corridor. Every moment, she attempted to dive her blade into a vital organ or to cut a vein. She seized each opportunity and thrust at her old enemy with such vigour that you would think nothing could hold her back. But the girl of a thousand tattoos failed each time against the sleepless, malicious old man's defences.

The figures, their dark suits perfect for camouflage in the gloom, moving like flickers of imagination, descended upon Thira. Krish, his heart beating as if it would break free of his chest, rushed at the figures, took up the unconscious Thira's staff and swung it haphazardly in the men's direction as he tried to regain his breath. Each man held a knife, glinting in the darkened corridor. They swerved to avoid the improvised staff. Then one took the full weight of the hunk of wood to the face and fell to the floor with a brief scream, collapsing over Thira's body.

Another slashed at Krish's wrist, cutting across his fore-arm. Pain and rage fuelling him, Krish rushed forward to engage the man, hitting him in the stomach with the staff. The man dropped his knife and took hold of the staff, pulling it away from Krish as he fell back into the compartment. Krish was pulled backwards with the falling man, landing on the floor, grazing his head against the bunk.

He stumbled to his feet but before he knew what was happening, a fist smashed into his cheek, pain reverberating through him. He lashed out at the aggressor, though he could barely make them out. He punched and punched and punched but to no avail.

The man's right hook sent Krish backwards into the top bunk. Knocking the outer pole from its holder, Krish swiftly brought his foot up and kicked the aggressor in the groin. As the man squirmed in pain, he grabbed hold of the top bunk's pole and hit him with all his might. The pole collided with the man's torso with such force that he was thrown backwards, smashing through the glass of the window as he was hurled from the speeding carriage.

Thira.

Krish dropped the pole and turned at once, foul air from outside the train whipping past him, to find the empty spot where the unconscious Thira lay moments ago.

Along the corridor, Aemea, filled with fire and fury, threw herself forward, grabbing hold of MalJack Strode's neck, feeling his stubble like tiny knives against her skin, his breath of warm sourness. She clung to him, letting her weight pull him down. They crashed into the window which shattered in an instant. Air, steam, the scent of metal rushed into the carriage. The teeth of what remained of the windowpane cut into Aemea's skin through her clothes.

An arm slithered round her, took her weight and tried to chuck her out of the window. She clung to the neck of the man as the air whipped around her. She looked into his malicious eyes, bloodshot and sleepless.

There was a glint of sentinellight on a blade from behind MalJack. Trying to shake Aemea free, MalJack had shuffled to the left as ShadowThief's knife hit home, embedding itself in the flesh of his upper arm. ShadowThief's free arm came down at the same time and seized Aemea by the collar. MalJack's soundless scream stank of rotting meat.

ShadowThief pulled Aemea up, across the shattered pane, and both fell back onto the carriage floor. MalJack yanked the blade out from his flesh, screaming silently again, dropping the knife in a splatter of blood on the floor and, with furious energy, resumed his assault on ShadowThief. He cut, sliced, shredded the air with his blade with such force that ShadowThief was knocked to the floor. She scrambled backwards on all fours.

ShadowThief tried to take to her feet again but lost her balance and fell back, forcing open the door leading to the caboose. The sour air of the City at night greeted them. MalJack bore down on her, his eyes excited. He took to his knees, spreading himself over her, holding his knife aloft. Fear jolted ShadowThief into action. She kicked at his chest and pushed herself forward, right to the edge of the caboose. Her head dangled over the edge, the spinning wheels of the train below. His knife came downwards, just missing her leg. He crawled forward and seized her by the neck. She gasped for breath. He held his blade aloft once more. He paused for an instant, lost in the malice of a smile, celebrating his victory a moment too soon.

In the fraction of a second before he struck, she saw her advantage – her leg was secure in the railings. With the other leg, ShadowThief kicked at MalJack's chest, heaving him upwards with all her might. His blade tore through the air towards her, just missing, as MalJack flew over the edge. ShadowThief was dragged with him, but her leg jammed in the railings kept her from falling.

And so, into the shadows of the City, MalJack tumbled.

ShadowThief dangled there, terror and relief pulsing through her. She clenched her stomach muscles to pull herself up, feeling the immovable metal post her leg was wrapped around might just snap the bone in two. Then the palm of a hand slapped into hers, as Aemea hauled her up.

'Are you okay?' said Aemea. 'You're bleeding!'

ShadowThief shook her head dismissively – *it's fine* – then held her hand to her wound.

'It was less than an hour,' said Aemea. 'I could feel this future... but it took less than an hour to come true.'

ShadowThief considered then noticed something else. The train was slowing down.

We're coming to a halt.

'You're right,' said Aemea.

The two took to their feet and re-entered the corridor, ShadowThief retrieving the amethyst blade.

The figures in suits were gone. Only Krish remained, emerging from the doorway at the other end of the corridor, which was flapping open and shut, revealing the lights of the City ahead rather than the carriage in front. They had been disconnected from the rest of the train.

Thira was gone.

34
THE GIRL & HER VOICE

'They took him.'

'Krish!'

'They took him. We've got to find him.'

'Krish! Have they uncoupled the train?'

'They took—'

'If they took him—'

'He's gone. We have to—'

'Krish, did they uncouple the—?'

'Uncouple...?'

'The carriage in front – is it detached? Did they uncouple it? We're slowing down. We've almost come to a stop.'

'Yes. They did. We have to find him. We have to find Thira!'

'Krish! We know where he is!'

Krish looked up at Aemea properly at last. Thira would only exist in the worlds of the Myrthali, reappearing with him when he arrived in the next world. But if he died in this world... what would happen?

'Where is he?' demanded Krish.

'That man,' said Aemea. 'The tall man with the eyes like—'

'MalJack Strode.'

ShadowThief looked up in shock, one hand on the wound on her shoulder. Aemea was equally puzzled.

You know him? said ShadowThief.

'We've met.'

Aemea nodded. 'He must be working for Ryker-Veere. I know he'd go for the best. So he'll have taken Thira back to him. They must be following us.'

'Then we should—'

ShadowThief banged her fist on the wall of the carriage in utter frustration. Aemea held up her hand to pacify ShadowThief.

'Krish, *you* hired *us*, we can go after Thira if you want, but listen,' said Aemea, 'they only took Thira. Perhaps because he was the easiest to take as he was unconscious, but perhaps because he was the only one they could identify from Kierbecker. What if you're right and Ryker-Veere doesn't know how to get into the safe? But he does know that the young boy who fell into the beer hall was one of those who tried to break into his safe.'

'Yeah and he might even have found the list of dreams that slipped out of Thira's pocket,' said Krish.

'Precisely! So, if he's put two and two together, he'll also be hunting for those dreams. And keeping Thira alive would be in his interests if he wants information. So, what if we carry on and find the rest of the dreams, then we head back to Ryker-Veere to rescue Thira and open his safe? Because if Ryker-Veere finds all the dreams first...'

'But if we catch up with them...?'

And then what? said ShadowThief. *They uncoupled the train! They could be miles away by now!*

'He'll be safe,' said Aemea. 'And we know exactly where he'll be.'

Krish was drowning in information and only just keeping his head above the surface. He processed it all in and nodded calmly.

'It's up to you,' continued Aemea, 'but I don't think we can catch up now. We need to keep moving.'

'You're right,' said Krish, still processing. 'We need to solve those dreams and get back to Thira.'

Well, let's go! said ShadowThief impatiently.

Krish returned to the carnage of their compartment. He couldn't distinguish the dreamglobe in the mass of shattered glass on the floor. Then he saw the expansive patch of oil, still spreading: the globe had been crushed.

'Well,' sighed Aemea. 'I hope you solved it.'

§

The next few fades were a blur.

Running across the tracks, sleeping in empty carriages, hunks of mouldy bread, water laced with grit gathered from the interiors of abandoned trucks.

The rains came. Bone-white sentinels leered overhead and the raingrates, hovering crafts of metal teeth, poured water down onto them.

On and on they ran. Through coal-black tunnels, shivering in the cold, soaked from head to toe. Whenever ShadowThief cut away the dark, they found little light filtering back in to give them any illumination. They were tired and their bellies were empty.

This way across the tracks was the best route, said Aemea. Streets and streets worth of train track, all the way to Tysbul'Niki. The rows of track never ended. Krish wondered if this was the closest equivalent KnockThrice had to the deserts of Ilir.

At last, they reached actual streets of people; in the bustle of busy souls, Krish's ears filled with unknown languages, words lost in the clattering and splashing of feet moving with haste through the ceaseless rain. Krish began to filter out even the words Aemea spoke to him in his own tongue, only tuning in if the name *Thira* slipped into the conversation.

'We'll get another globe,' she had said somewhere, some-when in their apparently aimless wanderings through the endless City. 'At least you still have the burner. And the list. You're sure the answer to the first dream is correct?'

'Yes,' he'd said with absolute certainty. 'The medicine bottle.'

Aemea looked baffled. 'The medicine bottle? How can you be sure?'

'The ship delivered the post. The dream wasn't about a rescue because everyone got out of the water safely. It was about the lighthouse keeper missing a letter about his daughter's condition. I found a letter to him in the wreck. It told him to get back to her as soon as possible and give her medicine. You could see she was ill because he had to help her stand in the photograph. And the house, *their* house, the one in the photo, was on the cliffs.'

How did you know where the house was? said ShadowThief.

'Because everything pointed that way!' said Aemea as the revelation hit her.

'Exactly!' said Krish. 'The chair, the compass, that skanky old sock. You just had to stand at the top of the lighthouse and look in that direction – you could clearly see the house on the cliffs.'

They found an overcrowded steam carriage to take them to the next street. They sat on the floor. A discarded newspaper by his feet caught Krish's eye. A locomotive pulling a tanklike carriage mounted with a long gun barrel was pictured in the sepia photograph on the front page:

Győri Conflict:
Gun-Carriages Deployed To Vihar Utca

'The war in Győr could destroy the entire neighbourhood any day now,' said Aemea, reading his mind. 'We're heading that way. We'll have to move fast. You know, it would be helpful to know what it is in that safe that you're both after...'

Well? said ShadowThief's raised eyebrow.

Krish looked away and Aemea sighed. Krish thought of Mum. He wondered whether she'd be horrified or proud that he'd fought several of them off. He just hoped that he'd solve the next two dreams and get back to see her mischievous smile soon.

'So, how do you know MalJack Strode then?' asked Aemea.

'Just before night was declared, I saw him attack a woman,' said Krish. 'For a moment I thought he'd cut her throat. Then I realised he'd taken this little cloudy marble thing. He stole some coin too. And NightTime started like a second later. It was almost like he'd triggered it.'

'A coincidence, I'm sure. He is the kind of wrecked creature who exudes the essence of night even in the light of day.'

'So would he have been working for Ryker-Veere then?'

'Perhaps, but more likely Ryker-Veere called for him. He has a reputation as a skilled hunter. And he is cheap as his motivations are never truly financial. No one knows where he comes from, who he really is, or how long he's lived. All anyone has ever known about him is that he is motivated by pure cruelty.'

ShadowThief hugged her legs to her chest.

'If you hadn't gathered already, Shad has also crossed

paths with MalJack in the past,' said Aemea. 'When she was very young. Before we'd met.

'The orphan-clan was trying to recruit her. Shad had a family, but she spent almost all her time away from them. She tends to be most at home on the street rather than being confined by four walls. And Shad had gained a reputation as a quick and surprisingly good fighter for her age. Her family lived in penny chambers. They came from a faraway neighbourhood.

'Anyway, MalJack, the scream-thief, was inspecting stolen trinkets the orphan-clan had acquired. He would sell them on the clan's behalf. And no one argued if the price he came back with was not altogether agreeable. Except Shad. Shad may have been one of the youngest, but she was one of the most vocal on the subject of underpayment.

'Then, one fade, he came to their house and, well, her mother—'

ShadowThief slapped the back of her hand against Aemea's shoulder. Krish had never seen her look so angry. Her face said, *Do not tell this story!* ShadowThief tucked her head into her crossed arms as she huddled on the floor of the carriage.

'It's okay,' said Krish as Aemea turned back to him. 'I get the picture.'

ShadowThief's eyes were closed now. Aemea leant over to Krish and spoke in hushed tones.

'I don't think you do. Shad's mother is still alive, as far as we know. What happened was worse than her simply being murdered. He was about to torture her to teach Shad a lesson when Shad turned up. Shad fought back but he took her voice. And then... her mother disowned her, seeing her silent child as a freak.

'That's why she fled. That's why she left her name behind.

Nobody knows it, not even me. It reminds her that her mother gave it to her.' Aemea glanced over her shoulder at Shadow-Thief, trying to work out if she was really asleep. 'Sorry. She doesn't like me speaking of this.' Aemea looked up at Krish. 'Apologies for my unremitting obsession with the macabre.'

'You're... sorry...?'

'These morbid, haunted tales comfort me strangely. Like I'm letting all the darkness out piece by piece so I can enjoy the light all the more. Sometimes I envy Shad for having a mother to despise.'

Krish watched as Aemea took a deep breath and looked over at her sleeping friend.

'Sorry, Aemea,' said Krish, 'I'm not always sure I understand everything you say.'

'Precisely. I talk too much. Shad has the right idea. If she makes the effort to say anything, she really has to mean it. Time to rest, I feel.'

Krish followed Aemea's lead and tried to close his eyes and get some rest. Although he wasn't able to dream in Knock-Thrice, visions certainly flashed before his eyes. He pictured Thira in various scenarios, not one of them featuring him in anything less than an incredible amount of pain.

She tried to run but the Woman had caught her

Now here she is soaked in rose-scented water

Bath time is no fun when you are stuck inside

About her secret room she would not confide

She lies back, breathes in the blossom and saylei

And mulls over the times when ceilings were high

'I hate you, Mum-Dumb!' Eva says to her kin

'Please don't call me that, child, you know it's a sin'

'What shall we do tofade?' asks little Eva

'We have no choice, child – all our plans have been made'

35

THE BOY IN THE GAMBLER'S CHAIR

The bolt tightened.

The metal felt as if it was directly against the bone of Thira's spine now.

The heavy cranking of the device.

He winced as the leather strap contracted around his neck, pressing into his Adam's apple.

Another wheel was turned and fine wire pushed down onto his fingers. He could only just move his head in the restraint and look down on his hands fastened to the arms of the chair.

'The gambler's chair... I take it you are not acquainted with this wondrous device?'

The man, Pesson they had called him, had a voice as deep as a well: oily, rich and a little gruff. He was bald and wrinkled, but in good shape for a man of his age. Eyes bulbous and bright like sentinels. He drank in every moment of the pain he inflicted.

The bolt was pushing into Thira's spine – it would achieve its awful purpose soon.

'Got anything to impart to us, dear boy?' intoned Pesson. 'Your companions? Their purpose? Your employer? Anything come to mind?'

Pesson spun another wheel and a wire cut into the skin just above Thira's ankle.

Thira winced again. He could sense the wire was wet with blood. 'Nuffin'... nuffin' comes to mind to be honest, mate.' He delivered the words through gritted teeth.

'Let me tell you something, then see if you fancy offering something in return... Give and take, dear boy. Now – the gambler's chair was developed to punish, as you might expect, *gamblers*. You tighten the screws, all the bolts and wires and straps start contracting, but there is no way of knowing which part of the machine will fulfil its purpose first. A gamble, you see?'

'Yeah, yeah, I get it, mate! I get it! I mean, not exactly subtle, is it? I definitely get the... get the... Oh! Whatsitcalled? Can't really concentrate in this do-dad! Can't we just do this torture malarkey in a nice comfy chair so I can think a bit more clearly?'

'Used to comfort, dear boy? Your employer is wealthy I imagine... I wonder, what value he would put on your li—'

'*The point*! I get *the point*! That's the thingamy I was lookin' for! Gotta be honest, mate – surprised you didn't crack that one out early doors. Nice little joke to relax yer, er... "clients"...'

'Feeling relaxed now, dear boy...?'

The neck-strap was starting to choke him.

'Tha... tha... tha... that meant to 'elp ya talk...?'

He felt the magic swelling within him. He must hold back. Emotions ignited magic. The magic held no weight, but it was awake, alert in every fibre of his body, ready to serve...

He saw the blade, lowering into position over his left forearm, glow purple and begin to shake, cutting the skin away... *No! No! Stop!* He must control it!

'Fascinating...' Sweat dotted Pesson's excited face as he leaned over Thira. Pesson's perspiration slowly rained down on Thira, slithering down his tense skin and nestling in his wounds, a salty stinging sensation coursing through him. 'So very fascinating... Observing this "force" of yours... Will you tear your own body apart before I can complete my work, I wonder? Fascinating...'

Thira felt as if a thousand tiny unseen life forces were squirming within him, ready to burst forth and save him; but would they? Could they...? Without a staff to focus it, the magic may simply tear him ap—

The door shot open, clanging against the wall, echoing in the cavernous chamber.

'How's it going, old chap? Going alright, is it?'

Ryker-Veere marched up to Pesson with the kind of jollity which very much ruins the mood of an interrogation. De Clercq was close behind her master. Pesson screwed his eyes up privately, the look of an artist who was moments away from completing his masterpiece.

'Still using all your normal jiggery-pokery, eh?' continued Ryker-Veere.

'If you feel the need to discuss interrogation strategy,' said Pesson, massaging his brow and looking down, 'I suggest we step out—'

'Let's ratchet it up a little, what? Make the young rapscallion really squirm – then he'll start spilling the beans!'

'I... appreciate that you are impatient for results, but I am making progress—'

'No 'e's not!' interjected Thira. ''E's got nuffin'! 'E's doin', rubbish, mate! I could torture meself better than this. I'd probably charge less an' all.'

'I am making progress,' continued Pesson. 'Perhaps we should step outside for a mo—?'

'Don't suppose ya could nab us a mug o' water before we crack on for round two?' said Thira. 'I am parched!'

'You speak when you're spoken to, you blackguard!' said Ryker-Veere.

'What the 'ell did you just call me?'

'Sir, please! If I am to complete my work with even a modicum of success—'

'Might I interject...?'

Everyone turned around.

Isri Stroever had a way of doing that, entering a room last and lingering in the background inoffensively, allowing a situation to reach boiling point before he chose to speak a word. He took the silence as acceptance and stepped up to Thira.

'Was the first question Mr Pesson asked you your name?' said Stroever.

Thira lifted his head, feeling the bloody soreness from the straps and head brace. Stroever's features were slight and indistinct. When he wasn't speaking, he stood like a statue. You waited for him to blink or you'd scan his chest to check it was rising and falling to see if he was alive at all. His sense of patience was infuriating.

'Don't fink it was, now ya come to mention it,' answered Thira.

'And was it the second or the third or the fourth or—?'

'Nah. 'E kinda skipped that one altogether.'

'Well, I should like to know it.'

Thira blinked. Several hastily constructed pseudonyms shot through his brain, but eventually he gambled on the truth. 'Thira.'

'And your family name?'

'Wessra. Ya'll struggle to look 'em up, though.'

'A farpilgrim?'

'You what, mate?'

'From another world...?'

Thira glared at Stroever for some time – *how did he know?* Then he cautiously nodded.

'What is your world like, Thira?'

'Well... ya know, less of all this dark-coloured stone and buildin's and stuff. More landscapes and countryside and that.'

'My apologies, Thira – what is "countryside"? I'm afraid I'm not familiar with the term.'

'Well, it's... like the opposite of all this cobblers. Ya know, big old buildin's made o' oblong stones an' all that. Not so much people an' buildin's and more wide open spaces and trees and nature and stuff.'

'I grew up somewhere similar, Thira.'

'I say, what the heck are you playing at, old boy?' interjected Ryker-Veere.

'Are you familiar with the word "empathy", Anders?'

'Rings a vague bell.'

'Please,' continued Stroever, 'humour me for a few—'

'Poppycock! We'll ratchet the chair up a few notches and he'll be spilling his guts in minutes!'

'I've no doubt about that. But how much sense do you think you'll get out of someone in the middle of being disembowelled? If you're lucky he may tell you what he thinks you wish to hear, but you'll have no way of knowing if it's true. And by then it'll be too late.'

Pesson's head was jerking in every direction impatiently. 'If you discuss your strategy with the subject, it renders the entire exercise—'

'He's not a "subject", Mr Pesson,' said Stroever. 'His name is Thira. And I have a proposition. Release him into my care and I will extract what you need. But I shall do so by treating him with respect and—'

'We don't have time for all this!'

'Yet hurrying will lead you to a dead end fast.'

Ryker-Veere pondered this for some time, not wanting to let his unease show. 'One moment, dear boy...' He stepped over to de Clercq and spoke softly. 'What d'you reckon, old girl?'

'He'll no doubt hand the boy over to Madam Ckrystafis,' said de Clercq. 'She is... an acquired taste from what I've heard, though her methods might be quite effective. But—'

'If he starts asking questions about—'

'Yes—'

'Hmm.'

'But, as I say, her methods are meant to be effective. It's a dangerous game to play though.'

'Well, we're all playing dangerous games these fades, what?' Ryker-Veere patted de Clercq boisterously on the back and marched over to Stroever. Ryker-Veere put his arm around Stroever and pulled him to one side.

'This, er, boy,' said Ryker-Veere, 'he and his associates are... meddling in my private business affairs.'

'I see,' said Stroever curiously. 'And may I inquire as to which business affairs these might be?'

Ryker-Veere considered for a moment. 'What's your interest in the boy?'

'His powers. They may be useful. One of my business ventures requires a little... assistance.'

'A venture you're keeping to yourself, old chap?'

'Yes. For now, at least.'

'So perhaps we can come to some arrangement?'

'What is it you want to know from young Thira?'

'Who his friends are and where they're headed.'

'I see. Consider it done. Be patient, but don't panic. You won't need to wait too long.'

'Hmm! Very well. And thank you for your discretion, old chap.'

'Think nothing of it.'

Ryker-Veere and Stroever broke apart.

'Now, Thira,' said Stroever, 'you shall be released into my care.'

'Wa. Hoo,' said Thira flatly.

'I will introduce you to my associate Madam Ckrystafis and she will teach you a little of her craft. And in return for your life, and for learning a trade that you can use upon your release—'

'Now, steady on, old boy!'

'Trust in my methods, Anders. Thira, in return for your life and learning a trade...you will give us information.'

'Not bloody likely, mate!'

'We shall see, Master Wessra. We shall see. I am a very patient man.'

'Ha! I'll give you that!' said Ryker-Veere. 'One thing your father lacked!'

Stroever ignored Ryker-Veere. He approached the gambler's chair. 'Thira, did you know we have trees in our world also?'

Thira did not answer. Stroever addressed Ryker-Veere and Pesson.

'Manacle his hands and feet and bring him to the factory floor.'

'Dishing out orders in—'

'In *my* factory, Anders,' said Stroever. 'You may have invested in my father's facility long ago, but you did not own him and you do not own me. I am happy for you to resurrect some of the more macabre corners of the factory my father and you built, but I will show you how patience and respect will yield more effective results. I shall learn the truth in return for your investment in our new little scheme.'

Ryker-Veere looked furious. 'That's still very much for my consideration. Find out what the boy—'

'Thira.'

'Thigh-ra knows. It is something of the utmost—'

'*Thear-ra!*' shouted Thira. 'Like 'ear', ya deaf bast—'

'PLEASE! Gentlemen!' erupted Pesson. 'Believe me, I am minutes from a breakthrough!'

'Thira will be dead within the hour with these methods and the answers you seek gone with him,' said Stroever and neither Pesson nor Ryker-Veere seemed keen to deny it. 'Now, how goes your campaign to seed the idea of legalisation in the minds of the people?'

Ryker-Veere retracted his attack, took a breath and spoke calmly. 'The papers have been briefed. They are all taking subtly different angles but all pushing in the same direction. It'll take time, old boy, but it has begun.'

'So, you will consider my proposal? My fleet of sun spearers is ready to go into production upon receipt of your 50% down payment. Dreams will flourish in the endless night. Though it shall not be night for us, dear Anders. Can you deny the power we will yield if we pool our resources? A firm grip over public information and control of the stars themselves!'

Ryker-Veere stared gravely at Stroever for some time, much to the intrigue of Thira and Pesson. Eventually, Ryker-Veere gave a short, sharp nod.

'Fifty percent,' said Stroever. 'I await receipt of the payment and will have the answers you desire shortly.'

'But do not think you can dictate—?' began Ryker-Veere.

'I can if you want answers. Mr Pesson, manacle him, wrists and ankles, and meet me on the factory floor presently.'

Stroever left the room before anyone could say another word.

36
THE SHADOWS ON THE WALL

The rain did not abate and fell in thick lines, splattering onto the streets with great pressure as if it was pouring down from taps high in the sky. Krish had never seen anything like this in his own world. They changed carriages so many times that he lost count. Eventually they reached Njivska Ulica.

Njivska Ulica was a higgledy-piggledy street filled with dips and troughs, which local carriages artfully managed to avoid. The spires on churches and the towers of some buildings tilted this way and that on the uneven ground.

Krish's outfit was stiff and heavy with rainwater, and both he and his clothes were not smelling pleasant.

They arrived at a guesthouse above an inn, which had the strong scent of ale and ham. The mattresses were rock solid, but Krish slept as if it was the softest material he'd ever laid upon.

§

To Krish it was seconds, but in reality it had been several hours. He awoke to the loudest whispering he'd ever heard.

'We have to wake him, Shad! We have to!'

His eyelids peeled back over his weary eyes. He felt like a great weight was tying him down to the bed. ShadowThief was gesturing at Aemea wildly, but she stopped as soon as her eyes met Krish's.

'Whas goin' on?' was all he could muster.

'They're on the streets,' said Aemea.

Krish staggered out of bed and gazed out of the windows to see a number of figures dotted about the street. He couldn't see their eyes, but he could sense them staring up at the window.

ShadowThief was acting out an escape through the back.

'Shad is right,' said Aemea. 'Too many possibilities. I can't see. We need to keep moving.'

'But I thought... I mean, if they've got Thira, why are they after us?'

Maybe we were wrong, ShadowThief was gesturing. *We thought it was Thira they were after but perhaps they've realised now they need all of us.*

'Or perhaps Thira gave them information already,' said Krish, fear and guilt spreading through him. 'Is it the same guys? The guys in suits on the train? They look different.'

'They are different,' said Aemea. 'Ryker-Veere has many contacts. He could send out descriptions by telegram offering rewards. A small amount of his money will go a long way out here.'

They crept out a window in an empty room on the opposite side of the guesthouse and clambered across the roof. Krish was convinced he'd trip on the wet tiles and fall. Despite his concerns, they managed to slip away without being detected.

The next guesthouse was much the same: figures waiting outside.

They turned their backs on the guesthouses, the inns and even the penny chambers. Opportunistic eyes were stationed on every corner.

Running was beginning to look far more appealing than hiding.

§

Krish, Aemea and ShadowThief took up residence in a derelict building. Most of the walls had collapsed; much of the remaining structure had subsided, and some sections of the dwelling they avoided altogether in case they crumbled. The bone-white eyes of the sentinels bore down on them from the polluted skies overhead, and shifting shadows crossed the wooden beams. The rains stopped just as the hunger and despair set in. And only hunger was keeping Krish from fearing for Thira's life every second.

Aemea and ShadowThief had caught several rats and cooked them over a fire, offering some to Krish. He hadn't had much luck catching any rats himself and had pretended not to see the stray black cat. He had little motivation; after tasting one rat he was not keen to eat another. Every other bite made his tummy gurgle and his whole body weak. He'd run to the building's toilet, which was its own cramped little hell, stinking and with no running water.

For a time, he chose to abstain from allowing anything other than water to enter his system. He sat, weak, drained and delirious, craning his neck up through the expansive hole in the roof, the cold whipping around his soaked, itching and stinking clothes. He watched a distant sentinel, way, way up in the haze, streaking slowly across the sky, leaving a blurry trail of light in its wake. He felt more alone in the chaos of the endless, overpopulated City than he'd ever done in the vast emptiness of the desert on Ilir. He'd do anything for a beam of yellowy-orange real sunlight to peak over the rooftops and dazzle him right now. He pictured himself in his cosy little garden at home, being embraced by his family as if he'd been away for years.

Aemea and ShadowThief returned each fade with few leads. Many dream-pedlars here had arrived from Vihar Utca, fleeing the encroaching war in Győr. And it had transpired that getting papers would not help them enter Győr. The fighting had intensified. Neighbouring Lanserhofstraße had sent gun-carriages to assist the Győri. They had arrived on the eastern streets of Győr, cutting off the retreating Ankaran forces, leaving them trapped and battling until the end, refusing the shame of surrender or defeat. The only real way in and out was the Necropolis Railway, transporting the dead of Szabó Utca, but that way too would be cut off soon if the fighting continued in much the same vein.

ShadowThief managed to question some of the dream-pedlars fleeing Győr about the dreams they sought, but each one shook their heads. Many of the specialists who dealt in such dreams were old and stuck in their ways. They were too stubborn to try and escape the war so remained in Győr. None knew how to mix the two remaining dreams, proving just how rare they were.

ShadowThief disappeared many times in the fades that followed. Aemea said that she was chasing up leads, but Krish could tell that something was unsettling her. He could guess what: the encounter with MalJack Strode, the demon from her childhood. The destruction of the clouded marble that contained her voice had made her even quieter than normal. She refrained from her usual habit of conversing in gestures. Krish had a feeling that she was wandering the streets, searching for her attacker, plotting some great vengeance upon him.

When she did return to their shelter in the derelict building, she'd huddle into a corner, wrapping herself in shadow, not allowing the sentinellight to illuminate the lines drawn onto her skin.

Several times Krish saw Aemea wander over and say a word that sounded like '*metalkova?*' and ShadowThief would briefly shake her head. Then, one time, Aemea marched up to ShadowThief, asked again, and waited for a long time until ShadowThief reluctantly nodded.

§

'Metelkova Ulica was a palace once,' said Aemea as they walked along a grey street of high, windowless buildings. 'Then the people rose up and kicked out the nobility who owned it. They never returned, so criminal gangs made the old palace their home.'

'You don't seem sure about this place,' said Krish. 'Is this a good idea?'

'No, but we have few options. And we can't just hang around doing nothing indefinitely. We're still alive in an hour, I can feel it.'

ShadowThief shot Aemea a warning look.

'Yes, yes, yes!' said Aemea irritably. 'Sorry – fifty minutes!'

'Your, er... future sense... thing...?' said Krish.

'Is no longer an hour, it seems. It's... it's curious... Anyway, Metelkova will be the best place to find contacts.'

'Oh,' Krish was taken aback. 'Then why didn't we just go straight there?'

Looks between Aemea and ShadowThief.

'Because,' said Aemea, 'we're known around there.'

'And that's... a bad thing?'

'On this occasion, yes.'

They approached some ruins in the raised street. Krish saw a structure built of limestone with large windows, many smashed. Various walls had collapsed in the once-great palace.

As they tucked into a misty back alley, discordant music filtered down through the air. They heard jolly yet off-kilter violins, clapping, laughter, and screams that could have been of either pain or delight, or both.

They passed through an archway and climbed stairs where many lay about intoxicated on alcohol or dreams, or substances unknown. Vacant expressions and slow smiles greeted them from those strewn about on the steps, aged beyond their years. Dreamcarts played mocking tunes, others were upturned on the ground, slim lines of smoke rising from them for the lost souls crouched on the ground inhaling the remains of sweet delusions. The sheer volume of people festering in this place both terrified and bewildered Krish.

They reached the top of the steps and walked among the once fine halls of the derelict palace. Walls had collapsed and the ceiling was almost entirely absent. People sat on battered chaise longues. They crouched on the floor around out-of-tune grand pianos or gathered near fallen chandeliers. Intoxication and debauchery infested every square metre of this place.

The three friends came to a large room, once a library, the walls cracked but largely still standing. The shelves had been emptied of books. They were now filled with dreamglobes and tankards, with a makeshift bar constructed of stacks of books at its centre. Bright lanterns were placed on the floor around the perimeter of the room, casting monstrously long and distorted shadows of the debauched patrons up the walls. ShadowThief walked cautiously across the room, visibly shrinking and hunched over, trying to draw any attention away from her lack of shadow.

Aemea ordered 'three kravahs', a cheap beer-like drink which contained no alcohol. Krish could hardly hold the heavy tankard, which was made out of several small sheets of metal welded haphazardly together. The taste was dull and metallic. He looked up at the swollen shadows flickering across the walls.

After a series of silent sips, ShadowThief braved speaking to the portly dream-pedlar with a bushy red beard.

'No freebies!' insisted Redbeard, placing his arm between ShadowThief and his cart. ShadowThief shook her head.

'The Three Dreams of the Forgotten Towers,' said Aemea.

Redbeard's ears pricked up. 'Not here,' he said. 'H-ha! We deal in very different fayre! How about something a little more...fanciful, eh, drummer?'

ShadowThief narrowed her eyes. Ignoring this, Aemea slipped a note from her sleeve to her palm, turned it over for Redbeard to see, then concealed it once more. 'And how about you tell us what you know and we leave you alone?'

The man's eyes betrayed his temptation.

Whilst this was going on, Krish noticed a group of shadows on the wall, marching purposefully in the direction of the bar. It was a sight very much at odds with the chaotic shadows dancing across the wall from the patrons in the rest of the shell of a room. They were unnervingly purposeful and heading their way.

ShadowThief leant forward across the bar, hiding between two strangers.

'Ha! If you think that's enough... No, wait!' Aemea had gone to leave without looking back, but then stopped when Redbeard had pleaded. 'Just... a little more and I'm sure—'

'No,' said Aemea, softly, forcing him to pay attention.

The gang of shadows arrived at the bar, accompanied by those who cast them. Krish realised that ShadowThief had now practically vanished completely.

'Okay, okay!' said Redbeard. 'Ya just notches the price up a touch or-or gets us a couple o' drinks...'

'No,' said Aemea firmly.

The gang leader held up five fingers, ordering drinks for each of them. There was something odd about the newcomers which Krish couldn't quite determine.

'Okay, okay!' said Redbeard. 'Gis us the money and we gis ya the number, yeah?'

Aemea ran her hand over Redbeard's palm and the money was quickly stowed away in the man's pocket. 'Number 404. At the eastern end of the street. Wonky door. Dunno 'oo told yer, yeah?'

'Indeed,' said Aemea. 'I don't know your name... you don't know mine, correct?'

The man nodded. Aemea went to leave.

'Aye, I wager I can 'ave a stab at the girl's name, boys.' A new voice had entered the exchange. It was gleeful in tone but also raspy, pained, as if the owner had exerted his vocal cords close to destruction. 'Let's see...let's see...' The man was toying with Aemea, who'd stopped where she was. 'I reckon... sum'ink thas the same backwards as it is forwards.' Aemea was trying but failing not to look rattled. 'And where there's she... there's also 'er.'

The man, the leader of the gang, their shadows stretching across the walls, had a short, trimmed black beard across the left of his face, the tattoo of facial hair covering his clean-shaven right. He wore a dark trench coat and was handsome but somehow haunted. Much of his gang were similarly attired, with the same partial facial hair, the shaved patches filled in with tattoo, long coats and fearsome expressions.

'Let's go,' said Krish to Aemea, but he spoke more loudly than he had intended over the din.

'Oh, I don't fink so, my pets,' spoke the leader. 'Ya always got to 'ave a croaker in Metalkova. And ours croaked quick, recognised a certain someone soon as she arrived...' The leader peered over at ShadowThief. 'Got unfinished business with this one, in't we, boys?' He swirled the beer in his tankard, half of its contents already gone.

'Look, if you want money...' ventured Krish. He immediately regretted entering the conversation. He was attracting scowls from Aemea.

'The new pet's got a mouth. Thas nice. Thas nice, in't it, my little ShadowThief...?'

Krish saw ShadowThief's eyes catch the light as she glanced over at the gang.

'Can't give it us back, can she?' said the leader, all his attention on the slither of beer left in his tankard, swirling it round and round. 'Can't give it us back? No, she can't.' *What was it?* 'Takes something of hers. Only fair. Only fair, we says.'

There was something very wrong. Something amiss about the whole gang, dwarfed in size by their shadows cast by the lights scattered across the floor.

'Takes something,' the man continued. 'A finger, a toe, a liver, a heart, an eye, a life. Only fair.' He swirled the liquid round and round, toying with the last of it.

The leader's four associates stepped up to ShadowThief, hands at their sides. Krish anticipated them producing weapons at any moment, but none appeared. *What was it? What was different?*

'Only fair, my pets.' The leader held his tankard up high and drained the last of his drink. And in that moment, Krish saw. He spotted straight away what was missing. Although a firm, gloved hand gripped the tankard, against the wall the shadow of the vessel rose on its own, a clear gap between the shadow of the leader's wrist and the tankard's shadow. The man's wrist-shadow ended in tatters. His hand had no shadow.

Krish eyed the other four and saw at once: stab marks torn into the back of one's shadow. Another had many gashes cut into his face's shadow. One's shadow was slashed clean in two, one half of his shadow-body disconnected from the other, a jagged gash shoulder to hip. The last's shadow had been hacked and slashed wildly until the shape on the wall was barely recognisable as a human being.

'You're a long way from your patch, Dar Fernier,' said Aemea, a quiver in her voice.

Dar Fernier moved a little closer to Aemea. 'Like you, pet, I 'as no patch,' he said. 'Not permanent, like. I was on my patch, mind you, only a few fades back. Emptyin' the odd over-burdened pocket. Not much goin' on in Fryin' Pan Alley. Then I 'ears that Jay Dodson's got a message for us. Message says that Mr Hickson and Mr Lovence, always a pair, wants to see us.'

Krish struggled to followed Dar Fernier's breathless ramblings.

'We arrives at the weir on Cattlecade Row, where Messrs Hickson and Lovence 'as Little Wally Eates dangled upside down over the water, as part of their ongoing investigations into the disappearance of some items from a local brewery that they 'ad until recently been very much invested in nickin' themselves.'

'Is this all strictly relevant?' chipped in Aemea.

'Now, Little Wally Eates,' continued Dar Fernier, 'with 'is own best interests at 'eart, naturally, don't know nothin' about no brewery bottles, or whatever it might be that 'as gone walk-abouts, 'e swears. But 'e *'as* been involved in a racket with Old Charlie at the telegram office, where the peelers 'as been storin' contraband. And *that's* where 'e sees my name and an offer in a 'gram from MalJack, plus a quart for 'ooever delivers it, to which I obliged with a clip round the ear to young Wally, complimentary, like.'

'And what has this got to do with us?'

'In 'is 'gram, Old MalJack says 'e's 'ad a sniff of an old friend. A drummer bitch—' ShadowThief, still leant over the bar, looking away, clutched her fist as if she was longing to have her blade in her grip, '—with lines o' colour on 'er skin and 'er compatriots, 'oo Old MalJack's been employed to locate. Asks if we remembers 'er. I says 'course we remembers 'er. 'Ard to forget! Apparently, she and her compatriots are in the business of stealin' dreams. Says if we follows the scent down to Čevljarski Most, stops 'em before they steal 'em dreams, there's a pretty penny to be 'ad.'

Dar Fernier toyed with the fingers of his shadowless hand, furling and unfurling them, gazing at where their dark shape should sit on the wall. 'Learned a lesson we did, tryin' to mess with this one!' he said, indicating ShadowThief. 'So just imagine 'ow pretty that penny must be for us to all be 'ere now, reunited, like.'

ShadowThief glared over her shoulder. Krish's mind was racing, trying to figure the quickest way out of this situation. Aemea inhaled deeply. Her calm tone was very much at odds with the turmoil within.

'Well, thank you for that informative if rather tangential yarn, Mr Fernier,' said Aemea. 'I'd hate to prolong your disappointment at travelling so far for nothing, so I'll bid you farewell.'

Aemea went to depart but Dar Fernier grabbed hold of her arm. ShadowThief stood up straight and turned to face Fernier and his comrades, staring daggers at them, her blade ready. Krish stepped forward but Fernier's men encircled them.

'You and yer drummer friends ain't goin' nowhere,' said Fernier.

'You say that word one more time...' said Krish, boiling with hate.

'Ha! What's that yer little drummer boy's sayin'?' said Fernier, directing his words loudly towards Krish.

He was sick of that word. He recalled his disastrous attempt to punch the policeman in Advocate's Close and he didn't care. This time he put the whole weight of his body behind his arm, not over-stretching himself, and landed his fist directly across Dar Fernier's nose.

There was a crunch, a scream of pain, spittle and warm breath across his knuckles. He pulled back and sucked in the white-hot pain. Before Dar Fernier's men could step forward, ShadowThief moved swiftly and held her knife to Fernier's throat.

Fernier's men stayed back. They appeared to be torn between waiting for their bloodied leader to issue a command and fleeing. All activity in the bar had stopped and they were now all watching the unfolding scene.

'Shad, this is not the place to commit bloody murder,' said Aemea steadily. 'Get your men to back away, Fernier.'

Fernier thought for a moment and then grunted at his fellow gang members.

Krish stared straight at Dar Fernier, all fury and determination. He breathed it all in and spoke with a steady voice.

'You in contact with MalJack?' he said. 'And whoever's got him looking for us?'

Dar Fernier, blood leaking from his broken nose, glanced at his men and then back to Krish. 'In a manner o'speakin'.'

'You pass this on thi—'

'Kr—' started Aemea before stopping herself.

'You tell him this,' Krish went on. 'My name is Krishna. Got it?'

'Naturally,' mumbled Dar Fernier.

'Say it!'

'Chris, or—'

'KRISHNA!'

'Krishna, okay! I got it! Blinkin' Krishna!'

'You tell him... I don't care if he beats me, if he wins, if he kills me... but he calls me Krishna... nothing else. Got it?'

Dar Fernier examined Krish for a time and then nodded.

Aemea, Krish and ShadowThief exchanged glances. The first two of Fernier's men began to back out of the room. Fernier looked up at ShadowThief, his face crumpled and bloodied. She released him then spun round to his front, holding the amethyst blade up defensively.

'Ya know what it feels like what yer shadow's ripped away...? Burns! Not shelterin' in the shade of yer own shadow.'

Instead of backing away further, ShadowThief took a step closer, a little smile on her face. 'You like me up close after all, eh, pet?' he said.

ShadowThief's grin broadened. She stepped even closer. Then he saw. She was now between him and the light, his own shadow across her front. His eyes widened in terror, but he wasn't fast enough. She held her knife with precision and tore across the shadow of his neck, ripping Dar Fernier's head-shadow clean away. He screamed wildly and staggered backwards, his face in his hands.

ShadowThief ran as the crowd filled in the path she left in her wake.

37

THE SLAUGHTER IN THE FOREST

The manacles were tight around Thira's wrists and ankles. He was guided out of the room and onto a gantry, eyes aching in the bright lights of the factory. The scale of the place was frightening. The red brick room was longer than the palace of Sccifihr'ei had been tall. He couldn't make out an end, it faded away into a haze.

He could just discern either side of the colossal oblong building. He craned his neck to look up. Lanterns the size of small dwellings were hung here and there from the ceiling. Over the gantry he now stood on, a portion of the ceiling was glass, revealing sentinels in the sky above.

On the factory floor were a large number of workers. They stood by the walls, tools in hand, awaiting their cue. Alcoves along the sides of the factory contained workbenches with tools laid out on them. The factory floor itself was a barren, dark brown earthen wasteland.

Thira heard a rumble of thunder.

'I've heard life is different in other worlds,' Stroever's voice reached him from farther along the gantry. Stroever surveyed the vast, featureless landscape below. He held out a hand, indicating the floor. 'The Iron Devil built the factories and created life within them. He lined each factory floor with soil and sowed seeds from beneath. Then He cultivated the pods from which life came. But in time humanity defied Devil, smashing His great plan to make us suffer in the confinement of the factories. Ah! They have caught one!'

Thira followed Stroever's gaze. He was shocked at the sight. Only magic, and very powerful magic at that, could achieve what he was witnessing right now.

A dark blue engine moved through the air, just below the ceiling. Instead of travelling across tracks, there were gleaming silver poles crossing beneath the engine, one running left to right and the other front to back. The poles stretched out across the length and breadth of the factory, attached at each end to wheeled cars, like small locomotives, on runners. The wheeled cars would move back and forth so the engine at the centre of the crisscross could reach any point on the ceiling. Underneath the engine was a slatted device, expelling great gusts of air, manipulating a familiar shape below.

Although they were infrequent visitors to the blue skies of Thira's world of Ilir, he recognised storm clouds. Even when bewitched with the strongest magic, he'd never seen a cloud quite so effectively under the spell of any person or device as this one beneath the dark blue engine.

'You have such things as these in your world, Thira?'

'Yeah, but not indoors!'

'Outside? How fascinating. We have only the raingrates outside. This is a crude equivalent of a raingrate. These are known as "lifebringers".'

'Oh. Right. We just call 'em "clouds".'

'Clouds? Like smoke? Fascinating. I suppose they appear similar. Only recent generations have truly harnessed the powers of these "clouds". They bring life to forests which we grow to harvest wood for construction – furniture, ships, houses and more factories. We grow crops here also. And animals for meat.'

'Wait, you *grow* animals?!'

'Indeed. All life was once grown in the factories. As I mentioned, humanity sprang from the factories, until we took control and ventured out into the streets, finding a world fashioned for our needs.'

'Flippin' weird.'

'The forests we grow for months, years, sometimes even decades or longer. My father used to specialise in vintage wood when it was in fashion and could be sold at a premium price. But some time ago, when populations were rising, there was increased demand for wood, fruit, vegetables and meat. So, we developed a way to mass-produce in record time...'

Stroever pointed at the cloud and Thira watched as a scene unfolded which no magic could replicate.

The storm cloud grumbled irritably, being forced to keep moving from side to side. Then came the rain. It poured down in one great shower and the engine began manipulating the cloud to water the soil on the factory floor, one row after another.

Thira was shocked to see little shoots of green wriggling out of the earth within seconds. They shimmied their way upwards and split into branches from which dangled fruits of rosy red, warming orange, vibrant blue, deep violet, forest green and purest white. Before their eyes the stems grew thick and changed from green to brown, from smooth to the coarseness of bark. Trees and shrubs and bushes and flowers sprang up all around. As the cloud was dragged away, crops were ready for harvest and the fruit ripe for picking.

The strangest and least familiar shapes to Thira's eyes

emerged from the soil as white stems, the tips of which swelled into large, bulbous, flesh-coloured sacks covered in grey pulsating veins.

A brisk hand gesture from Stroever and the workers marched forward, scythes and axes and all manner of cutting implements in their hands. They slashed and chopped and cut the life out of everything. Fruits were picked and trees were felled. The canopy of the forest, fresher, purer and greener than any Thira had ever seen, was torn down within minutes of being grown.

The unusual shapes turned out to be flesh-pods. As they were cut open, low, gurgling cries escaped from within. It was the braying, groaning, and desperate whimpers of young live-stock. Pulled from the pods were grey-white sacks without heads or limbs. Somewhere they must have had mouths from which the terrible cries emanated, but all Thira saw were struggling, squirming bags of flesh which were led over to drains at the edge of the factory. Vital arteries were cut to extinguish their brief lives. The air was thick with the scent of blood and the clamour of screams.

Within minutes the factory had been transformed from a lifeless void to a forest teeming with life, and finally to a slaughterhouse.

'Few get to see this incredible sight, dear Thira,' said Stroever, booming with pride. 'My father, damnable though he was, was a genius. He condensed the entire process. The meat is inferior, the fruit largely tasteless, and the wood relatively weak, but the yield is enormous and can be sold at an afford-able price. My father was one of the innovators of mass-production –- the zenith of humanity's mastery of the facto-ries! But now prices are becoming even more competitive. The process which once made us market leaders now barely covers its costs. So perhaps my work shall indeed overshadow his. In time...'

Stroever glared pointedly at Ryker-Veere who was loitering uncomfortably in one corner away from the edge of the gantry. 'We shall see, Thira. We shall see... Come! Come and take a closer look...'

Thira was led down the clanging metal stairway to the factory floor. The scent of fresh cut wood and vines, and the aroma of fresh fruit mingled with the iron tang of blood. He observed the workers stripping a felled tree of its branches. At a distance, Stroever was now talking business with Ryker-Veere, who shook his head vehemently.

While no one was paying attention, Thira shuffled forward, trying not to let the manacles jangle too much. The forest wrapped itself around him...

A memory resurfaced from when he was young. Before he was *he*. In his mind, he walked alongside a recollection of his old self and together they became lost and alone in a strange and wild place. The dense forest of Ka'hi wrapped itself around them. Smells and sensations they had not experienced since...

Thira returned from his daydream. He toyed with the manacles. He looked up at the tree towering above them... So much of now was transporting him to back then. That time had returned with such freshness, never more vivid than it was right now and... yes... that was when it had started... the day when...

Workers swarmed around Thira, hacking at the life all around him. Trees were hewn, life cut away. The memories sunk within him, faded to less than dust and the cold light of the factory bore down on him once more.

The workers were gone and his recollections vanished with them. He collapsed to his knees and stared glumly at the soil.

Seconds poured away as he waited there.

Then... the faintest sound... like the fizzing of kindling catching alight...

He turned to his left...

Tiny stars of midnight blue twinkled in and out of existence over the soil. In moments they were gone as if they never had been. A creaking of young wood, then a shape emerged from the earth. A long, golden branch, no thicker than his little finger. It sensed his presence and snaked towards him.

Thira sat and calmly let the golden branch travel up his sleeve. The whole thing was just a touch longer than the length of his arm. It curled its way around. It settled there, warm, safe and comfortable. Under his sleeve it was not visible to anyone around him.

Thira looked from side to side. No one was watching.

Moments later, Stroever wandered up to him as if in a daydream. Stroever crouched and picked up a leaf sliced in two. 'After my father's death, I ran into the forest and hid here for many years.' Stroever held the maimed leaf in his palm and stroked it tenderly with his thumb. 'I never found a cure for my illness in the forest. Perhaps one day, given time, I shall, but it did give me some fine ideas about the future of the City...'

He stared up at the gigantic lanterns on the ceiling for a time. 'All property passed to Lord Ryker-Veere until I came of age,' continued Stroever, 'and he neglected the forests, concentrating on his own business endeavours. The trees grew tall and the undergrowth thick...' He seemed lost for a time in his own imaginings.

'Take it 'e gave everything back to you in the end?' said Thira.

Stroever awoke from his trance, stood and dropped the leaf. 'He may have kept the odd trinket of father's, but I believe nothing of significance.'

Thira noticed that Ryker-Veere stood anxiously some

meters behind Stroever, framed by the greenery, leaning forward a little, trying to hear what was being said. Stroever turned to see him, wandered over to Ryker-Veere, then ushered to Thira to join them.

Thira got up and followed obediently, glad of the long sleeves and manacles masking the golden branch curled around his forearm.

As he stumbled towards Stroever and Ryker-Veere, he remembered that day long ago. How could he ever forget?

It was sleeping now, the thing wrapped around his arm.

Resting, contented.

Waiting.

38

THE HOUSE, ITS DOOR & WHAT LAY BEYOND

The rain was teasing a return on the broad, empty backstreets; the damp cobbles shining in the sentinellight.

The three marched briskly forward, ShadowThief walking ahead of the others, still catching their breath after escaping Metelkova.

'Why did you say that?' said Aemea.

'I don't know,' said Krish. 'Sounded impressive.'

'And now they know all our names.'

'Good. And anyway, is it really going to make that much of a difference?'

'Well, no. Probably not but... perhaps think these things through next time, *Krishna*!'

'Who were they? Dar Fernier and all that lot?'

ShadowThief looked warningly back over her shoulder at both of them. She made some pretty strongly worded hand gestures.

'We should have just fled!' said Aemea. 'You didn't have to

go and make some stupid point! Why were you so angry anyway?'

'Guess you don't even have words like racism and ableism and stuff like that here?' said Krish.

Aemea considered this for a while. 'They don't sound familiar.'

Krish laughed bitterly. *Of course they didn't.*

They were approaching the address Redbeard had given them.

A house loomed up in front of them, whitewashed with black beams criss-crossed over the front. Every floor was a tad bigger than the last, each set of eaves protruding over the floor below, leading up to a large triangular roof. The whole building appeared to lean a little to one side, its red parallelogram-shaped door finishing the wonky image. There were no lights on.

'You think someone's already been here?' said Krish.

'It's not a good sign,' said Aemea. 'No lights. We should be quick.'

'Through the front door?'

ShadowThief shrugged.

'At this juncture and on an empty street like this, I feel it could be a waste of time to try and be inconspicuous.'

'Fair enough,' said Krish.

ShadowThief ventured forth, cut away some of the shadow by the door, produced a small piece of wire, jiggled it up and down in the keyhole for a while, then withdrew it impatiently and kicked the door down in a few short moves.

No light lay beyond. The darkness was inviting. Shadow-Thief entered. Krish and Aemea followed.

As ShadowThief cut back the shadow, a room which looked like a sterile sweetshop was unveiled. There was a counter and many shelves full of jars. Krish felt a crunch. He looked down.

There were numerous smashed glass jars strewn across the floor. And something else. A smell, metallic, like iron.

They walked cautiously into the next room. The smell grew stronger. ShadowThief began to tear vigorously at the gloom, a flicker of light appeared in the corner of Krish's eye and then—

Total darkness descended again in an instant. Krish felt a mighty emptiness within. He wanted to run but he was stuck to the spot. No force was holding him down, but still he did not move.

A light appeared in the doorway. A figure stood there, slanted, hunched, its face pale and deformed, swollen unnaturally in places. As the figure came closer and closer, the smell of iron, of blood, grew much stronger.

Krish couldn't budge, he was stuck to the spot.

The figure staggered forward.

He wanted to fight, to call for help but nothing happened.

Then the creature screamed. A mighty scream, primal and desperate. Skin began to fall away from its face, shredding, peeling off in different directions, until a great mottled skull of yellow and black was crying animalistically in Krish's face. He couldn't feel the breath of it and the scream...the scream was a memory of a scream, and the place was not this place, but he was here, and there was no sense, just the scent of iron and—

The sound of a small glass object being crushed underfoot. The stench of blood intensified for a moment then vanished completely as ShadowThief's arm waved the hellish vision away.

Krish looked down at the smashed dreamglobe on the floor then up at the room. He was back in the wonky house, standing in a workshop. The room was full of tools and shelves of jars and small boxes. The place had been vandalised, everything crushed or removed.

'What... what was that...?' said Krish. 'A trap?'

Aemea looked around. All was unnervingly still.

'I don't know,' she said. 'A deterrent, I'd guess.'

They spent a few minutes searching the ground floor of the building until they concluded that there was nothing to find. With one last burst of determination, Krish marched up to the main counter, realising it was the one place they'd neglected to search. He found a large jar filled with liquid. There was something in there, but he couldn't make it out. He lifted the heavy cylinder.

He banged it down on the counter, very nearly dropping it. Clouds of blood were spreading out from the object – a severed arm. It was muscular, with thick black hair and dirty fingernails. On the forearm was a tattoo of a cobbler, hard at work mending a shoe.

'A dream-pedlar,' said Aemea solemnly.

ShadowThief knelt on the floor, cut away the dark under the counter and revealed a whole series of jars – they had found the rest of the dream-pedlar.

'I sense that Dar Fernier may have stopped here before Metelkova,' said Aemea. 'He did mention the dreams. I imagine part of the fee he alluded to was to retrieve the dreams for Ryker-Veere.'

Krish took a deep breath and walked slowly to one side of the room.

'Krish...' said Aemea, defeat in her voice.

'I know, I know,' he said. 'It's gone. We're too late. They've taken the dream and destroyed anything that could lead us to it.'

Aemea and ShadowThief looked from Krish to a jar with the dead man's head in it. ShadowThief gestured violently and stormed out. Aemea followed.

'What?!' said Krish. He run after them, exasperated. 'What?! What is it?!'

'A man is dead because of you!' said Aemea.

'No! No, not because of—'

'Ryker-Veere is looking for the people who are following the clues, trying to open his safe. I'm pretty sure this confirms that he hasn't opened it himself already; but, Krish, people have died because of this! So perhaps you could tell us now what's actually in the safe?'

'I'm sorry, I can't do that.'

ShadowThief turned, fire in her eyes, grabbed Krish and banged him against the wall.

'Get off me!' shouted Krish.

'Why?' said Aemea. 'Why should she? Do you know who those men were? What they're like? Why should we be risking our lives for you? For money? I'm not sure it's worth it!'

'For Thira!'

'Fine! Then why don't we pay him a visit?'

'You were the one who said we should solve the dreams first! And I don't know what Ryker-Veere'll do once he opens the safe! He won't need him anymore! He might take it and—'

ShadowThief pulled Krish towards her and then banged him even harder against the wall, her eyes screaming *What?!*

'What's in there?!' said Aemea. 'What's in the safe?'

'Myrthali!' said Krish.

'What is—?'

'If you don't know, I don't know how to explain! It's something to save my mother's life!'

'Ha! That's what this is all about? Really?! Is all this *really* worth it?'

'YES! Yes, it is!'

ShadowThief and Aemea exchanged glances. ShadowThief released Krish and he fell to the ground, gasping for breath.

'And it's... it's my only way home,' he said.

'And what about Thira?'

Guilt clouded Krish's mind. 'What about him?'

'I can't tell if he's the most important thing in all existence to you... or if you don't really care that much about him.'

'I'm... I'm not sure if I can tell either.' He could feel tears welling up inside him, waiting to burst forth. Then shame kicked in and he covered his face. Trapped in the closeness of his own palms, the quivering breaths stuttered out of him. In a second it all came gushing forth.

A moment or two later, Aemea knelt beside him and stroked his arm tenderly in a way which unnerved Krish.

'I didn't want this to happen,' he said in a croaky voice that was largely unfamiliar to him. 'For people to die... To lose Thira... He could be dead...' A tear ran down his face, hidden from Aemea and ShadowThief. 'He could be dead! Mum could be dead!'

'Krish,' said Aemea, 'I think we should head back. Find Ryker-Veere. Perhaps... I don't know, if he's already opened the safe—'

'No, no! We have to keep going. Find the solutions before he does.'

'The safe is probably well-guarded now, but—'

'But we know where it is! And he can't get into it! If he opens that safe now, he could take the Myrthali somewhere else. If we find the solutions first... Yeah, we can do it.' Krish ran his hands down his raw and puffy face, wiping away the tears in the process. He looked up at Aemea and ShadowThief, his strength renewed. 'We can do it.'

'Well, think about it like this,' said Aemea. 'They clearly have one of the dreams that we don't, but hopefully we can get ahead of them by getting to Győr first. So, they'll have one dream we need and we'll have one they need. Could be a bargaining chip when we rescue Thira.'

ShadowThief mimed opening the safe.

'Exactly!' said Krish. 'The safe is there too. Everything in one place. We just have to get to Győr first.' He carried on nodding to himself, slotting it all together in his mind.

Aemea looked to ShadowThief then back to Krish.

'Tell us what Myrthali is, Krish,' she said. 'What are we fighting for...?'

Krish thought for a moment, but he already knew he was going to tell them.

'It's the essence of time itself. It gives you more time to live. And... well, it might do other stuff, but I don't know. More time is what I want. To save my Mum. So there. That's what it's worth to me.'

Aemea chewed over this in her mind then nodded.

'That's some pretty insane stuff you just said. For now, we'll go with you, but ultimately I think there needs to be something else—'

'I can't make bargains to split the Myrthali!'

'Why not?'

'I don't know, but I was told... I was told it won't work.'

'That's a shame. We could always just take it for ourselves, I suppose.'

'You could... but I reckon you won't,' said Krish.

ShadowThief smiled slyly.

'No. We won't,' said Aemea. 'But there has to be something else you can offer us.'

Aemea looked over at ShadowThief for a few seconds, discussing silently with her friend, then she turned back to Krish.

'So, where you're going, the borough you're returning to, will you be able to use the money you stole from Ryker-Veere there?' said Aemea.

'No,' said Krish.

'And you have, what, roughly—?'

'You know exactly how much I have.'

ShadowThief's sly smile again.

'We do. That's more than enough to get us to Győr and back. And then... Who knows?'

'A clean break?'

'You make it sound more like breaking bones.'

'I mean, you can get away from all this. Do something different.'

ShadowThief nodded encouragingly at Aemea, whose eyes were placid, lost in a serene vision for a moment or two.

'Yes,' said Aemea dreamily. 'It could certainly be enough to travel to a faraway street and find a new profession. Something a tad more... legal.'

'I'll think about it,' said Krish.

He sniffed and wiped away the tears. He looked up at Aemea and ShadowThief, feeling embarrassed.

Hey, said ShadowThief. Then she signed something about him crying that he only just caught up with: *This isn't weakness.*

'Thanks,' he said, braving a smile. He felt, by the way she turned away with a smile, that this was a note to herself just as much as to him.

The Woman instructs Eva, tired and low

'Why can't the stupid game just wait 'til primo?'

The board and pieces are laid out on her bed

'I don't understand, I've made most of them dead!'

'I don't like it either, but please kill all pawns'

'Alright then, I will!' Eva lays back and yawns

'I'll poison their thoughts and black I'll paint their sky

Make them all so sad that they'll jump from on high'

The Woman nods with teary complacency

Begging within that one fade she will be free

39

THE POISON IN THE KITCHEN

Beneath the low-arched ceiling of the black-walled, windowless room, the kitchen was dotted with colour.

The lilacs of the freshly cut foxgloves and the pinks of oleanders, the whites of the dainty little heads of the lily of the valleys, all were arranged in a broad wicker basket on the sideboard. Fragrant rosemary, blushing red crab apples and the pinky-red stalks of rhubarb with their cabbage-like leaves, all neatly laid out on pearl white plates. Willow and yew and mistletoe and prickly holly, deep green with bright orange berries, laburnum and snowdrop bulbs, each gracefully displayed on the many surfaces in this wonderland of colour.

'Everything in this room is poisonous.' Madam Ckrystafis placed a hand on Thira's upper back, guiding the handcuffed boy into the kitchen.

'See this?' There was an assuredness to everything Madam Ckrystafis said, but an untrustworthy amount of warmth too. 'Snowdrop bulbs. Often mistaken for onions. A terrible error.

Rhubarb. Very tasty, but see the leaves? Good substitute for cabbage, they say. But, no! Gives you nausea, vomiting, convulsions, bleeding on the inside. Eat the oleander and it is death. Red spurge sap will cause temporary blindness if you get any in your eyes. And you see this? Traveller's joy. Another name is devil's guts, hag-rope or maiden's hair. Many names – most from other worlds, they say. To create sympathy, some beggars rub traveller's joy on their skin and the irritation makes it look like sores. If chewed the tongue will erupt in blisters.'

'Wow, all sounds lovely,' said Thira, glad his sleeves continued to obscure the golden branch wrapped around his arm. 'Any pretty flowers what don't kill ya? What's this? Smells alright.'

'Rosemary. It is fine in small amounts when used as a herb to add flavour. But consuming large quantities of the leaf or consuming undiluted rosemary oil can cause vomiting, bleeding of the uterus, kidney irritation or redness of the skin. Some let rosemary grow by graves to keep the dead from walking. And this? Angel's trumpet.'

'Looks pretty.'

'It does. Eat it and you will feel very relaxed. Very, very relaxed. Then there will be hallucinations, then sleep. Then more sleep. And more and more and more and then... No waking. My favourite. Very useful for a quiet death.'

'Oh. Great.'

'Come, child. Sit! You will help old Ckrystafis with her work.'

She sat at the workbench on a tall stool. She wore a simple black dress patched with the odd square of pastel colour; reds, oranges and yellow. There was a belt pulled tight around her middle and she wore an orange headscarf.

'So what the 'ell we doin'?' said Thira, seating himself on a stool on the opposite side of the workbench to Madam Ckrystafis.

'Gloves is what we are doing,' said Madam Ckrystafis. 'Always gloves first if we are wanting to stay alive.'

'Perhaps we could slip these bad boys off?' ventured Thira, indicating the cuffs.

'No, child. You will cope.'

Thira rolled his eyes and pulled on the gloves, with some difficultly thanks to the manacles.

'Now,' said Madam Ckrystafis, picking up a flower with yellow petals, 'you remove the bulb, slice it in two and squeeze it into the vial. And then you go back and squeeze a little more – there is always more in these.'

'And this tiny amount is enough to stop ya gettin' up and doin' all that breathin' malarkey, yeah?'

'No, child! This is only very mild. It won't kill you.'

'Oh. Well, what's the point? I thought killin' was basically your thing?'

'No, no, no, child! Poisoning, yes, but poisoning is not always killing. These fades I am mainly engaged in the more subtle arts of poisoning.'

'Like...?'

'Like creating ingredients for dreams. I specialise in providing the key ingredients for the finest nightmares.'

'Oh. Charmin'.'

'So, come. Talk to me. I heard you are from another world – not so hard! You will squirt it in your eye. And you will not be looking at much with it after that. Now, tell me – where are you from? How did you get here?'

'Well, I don't know really.' It was easy for Thira to give Madam Ckrystafis vague, unhelpful answers, as that was all he had. 'I'm from a long way away.'

'How far?'

'I... dunno.'

'How long did it take you to get here?'

'Well, kinda no time at all.'

'Ah! A gateway! I have heard of such things! There were many in and out of the City once, so the stories say. Did you perform rites, a ceremony, to arrive here?'

'What?! Nah, nothing like that. Just sorta happened. Wasn't my choice. Well, it was but... it's complicated.'

'But how did you get here, child? You must have done something.'

'Nah, I really didn't. In fact, I sorta didn't come here... I... well, I might still be there. Another me. Back where I was born.'

'Dear child, you're not making sense! Perhaps the poison in this room is seeping into your brain through the air. Now stop! Think! Give me some plain words.'

'Well... I think I might still be there... I mean, it's not really my body. Well, it is *now* but... It's like this but it's... different...'

'Different? Different how? You were shorter?'

'No!'

'Taller?'

'No.'

'Fatter? Slimmer?'

'No, no, no! I was different but... the same.'

He was now mulling over Madam Ckrystafis's inquiries and began to formulate the answer to a question she had not *quite* asked.

'Are you all right, dear?' said Madam Ckrystafis, looking at him side on, narrowing her eyes. She handed him a cup. 'You look lost in your own thoughts! Here – have some water...'

Thira's mind was reaching conclusions at a rate of knots. He leant over and took his cup of water and drank deeply. Then he stopped. He glared at her wide-eyed.

'It's poison, innit?'

'No, child. You saw me pour from the same tap into both our cups.' She took another swig from her own. 'No, no. It is the cup that is poisoned. Velwood lined with hapsoley. Weak but lethal within minutes...'

Thira placed his hand on his stomach. It began to gurgle and he could sense his organs aching, switching into overdrive to find a solution to his predicament.

'I have the antidote, which I shall give to you, of course, but first, a quick question. Your friends... they have paymasters?'

Thira considered. The aching within had turned to red hot pain. 'No.'

'They operate alone for their own ends? Interesting. And where are they heading now? Odensegade? Paternoster Row? Strada Serrabolino? Győr?'

Thira felt his eye twinge nervously.

'Aaah!' said Madam Ckrystafis gleefully. 'Of course... Now, tell me their names. And let me advise you to hurry, child.'

Thira felt his organs were about to burst. The branch was glowing around his arm, warm and loyal and ready to serve, but he was frightened to unleash it untested.

'Er... well... alright! There's, er, Jarhi... er... Sia... and Hri.'

Madam Ckrystafis shook her head. 'You would rather die with terrible lies on your lips?'

'That's about the size of it.'

'Hmmm... But what are they up to, child? What is their objective, these friends who abandoned you?'

'Ooooh, ya know that 'as slipped my mind. Perhaps it'll come back to me in a min...'

'Ha! You are not a traitor. Most admirable. Still, this has been most helpful. Now take this...' She tore a large green leaf from a nearby potted plant. 'Place it on your tongue and suck. The pain will be gone shortly, though make sure you eat a full meal within the hour and go to bed early. This is a very simple poison. The only one I have the antidote for here. That will be all for tofade. Well done, child.'

A minty freshness filled Thira's mouth. His insides were soothed, and moments later the aching sensation already felt like an obscure memory.

'Stay here for a minute or two, child,' said Madam Ckrystafis, getting to her feet. 'I shall have a quick conference with our friend Mr Stroever. I would not advise eating anything in here.' She placed her cup in front of Thira as she left. 'Attempt to poison me if you will. I shall let you know if you have concealed the scent well enough. And you will find no other antidotes here, but feel free to look if it amuses you.' And with that she left.

Thira listened to the key turning in the lock, waited a handful of seconds, not budging a millimetre, then straightened his arm with enough force that the length of golden branch shot out. It was lean, twisted and a bit knobbly, but elegant nonetheless.

Bloody 'ell, look at ya! he thought. *Different to the last one... so different... Now, let's see what ya can do...*

§

Madam Ckrystafis approached Isri Stroever, who was waiting in the shelter of one of the trees on the factory floor.

'They're heading for Győr,' she said.

'Into the heart of the war,' said Stroever. 'They are determined.'

'So it would seem. He will not give us names.'

'No. I did not expect him to. But a lead will no doubt keep Anders occupied for a while. I shall pass it on. As for Thira, in

time perhaps he will help us solve our little problem. Győr...
Any idea why they are heading there?'

Madam Ckrystafis grinned. 'Some of the borough's finest
dream-pedlars are Győri.'

His eyes narrowed. 'How curious...'

40

THE DARKNESS IN HIS
OPEN EYES

K rish and Aemea waited on a gloomy street corner. ShadowThief had snuck into an abandoned telegram office in a desperate attempt to send some messages covertly to contacts in Győr.

They were in luck. Many of the more specialist dream-pedlars of Győr had indeed remained despite the escalating conflict, though the reasons for this were worrying. Ankaran gun carriages had blockaded the neighbourhood. The Necropolis Railway was, as Aemea had suspected, their only choice. The Ankarans were keen to shift the corpses littering the streets out of Győr, permitting them to be buried in the Győri cemetery at Dravska Ulica. A contact at the railway had agreed to take them across the border to find a dream-pedlar for a fee. They had asked for surprisingly little, which made Aemea uneasy. Their motivation for taking them must be more than financial, she said.

ShadowThief's contact at the Necropolis Railway also confirmed that they'd received no communications from anyone else about reaching Győr. So unless Ryker-Veere had an alternative plan, they were a move ahead of Dar Fernier or whomever was hunting for the dreams.

'We must be careful though,' said Aemea. 'It's a small world when you're searching for dreams. We tried to avoid Metelkova because we knew characters like Dar Fernier would head there looking for answers. In war-torn Győr, I'm imagining there'll be very little left to explore. Our world could be even smaller.'

The idea of going into a war zone terrified Krish, but Aemea simply nodded solemnly and off they headed.

They descended many stone staircases, going deeper and deeper into this corner of the City, roofs towering above them, leaving little space for the light of the sentinels to penetrate. They ventured along seemingly endless narrow back-alleys, high buildings on either slide.

At last, they emerged into a large yard intersected by tracks. It was the largest open space Krish had seen in the City and it was relatively quiet, save for the distant chuffing of trains and the odd clang of metal. Trucks were being shunted around by squat little steam engines towards large wooden gates. All was plastered black by soot and coal dust. Armed guards rode on the rear trucks of most trains, but none seemed to anticipate much trouble.

The four of them approached a large locomotive, predictably black, its squat frontage reminding Krish of a bull in mid-charge.

Aemea spoke to a guard sporting a fine horseshoe moustache, his rifle comfortably shouldered. Krish's eyes scanned the long train, trying not to dwell too much on the cargo they usually transported.

After a brief explanation, the guard nodded knowingly and opened his hand, which Aemea swiftly filled with notes. He ushered them onboard.

§

They sat on the hard metal floor of the deep, empty carriage. Krish hugged his knees. He tried to sleep to conserve energy. In fleeting moments of consciousness, he saw a plume of smoke caught in the dazzling light of a low-flying sentinel, the guard scraping the wood of his rifle's barrel with his bayonet, but mostly he saw only the never-ending blackness. Right now, the world barely looked different from either side of his eyelids.

He recalled Mum leaving the room when he was younger and leaving the door ajar. He'd cry until she turned off the light in the hallway. He'd do anything to see that light again, and her rolling her eyes at him and chuckling as she switched it off.

Aemea and ShadowThief nibbled at their supplies. Krish managed to stay awake for long enough to eat a little too. They discussed plans but with scant details. There was no real way to prepare for a war zone. They would arrive at the main station in Márai Utca, and it was a short walk from there to the parallel street of Szabó Utca, where the dream-pedlars were based. All they needed was a guide to suggest an address. They had to be in and out of Győr as fast as possible.

A handful of hours drifted by. There was orangey light above and low thuds in the distance. The sounds didn't grow any louder, but they did increase in number.

Then – an excruciating screech as the locomotive's brakes ground them to a halt. Two figures in long coats and caps, rifles on their shoulders, jumped aboard, and then the train continued on its way. The guard briefly acknowledged the figures then turned away.

The two men climbed down into the truck and approached them.

'My name is Elek, this is Ferenc,' said one of the men. He

had bulbous eyes, swollen-looking in their sockets, a long sharp nose, and facial hair growing in scraggy patches.

Ferenc was shorter, his eyes narrow. Every corner of his face was covered in scars, scarcely a scrap of skin between one old war wound and the next. He didn't say a word, looking away most of the time, keeping watch.

'You're here to help?' Elek asked.

Krish, Aemea and ShadowThief all conferred silently. 'Help?' said a puzzled Krish.

'Sure,' said Elek. 'We find your suszter.'

'Suszter?' said Aemea.

'Dream man! Dream maker.' said Elek. 'Then you helping us.'

'Doing what?' said Aemea.

Elek and Ferenc exchanged glances. 'Carry the...' he waved his arms about, indicating the emptiness of the truck.

A cold wave spread through Krish – they were to help load the trucks with bodies.

'Well, erm, of course,' said Aemea.

Elek sneered at Aemea. 'You in charge?' he said. 'Girls not in charge! This is war. Girls cry and hide in the corner.'

'Excuse me!' said Aemea sourly.

ShadowThief took to her feet and pulled out her knife though Elek and Ferenc paid her no heed.

'Ha! This one even more in charge!' said Elek. 'Okay, maybe this one don't cry so much.'

'They're both tougher than me,' stated Krish.

Elek glanced at Krish then looked directly at ShadowThief for the first time, her tattoos catching the light of a passing sentinel. Elek put his hands up. 'Okay, okay!' he said. 'You help us, we help you. Is fine. We find suszter.'

'We're after a particular one,' said Krish.

'The best,' added Aemea.

Elek nodded. 'I know the one. We take you to Ferenc. Not this Ferenc, another Ferenc. Feri Bácsi. Why you need him?'

'He has to make a dream for us,' said Krish. 'He makes it for us and then we leave. We can help in any way we can on the way out.'

Elek grunted. 'Serious?! You pay for this?'

'You've no idea what it's worth.'

Elek laughed heartily, his breath stale, and slapped Krish encouragingly on the shoulder. 'It's your money, my friend! Yes, we find Feri Bácsi. He is not the best, but he is very, very good. And he is alive. Is alive good for you, my friend?'

'It's good,' said Krish. 'We'll pay you half now.'

Aemea and ShadowThief scowled at Krish.

'H-ha!' laughed Elek. 'It's war. Only payment in advance. I want to be rich when I die. When they find me, the enemy, they torture me and kill me, I will eat my money first and laugh that they not get it. I will be rich in the next life! You will see! Rich in the next life!'

Moments later, money was exchanged. From then on, the conversation dwindled as the train hurtled onwards, the sounds of low thuds growing in the distance.

41

THE WAR IN THE STREETS

The low thuds increased.

The air was rich with a scent which made Krish think of Mum's nail polish remover. The sentinels cast few beams on this corner of the City. Darkness was all around with scars of light from mortars ripping across the horizon. War was near.

They sped past a great fence, towering over them, covered in barbed wire. There was a bright spotlight bearing down on many figures climbing. The scene was gone again a moment later.

'First border,' said Elek. 'There is another.'

They zipped past another great barbed wire barrier. Krish looked more intently this time; Many of those scaling the fence had bloodied hands. He heard gunshots as the horrific vision vanished from sight.

'They open for us, but we must be quick,' said Elek.

The train arrived just outside of the grand station at Márai Utca. Krish could hear chants and cries from nearby. They walked along the track. A guard toyed with a loose bolt in the truck ahead of the one they'd arrived in.

'When we return,' said Elek, 'you help with bolts. You take one truck each, spread out. We load fast. Okay? Pull bolts! Open truck side! Load!-Load!-Load! Must be quick!' He led them onwards.

Elek looked up at the station. Krish could see guards standing on the walls separating the streets from the tracks. Beyond, he heard the clamouring crowds.

'Government don't want people to run,' said Elek. 'To get on trains. Think it be chaos.' Elek grimaced at the guards up on the walls and vented his frustration by coarsely cocking his rifle. 'They prefer everybody be dead than show weakness. We back here in one hour.'

From behind the building there were flames. Guards were scattered around the many tracks which led into the main station. Aemea's eyes were open wide and moving in every direction. Something was happening to her, Krish could tell; there was a storm in her mind. ShadowThief's eyes framed a question that normally Aemea would understand and answer. She said nothing. Her breathing became increasingly erratic.

They veered off from the main station and came to a small shed-like building. Elek muttered something at the guard outside and dropped a few coins into his hand. Elek pulled the door open and—

Aemea took in a gigantic breath and fell to her knees, gasping as if she was drowning in the very air around them. ShadowThief hauled her back to her feet. The guard barked at Elek, pointing at Aemea, but Elek simply shouted back dismissively.

'Aemea! What is it?' said Krish, helping ShadowThief lead her forward. 'What is—?'

'Hold onto me! Don't let me go! Both of you! Don't let me

go! Please! *Please!* It'll happen! They'll try and pull us apart, but we mustn't! We mustn't!'

They followed Elek down a flight of steps into a narrow corridor, only a couple of metres wide, lit intermittently by gas lanterns. Krish and ShadowThief's shoulders scraped along the wall as they supported Aemea.

'Don't let me go! We can't be separated! We can't! *We can't! No* There's only one way... there's only one way! We can't go back! It's chaos! Madness! Fire! Fire everywhere and-and-and-and... no! Please! We can't...we can't... we can't stop it...'

ShadowThief held her friend close, asking many silent questions as they walked.

'Aemea, please!' said Krish. 'Please! Tell me – what is it? What's wrong? What do we have to do?'

'We can't... we can't... there's nothing... no way back...'

Aemea began to shake. Krish now felt as if he and Shadow-Thief were holding her to try and stop her limbs from shaking themselves loose.

'Too soon! Too soon! The future is too soon! Too soon...'

They followed Elek and Ferenc up the stairs. A door opened and they entered a cramped room where several soldiers sat about, clutching their rifles, staring glassily at the three young arrivals. A service door set into a column opened and they found themselves exiting onto a small bridge.

A cacophony of chants and screams whipped around them. Krish looked down to see a crowd gathered around the entrance to the station, bashing the stone walls and wooden doors, shouting and kicking and holding up infants, some being passed to the front for strangers, begging for their children to be taken to safer streets. The guards fired rifles into the air, but this had little effect on the incandescent crowd.

'We go down there, then under bridge,' said Elek.

Krish looked down in horror at the tangle of people. It felt as though a spark could come at any moment and ignite the crowd.

'Come!' said Elek.

They began to descend the steps when Aemea grabbed hold of Krish and ShadowThief. She was crushing Krish's hand.

'Aemea! You have to tell me! What do we do?'

'I can't, I can't-I-can't-I-can't-Ican'tIcan'tIcan'tcan'tcan't-seecan'tseecan't—'

'Aemea!'

'This way!' cried Elek.

He ushered them down the steps and Krish and Shadow-Thief pulled Aemea with them. Krish looked one way at the pandemonium in the streets, and then the other where there was an archway under the bridge. Aemea clasped his hand so tight he felt the bones would break.

'STOP!STOP!NO!IT'SHERE!NO!PLEASE!STOP!'

She looked in every direction, words screaming out of her, not even sharp gasps for breath slowing the torrent of words pouring from her.

'NOTTHERE!NOTTHERE!NO!NO!NO!NO!NOTTHERE!'

Elek led them towards the archway but Aemea yanked them back.

Then the world fell on them.

A thundering *WHOOSH*! then a mighty crash.

Krish felt the explosion as if it had directly hit his eardrum, and the whole street shook as the bridge behind them disintegrated, piercing screams, half of them silenced in an instant and Elek rushed forward towards the archway and safety beyond, they sprinted after him, reaching the midpoint under the arch when Aemea suddenly jerked them backwards then a deafening blast all around and ShadowThief ...roar of air...

Aemea

Krish ...world caving in...

...thrown backwards...

...hurled forward...

THUD!

THUD!

THUD!

...stones falling...

Faces!
Screams!
Hands!

...hitting the ground...

...dust in mouth...

...dragged away...

...dirt in eyes...

...archway gone...

SHAD!

AEMEA!

§

A firm hand yanked her from the rubble.

Aemea clasped the figure who had rescued her from the collapsed archway. Her breath was out of control, her throat dry as she choked on masonry dust.

Breathe and breathe and breathe and breathe...

As she calmed, realising she had not run out of oxygen, she began to sense that the person she had wrapped herself around was not her friend. The stale sweat and the feel of their torso was not familiar.

'It is, it is! I swears it!'

'Shut yer noise!'

'I tell you it is!'

She tuned into the voices. She knew them and they were not friendly.

'Looks like I got myself a new pet!'

She pulled away, recoiling in horror.

There, shadows shredded, torn, stretched long against the cobbles, flickering in the flames of a decimated wooden hall which was now ablaze, immovable amongst the tide of fleeing humans, were the tattooed figures of Dar Fernier and his comrades.

'Oooh... the resemblance is somewhat uncanny under all that dust,' said Dar Fernier, cruel glee in his broad smile. 'Let us cut it open, see if it all looks right.'

'Well... as... pleasant as this... unexpected reunion is...' began Aemea, catching her breath, 'I feel... I should be on my merry way.'

'Ya find 'im? Yer dream-pedlar?'

Aemea was taken aback.

'Oh, yes,' said Dar Fernier bearing down on Aemea. 'Mal-Jack says you's 'ad a taste of what 'is master's after. Got to get there before 'em, 'ee says. Track down another stinkin' old dream-pedlar. 'Fore it's too late. And 'ere we are, my sweet...'

Aemea jumped as two hands were cupped tightly around her shoulders. One of Fernier's underlings had circled round behind her.

'They find 'im?' said Fernier. 'Your compatriots?'

'How should I know?' spat out Aemea. 'We were separated.'

Fernier jerked his head to the left, a signal to the others who quickly departed to scout the area. Aemea's captor remained. He shoved her forward into Fernier's grasp. She attempted to pull away, to grapple with him, to claw at his filthy skin, but to no avail.

'Oh dear, oh dear, fink this might be the end of the road for you, child.'

Aemea looked into his eyes. She felt it, the path they would now take, and the horror overwhelmed her. She began to shake uncontrollably.

'Please... please... no... don't... don't....'

'Ssssh! Sh-sh-sh! Look at ya quakin' in yer little booties!'

'Please!'

'I hears you sees the future. Nah, nah... *feels* it! Always just a little ahead of what's 'appenin'! Don't feel much in your future, does ya, girlie?'

'Oh, you are infinitely wrong, Dar Fernier! You are so, so wrong!'

'A-ha! Don't try foolin' me! I won't be in this sinkin' 'ell'ole for much longer, trust me! But I can still make it good and slow 'fore the others return...'

'Please!'

'Nothing untoward. We're gentleman, like. But I got to make it hurt...'

He dragged her into the ruin of a building, snaked his right leg around her, pressing into the backs of her knees, forcing them to bend as he lowered her to the ground. Dar Fernier pulled out a jagged knife, leant over her, his sour breath spilling into her mouth and nostrils, the bristles on his chin jabbing into hers. 'Like your friend made it hurt for us...'

'Please! Please don't!'

'I'll make it quick at the end, don't worry...but first—'

'Please! Please! Don't!'

'Ha-ha-ha!! This is just how I likes it! Likes to smell the fear on 'em 'fore the end! Make 'em beg for their lives!'

'I'm not begging for my life, you filthy, rotten, despicable imbecile! I'm begging for yours! And for her soul...'

As Dar Fernier held his knife up high, he saw both terror and defiance in Aemea's eyes. He froze, sensed she was talking to a figure she'd spotted out of the corner of her eye.

'Please... please don't...' She wasn't talking to him.

Fernier looked one way then the other and saw her too late. 'PLEASE! Shad, don't!'

Dar Fernier's accomplice went for ShadowThief, but he'd scarcely moved an inch before her blade was in and out of his neck. He crumpled to the ground just fast enough for Shadow-Thief to step over him and up to Dar Fernier.

Never had he seen such pure fury in someone's eyes, blazing with hate, caught in a blur as the figure, every line of every tattoo shimmering across her skin in the light of the flames, leapt forward, her blade finding a new sheath in the flesh of his purlicue, forcing him to drop both Aemea and his blade.

'SHAD, PLEASE!'

A guttural cry from Dar Fernier; the shriek of an infant fearing it will scream its last. ShadowThief slashed upwards, slicing the flesh between Fernier's thumb and forefinger in two and splattering his blood on all three of them.

'SHAD!'

She drove her elbow into his stomach. He fell onto his front, winded, so she kicked him onto his back.

'SHAD! SHAD, NO! STOP! PLEASE!'

ShadowThief straddled him. She shook with anger, looking into the man's pleading eyes.

'SHAD!'

She held the amethyst blade aloft.

And then she began.

§

'Elek....! Elek.....!'

Krish's lungs ached, his throat was hoarse. He ran and ran and ran away from the destroyed archway that had cut him off from Aemea and ShadowThief. Dust stung his eyes, his back was bruised and raw.

'Elek!' He was against the flow of those fleeing. 'Elek!' He could just see him. Every time he vanished from sight, he turned a corner and spied him up ahead.

Were they dead? Were they gone? Was Thira dead? He ran and ran through the hell of war-torn Győr. Buildings were crumbling all around. Another shell hit a tower ahead, tearing it apart and it crashed onto the street. Krish turned at the last minute to avoid the raining debris and rushed after Elek.

He darted around another corner onto a street where the crackling of fire married with a blast of heat. A large building ahead of him was ablaze. Charred beams of wood dropped from the facade, and he spotted Elek, caught, nowhere to run, turning to flee.

Krish ran up to him. Elek aimed his rifle but Krish, swimming in fury, whacked the rifle away, forcing Elek off balance. Elek tumbled to the ground and Krish shouted fearlessly in the face of a man twice his height.

'You take our money, you run! You try and shoot me! What's wrong with you?!'

'You run up behind me! What you expect?!'

'Where are they? Aemea and ShadowThief. Where—?'

'How I know?' Elek got to his feet. 'Come on! It's too late!' He went to leave, but was waiting for Krish to move.

In a fraction of a second, many emotions washed over Krish:

Fear – any moment he could be dead.

Guilt – he pictured Mum waiting on her bed, staring at an open door that he'd never walk through.

Determination – there was only one way back.

'Elek—' with every syllable he tried to mask the quivering child within, '—you have to find them, but tell me... Where's Feri Bácsi?'

'You will die!'

'Then you'd better get them to safely. Where is he?'

Another beam crashed to the ground, a blast of heat sweeping over them. Elek glared at Krish then pointed to the neighbouring street.

'Three-nine-two!' he Elek. 'Red door! Be quick!'

Elek and Krish ran in opposite directions.

Krish sprinted through the street of fire. Every building here was made of wood and looked subsided, each apparently leaning on its neighbour to stay up. Krish found the door hanging open. He barged inside.

The room was covered in rubble and books and smashed jars and dream ingredients. The far wall had collapsed revealing a kitchen beyond. The dim room was lit by the light of a single lantern in one corner.

A figure, curly iron-grey hair, a thick moustache across his upper lip, scurried into the room and then out again. Krish marched in his direction.

'Feri Bácsi?'

Sudden stillness from the next room. Then movement. The old man returned, eyed him suspiciously, shouted something dismissive in his own tongue then disappeared again.

Krish walked towards the kitchen. 'Feri Bácsi!'

'Ha-ha! Feri Bácsi! Feri Bácsi! *Mit akarhat bárki Feri Bácsitól most?*' said Feri Bácsi, waving him away.

'I-I need a dream. *This* dream.' Krish held out a scrap of paper with the dream code written on it.

'Ha-ha-ha! *Ez valami vicc?!*' said Feri Bácsi as he went to pass Krish.

'Please!' Krish pulled out a handful of bank notes. 'Please! You must help me!' He placed the notes in the old man's hand.

'Ha!' The old man cried out, threw the notes in the air, dispersing them everywhere and shouted back at him mockingly.

The old man turned to leave, but Krish grabbed hold of him and turned him back around. He swooped down, snatched a handful of the notes and thrust them into the dream-pedlar's pockets. 'Please, please...' He stayed calm and stared right into the old man's eyes unblinkingly. 'Please...'

Feri Bácsi stared for some time then mumbled. He walked away, laughing heartily, making a gesture as if he was tossing something over his shoulder.

The dream-pedlar got to work at a furious speed. He grabbed ingredients – wood, bone, animal fur, dried grey herbs – chopped them, ground them, pummelled them to dust. He tossed the ingredients into the globe and before Krish could say anything more, he chuckled, made the throwing over his shoulder gesture again, lit the flame and left the room.

'No! Wait!' cried Krish.

The man walked away as a cloud filled the room. A scent like a struck match wafted into Krish's nostrils...

42
THE SECOND TOWER

THE WΛY IS CLOSED

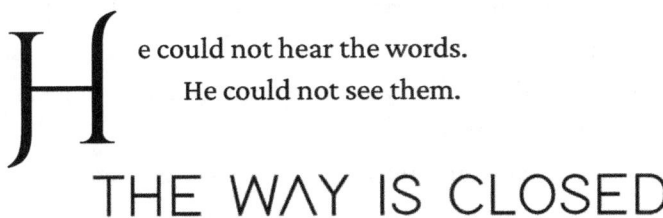 e could not hear the words.
He could not see them.

THE WΛY IS CLOSED

But they were there.

As the mists of this dream soaked his senses, he tasted the words.

THE WΛY IS CLOSED

The odour of a pavement after a sudden downpour in summer. The sparkling scents of electrical activity.

His vision cleared and there it was...

He could not have been ready for this world.

His own world was a small rock of blue and green, hanging in the nothing, much like Thira's world of Ilir. And Knock-Thrice was a never-ending city, a flat world of stone and metal encased within a gigantic box.

But this world was something else.

There was no sky of blue with a blazing local star above. No blanket of stars and glowing moon. No roaring gas-stars and eery sentinels.

Instead, he observed a concave landscape, a valley made of fragments of rough, diamond-like shapes. The land, if that's what you would call it, was brittle and grey, like dried up shells.

Above, a mirror image of the terrain below, another parched patchwork of shell-like platelets.

You could not see, even on the tiny world of Ilir, the world moving in the void; but here, movement was perceptible.

The more you looked, the more you saw that it was moving, oh so slowly, the two expanses travelling in opposite directions from one another.

The desolate, scaly land was scattered with the remains of many pulverised structures. Flattened. The destruction reaped on this land made Győr appear in comparatively good shape.

And every moment was accompanied with a crackle of electricity as lightning tore through the air and struck the barren terrain.

Great electric claws lashed out again and again at the dead world, emanating from nowhere but the space between the two drifting landmasses. A flash of existence then nothing.

He craned upwards and took in, through the ceaseless lightning and the bone-white destruction, a hole, the tiniest fracture in the surface above. A small aperture which must be much bigger up close. Beyond was a hint of colour, of green and orange and blue.

And in a flash, it was gone.

He was looking down at the ground and seeing beams of metal, many 'X' or 'L' shapes, scattered across the land. They all appeared to fit together, perhaps forming a large structure that had been destroyed.

THE WAY IS CLOSED

This world refocussed itself, twisting and curling around. Lines of ashen white and the blackest shadow whirled around then ceased. He was somewhere else now. The room appeared solid enough but was like a shape not yet formed, as if those swirling shades of white and black were paints mixed roughly together then left to dry. A warren-like subterranean world beneath the barren land above.

He drifted from one rounded, low-ceilinged chamber to the next. People slept under blankets in ragged, largely colourless clothing. He sensed whispering, muttering, but heard nothing. As he moved into the largest chamber, not much bigger than his classroom at school, he heard voices. He recognised the words as the lips moved, his mind received and understood them, the tone of voice, the emphasis, everything, but not a sound reached his ears in the dream.

The way is closed, but there is hope, spoke a woman; she had light grey shoulder-length hair, and was stern, direct, but not unkind. She wore a long, regal cloak of black with grey fur trim, like a queen who had not yet been allocated her throne. Her name came to him. He knew her name, as you often know things in dreams you did not know before. Everyone knew her name. Her name was Mariga.

Yeah, well, you may think there's hope, but as long as SHE's still here, there might as well not be, spoke a man. Tall, slim, with short, curly white hair, a face which could have been friendly yet had chosen to take a different path.

He paced up and down, gesticulating with his arms on every other word for emphasis. He wore scuffed shoes and an apron. His sleeves were rolled up, signifying that he was always ready to get his hands dirty. His name came to Krish too. His name was Andro.

I've heard she's come up with a new invention, said a woman who was too old to be a child in everything other than attitude. She was stick-thin, tall and lanky, but had a habit of standing slightly hunched over, as if she was attempting to diminish her own height out of embarrassment. *I do so love her inventions. It's what she does best. I hope it's a good one.*

She wore grey dungarees and a black-and-white striped shirt underneath. She was the only person in sight to display any colour on her clothing. The braces of her dungarees were spotted with badges. 'Haven't seen that smile in a while!' read one with a bright yellow face upon it. 'Mother saw the Star-bright & so will you!' was in the centre of a shiny, golden white star, beams of light spreading in every direction. Other pins depicted animals: tropical birds, great whales, and at the very top a large shiny metal pin cut into the shape of a majestic grey dog. He knew her name also. Her name was Lu'shaya.

Er, excuse me, where in the job description for 'leader' does it say 'has to be good at inventing stuff'? said Andro. *V'shiri is meant to lead, not invent!*

To be fair, that is what we need right now, said Mariga. *If there is a way across the Stormveldt, V'shiri's the one to find it.*

There is no way! said Andro. *People are starving! We need an election! Someone else to take charge while she focusses her energies on finding a way across! If there is one!*

An election would be too disruptive right now, said Mariga.

Eight months ago, maybe, but right now we need action. We can hold an election on the other side of the Stormvedlt.

IF we get there! said Andro. *And if we do, she'll win by a land-slide for leading us to safety! You know this! Why doesn't she stand down?*

Who would take over? said Mariga. *You, Andro?*

Andro huffed and looked at his feet. Under his breath he added: *'Course YOU'd defend her...*

Oh, I would see a sky again, said Lu'shaya dreamily. *Do you remember the pasturelands, Mariga? There were birds in the sky and fish in the rivers!*

I remember, said Mariga, inhaling deeply. *If only the towers were not struck down by lightning! There used to be mad notions of flying machines to take us to safety too.*

It'd strike a flying machine too! said Andro. *If that's what V'shiri's working on, then we have no hope!*

We travelled up through the plates over the centuries, said Mariga. *We've been stranded between plates before and we've escaped before. We must wait for V'shiri. She will have a plan.*

Waiting will kill us, muttered Andro.

There was a stirring in the gathering. A figure hobbled into the chamber. People moved aside. The woman moved on wooden crutches, one leg cut off just below the knee. As she came closer, a face emerged from behind her long, grey hair. The eyes were sharp and scanned the room indifferently.

Her name was known to all, for her name was V'shiri.

V'shiri made her way across the room, leaving silence in her wake. Lu'shaya produced a chair for her. V'shiri did not acknowledge the gesture but instead turned on her crutches and surveyed the room.

Well, well, well, said Andro flatly before V'shiri could speak. *If it isn't our glorious leader, at last.*

V'shiri was unmoved by Andro's sarcasm. She waited for a

moment to make sure that everyone was listening, the silence washing away Andro's words as they waited in anticipation.

I promised to return either with a solution or to pronounce our civilisation doomed, said V'shiri. *And I swore long ago never to do the latter. As long as we breathe, there is hope, and hope is what I deliver today. You are perhaps aware of the experiments I have been carrying out.*

Yeah, and flippin' noisy they've been as well! said Andro.

They have indeed made a great deal of sound, said V'shiri, not looking back at Andro. *And they will continue to do so. My friends, today is the day. Pack your belongings, prepare to leave! Take only what you can carry as you climb. This very day we shall escape into the next passing opening. A return to lush fields once more.*

Karsha, please! said Mariga softly. Only she would dare use their leader's first name. Her fingers curled around V'shiri's upper arm and many had mental images of the two of them lying entwined in bed. *You talk of climbing but there is no tower that can be built in a day and none that can withstand the Stormveldt.*

I will build such a tower and it shall be built today. There were gasps. *And yes, we shall ascend it to our new lives on the up-plate. Believe me, it will not be vulnerable to attack from lightning.*

She raised her hand. Several lab workers entered the room wheeling a trolley. On the trolley was a shining silver aerial, like a sword twice the length of a human with a thick metal base.

Conductors such as these will be placed around the valley by my operators and will absorb the worst the Stormveldt can throw at us.

Andro laughed hysterically. *Madness!*

V'shiri's face broke into a rare smile.

Lu'shaya poked her head forward sheepishly and spoke:

But... but surely the tower, if... if indeed you can erect such a

tower as fast as you say, which... I'm sure you can... being so much
taller, it will still surely take the brunt of the damage.

V'shiri shook her head and everyone waited, leaning in
somewhat.

Another hand gesture and a lab assistant entered holding a
small object. The item was placed on the floor. It was barely
knee-high. The object was a simple black metal cylinder,
welded into a cradle at a 45 degree angle, mounted onto a
square plate. A wire ran off the object to a machine covered in
many cables and dials being wheeled into the room by yet
another assistant.

The crowd's puzzlement threatened to bubble over into
frustration but still they waited for V'shiri to speak.

Have you ever stood close to a child as they screamed? To a
choirgirl as she holds a note? Or felt the thunder strike in your heart
as it arrives, every molecule in the air around reverberating? Yes...
sound is a tangible thing... If made physical, it would surely be a
force to be reckoned with, no? Every time I see a problem, I search for
a way to turn it around. Tortured by the sound of thunder in my
laboratory, desperately trying to conjure up a way to escape...

V'shiri waved her arm and everyone in the path of the
cylinder moved aside. Then her finger rose and fell a very short
distance. It was such a small action, but all saw it, and an
assistant took her cue. The assistant turned a dial and a
sonorous assault ushered forth from the cylinder on the
ground. A high, sharp drone, like a wetted finger around the
rim of a wine glass, cut through the air. Everyone placed their
hands on their ears as the great sound distorted and then
vanished.

Hands went slowly to people's sides. The only sound was
the pat-pat-pat of V'shiri's crutches as she hobbled forward.
She stopped short of the path of the cylinder. She removed the
glove of her left hand and lay it over the path. It hung there,

apparently laying across an invisible tube. There were gasps of astonishment.

This is how the path shall open for us once again. V'shiri gripped the invisible tube with her right hand and pulled up the entire weight of her body. People shrieked at the impossible sight. *But be mindful of one thing...* She lowered herself to the ground then removed the glove which still sat on the unseen tube. She turned it over to reveal how it was frayed on one side. *Hold on for too long and the sound will cut into you. And even when spread out, the top of the tower will be very steep.*

V'shiri waved her arm wildly. The cylinder was deactivated then many more assistants wearing gloves entered holding scores of cylinders mounted on plates, just like the first, but some at different angles. The people stood aside to let them through.

THIS IS IT! cried V'shiri. *This is how we make our way from this dank warren to the free lands and the pastures of green! We will live again! We will climb the tower of sound and I shall lead us to freedom!*

There was much cheering and celebration, and then time moved on, swirling seamlessly into a moment when almost everyone had filed out of the room. V'shiri concluded a discussion with one assistant then hobbled over to Lu'shaya. Together, they observed Mariga and Andro on the fringes of the room conversing in hushed tones.

They want me to step aside? said V'shiri.

They do, said Lu'shaya.

I would, gladly. But there is no time now. It will be a tough climb for many, me in particular. If I am left behind, then no matter. If my invention gets you all to the other side, you will find a way.

Oh, V'shiri! Please don't speak like that! You will make it!

And if I don't? Or if a new leader is decided... who will it be? Andro?

No. I think he prefers to be the voice of rebellion, shouting you down at every turn. He knows in his heart that he could not lead, but many may expect him to take the post.

He does not truly hate me. He just despises authority.

Yes. I think he'd fall apart if anything happened to you.

And what of Mariga?

She is decisive and fair but fears that none will accept her because of her class. Her love for you is also a barrier – she feels there is nothing she can do that you would not do better.

She will not always be in my shadow.

Oh, please don't say that, V'shiri! You have many years left!

Her time will come. And what about you?

Me? I am too young! I do not feel confident enough either.

You have experience from a young age. You possess wisdom and insight beyond your years. Never doubt it. V'shiri rubbed one of Lu'shaya's badges with her thumb until it shone. *You cling to childish things and some mock you for it, but your self-awareness, your lack of ego, even your doubts are your greatest strength. They ground you in compassion. Never let anyone tell you they are weaknesses. I will lead the pack to safety, but it is up to you to make life better for them on the other side.*

When you say 'you', my dear V'shiri... do you mean me or...?

V'shiri only smiled. Then she let go and moved away. Lu'shaya observed as V'shiri folded her arm into the small of Mariga's back and whispered in her ear. A startled Mariga departed. Then V'shiri spoke for some time with Andro in hushed tones.

Lightning ripped across Krish's vision and the dream shot forward in time to the sight of a desperate exodus. The ruin-strewn plate below and the great plate moving above, the enticing green patch directly overhead.

Lightning flashed in every direction, finding its way to the aerials, thundering into the ground. The world was rich with electricity. The mounted cylinders were stationed all around. Tiny people climbed an unseen structure stretching up through the sky, bisecting the heart of the Stormveldt.

And then, closer... closer...

Women, men and children, the latter often clinging to the shoulders of their parents, ascended with haste, their worldly possessions in backpacks. The lightning crackled all around. People shuddered but kept on going. They were close, so close! They could see it so clearly now – a hole around which the green of lichen and moss grew, a blue sky with wispy clouds stretched leisurely across it. Freedom was minutes away...

Bringing up the rear were Lu'shaya, then Mariga, then Andro. Just below them was V'shiri, her crutches fastened to her back.

Not far... not far... not far...

And then, coinciding with a mighty roar of thunder and a flash of lightning, was a cry from below.

V'SHIRI! screamed Lu'shaya. She scrambled down but Mariga cried out to her, shaking her head. Andro, closed his eyes, bowed his head, then kept on climbing.

A bolt from a crossbow had pierced V'shiri's chest. Blood started to pour. She winced as she tried to haul herself upwards, but she had no strength left. Her gloves became frayed. Then, with eyes screwed up tight and teeth gritted, blood came from her fingers.

Then it was over. She released herself, closed her eyes, allowing the gale to carry her away as she fell to the ground.

Lu'shaya screamed silently in the dream. Mariga called out to her lover. Then both kept climbing. The green of the hole leading up to the plate above surrounded them. Time condensed and space unfocussed and swirled into colours, and colours faded into blackness tinged with the orange of the fire burning on the other side of Krish's eyelids.

He awoke to a world aflame.

Heat bombarded him, suffocated him. He coughed and spluttered and blindly ambled forward. Then there was a great crunch underfoot. He looked down, observing the crushing truth of the situation he faced, here in the burning home of the dream-pedlar – the smashed dream-globe.

§

The old man watched his feet as he crossed the cobbles. The dream-pedlar had not run this fast in years. He swore it would kill him. He was wrong.

His path was blocked by a group of gentlemen. They did not seem eager to let him pass. In fact, they appeared, in comparison to all those fleeing all around, especially interested in him. He did not know the words they spoke, but he understood their intent from the knives in their hands.

They showed him the code for a dream. It was the same one as the boy's. He would do as they said, but he was not counting on as lucky an escape once his work was complete.

It's medicine time, always just before bed

But now Eva decides she'd rather be dead

It tastes all funny and doesn't really help

Once the Woman is gone, she'll spit and she'll yelp

So into a bottle the liquid she pours

She has chosen, she'd rather be in the wars

The Master calls it a draught, names it a cure

Eva pours it away, she'll live her life pure

43

THE ASH IN THE SILENCE

Ash fell on emptied streets and silence festered, gnawing at a friendship.

The two figures sat on the ground by the charred remains of a smouldering building, the warm scent of burnt wood drifting through the air. The shelled house was filled with rubble, the wall to the street collapsed and open to the world. The sink had been swept away with the wall and what remained of the pipe spurted freely onto the ground. The stream flowing through the gaps between the cobbles was thick and red.

Aemea struggled to look at ShadowThief. ShadowThief on the other hand, would not take her eyes off her friend.

Aemea and ShadowThief were still dripping blood into small puddles on the table. It was there, under nails, splattered across their clothes and emblazoned across their minds.

'I... I will forgive you for what you did, in time. I will thank you. I *do* thank you now... for saving my life. Again. So, so many times have you saved my life.'

ShadowThief nodded in her direction, her eyes deep with meaning. *And you. You have saved mine SO many times.*

'Yes. But... I have to process this... I have to... I know it will take time but.... What you did to him—'

She banged her fist on the table. Only Aemea could understand every word she gestured, all the meaning in her expressions. *He was a vile, evil man who deserved everything he got! It lasted a second! I did not know what I had done until it was over!*

'Shad... No one should live through that pain... We... we shouldn't kill anymore, Shad. I will not see another person die like that. Not by my hand or yours.

It couldn't control it! It was so fast! I had to stop him from getting away! From ever hurting you again!

'We must go. Get away from these streets. Follow the lost millions who venture beyond the borough and explore the farthest reaches of the City. We should go as far as we can go and then go farther! Far enough away for our pasts never to catch up with us. And we must be different. What you did to him... you did it to yourself... You carved up your own soul until I couldn't see my friend anymore...'

Aemea looked up with teary eyes at the pleading expression on ShadowThief's face.

I'm sorry! He was going to kill you! I'm sorry... I'm sorry... Please...

Aemea took a deep breath, calming herself. She spoke simply.

'I think I should tell you, ShadowThief, because people don't say things when they should or until it's too late for the other to say anything back: I love you, ShadowThief. Not in the way that people do when they kiss or get married or all that other stuff. I love you as a friend who understands me so completely that I don't have to utter a single word, and it causes me great pain to think of being apart from you for any substantial length of time.'

ShadowThief closed her eyes, sucked in all the hurt and love, and placed her hand on Aemea's face. In answer, Aemea matched the gesture, shutting her eyes and cupping Shadow-Thief's face in return. They sat there like this for a time, not daring to look to see if the world had collapsed around them.

§

Krish wandered in a daze through the abandoned streets to find the grand station stretching out in a square before him. The crowds had smashed the windows of the station and forced their way in, the guards shouting after them.

'Krish!'

Krish turned to Aemea and ShadowThief rushing towards him, Elek not far behind. Krish embraced his two friends tightly.

'People are storming the station,' said Aemea. 'They're trying to get onto the train, but armed guards are holding them back.'

They headed in the direction of the entrance to the service tunnel.

'Did you find it?' enquired Aemea.

'Yes,' said Krish. 'But the dreamglobe ended up smashed.'

What?! exclaimed ShadowThief.

'Oh, no, no, no! I saw it! I watched it! I'm trying to remember all the details...'

Aemea took out a wad of paper and began to take notes as they walked. They stopped for a while as they reached the tunnel.

'Such a strange world,' said Aemea. 'I can't quite picture it with all its floating plates and all those storms appearing out of nowhere. Come on! We'll discuss it on the train.'

Elek looked around carefully before leading them into the tunnel. 'The guards know nothing of this place. They explode all tunnels. They want no one to leave.'

'Why?!' said Krish.

'Government says stay and fight. Nobody surrender! Only coward.' Elek spat on the ground in disgust then led them into the tunnel while the guards at the station were distracted by another bashing at a boarded-up door.

Elek led them through the dark tunnel and onto the tracks. Krish looked back. The high walls and well-guarded station cut the population off from the tracks. A great number of frenzied Győri citizens were now trying to climb onto the walls to get to the train, but guards were shouting and pointing their rifles at them to quell the pandemonium.

The Necropolis Railway locomotive sat steaming at the opposite end of the train of trucks from earlier, ready to depart. Elek rejoined his men, and they stretched out along the train, rifles ready. The sides of the trucks were open, revealing empty interiors. There were no bodies in sight.

'Hurry! Hurry!' said Elek, ushering them over. 'Get on board! One truck each! You help them onboard!'

'Where are the bodies?' asked Krish as he clambered onto an empty truck.

'The dead can wait...' said Elek, his gaze remaining on central station.

ShadowThief and Aemea climbed onto the next couple of trucks.

Minutes passed and then it happened. A great BOOM! and one of the walls at the end of the station exploded. A guard was hurled into the air and a crush of people rushed forward towards the train.

Krish braced himself as the waves of fleeing citizens came into view, desperate and fierce, tearful and screaming, all manner of people headed directly for them.

Elek cried out and the locomotive began to *chuff* and inch forward. The guards along the wall by the station shouted and aimed their rifles high, but none fired. The train picked up speed as a group of young men overtook the rest and were helped aboard by Elek and his men. Next, young women and men began to jump aboard, dragging their children and some of their older family members with them. Krish tried to help them up, but he hasn't the strongest and most hauled themselves aboard.

There was a far-off BOOM! as the Ankarans continued shelling the streets of Győr. The sound became distant as the locomotive accelerated. Those who were not fast enough or strong enough were left behind, many of them elders.

Everyone sat there in a sweaty heap, laboured breathing mingling with the sounds of the speeding train. Krish looked about; the trucks were scarcely a quarter full.

44
THE FLOWERS ON HER GRAVE

There were no flowers on his grave. On hers, freshly cut lilies.

Isri Stroever cut back the rosemary growing through the metal slats of the graveyard from the woman's grave, but would not touch where the shrub was spreading across the man's.

The graves read:

ISAIRIS STROEVER
BELOVED HUSBAND OF JANE
FATHER OF ISRI AND HELENA
TAKEN FROM US BEFORE HIS TIME

JANE STROEVER
BELOVED WIFE OF ISAIRIS
MOTHER OF ISRI AND HELENA
DELIVERED HERSELF UNTO HIS MERCY
DEVIL SPARE HER

The raingrate overhead dripped but did not unburden itself. Stroever waited for his anguish to be quenched but the moment did not come.

§

The graveyard, on the roof between two taller buildings, was a short walk from the ancestral home of the Stroevers and their factory on Ha'penny Row.

In the poison kitchen at the factory, Madam Ckrystafis was at work brewing dreams as Thira watched intently.

'This one Mr Stroever commissioned me personally to make,' said Madam Ckrystafis, indicating a globe full of inky liquid. 'It is the life of Jane Stroever.'

'That's Stroever's mum, yeah?' said Thira.

'The wife of the late Isairis, yes. It's very carefully constructed but he finds it a little painful to watch, I fear. He watches it rarely but mulls it over frequently. With memory-based dreams you can use items such as pages of a diary. We used fragments from her private journals. Some moments were added by Stroever. She stopped keeping a journal towards the end of her life.'

'Can I see?'

'If you wish...'

Ckrystafis lit the flame under the dream. Smoke of all the colours of the night hiding beyond the black rose from the dream-globe. It passed over Thira and a NightTime scene unfolded. As the dream took hold, he skipped through the life of Jane Stroever, starting with the warm, comforting smell of cakes being baked for a young girl's birthday many years ago...

...37...38...39....40...41...42...

As the boy counted, the young girl with long, straggly brown hair raced around the yard.

...46...47...48...49...50...51...

She scrambled up the drainpipe.

...55...56...57...58...59...60...

She hauled herself up.

...71...72...73...74...75...76...

She tiptoed across the roof.

...83...84...85...86...87...88...

She stopped for a moment and peered back down into the yard.

...90...91...92...93...94...95...

The young boy was in the corner, his face against the wall. It was dark, only sentinellight in the long night. If the boy turned, he'd see her clearly. She bent forward, keeping her eyes on the boy in the yard. She placed her hand on the glass of the skylight then, as she shifted her weight onto that arm, the glass cracked...

The mists of memories swirled as the young Jane fell...

They cleared to reveal Jane in a hospital bed, her head shaved and bandaged, her arm in a sling. She looked up at the orangey starlight of a hot day pouring through the intact skylight overhead.

The girl next to her spoke...

Hannah Thurlow is having orange juice! I bet it'll make her go to the toilet lots and she'll have to use that machine where you can see the wee! You have to come and see, Jane!

No, I can't. I can't get out of bed with my arm.

Ugh! You and your silly arm! When's it getting better?

I don't know. They said it might not. My left arm might never work as well as it did, they say. But not because it was broken, but because my head was too.

Ha-ha! Jane broke her brain!

Stop it!

Okay, okay! Look! Daddy made me a quiz! Let's play! Though I bet I win!

I don't want another stupid quiz! And I don't care who wins! Why can't we just play to have fun? I hate it when someone has to lose...

The mists twisted round again and the scene refocussed...

The young Jane, now in her early twenties, stood at the grand drinks reception. Her shoulder length hair was chestnut brown and slightly curly. She was the only woman present who was not a predominantly silent accessory on the arm of a man. She held a vael glass in her right hand while her left hung limp at her side. Occasionally she flexed her fingers then curled them into a ball as if to keep them warm. She stood there listening to the words of a well-dressed gentleman who very much resembled a young Isri Stroever, but was far more boisterous.

You work? My word, that is most admirable! said Isairis Stroever. *I know just how you feel. Just how you feel! It is tough! And if your concern is the disparity between men and women's salaries, have no fear! Once I've completed my current project, I shall try my utmost to persuade a local dignitary I know, lovely chap, to bring it up in parliament. But I have to say I'm most impressed that you've managed to sustain yourself as an unmarried woman. Most impressive!*

Jane forced out a bitter smile. *Well, thank you, Master Stroever, for your kind yet patronising words, but I would rather roast to death in Devil's fiery arse than entertain another conversation with one of your ilk. And, no – you do not know how I feel.* She flexed her left arm in irritation. *Not that you would understand, but getting work as a typist when you have a certain...'condition' is not easy. You are paid by the word and if you fall behind, they sack you and others are reluctant to hire you. And that's before the disparity you mention even comes into effect.* She swiftly finished her vael then went to depart. *A pleasure to meet you,* she added flatly.

You're right. Something in his tone made her stop and turn back to face him. It was as if she had not truly been looking at him previously. *You are of course correct. Everything I say I twist to become about myself. I am truly sorry. Tell me more of your work and I will listen, I promise.*

Their eyes were locked together as the scene changed first to the joyous occasion of their wedding and then to the birth of their first child. The dream lingered on the second scene for a moment, Jane in the hospital bed clutching a baby, while Isairis Stroever stood by the window watching the sentinels looming overhead.

What better name for a child born the fade before Ironfeast...? said Jane.

We can talk about it later, said Isairis Stroever, not looking away from the table. *It is hardly important.* The cold distance in Stroever's voice was now sounding more like his son's tone of voice, thought Thira.

You are disappointed...?

Isairis Stroever inhaled deeply. *We can talk about it later. For now...* He turned and pointed to the paperwork laid out on the table.

Jane scowled, clutching the child close. *Urgh! If we must continue with this charade, then I imagine you'd prefer Isri after yourself?*

Yes... he said. *Isri will do...*

The odd scene remained for a moment, a cloud of awkwardness hanging over them.

Then it faded into another time, another hospital bed, another child.

Helena, she said. *I suppose this time you'll permit me to name her?*

I suppose, he said.

You used to listen to me. Now Jane Stroever is just a name you drop into conversation to remind people of your status as a married man.

Whatever you say, my dear...

The scene shifted to the family in front of a roaring fire, wrapping paper and presents on the floor.

The younger child was chasing her older sibling. The latter ran into another room, dropping something on the way. The younger picked it up and went and sat in her mother's lap.

Mummy! Mummy! It's broken! said the younger, passing an ornate, shiny little red sleigh to Jane.

Helena, my dear, it's fine! said Jane. *Your father will fix it.*

It's my favourite and a certain someone broked it! Helena glared across the room at her older sibling.

Now, now, let's not make silly accusations.

Why not? SOMEONE's always breaking my things and ruining everything!

Now, come on, Helena! Do you remember when you first got this? It was one of your first Ironfeasts! It snowed then, too; the rain-grates froze and filled the streets with whiteness! It was so, so cold, but the stars were out and it was wonderful! You both went across the ice at Chronometer Dock on your beloved sleigh. You were the best of friends back then!

I'm never letting it out of my sight again! said Helena, clutching the little red sleigh close. *It's my favourite!*

A moment later the sleigh was snatched away from her again. The two parents laughed at the children chasing each other around the room as the scene faded into another.

The same room came into focus but all light and colour from the Ironfeast celebrations were gone. The embers shimmered dimly in the grate. Jane leant forward over the dying fire, Isairis a few strides away. She quivered and sobbed.

Jane, please... A divorce would be...

Of great disadvantage to your public image...?

Jane—

No... NO! NO! NO! NO! As she spoke, she lashed out with her fist, smashing it against the wall. Then she redirected the final two strokes to her own face.

Isairis Stroever did not react.

Suddenly, Jane turned to her husband. *Will you do nothing? Say nothing? I am happy to receive help, but first you must accept the diagnosis I offer you!*

You are suffering from no malady, Jane.

I beg to differ.

The doctors can find nothing physically wrong with you.

That is because there is nothing PHYSICALLY wrong with me!

Jane!

I will take the children! We cannot continue if you will not accept my illness is real, Isairis!

You must cease drinking, Jane.

When I drink, I am thinking clearly! I know the tough decisions that must be made! But I have the sense and restraint to wait until the morrow to see if my conclusions remain the same. The drink is not the cause of my sickness, and neither are you. But you are becoming a barrier to my recovery, Isairis.

I will pour that dammed rum into the river-street!

I am not mad! I am sick, Isairis! I know that life is the only way and that nothing is worse than nothing, but I fear that a moment will pierce me and I shall inflict upon myself a permanent solution to a temporary problem.

Jane...

I ask for your help in accepting my diagnosis, Isairis. I cannot be alone in the belief that sickness of the mind is a very real disease! Tell me you believe me!

There was a weight in the air between them.

Take Helena, said Isairis Stroever. *But please...*

Jane was shaking, her mouth shut, quivering breaths escaping her nostrils. *I will not go without her...*

A moment passed, then both turned to see Helena standing at the bottom of the stairs, fuming.

It's always about her now! screamed Helena. *Why is it always about her! She ruins everything!*

Jane Stroever rushed over to her daughter. *Helena! Please!*

As Jane held the agitated Helena, Isairis looked up, catching the eye of the eldest Stroever child, who stood caped in shadow at the top of the stairs, coldly taking in the scene below.

The mists cleared and the poison kitchen came back into view. Madam Ckrystafis gave Thira a little smile.

'Blimey, Stroever's parents didn't have the happiest of marriages,' said Thira.

'Hmmm...' said Madam Ckrystafis.

'And what 'appened to Jane in the end...?'

'Her prediction proved correct, tragically. As you may have heard, Isairis Stroever was murdered by associates of the criminal Valkyrys Hanch. Jane was navigating a spell of mind-sickness at the time and, although she seemed about to recover, her husband's death tipped her over the edge. Helena was taken into the care of Jane's sister, while young Isri, as everyone knows, hid away on his father's factory floor, growing up in the wilds.'

'And does 'e think that, what d'ya call it... "mind-sickness" is real?'

'Isri does, yes.'

'Unlike 'is dad.'

'Yes... As I said, he dreams this dream with increasing rarity, but it is frequently on his mind.'

§

In the rooftop graveyard some streets away, Isri Stroever peered at the grave of Isairis out of the corner of his eye, but he would not look away from Jane Stroever's.

The raingrate continued to dribble on him from above but the downpour was not forthcoming. The living had no place here yet still he remained.

Eventually, he departed, leaving the dead to their own devices.

45
THE ARROW & THE INDECISION

Aemea ran her pencil over the page of the notebook in her hand, drawing a line through one of the names on her list:

V'shiri - leader, wise, fair
Mariga - second in command, V'shiri's lover, good leader, not intellectual
Andro - very vocal, wants to be in charge, irrationally angry
Lu'shaya - kind, intelligent, lacking confidence

Krish, Aemea and ShadowThief were sat on the floor of the truck as it thundered through the night, surrounded by several groups of exhausted Győri citizens who were too tired to talk. Krish also had his list of the pictorial safe tiles to hand:

Arrow
Medicine bottle

Water

Rope

Lantern

Stove

Dagger

Hand

Herb

Piston

Mirror

Needle and thread

Shoes

Wolf's head

Waves

Ear horn

Crutch

Stairs

Cherries

Ruby

Pestle and mortar

'So, their leader,' began Aemea, 'V'shiri, is killed. I suppose in these stories it's all about who did it.'

ShadowThief shrugged and brushed an imaginary speck of dirt away, *No, that's not the important thing.*

'Yeah,' said Krish. 'It doesn't seem like it's about that. Besides, it seems pretty obvious who did it.'

ShadowThief pointed at the name 'Andro' on the list.

'Indeed', said Aemea. 'He is clearly a vocal opponent of V'shiri, according to your account at least.'

'But then Lu'shaya was saying that Andro would never do anything other than complain,' said Krish. 'No one seemed to think of him as a real threat.'

'But you did say he was farther down the tower when

V'shiri was assassinated? And that he looked guilty? So it must be him?'

'I mean, it must be. And she was shot by an arrow so...' Krish tapped the word 'arrow' on his list of tiles.

ShadowThief countered this by pointing at the word 'stairs'.

'Yeah,' said Krish. 'Climbing stairs, a tower, whatever, was kinda what it was all about.'

'Though getting shot by an arrow seemed to be the point the dream was leading up to,' said Aemea. 'But also...' She pointed at the words 'ear horn'. 'It was all about building a tower to escape the place they were trapped in. And it was made of sound so...'

ShadowThief shook her head: *It can't be all three!*

'Yeah, and V'shiri was on crutches,' said Krish. 'So it could be that too.'

'And these kind of puzzle dreams are not meant to be immediately obvious,' said Aemea. 'It must take some deduction. So perhaps the murderer is not who we suspect.'

'Yeah, but it *was* obvious,' said Krish. 'It was definitely the bloke Andro.'

They sat in silence for some time and Krish stared up at the trail of smoke from the locomotive, only just lighter in colour than the endless expanse of night beyond.

ShadowThief shattered the quiet by gesturing animatedly, almost knocking into some of the citizens crouching nearby: *It's not about who killed V'shiri! It's about who she wanted to replace her!*

'So, not Andro then,' said Aemea.

ShadowThief examined her own tattoos in the light of a passing sentinel, showing all the figures embracing. A thought struck her and she began gesturing at all three of them: *It's about working together.*

'Yes!' said Aemea. 'V'shiri wants Mariga and Lu'shaya to rule jointly. It was something she was heavily implying.'

'But what about Andro?' asked Krish and the answer came to him as he ran through the dream again in his head. 'Mariga and Lu'shaya feared that Andro would undermine them. And V'shiri was worried that there was no good time to hand over power, so she persuades Andro to assassinate her during the climb. Yes! I saw Andro and V'shiri chatting quietly to each other! V'shiri knows that that's the only time her lover Mariga won't turn back. Mariga's strong and decisive and I think she probably had an idea about what would happen.'

'And Andro would be too ashamed to take over after that?'

'I think so. He looked pretty down after V'shiri died.'

'So it's about Mariga coming to power?'

No! said ShadowThief, pointing at her tattoos again. *It's about togetherness! I don't know how but it's about that!*

'I think you're right, Shad,' said Aemea. 'It must be about Margia and Lu'shaya ruling together. The only issue is, what on this list symbolises that...?'

They descended into silence again. The three of them sat back, lost in thought, enjoying the rocking of the train, though creeping dread was sweeping over Krish. Even after cracking the second dream, they still had to rescue Thira, find and solve the final dream, and get back into Ryker-Veere's house.

ShadowThief noticed Krish's unease. *You okay?* she said.

'Er, yeah,' he said. 'Yeah, I'm just... not feeling great.'

ShadowThief's eyebrows furrowed, asking a question as she rubbed her tummy then tapped her head. Krish tapped his head in reply – it was his mind, not his body, that was unwell. ShadowThief nodded.

Then, after some reflection in which Krish browsed the list of safe tiles again, she held out her hand. Reluctantly, Krish handed her the slip of paper. She turned it over, took a pencil and scrawled a note:

To heal, first you must name your disease.

Krish digested this phrase for a time, then nodded.

Family motto, said ShadowThief.

Then she shifted to one side, tucking her knees under her chin, clenching and unclenching her fists.

Krish then noticed that Aemea had been watched, her eyebrows raised.

'That's very unusual,' she said softly to Krish. 'She hardly ever writes and almost never speaks of her family.'

'Is she okay?' He observed ShadowThief continuing to clench and unclench her fists.

'There's a lot she's mulling over.'

'Unprocessed trauma,' said Krish, suddenly remembering the phrase his sister Joshi had used when talking about his dyspraxia diagnosis.

'I suppose...'

Suddenly, Aemea seemed to jolt as if she had silently hiccoughed.

'Something on the track...' she said.

'Should we... do something...?' said Krish.

'No, it's fine. Just keep an eye on the time.'

Not long after, the truck shook violently for a moment, but kept going.

'What was that?' said Krish.

'I don't know,' said Aemea. 'Just something on the track. But how long has it been?'

Maybe ten minutes, said ShadowThief.

'Ten minutes?!' exclaimed Aemea. 'It can't keep getting

shorter... It has to stop at some point or... I don't know... I don't know...'

At the next junction they jumped off and made their way across the tracks, cutting through a depot filled with rusting old engines and found their way to the port street of Barkan. They boarded a steamer and headed for a cramped cabin with four bunks on the lower deck.

'I think we've come to a decision,' said Aemea. 'Once this is done... we're done. Thanks to you, Shad and I will have enough money to go a long way from these streets. Many neighbourhoods away.'

Another borough, perhaps.

'Well, I mean, that's a mad idea but... maybe. A whole different borough...? Who knows.'

'Cool,' said Krish, reminding himself that boroughs were the size of planets in KnockThrice. 'Mad dream but yeah, go for it.'

ShadowThief narrowed her eyes at Krish. Aemea was pulling a similar perplexed expression.

'Cool,' said Krish. 'Sorry... "cool" means like... "good", ya know.'

'It wasn't that word,' said Aemea. 'What did you mean "mad dream"? We won't be going anywhere near dreams after this. We're through with dreams.'

'Oh, erm, I meant... it's like "dreams" in my world doesn't just mean, well, you know, "dreams", "visions". "Dreams" can mean... like... ideas, ambitions. Things you want to do. Dreams are good things. Stuff you aim towards.'

Aemea sat for a time as if a tranquil and wondrous vision was playing out before her eyes. She awoke from her daydream and looked at ShadowThief, who gave her an encouraging nod.

'Dreams... as a positive word. How interesting. I'd love to travel far enough away to find where dreams are something good. Dreams... Perhaps there's a borough out there were people dream naturally...'

'Yep! That's what happens in my world. And in Thira's. Dreams are free! You don't need dreamglobes or anything!'

'Dreaming for free...' The idea shone before Aemea's eyes. 'Cool!'

'So where are we heading now?' said Krish.

Aemea looked at ShadowThief who elaborated with hand gestures: *To see an old associate.*

46

THE STAFF IN HIS HAND

'I tell ya, seriously, I ever see 'im again I'll punch 'im directly on the nose! Bloody idiot!'

'He makes you mad?' said Madam Ckrystafis to Thira. 'This friend of yours? Krish...?'

'You're bloody right 'ee makes me mad! Selfish bugger.'

'You think of him a lot...'

Thira had been caught off guard. He stared at Madam Ckrystafis across the workbench, a knowing smile on her face.

'Guess so,' said Thira, looking down at his work, chopping drashig leaves. He just wanted to keep Ckrystafis talking, see what he could discover, but his anger at Krish was genuine. If the selfish git was there right now, he'd absolutely punch him. But the important thing would be to have him there. He didn't want to be in this world at all, but hanging around with Krish wasn't bad. Not bad at all. Most of the time.

'Goin' through all this for 'is benefit. Not mine!' Thira went on.

'You think he is coming for you?'

'Maybe,' he said softly, coming to be resigned to the fact

that Krish had abandoned him. He could detect a smile out of the corner of his eye.

'There, there, Thira. You are at home here now. We will make many excellent poisons together! Even without the help of you "m-gick".'

'Magic!'

'Ah, yes! "Madge-ick". An elemental force not present in the City. Until you arrived, so I'm told. Maybe we will let you practise it again soon. It will help us, perhaps.'

Madam Ckrystafis was currently weighing ingredients on small brass scales then adding them to a dreamglobe.

'This one is memory based,' said Ckrystafis.

'Thought you said they were all oil-based?' said Thira, just adding a hint of stupidity to his tone of voice.

'They are. But some are fantasies, wild imaginings, while others are based on memories.'

'Oh! Like Jane Stroever's? That 'ad some of 'er diary in it, right?'

'Exactly. I used a corner of the page from her journal. It didn't even have any writing on it. It was a scrap of the page. The oil fills in the rest from that tiny piece. This saves us from wasting the whole page and we can create the dream over and over again until the page is gone. And if the dream has to contain something very specific, such as a photograph, it must also have a small amount of the original picture.'

Madam Ckrystafis produced a sepia photograph of a young boy, tore off the tiniest amount from the corner and dropped it into the flask. She drenched the ingredients in oil then placed the flask on an unlit burner. She scanned the room and, not finding what she was looking for from her seat, settled on Thira. The smile on her face was mischievous.

After a few moments, Thira realised it was an invitation. He leant forward and held his finger under the burner. He thought of fire and fury, concentrating hard on something that made him angry (which right now was Krish) but he didn't allow the anger to overwhelm him. Red sparked from his finger for a fraction of a second and then the burner was alight.

'You are most kind, Thira,' said Madam Ckrystafis, her smile both affectionate and a little patronising. Thira was pleased that she was treating him like a stupid child – if he kept this up, he could learn more than she would realise.

'There's a lot your magic could help with in dream brewing. Perhaps we shall bend the rules a little. But be wary, young Thira. You'll never know when something you eat or drink is poisoned, so be careful not to dispose of the only person who knows how to cure you. Now, let us add a little hasrakine and dastari.'

'Thought you said they weren't poisons...?'

'They are not. They make the dreams catch hold of you and not let go. How do you say it?'

'Addictive?'

'Yes! Exactly! Exactly right, young Thira! Keep people coming back for more. Now, what poison shall we try on you today, Thira?'

'Why don't you just ask me some more questions or something?'

'An excellent suggestion! And I shall only poison you if I am sure you are lying!'

'Er, yeah. Sure.'

'But first...' She produced a large globe from one of the cupboards. The liquid within was inky-black. 'Perhaps you can help me with this.'

'What is it?'

'A most special project that I am working on for Mr Stroever. Now, I pride myself on my skills in creating slow-release poisons, but this one has evaded me. It requires a touch more heat to pass through it all at once, but it must not boil. It is hard to do this correctly. But perhaps you...?'

'I can't really... my magic—'

'Not to worry! Not to worry, little Thira! I was going to pop out for ten minutes to check a few things with Mr Stroever, but instead I shall spend a few hours trying to fix this problem once more.'

Madam Ckrystafis stared at him expectantly. Time alone would mean more time to experiment with his staff. It was all a little too tempting.

Thira extended his finger and touched the globe full of inky liquid. A spark of red and the globe glowed. Madam Ckrystafis smiled darkly, shut her eyes and inhaled through her nostrils, enjoying the bitter scent in the air.

'Superb!' She put away the dreamglobe and produced a silver flask, which she placed on the workbench. 'I shall return shortly. Kindly refrain from poisoning yourself while I am gone.'

'Sure.'

Madam Ckrystafis made her exit, turning the key in the lock, and within moments Thira had pulled out his lean, golden staff.

'Yes! Come on... come on... Slowly... slowly...'

He turned the golden staff in slow circles. Every cell in his body became excited and tingled with magic, which now flowed into the staff. Gradually the lines it traced in the air turned into swirls of colour. Instead of magic jabbing violently at the world, it was concentrated, refined.

He pointed at the cup and gently lifted it up.

'Yes...! Yes!' He looked around. He was still alone, but he had to be cautious. He lowered the cup. 'Blimey, it's like learning to walk again.' He glanced around once more and then his gaze fell on the manacles.

'Right... let's see if we can try somethin' a little more sophistimacated...'

He concentrated hard on the top of the bolt that slotted into the lock of the manacle. He glared. He hated it. He despised it. He sliced through it in his mind, like it was a finger through water.

A ring of red around the top of the bolt. *Just a little more, just a little, just—*

Panic flooded his mind. He'd been aware of the footsteps for a few seconds but had paid them no heed. He flinched at the sound of the key turning. The door opened. Thira jolted his arm downwards and dropped the golden staff which clattered to the floor. *Did she hear it? Did she see it?*

Thira turned and was surprised to see not Madam Ckrystafis but Stroever standing in the doorway, his clothes dotted with raindrops, his hair soaked, his skin shining wet. They exchanged glances and Thira was aware of how startled he must appear. Stroever looked haggard. He stared at Thira for a time.

'Go ahead, Thira,' said Stroever. 'Try and poison her. She'll be most amused.'

Thira followed his line of sight to the chopped drashig leaves and the two cups in front of him.

'Madam Ckrystafis always expects her pupils to try and poison her,' said Stroever. 'Though she generally turns the tables on such behaviour. Just so you are aware. Is she...?'

'Just popped out to find you.'

Stroever raised an eyebrow a touch. He let out a brief chuckle. He noticed the silver flask on the workbench, picked it up and broke the seal. 'To tell me this is ready, no doubt. Though I have some other business to discuss with her.' He drank down the thick black mixture in one gulp and then pulled a grotesque face. '*Heggarum santai.*'

'Oh. What's that?'

'None of your concern, is what it is, Thira. Though I don't mind sharing that it is most unappetising and I am glad that I only have to take it every few months.' He pulled another face.

'Some kinda medicine?'

'No. I could live the rest of my life, however long that may be, perfectly well without it. Though, for certain reasons, it is useful.'

Stroever eyed the grand, cushioned chair on the edge of the room. He strolled up to the chair, slumped into it and folded his gloved hands in his lap. He immediately closed his eyes.

'Carry on with your work, Thira. I shall wait for Madam Ckrystafis's return. I require an update on a certain project from her before the launch.'

'Oh, right. Guess I'm not invited to this swanky do?'

'That will be for us to decide. You may have your uses. I shall discuss with Anders upon his imminent arrival.'

'Right ho. 'E gonna be chained up in a kitchen or stayin' somewhere nicer?'

'I have booked him into the Starwane, his regular haunt in these streets.' Stroever half opened his eyes. 'You know, Thira, I contacted the Starwane to make sure his room would be prepared, and they mentioned a rather curious request his assistant de Clercq had telegrammed through.' The drowsy Stroever allowed his eyes to close again.

'Oh, yeah...?'

'He has asked for four porters to be ready upon his arrival.'

'He don't travel light, I guess?'

'Interestingly for such an extravagant gentleman, he does.'

'Perhaps 'e needs somethin' 'eavy carryin'.'

There was a hint of a smile on Stroever's face. 'Yes... perhaps he does...'

Stroever lay there silently in the chair with his eyes closed.

Thira hesitated for a time, his eyes looking at the tabletop, knowing that the staff was somewhere underneath.

'She's good, isn't she?' said Stroever.

Thira had been silent for too long. He was convinced that anything he said would somehow give away the object under the table.

'She got the truth out of you yet?' said Stroever, his eyes still shut.

'Er, not yet, sir,' said Thira, playing the loyal little puppy dog.

Stroever let out a little laugh. 'She will.'

Thira digested this and then, as Stroever seemed to move towards sleep, continued chopping. His foot searched the floor but couldn't seem to find the staff. It couldn't have rolled – *ah! There it is! If he could jus—*

'She worked for my father, you know,' said Stroever, quite suddenly. 'Towards the end. When I... I was ill. He was looking for a cure.'

'Oh yeah,' said Thira. 'You ever find one? A cure?'

Stroever flexed the fingers of his gloved hands. 'I am surviving, Thira. Surviving. But given time... we shall see...'

'So, what does she do now? Ckrystafis?'

'Vital work,' said Stroever. He smiled broadly, his eyes still shut. 'The City will change soon, Thira. Believe me... it'll all change...'

'Still knocking about is 'ee?'

'Who?'

'Yer old man?' Thira hoped that the more he pretended not to know, the more he may learn.

Stroever did not stir, but his hesitance to answer was something Thira took as a warning to tread carefully.

There was silence for a good minute. As slowly as he could,

chopping loudly to mask the sound of wood scraping across stone, Thira brought the staff closer to him.

'It is a strange feeling.' Stroever's words made Thira jump. 'To realise you are older than your father. He was no great age when he died.'

'Might I ask——?'

'He died of...' Stroever was quiet for a time. 'There is no pleasant way to say it. Isairis Stroever was murdered.'

'Oh.'

'Who did it? That was what you were going to ask...'

'Well, to be honest——'

'A man by the name of Valkyrys Hanch. Hanch was one of ——' Isri Stroever, his eyes shut, leaning back in the chair, was becoming more and more groggy, '——one of his earliest investors. And uncle to... to his wife, Jane. My mother. Hanch... unpleasant character. Long dead now, of course. Threatened him over unpaid debts. Many times. Father never took him seriously. 'Til it was too late. Hid in a room above the Beggar's Lantern. Hanch's men found him. Cut his throat. Dumped his body in the river. Though it was his own fault really. Idiotic man. Was the end of the Eighty Fade Night. The darkness...' He inhaled deeply. 'The darkness combined with this was too much for... for... Jane....'

'Your mother?'

'My... yes.'

'And you mean she...?'

'Yes... I never knew... of course...'

Stroever yawned broadly.

'I was... lost...'

Stroever was practically asleep now.

'On the factory floor... It was her fault... but I forgave her...'

'Who? Yer mum?'

'What?'

'Whose fault was it...? Ya said it was her own fault...? Was it?!'

Stroever did not answer.

Thira had the staff balanced on his toe now. He delicately brought the tip up towards his hand.

'This was where ya grew up, yeah?' said Thira, fearing silence would give him away. 'In the factory?'

'Factory... Trees... so tall... So peaceful... peaceful...'

'So, you was lost...when your father died...?'

'Ecarian flu...'

'Ecary-what?'

Thira gripped the staff between his thumb and index finger. He lifted the staff up, straightened it out and pointed towards the sleeping man. Thira turned the staff in circles in the air, purple and blue and green light washing soothingly over Stroever.

'Ecarian flu,' repeated Stroever, his head dipping down, now no more than muttering in his slumber.

'But you just said he was murdered...' Thira was genuinely puzzled.

'The trees... green... so peaceful... so peaceful...'

'You were talkin' about your father... What 'appened to 'im...?'

'So peaceful... peaceful... She... so peaceful...'

And then, for some time before Madam Ckrystafis returned, Stroever spoke in his sleep. Thira listened with increasingly wide eyes and keen ears as Stroever spoke the truth.

'Eva, now we must play, the Master insists'

Pieces thrown to the floor, young Eva resists

'I don't understand why we're playing again!

I know I'll lose worser than I did just then!'

The Woman retorts, 'It's all about learning'

Little Eva wishes the board it was burning

'Silly mum-dumb!' says Eva, now she is riled

The Woman is angry, 'Don't call me that, child!'

Eva hurls the board to the floor, flees the room

She'll find her secret place and hide in the gloom

47

THE CAPTAIN & THE THIEF

Fenric Stavast, former captain of Isri Stroever's ship, sat patiently waiting, his hat and a tot of rum on the table in front of him.

Across the bar from the old captain, an accordion played, sailors drank and jollity infested the air. Stavast was content to be lonely, keeping to the shadows at the side of the room, away from the merrymaking.

He was not alone for long.

The girl stalked into the inn from the oft-neglected eastern door, leading to the smaller of the river-street island's wharfs. The gas lanterns hanging from the rafters shone light onto the glimmering tattoos which marked her face and arms, but no one paid her any heed. The shadows appeared to lean in towards her, as if to hide her from prying eyes.

Stavast did not move. His eyes, no more than rusted nails driven into the sockets many a year ago, could only see when the wind threw salt and moisture in his path. Away from the sea he saw very little, least of all the knife held comfortably in her grip.

The girl slowed as she came up behind the captain. Her footsteps made not a sound. In the shelter of the shadows, she was no more than a ghost. She held up the knife and leaned in towards him. She saw the scar slashed across the back of his right hand, like a mouth cut into his skin. She then placed the blade across the years-old scar, firmly but without enough pressure to break the skin.

Captain Stavast looked up, warm familiarity in his eyeless gaze.

'Aye, many a stormy fade has passed since this blade last made its home upon my flesh. It was welcome then... it is welcome now.'

ShadowThief removed the blade and pulled up a chair opposite the captain.

'Back then, the currents of that sea-street were calm, but there was a squall in my blood. If it were not for the landlubbin' maiden who I am told casts no shadow, that cursed splinter from that fallen mast would have completed its assignment to deliver my soul to the depths from which ye never returns.'

ShadowThief bowed in appreciation and the captain, sensing a slight disturbance in the air, nodded in acceptance.

'Turbulent waters for us both at that time. Me, cast adrift, my body reeling still from the great nails moored in coves where they had no right to dock, on the long road back from Calle Cienfuegos. She and her orphan-clan betrayed by one not fit to bow 'fore a barnacle. Together we learned to sail back to land-streets familiar and much more beside.'

ShadowThief sat attentively, listening like a child transfixed by a bedtime fable.

'Without sight, She was all I could feel, the only sensation I could endure,' Stavast continued. 'The Sea. I was ready to be swallowed up by the Majesty of Her. The Mistress I had known

my whole life. But your need to survive reawakened a desire in
this salt-crusted mariner to keep his head above water. And
into the bargain, a friendship was forged stronger than any
this old dog could have had with any of the daughters he'd
never fathered.'

He could not see the tear extending down her left cheek.
She wiped it away with haste.

'Aye, upon the dry stone cobbles she makes her livin', but
even I can see her salt-soaked soul. If ya be in need of any
assistance, ya put away yer shell-pennies and tells me straight.
I will do what I can.'

ShadowThief placed her hand on his, squeezed affectionately, then began to tap rhythmically. Stavast listened then
replied.

'Aye, 'course I remembers! Young 'un with the curious
powers o' seeing that which has not yet come to pass. Any
friends of the ShadowThief are welcome to share a tot of rum
with old Fenric Stavast!'

ShadowThief squeezed his hand again and departed. Less
than a minute later she returned with Aemea and Krish. Aemea
made introductions and Krish shook the rough hand of the
captain, finding salt on his skin as he pulled his hand away.

'Captain Stavast,' said Aemea, 'do I understand you were
once in the employ of one Isri Stroever?'

'Aye, I was 'til very recently in that mangey lubber's
employ.' Stavast downed his rum.

'And is it true he's been associating with Lord Ryker-
Veere?'

'Most certainly.'

'Captain Stavast,' Krish entered the conversation, 'we'd be
keen to employ you to take us to Ryker-Veere's on Kierbeckerstraße. And any information you have which could help us
infiltrate...' Krish, who until that moment had been rather

proud of his use of the word 'infiltrate', trailed off as Stavast began to shake his head.

'There be no need for ye to sail all the way to Kierbecker. Ryker-Veere makes port at Ha'penny Row. He stays at a hotel nearby Stroever's residence. They is stuck together like mussels to a pier these fades! In a few fades time they're launchin' some new scheme. Gettin' investors into Stroever's factory, just a couple o' doors down from his place. And if ye wants access to that most prestigious of events, I can't help you. But there is one who might.'

It was Captain Stavast's turn to leave the inn. Five minutes later, he returned with a young woman with shoulder-length brown hair.

'This is Emese,' said Stavast. 'Not that long ago I found myself in a discreet conference with Annemieke de Clercq, Lord Ryker-Veere's private secretary. We struck up something of a companionship and then late one fadenigh, I gets a telegram from her. *I needs yer assistance*, she says. Smuggle some bodies out of the neighbourhood. Though these bodies ain't destined for the seabed, she says. They's fresher than the freshest o' catches, only they don't look that way. She pays me a pretty shell-penny to deliver these lubbers to streets new. The other three hole themselves up below deck, waitin' for a kind tide, but this one stays close. Listen now, hear this tale o' hers...'

A quiet rage brewed in Emese. She spoke with a heavy Győri accent.

'Ryker-Veere is a monster,' said Emese. 'Cruel and selfish. A child, only worse. I had an opportunity to shoot him, but it did not work. I will go back. For enslaving us, for the humiliation, for everything he did and will do. My parents became poison-dream addicts and died from it. Now he wants to legalise dreams and make large profits! And he has plenty of time to achieve this goal. He has some medicine in a safe that will make him live long, but he cannot get inside it.'

'Are you still in contact?' said Krish. 'With... erm...'

'De Clercq? Yes,' said Emese. 'She uses a telegram machine inside the house of Stroever, though she must be careful. They are planning an event at Mr Stroever's factory. Many potential investors. It is well guarded and my face will be familiar, but I must get in. I must kill Ryker-Veere.'

'So, you have a plan?' said Aemea. 'You know how to get into the factory?'

'Yes,' said Emese.

'And you know much of the layout of the factory?'

'Yes, Fenric helped me. I have the...' Emese turned to Stavast for help.

'Schematic,' said Stavast.

'The schematic,' confirmed Emese. 'De Clercq cannot say much but there is a room at the factory that Ryker-Veere is using for his dreamers. For years, he has looked for three dreams which will help him unlock the safe, but until recently he did not know which three. De Clercq says they have solved one, are close with another, but there is one, from Njivska Ulica, they still cannot solve.'

Krish, Aemea and ShadowThief exchanged glances – Njivska Ulica, the only place where they had not been able to find the dream.

'So, he has this room for dreamers, wants them close, but tries to pretend he uses the room for something else. He is keeping a lot of secrets from Stroever. I think the safe once belonged to Stroever's father, Isairis. He is dead now. Ryker-Veere does not keep the safe at the factory or Stroever's house. He keeps it at his hotel, the Starwane.'

'Is there someone else there with Ryker-Veere or with Stroever?' ventured Krish. 'Someone new? A young boy...?'

'I don't know,' said Emese. 'My messages with de Clercq are short. But they are looking for the people who are trying to steal what is in the safe. I know they are still looking for three.' She looked knowingly at Krish, Aemea and ShadowThief.

'Do they know anything about us?' said Aemea.

'I don't know!' shouted Emese. 'How would I know? Our messages are short!'

'Okay, erm, Emese,' said Krish. 'Sorry.'

ShadowThief banged her fist on the table and waved her hand in front of her own face in frustration.

'Yes, you're probably right,' said Aemea.

'What was that?' asked Krish.

'Shad makes the point that she is somewhat conspicuous. If anyone spots her, they know you and I will be nearby, Krish. It's probably why Dar Fernier tracked us down so easily.'

ShadowThief nodded vigorously, sighed deeply and began gesturing: *If we are to infiltrate this event, I will have to remain behind.* She buried her head in her hands in defeat.

Aemea gave ShadowThief a friendly pat on the back then addressed Emese. 'Did you ever ask de Clercq if she would kill Ryker-Veere?'

A bitter laugh from Emese. 'No. She will not.'

'Why—?'

'I am telling you she will not!' Emese looked down at the table as she spoke. 'I have worked with her for many years. She hates him, she insults him under her breath often, but the rest of the time she shows respect. She does not want to stay, but leaving is too much for her. She helps me, but she says little. I think she would let you into the factory, to the event, but only that.' Emese looked up and into Krish's eyes. 'You will kill him?'

Krish, Aemea and ShadowThief exchanged glances. Krish plucked up the courage to answer. 'No.'

'Then you get no more help from me.'

Krish considered then spoke again. 'What'll happen if someone takes the Myr... the stuff in the safe?'

Emese looked lost. She stared curiously at Krish for a time.

'Because I'm going to take it,' said Krish.

'He will find you!' said Emese.

'He won't be able to.'

'You lie! He will find you!'

'Emese, if I wanted to lie to you, I'd say, "Kill this Ryker-Veere? Sure! How d'you want it done?" But I'm telling you the truth. This medicine of Ryker-Veere's is called Myrthali. It helps people live longer and I'm going to steal it from him. You saw my friend Thira in the beer hall with his powers? We'll use a power very much like that to travel far away. Far, far away. And all we have to do is touch the Myrthali. So, believe me, he won't find us. Now, tell me, what would it do to him? If I emptied that safe?'

Emese looked down at the table, allowing Krish's words to seep in. 'Destroy him. Totally destroy him. All his plans... they will take a long time. He needs it. You take it... it would destroy him.'

Krish nodded. Then Emese nodded. She spoke at length while Krish and Aemea scribbled down notes. Finally, when her knowledge and energy were depleted, Stavast escorted Emese back to his ship. Before he went, he ordered charril for everyone and they toasted their partnership. Charril was hot, sweet and aromatic, but with an odd, salty aftertaste.

The group then split in two, ShadowThief and Stavast communicating at a table while Aemea and Krish spoke in hushed tones a few meters away.

'So, if Ryker-Veere has the dreamers working on the dreams in a room at Stroever's factory...' said Krish.

'Then all we have to do is infiltrate the factory and get to the hotel room where Ryker-Veere has his safe.' Aemea finished her charril and screwed up her face in disgust. 'I felt that. Five minutes ago... I felt it.'

'Why is it so close now?'

'I don't know. But something's going to happen. I don't know what, but it's soon. It's odd. In a way I feel calm now. The closer it gets, the less I feel I have any choice in what I do.'

'And that relaxes you?!'

'Feeling the direct consequences of every path you might take in an hour is very draining, Krish! I'm constantly riddled with anxiety, and perhaps just letting things happen and not worrying would be best for me in the future.' Another thought spread across her mind. She looked directly at Krish. 'I take it that's true? That thing you said about you being transported far, far away? As soon as you touch the Myrthali?'

'Yeah,' said Krish. 'You don't believe me?'

'No, but I'm sure when I see it I will. And Thira will go too?'

'Yeah. He'll only exist in worlds where I'm searching for the Myrthali.'

Aemea recoiled at this idea. 'And he's okay with this?'

'Er... well, I don't think he's that keen but... well, he sort of didn't exist before. Well, he did but he's more like a copy of someone from another world.'

'This is all a tad strange, Krish.'

'Yeah. I just wanted to see him again.'

'So, if you're not together when you touch the Myrthali... does he go too?'

'I guess.'

'So, the priority is to solve the dreams, find Ryker-Veere's safe and then go...?'

Krish pondered this for a while. 'No. We have to find him. He might be hurt or... I dunno. We have to find him. That's the priority.'

Aemea nodded. She smiled and took a deep, satisfied breath in. 'You know, I've been "dreaming" of escape with Shad, and suddenly I have to admit I'm little sad at the prospect of us parting.'

'Yeah... me too, Aemea.'

'But I suppose what will be will be. Shame in a way to break up the pack.'

Krish's eyes widened.

'Oh, sorry!' said Aemea. 'When I say "the pack", there was this storybook I read as a child about these creatures like dogs in another world and they—'

'It's the wolf's head!' said Krish suddenly. He got out the list and checked – he had indeed written down 'wolf's head' as one of the slides. 'Someone mentioned "howling"! V'shiri called their group a "pack"! And she pointed at Lu'shaya's badge when they were talking about who would take over as leader. I thought it was just a large, grey dog but it was a wolf! ShadowThief was right! It's not about who killed who or about one person being in charge – it's about togetherness! And they thought of themselves as a pack, like wolves!'

'Of course!' said Aemea. 'And the idea of large groups of animals moving together is almost unknown in the City, unless you read some rather rare books. So it would be hard for many to work out!'

'I saw it on a documentary! Packs of wolves have to work together as they move through the wilderness to safety. That's what it's all about!'

'Well, one more dream left to solve...'

Minutes later, as the excitement died down, Stavast showed Krish to the cabin on his ship and then returned to speak to Aemea and ShadowThief at the inn.

'So, what'll it be, shipmates?' said Stavast.

'Well, "shipmates" is something we very much had in

mind,' said Aemea. 'Perhaps, when this is all over, if we worked on board your vessel and...'

Stavast waved Aemea off with a smile.

'Aye, there be no working on my ship for the rest of my fades. We looks after the ship and one another and the Sea does the rest. How far ye thinkin' of goin'?'

ShadowThief mimed heading off into the horizon.

'As far as far will stretch.'

'I may know something that will suit ye very well. Long voyage but it's the long voyages I am in business for. I will take ye there and bid ye farewell with all the blessing an old seadog can offer.'

Stavast stood and made his way to the door.

ShadowThief tapped out a message urgently for Stavast: *But after that, where will you go?*

Fenric Stavast looked up at them with a broad and wily smile.

'To Sea, to Sea! She is power, She is glory!'

48
THE NAME ON HIS LIPS

The scents of salt married with spice, mixed in with oak, red meat and brass. A cloud of black and grey mingled with another of red and purple emanating from the opposite side of the room. Two groups of dreamers sat in chairs on either side of the room, each engrossed in separate dreams. The room had once been a workshop, now emptied out to create a makeshift dream station.

Outside the room, on the factory floor, next to the stage being constructed on the edge of the forest, several dreamers who had just completed their shifts in the neighbouring room were now scrawling notes. One slapped her hand decisively on the floor on which she crouched. She got up and marched excitedly up to the man pacing about impatiently.

'Lord Ryker-Veere! I have it!'

'Keep your voice down!'

'I'm sorry, I'm sorry, but here!' She passed Ryker-Veere a slip of paper.

'You're certain?'

'Absolutely certain, sir. I've gone through it several times and I'm sure. I can write up my notes for you.'

'I don't have time to read all of that claptrap!'

'I'll check with—'

'I said keep your voice down!'

'I'm sorry, sir.'

'Hm. Two down, one to go, what-what! Any progress on the one from Njivska Ulica?'

'Not yet, sorry, sir. There's been a lot of debate over that one.'

'Hm! Once you have a solution, report to me post-haste. Discreetly.'

'Yes, sir.'

Ryker-Veere exited the factory, crossed the street and entered the Stroever household to reconvene with de Clercq. The drawing room could be dingy in full starlight, and even now, with sentinellight pouring in from the single window above, it still appeared dark and empty.

'The papers are rallying around you, your preposterousness,' said de Clercq, circling round Ryker-Veere.

'What?! What was that?!' said Ryker-Veere, a hand cupped around his ear.

'The papers!' said de Clercq, thrusting two newspapers into his hands.

Ryker-Veere studied the front page of *The Fadely Star:*

GYőR: THE BLOODIEST FADE

Underneath was a photograph of devastated streets.

'And what concern of mine is Győr now, hm?' said Ryker-Veere. 'Though perhaps it'll put to rest those rumours of economic recovery. It'll be a dash sight easier to sell Stroever's mad scheme while night persists, what-what!'

'Economic recovery does seem inevitable, sir,' said de Clercq. 'See page five. Ankaran separatists are plotting to overthrow the current regime. The end of the war could trigger the end of NightTime.'

'I've no doubt we can get things moving before that, old girl!' Ryker-Veere lowered his voice even further. 'Sounds like the solution to the final dream is already within our grasp! Playing with fire setting up camp in the factory, but if it's cracked during the launch, I want the answer close at hand.'

'Sir—'

'Does he suspect anything, you think?' Ryker-Veere's eyes did a quick circuit of the room. 'How would he know anything of the affairs of his late father, hm?' A memory nudged him from years ago. An event that had taken place in this very room. He brushed it aside.

'Sir!' said de Clercq. 'I was actually trying to draw your attention to—'

'What?! You're on the wrong side again!'

De Clercq repositioned herself but kept her voice down.

'I was drawing your attention more to the second page of *The Fadely Star*, and the third in *The Illuminator*.'

Ryker-Veere flicked through to the article:

'DREAMING HAS HEALTH BENEFITS', FORMER MINISTER

The health benefits of dreaming have long been overlooked, a new report from leading medical research body Gordonbrock Row Health suggests. 'We have conducted various experiments and have determined that, if administered correctly, dreaming is extremely beneficial in relieving stress, relieving anxiety and may even...

'Gordonbrock Row Health...' Ryker-Veere pondered. 'Where do I know that name?'

'You asked me to set it up some months ago,' confirmed de Clercq.

'Oh, yes! Hard to keep track of all our new outfits, what-what?'

He brushed past *The Illuminator's* headline – **16,000 DEAD IN GYŐR CRISIS** – to find a similar story in that paper:

THE COMMUNE PROVING US ALL WRONG ON DREAMING

It's easy to be dismissive about the strange characters inhabiting the Balis commune in Kirkmir Street, with their garishly coloured clothing and home-factories; but this collective of artists and philosophers has existed here in relative peace, with no murders and very little crime, for the past 26 years. The reason they have remained in a state of perpetual harmony? Many have their theories, but the finger is frequently pointed decisively at their proclivity for dreaming.

'Excellent, excellent, superb!' said Ryker-Veere, tossing the papers aside.

'The word "proclivity" means—' began de Clercq.

'I don't give a dash! Ha! Such a fantastic notion to dig out the story of an old squat full of layabouts to appeal to the liberals! H-ha! Legalisation shall take time, but the seeds have been sown. Bravo, bravo!'

'Bravo indeed,' came a voice from the edge of the room.

Ryker-Veere turned to see Stroever framed in the doorway. How could he not sense when he soundlessly snuck into a room by now? He dearly hoped that Stroever had only just entered. Stroever stood between the sliding doors, currently wide open.

'Ha-ha-ha! Isri, old chap! Ha! You probably don't remember...'

'I recall.'

'On this very spot, between those doors, I saw your chubby cheeks for the first time.'

Stroever nodded. 'May I request your support in staffing for the event and our little demonstration?'

'Why... why of course. You shall have plenty of my chaps at your disposal. Couple that carry concealed knives, just in case, what? Few extra pairs of hands returned from a recent job as well. Will spare as many as I can.'

'Thank you, Anders. That would be greatly appreciated. And the Selkirk and her ensnared star require some additional protection. Do you have anyone... *special* who can assist?'

'I'll send the very best.'

'Wonderful. Oh, and the dream business... that is going well...?'

Stroever's tranquil countenance was deeply unnerving. Ryker-Veere was convinced for a second that he knew, that he'd always known, about the safe.

'Dream... business...?' said Ryker-Veere.

'The stories in the papers. I saw them dotted about. All your doing?'

'Oh! Yes! Yes, my boy!' Ryker-Veere mentally breathed a sigh of relief. 'Once the public comes round to the idea the governments will soon follow. It will take time, but it has begun!'

'And time you have...'

He knew. Ryker-Veere was certain of it. He was caught. His heart hammered a warning in his chest.

'Isri...' Ryker-Veere attempted to calm himself with his own words. 'I take my hat off to you. Your proposal is genius. Shocking at first, I must admit, but you know what, old chap, all this talk of health benefits, very convincing! I mean, I myself have used dreams for years, don't ya know. And the opportunity to sell gas from the stars themselves! Ha! Even your father couldn't top this!'

'My father was a fool and now he is dead. Perhaps when our meeting this evening is concluded, we shall talk about inheritance.'

The guilt stabbed directly at Ryker-Veere's heart.

'Inheritance...?'

Ryker-Veere became aware that someone was drifting through his peripheral vision. He turned and saw a figure in a faded, loose-fitting purple dress, who may well have been a ghost. There was no colour in her face, and like her older brother she was aged beyond her years, her hair prematurely grey, matching her colourless eyes.

He recognised her immediately. Ryker-Veere's heart beat so hard that in one ear he could hear his own pulse, throbbing away. In the other, his deaf ear, he could only feel it. Staring into the woman's eyes, he recalled the day he had last been able to hear on his left.

POUNDING and POUNDING and in an instant, he was there, reliving memories of the fade he had constantly been attempting to suppress. POUNDING and POUNDING, each blow landing as if it would crack his head in two. POUNDING and POUNDING against his left side.

A ringing, throbbing pain, his heart beating desperately. He raised his head to look up at the men who had dragged him into the alley off Krelborn Row.

WHERE IS HE? WE KNOW YOU KNOW!

I don't! I don't! Please!

WHERE IS HE?

PLEASE!

Always braggin', aren't ya? 'E's yer closest associate, eh? And now ya're sayin' ya don't know where 'e' is, eh?

I haven't seen Isairis for weeks! Please!

They left him in a bloody heap. He peeled himself off the ground and stumbled away.

Later that fade, Jane Stroever was tending to his wounds in the Stroever drawing room.

They're serious, Jane.

I know.

If they did this to me...

I know.

He'd better be a long way away.

He is.

A long way—

They won't find him, Anders.

Your uncle is ruthless. Ruthless!

He wants to make a point. He won't harm Isairis.

Look at me, Jane! Look at me! He has no notion of what his goons will do to appease their bloodlust!

Isairis is far from here, Anders. A long, long way away...

Jane Stroever lingered for a time and Ryker-Veere could see that another spell of mind-sickness was plaguing her. She was too quiet to be well.

When she left to find a fresh cloth, he sat there, head back, eyes closed, exhausted and in agony.

Then he opened his eyes again and looked down at the child sitting on the ground just in front of him. She clutched a gleaming red sleigh to her chest. She looked fearful.

It's okay, said Ryker-Veere.

Uncle Anders? said Helena Stroever.

It's okay, my dear.

I want to go and play with my sleigh.

Well, there's no snow. He looked back in the direction of the kitchen where Jane was boiling more water for the cloth. Ryker-Veere glanced upstairs to see if there was any sign of Isri and then looked back at Helena. *And there is a certain young lady who is somewhat unwell. We must take care of her.*

He motioned a touch towards the kitchen though Helena seemed uninterested. She threw the red sleigh to the ground in a fury.

It's always about her these fades! When will she be better?

I don't know, young Helena.

He opened his arms in invitation. She ran over and placed her head on his knee. He put his hand on her head, holding her there protectively.

Your father will be okay, little Helena. He's far, far away.

Why is Uncle Val doing this?

I don't know, child. I don't know.

He felt her tears seeping through the fabric, dampening his knee.

Nobody plays with me anymore! Nobody listens to me!

Now, that's just not true!

Daddy loves me! I told him he has to go far away to be safe, but he didn't listen!

He did, child! He did!

No, he didn't! He's only at the Beggar's Lantern! Why doesn't he go farther? I walked all the way there the other fade. Why doesn't he go really, really far away?

Child—

Mummy says no one ever goes to the Beggar's Lantern so the room overtop is best. No one'll guess but what if Uncle Val checks anyway?

You shouldn't talk about things like this, Helena. Have you told anyone?

No.

Then you mustn't tell anyone else, Helena. Understood?

Okay.

It's a secret. Just a fun little secret.

Okay... okay... a fun little secret...

Hours later, he was drunk in a rum palace, feeling his swollen left side, paranoia taking control.

As he staggered back down Krelborn Row, the raingrate gushing down on him, he saw Valkyrys Hanch's men again. They'd been watching him. They knew he'd come from the Stroevers'. He wept and crumpled onto his knees. He could feel the phantoms of the pain they were about to inflict as they circled around him. Before they opened their mouths, he spoke...

Beggar's Lantern...

They departed.

He curled up in a heap, the rain pummelling him as he convulsed, crying then screaming, guilt tearing him apart.

Isairis's body washed up the next fade.

In the fades to come, he learned that he was to inherit the safe, and with it the secret of what it contained. He had no idea how to open it, but it motivated him. Greed began to transform him and he buried his guilt deep.

But one particular detail from those terrible fades still haunted him. Something that he'd perhaps imagined but...

When Helena had told him about the Beggar's Lantern, he had looked up at the gap between the sliding doors at the end of the room. There had, perhaps, been a flicker of movement.

'Helena...' said Ryker-Veere back in the present. 'My word, it has been years! So many years! Ha! You remember when we played here together...? In this room...? Your Uncle Anders...?'

'She remembers,' Isri spoke for the woman standing uncomfortably at the bottom of the stairs.

'I thought you lived with your aunt.'

'She did until her death. Then she moved back to her ancestorial home. Around the time I returned from the factory.'

Helena Stroever stood there, her expression vacant, waiting for a cue.

'Are you done with me now?' was all Helena Stroever said.

Isri Stroever nodded and the woman drifted back up the stairs, entered a room and closed the door quietly behind her.

Ryker-Veere glanced at de Clercq, who stared helplessly back, before he addressed Stroever. 'What is the meaning of these theatrics, old boy?'

'To make things clear,' said Stroever flatly. 'Fadenigh, you will introduce me and then you will take a back seat. You will allow me to conduct the proceedings and afterwards we shall discuss my inheritance.'

'Your poor sister, locked away in—'

'You will do as I say and that is that.'

Ryker-Veere abhorred the stinging silence festering in the air.

'I want the boy there,' Ryker-Veere mustered.

'Thira?'

'The young scallywag with the unnatural powers. You say you can control him?'

'I can.'

'Well... he must be there.'

'As bait?'

'Yes. We have the description of one at least. A hairless drummer child.'

'I see. Very well.'

'And you found out nothing else from the boy?'

'Only that he would rather die than betray his compatriots.'

'Hm. And the only other thing my contacts were able to glean was the name of the other boy, the ringleader.'

Stroever remained motionless, asking the question without speaking a word.

'Krishna,' said Ryker-Veere. 'The boy's name is Krishna.'

49
THE THIRD TOWER

'Here, child,' said Madam Ckrystafis, placing an open-topped wooden box on the workbench in front of Thira. 'Tofade, something different.'

She began to empty the box. He observed a lump of dull yellow wood, a scrap of shoe leather, a jar of clear liquid, a spool of cotton thread, a collection of nails and a vial of blood.

'Would you like to create one yourself?' she asked.

'What's all this cobblers?' said Thira, as if he didn't recognise the ingredients for a dream.

'Bless you, child! You will learn. Follow my instructions and we shall see how well you do.'

They soaked the nails in the clear liquid then slowly warmed them over a flame until bubbles began to appear. Ckrystafis showed Thira how to snap the wood in two and then soak it in oil which smelled rich and sweet. They then singed the shoe leather and placed all the remaining ingredients in the dreamglobe.

'What were you doing when I walked in on you and Mr Stroever?' asked Madam Ckrystafis abruptly.

'Nuffin',' said Thira. In truth he'd taken a calculated risk, after hearing what Stroever had said in his sleep, that his best course of action was to remain where he was. He'd hidden his staff up his sleeve and had even locked the restraints again, though Madam Ckrystafis had actually decided to remove them altogether. The amount of trust she'd suddenly placed in him was unnerving.

'I see...' said Madam Ckrystafis, narrowing her eyes and smiling coyly. 'Now, let's try it. Just a little...'

Thira lit the flame under the dreamglobe, and after a minute or so a wisp of deep red smoke escaped the funnel and reached Madam Ckrystafis's nostrils.

'Oooh! Not quite, not quite! Need to infuse a little longer...' She gave him a sickly-sweet smile and Thira obliged with a miniscule injection of magic.

'There we go! Perfect, child! Now, can you guess which dream in particular this might be...?'

Thira was overwhelmed with emotion for a moment. Had Ryker-Veere beaten Krish, Aemea and ShadowThief to all the dreams? Were they all still alive? Was Krish still alive?

'Er, no,' said Thira, playing innocent. 'What is it?'

'Lord Ryker-Veere has requested a room for his own private use at Mr Stroever's factory,' said Madam Ckrystafis. 'He is trying to be very secretive, but we have an idea of what he might be doing. Discretion is not one of Lord Ryker-Veere's skills. Information arrived recently by telegram from the Győri border.'

A pang of fear shot through Thira – had Krish and the others made it as far as Győr?

'One of Lord Ryker-Veere's men reacted immediately and began collecting ingredients for a dream,' continued

Ckrystafis. 'Most curious, is it not? Now, I was not able to observe his work, but he did leave a box of the previous dream's ingredients on the worktop for a short time. This I was able to observe momentarily. I have a fantastic memory! And I have been able to replicate the ingredients their dream-mixer had prepared. Mr. Stroever is curious about the dream so has asked me to inspect it.'

'Oh. What kinda dream is it?' Thira still had every word Stroever had said to him in his sleep ringing in his ears.

'Well, let's see...'

Madam Ckrystafis began adjusting the nozzle of the dreamglobe. Thira sensed his staff, wrapped once more around his arm. It was tense, ready. He just had to wait for the right moment.

The deep red mists filled his vision, the scents of sweat, of iron, of blood, of dry stone which put him in mind of Ilir. The dream wrapped itself around him.

The mists cleared quickly and a strange landscape appeared. Nothing moved, no sense of sound. All was uncomfortably still.

The stars twinkled in the night sky. One large moon loomed on the horizon, bisected by the land. Another misshapen moon, like a blob of clay pocked with craters hung farther away, high above the first.

A vast plain bathed in moonlight was laid out before him, walls of rock twisting upwards like frozen waves of stone all around. The ground was a sea of jagged, spear-like, blood-red rocks zigzagging across the terrain.

The centrepiece of the landscape was a tall tower of dark yellow stone, rising straight up, featureless and foreboding, a spiked crown at the top. There was no sign of life anywhere on the structure.

Closer and closer he drifted, the dream craning his vision

upwards. The structure was taller than the great tower of Scci-fihr'ei on Ilir, but unlike that construction of wringing bodies, never still for a moment, this budged not an inch.

A smooth road had been hewn through the land to the tower. Several sentries were on duty outside, rifles on their shoulder. A broad staircase led up to the only entrance to the building.

The dream guided him through the wall, and he was now in a spartan entrance chamber where an entire legion of troops watched, rifles raised, as a prisoner in a cage was hoisted into the air. The captive was lifted to a landing several storeys up – a fall from the platform, which had no railings, would surely be fatal.

He drifted up the central shaft of the tower where the prisoner was escorted to a cell, not much larger than a broom cupboard. This was the only cell on the level and a six-strong force of guards waited outside, eyes always on the room.

As you looked up, there were many more platforms, each featuring a single cell, along the interior of the great chimney-like structure.

At the tower's pinnacle, guards were stationed at vantage points along the crown's spikes, looking down at the sheer drop, rifles always by their sides.

Down and down again the dream transported him to a cell, a little larger than the others, halfway up the tower.

A beam of light from the small window, high up in one corner of the room, travelled diagonally down to the corner near the door, revealing a figure slumped on the bed. She was middle-aged and slim, though judging by her loose-fitting clothes, she'd lost a lot of weight recently. One eye was swollen and puffy. Cuts and bruises covered her body. Her feet were bare. A young moustachioed guard stood in the doorway, perhaps another twenty guards a little way behind him.

Rest, said the guard. *They will have fewer questions tomorrow.*

Ha! replied the prisoner. *Because tomorrow they shall kill me!*

Hush, Dhriti! The Viceroy will come tomorrow. They will not want to shed blood in his presence.

You are naïve, Kala. They will want to finish me off in front of him. To make an example of me for my crimes against the colony.

I don't believe this, Dhriti.

Urgh, don't worry, Kala! I'm sure they won't make you do it. Perhaps I'll leave you my teeth, eh? You'd make quite a bit selling them, ha!

I'm sure if you are honest tomorrow—

Then they will make it quick? No. They're bloody monsters and they like to stretch it out for the Viceroy. I've seen it before. Urgh! All the interrogators fighting to be the one to finish me off. It'll be a pretty tiresome way to die.

Please, Dhriti. Rest.

Hate to break it to you, Kala, but I'm dying tomorrow and unless you get me something scrumptious as a last meal, I intend to leave you, or whichever other unfortunate has to clear out my pisspot, a particularly nasty surprise in the morning.

The prisoner, Dhriti, slumped back onto the bed. Moments later, detecting that the young guard, Kala, was still there, she sat up and stared at him with her good eye.

Is there anything I can do? said Kala.

Dhriti mulled this over for a long time.

The Viceroy, eh? said Dhriti. *We were good friends once. Before I tried to kill him, of course. Best be presentable, even if I risk the first interrogator ripping me a new one in the first few minutes. Perhaps... a needle and thread.*

Dhriti, they will not allow you—

A needle, Kala! A needle! You tell me how I'm going to kill someone with a needle?! And... oh! You know what I'd like? Some cherries. Reminds me of childhood! Forget the last meal and just bring me as many cherries as you can. Dhriti looked down at her bare feet. *And a pair of shoes, come to think of it.*

Dhriti, I tell you, they will not allow shoes! They worry that you will hang yourself with the laces.

Well take them out then! I will not face the Viceroy like a bare-foot beggar!

You are most brave, Dhriti. You do not seem afraid of death.

Why should I be? Not as if I woke up this morning realising that life wasn't forever.

Most brave, Dhriti. Most brave. I will let you rest and see what I can do.

Shoes, needle and thread, and plenty of cherries!

I will see what I can d—

Something sliced into Thira's skin and infiltrated the vein. The mists vanished as he tossed his head back, a reflex to the pain. He flinched but she held him close from behind. He felt the plunger being pressed and cool liquid mixed with his blood.

'Hold still, now, hold still,' came Madam Ckrystafis's voice. He was brimming with magic, the staff ready to spring into action, but it was too risky with a needle currently in his vein. 'If you desire us both to die, unleash your powers. But if you want to live... don't worry. This is just a deterrent. A warning. You are to be our guest at the reception. To greet any inter-lopers who may appear.'

Thira's heart soared – *Krish*. He must still be alive. And he would be bait to catch him. 'Shrilwood's Knee,' said Madam Ckrystafis. 'It will kill you, child. It will! In a few fades all heat will go from you, you will experience convulsions for several minutes, and then it shall be done. But do as we say, and I shall administer the antidote. So, listen close – if your friends, this Krishna and the illustrated girl, and whomever else, if they appear, you will let us know. You understand? You let us know.'

50

THE NEWCOMER TO THE CONVERSATION

The colossal factory at the far end of Ha'penny Row was so large that it stretched right across the street, the road continuing through a tunnel under one section. The imposing building of red brick was almost featureless aside from a row of windows along the top and a series of tall funnels billowing smoke.

Elegant carriages exited the tunnel and twisted up the road to the raised level where the main entrance to the Stroever factory could be found. Armed guards, supplied at great expense by Ryker-Veere, lined the road leading to the factory. More were clustered around the entrance. A registrar in a smart black suit at a podium welcomed the arrivals. Refined guests were ushered into the humble doorway leading into the factory after being searched for weapons by the guards. Many protested but eventually gave in, shaking their heads. Madam Ckrystafis loitered in the background, watching each guest pass by through narrowed eyes.

A large horse-drawn carriage arrived, shining black with

dashes of gold. Compared to the discreet carriages, which had already decanted their guests, it was rather garish. Lord Ryker-Veere exited in a splendid black suit, cape and top hat. De Clercq followed her master, closing the carriage door behind her.

'Lord Ryker-Veere?' said Madam Ckrystafis, emerging from the entourage of guards. 'Fashionably late to your own party?'

A flash of unease from Ryker-Veere but a brash smile masked it. 'Ah! You must be the talented Madam Ckrystafis.'

'I am. Pleasure to make your acquaintance at last.'

'Likewise.'

'Would you mind...?' she extended an arm in the direction of a burly guard.

'I most certainly would!' Ryker-Veere protested. 'At a function I poured so much of my own money into!'

'And what if some rogue assassin were to find out you were carrying a weapon and turned it against its owner?'

'Yes, yes, yes! Alright!'

The guard patted down both Ryker-Veere and de Clercq to much exaggerated huffing from the former. The guard produced a small pistol from Ryker-Veere's pocket and passed it to Madam Ckrystafis.

'Why, I believe it was a pistol like this which was pulled on you at Kierbecker,' said Madam Ckrystafis playfully. 'Tell me, Lord Ryker-Veere, would this be the same one?'

'It is so. Taught me you can never be too careful.'

'I'll have it locked away.'

The guard finished searching Ryker-Veere and turned to Madam Ckrystafis expectantly.

'Enjoy the event, Lord Ryker-Veere,' said Madam Ckrystafis.

'Hm!' Ryker-Veere went to enter. He stopped again as Madam Ckrystafis spoke, just as he had drawn level with her.

'If you are curious about my poisons, I am of course always happy to provide a private tasting for you...' She offered Ryker-Veere a deliciously dark smile.

Ryker-Veere blinked away his discomfort. 'Hm! Take it you're not doing the catering tofade?'

'Sadly not.'

'Hmph! Lovely to meet you.' He breezed past Madam Ckrystafis, his cape flowing behind him.

'Taste everything before me, there's a good girl,' Ryker-Veere uttered over his shoulder to de Clercq.

'Perhaps you could sup later, sir,' said de Clercq.

'You are deliberately standing on my deaf side, woman!' said Ryker-Veere, turning to face de Clercq. 'What is the matter with you?'

De Clercq sighed deeply.

§

Hidden from the light of the sentinels, Krish, Aemea and ShadowThief crept along the slim shingle beach, the foul waters of the river-street to their left, looking up at the buildings along Ha'penny Row on their right. They had left Captain Stavast on his boat, moored about a mile upriver at Henstan Quay.

'That's 47 Ha'penny,' said Aemea. 'The Stroever residence.'

Krish craned his neck to see the rectangular tower capped with a cupola. Not much compared to the dizzying heights of the towers in the dreams, but there was a quiet menace to its silhouette.

They reached a wide pipe stretching out over the beach, spewing water onto the shingle. A figure loitered near the opening, a rifle in his hands. ShadowThief, the shadows sticking close to her, sized him up.

'Shad...' whispered Aemea.

ShadowThief nodded, anticipating her question – *I'll be careful.* She hurtled forwards, knife raised. The man looked at the last moment, but it was too late. She brought the base of the knife down on his skull. There was a sound like the crack of two billiard balls knocking together. The figure folded onto the ground. Krish and Aemea joined ShadowThief to gag and restrain the guard.

In the half-light, Aemea and ShadowThief exchanged glances, a glint of sentinellight catching their eyes. They embraced. Krish was not sure they would break apart. They separated, ShadowThief heading back towards Stavast's boat.

Aemea and Krish entered the pipe and trudged through the shallow stream of wastewater. They were resplendent in fine dress for the launch event, purchased from a tailor on Frying Pan Alley.

'I'm hoping the oils I bought are enough to mask this stench when we get up there,' said Aemea. 'It's maybe a minute now. I can already feel that we are climbing upwards through the hatch.'

A minute later, they found the hatch they were searching for. Krish knocked twice. The hatch opened straight away and de Clercq looked down at them. She stood to one side as they climbed up through.

'Stick close to the Shree Maharjan from Pashupati Sadak, red suit, and his friend, Lady Hennessy, green dress,' said de Clercq, barely looking at them. 'People may assume you are with them. The room you're after is on the lower level, on the factory floor. Four doors along from the main stage. The rooms either side are unoccupied. There is a back entrance to each room, but be wary of guards. Do not talk to me.' And with that, de Clercq marched away having never looked at either of them directly.

Krish and Aemea brushed their shoes dry with some nearby napkins, poured some oil on their footwear to neutralise the stench, then followed in de Clercq's wake along the dark corridor.

De Clercq exited the corridor through a door which she left ajar. Krish and Aemea caught up and peered through the crack. Light and the hubbub of the drinks' reception filtered into the gloom of the corridor.

Many finely dressed noblemen and noblewomen were scattered about the forest on the factory floor. There were a number of children too, just as well-dressed, staying close to their parents.

The two of them took deep breaths and marched into the reception with as much confidence as they could muster. Many of the guests held shining silver canisters and were turning them over in their hands as if they were something entirely alien. Occasionally waiters passed and handed out a canister to someone who didn't already have one.

Krish looked up in awe of the trees. He had not been this close to the sights and smells of nature in so long. The scent of pine filled his nostrils and he was transported back to camping holidays with his family. But as they wandered through the forest past clusters of guests, Krish was feeling more and more out of his depth.

'Aemea, we stand out too much!' whispered Krish. 'I can't see any kids without their parents!'

'Just be all stuck up and arrogant,' Aemea whispered back. 'All the kids look like they're playing silly, over-the-top versions of the adults. Act like you own the place.'

There was a clearing in the trees and they spied a stage erected up ahead. A large number of guests were congregating around this area. Beyond the stage was a brick wall lined with metal doors. There was a light on in one room.

'I can't see Thira anywhere,' said Krish.

'I'm sure he's about,' said Aemea. She pointed through the leaves.

'There...'

There was an entrance to a corridor running along the other side of the rooms. A guard stood nearby, arms folded. Aemea pulled a box of matches out of her pocket and passed them to Krish. He knelt, nerves taking hold of him. They were lucky that the guests were so self-absorbed that they weren't looking their way, but the odour of the sulphur dioxide from the match could give them away.

The tree began to burn. Krish and Aemea stepped away.

Seconds later the guard caught a whiff of smoke, rushed forward and stamped out the flames. He missed the two figures darting around the corner.

Krish and Aemea could see a guard at the other end of the short corridor, guests milling about beyond him. They ducked into the room next to the room with the light on. They found themselves in a cluttered storeroom. Aemea left the door open a crack so they could see out.

'We're in luck,' whispered Aemea, pointing at the small window above the workbench, light for the next room shining through. Krish climbed up onto the bench and opened the window.

A deep red cloud began to pour into the room. Krish and Aemea stood on the bench.

'Let's hope it's the right dream,' said Aemea.

'Sounded like the one from Njivska Ulica was the one they were still struggling with,' said Krish. 'So there's a good chance.'

Aemea nodded.

They breathed in.

Blood, sweat, staleness. The dream took them to the prison in the tower. They observed the single entrance, the prisoners lifted in cages, the disproportionate numbers of guards per prisoner, the guards in the spiked crown of the tower looking over the sheer drop. They saw Dhriti and listened to her request to the guard.

Shoes, needle and thread, plenty of cherries!

I will see what I can do, Dhriti. I will see what I can do.

'It was short!' said Krish.

'Indeed,' said Aemea. 'What do you think?'

'I don't know. Do you think it's about escaping?'

'Yes. This time I think it's exactly what we think it's about. The woman Dhriti must find a way out before she gives out too much information or is tortured to death.'

'Yeah. Poor woman.'

Aemea pulled a face. 'She sounds like she was happy to kill other people, Krish. In fact, I've no doubt she must have done something pretty awful to have ended up in such an impenetrable fortress.'

'Yeah. But she just seemed... Dunno... Didn't seem like a bad person.'

'Perhaps not. More a political prisoner. But anyway, how would she escape?'

'Parachute!'

'I beg your pardon?'

'A sheet that helps you float to the ground. That's why she needs a needle and thread! To sew her bedsheets together so she'll float down the central shaft or off the sides! Must be the needle and thread tile!'

'I'm not sure that that would work, Krish. Besides, there were guards watching her cell the whole time; she wouldn't be able to sew the sheets together without being observed. And there were guards everywhere. In the shaft, at the top of the tower and on the ground. There's no way she could just float gracefully to freedom.'

'What if she poisoned the cherries and offered them to the guards? She could use the needle!'

'Poison them with what, Krish? And how is she going to poison every single guard? And how would she even get down the shaft? Additionally, what you are suggesting appears to involve the needle *and* the cherries, so...'

'I've got it!'

'What? And I advise you to keep your voice down. We should leave soon.'

'The shoes! I saw it in a film. They dug their way out and put the dirt in the shoes then dropped it off and... and... You're looking at me like none of what I've just said makes sense.'

'That's because it doesn't.'

'Yeah. You're right. If everyone's watching all the time...'

'And you can't dig your way out through solid stone. And she'd be digging for a long time at that height...'

Silence descended.

'Do you think it's a memory?' said Krish. 'The dream? Do you think she was a real woman?'

'Possibly. Come on. We should leave.'

Aemea eyed the door ahead of them rather than the one behind they'd entered through.

'Shouldn't we go back the way we came?' said Krish.

'It's curious... Once I saw options, but not anymore. Now I only see one way...'

Aemea drifted forwards to the door which led into the party. She waited a moment. Suddenly there was an array of popping noises and Aemea pushed the door open, slipping into the party, Krish following close behind.

There was a collective 'Aaaah!' from the guests as they

observed a number of waiters spread out amongst them, who'd just popped corks from bottles. They filled glasses with bubbling liquid and there was much excited chatter as they were passed around the guests for a toast. Many pocketed their silver canisters to keep a hand free.

Madam Ckrystafis lurked amongst the trees, her eyes scanning the crowd.

'The man in the red suit!' said Aemea, indicating a nobleman with a fine beard chatting to a lady in a green dress who was making him laugh.

'And the lady in the green dress,' said Krish.

They hung back, a few metres away from the nobles they were pretending to be related to. They peered through the trees and saw next to the stage a rotund gentleman in a fine suit who was talking loudly and gesticulating wildly, much to the amusement of the crowd.

'Is that him?' said Krish. 'Ryker-Veere? Looks like the guy at Kierbecker.'

'It is,' said Aemea. 'Seems to have rid himself of that ridiculous beard, though.'

'Yeah...' Krish was distracted. Perhaps it was his imagination, but he seemed to have noticed someone familiar across the room. When you know someone well enough, you may well recognise them from the back of their head. 'Thira...'

Krish marched forward, Aemea following.

'Ah'

A red-faced man with a diminishing patch of white hair and a bushy white moustache strolled up to them and blocked their path. On his arm was a woman in a blue dress with a broad smile plastered over her face which she was reluctant to let droop for even a second.

'You must be Biini's boy,' said the man enthusiastically. 'My-my, haven't you grown? Hasn't he grown, Tilly?'

'Yes!' said the lady on cue. 'You've grown so much!'

'Er, thank you,' said Krish.

'And you must be Samuel and Margret's girl?' said the man.

'I... do belong to them, yes,' said Aemea.

'Marvellous! Marvellous! Isn't it marvellous, darling?'

'Oh yes, simply marvellous, dear!'

'Lord and Lady Rooksmoor,' said the man. 'I imagine you're too young to remember us.'

'So young!' said Lady Rooksmoor.

'So nice to meet you, Lord and Lady Rooksmoor,' said Aemea.

Lord Rooksmoor completely ignored Aemea and spoke directly to Krish. 'You know, grandfather always said Pashupati Sadak should be independent!'

'He always said that,' added Lady Rooksmoor.

'They used to string up your kind, you know?' continued Lord Rooksmoor. 'Can you believe that? Terrible times. Our family were all against it. And look at you now! Young scally-wags like you, your generation, you could hold official offices one day. And jolly good, I say! Jolly good!'

'Jolly good!' chipped in Lady Rooksmoor.

'Tell me, Lady Rooksmoor,' said Aemea. 'Do you have opinions of your own?'

'Of course she does!' barked Lord Rooksmoor. 'You need to have respect for your elders, young lady! Now, tell me, young man – Tilly and I are thinking of visiting Potala when day comes. Plenty of your type down there! Wonderful chaps! Any recommendations?'

'Er, I don't really know Potala or if any of "my type" are there, but I'm sure you'll naturally gravitate towards plenty of other condescending bastards when you arrive.'

Aemea stifled a giggle while the Rooksmoors were lost for words.

As Lord Rooksmoor went to open his mouth, a new voice cut into the conversation.

'Melvin is a little antiquated in his words, but he means well.' The speaker was a slim man in a fine suit who spoke softly. 'He's an unashamed relic from a glorious age and his vast experience of all corners of the borough is always welcome here.'

'My dear boy! You are the spitting image of your father!' said Lord Rooksmoor animatedly to the newcomer. 'Isn't he the spit, Tilly?'

'The absolute spit, Melvin!'

'You are too kind,' said the newcomer. 'Please, make certain you have a canister with your free sample and have yourself another drink. The speeches will begin shortly.'

The Rooksmoors departed without giving Krish and Aemea another look. The newcomer remained. He looked from Krish to Aemea.

'You are the children of Maharjan and Hennessy respectively?' he said.

'Yes,' Krish and Aemea answered simultaneously.

The newcomer nodded then turned to Aemea. 'You were not charmed by the ever-accommodating Matilda Rooksmoor?'

'No.'

The newcomer willed her to continue.

'She is a parrot in a dress. If I were her, I'd fly off next time he opened the cage.'

The newcomer let out a silent chuckle. He turned to Krish.

'You did not enjoy Melvin's comments?'

'He was patronising.'

'Go on.'

'It was like he wanted to prove he was better than us while also reminding us that we're... I dunno... different.'

'And you do not think that the differences between one person and the next should be discussed?'

'Well... they can, but... it's more like the way you talk about it.'

The newcomer nodded several times.

Aemea stared at Krish, her eyes widening as if in warning.

'I sense that much change is afoot in the City,' said the newcomer. 'Perhaps a fade will come when we recognise our common humanity and turn our backs on prejudice, only choosing to highlight our differences when celebrating the great variety within our species.'

'Yeah,' said Krish, nodding enthusiastically. 'Yeah, exactly!'

The newcomer smiled warmly and held out his hand. 'My name is Isri Stroever. A pleasure to meet you, Krishna.'

'You too, Mr Stroever.'

As his hand slid into Stroever's firm grip, he realised his mistake. The smile on Stroever's face broadened.

After a moment Stroever withdrew his hand, turned and left. He nodded to a guard, who signalled to another on the opposite side of Krish and Aemea. They could feel a ring of eyes encircling them.

'Aemea...'

'I could sense it, but it was too late. I was trying to warn you!'

Krish swore under his breath.

'Krish... it's seconds now. Thirty seconds, maybe less but... it can't be long now.'

'We need to find Thira and get out of here.'

'I don't think either will be that achievable at present.'

'No. And we're no closer to solving the final dream.'

'I know what it is,' came a familiar voice.

Krish and Aemea turned. They saw Thira approaching them dressed in a suit of midnight blue, his hands uncuffed, his hair tied back. He was strikingly handsome in his new outfit.

'Thira,' said Krish.

'Well done, mate,' said Thira, quietly, drawing close to them. 'Think I was meant to be bait but looks like you managed to trap yerselves perfectly well without me.'

51
THE WORDS ON THE PAPER

The ink was drying. Their two signatures were at the top of the page:

Lord A. Ryker-Veere

Mr. I. Stroever

Below, there was space for many other signatures.

The paperwork was laid out neatly at the centre of the table on the raised stage between the edge of the forest and the metal stairs leading up to the gantry overlooking the factory floor.

Ryker-Veere was boisterously addressing a cluster of guests, laughing as heartily as he could muster, though every time his eyes caught Stroever's or the room where his dreamers were at work, his grin wavered.

Every now and then he glanced at the paperwork on the table. He'd checked over and over again for a clause that would catch him out. There was none. Stroever had set no traps in the agreement that he could find.

De Clercq remained close at hand. She spied Madam Ckrystafis near the edge of the forest.

'You are ready?' Stroever's words made Ryker-Veere jump.

'Of course I'm ready, old chap,' said Ryker-Veere. He attempted a smile and then thought better of it.

Stroever nodded and headed up onto the stage, Ryker-Veere following behind.

§

'Thira, are you okay?' said Krish.

'Fine, mate, fine,' said Thira. 'Could be better, but I'm alive. At the mo, anyway.'

'What do you mean?' said Aemea.

'I'm sorry, Thira,' blurted out Krish. 'The train separated us and we couldn't find you and—'

'Yeah, yeah, yeah,' said Thira, casually. 'It's fine, mate.'

Krish was almost annoyed by Thira's placidness. 'Fine? What do you mean fine? Thira, what's happened?'

'This your idea of a rescue?'

'Well, it was meant to be.'

'Mucked it up a bit, eh?'

'We're working on a solution,' said Aemea.

'Gettin' out's not the problem,' said Thira, flexing his staff-arm.

'What?!' said Krish.

'Gettin' out's the easy bit. It's what happens next.'

'Well, we get to Ryker-Veere's safe, if you *really* know the answer, and go.'

'Yeah, it's the goin' bit I've got an issue with.'

'What issue? Thira, what's been happening? You really know the solution to the last dream?'

'Krish! Keep your voice down!' whispered Aemea.

'I am! Ryker-Veere won't hear—' said Krish.

'And who do you think all these people work for?' said Aemea.

'I'll tell you one person what don't work for Ryker-Veere,' said Thira, nodding in the direction of a lady in a black dress, patched with the odd square of pastel colours, surveying the room through narrowed eyes, frequently resting her gaze on Thira and his companions. 'Madam Ckrystafis. Professional poisoner and proper nasty piece of work. Been 'angin' around with 'er. Learnin' a thing or two. Anyway, point is, she works for Stroever.'

'I don't get it,' said Krish, exchanging looks with all the guards surrounding them. 'If Ryker-Veere knows we're here, why doesn't he just lock us up?'

'Ryker-Veere's not runnin' the show,' said Thira. 'Stroever is. 'E's playin' with us. Playin' with Ryker-Veere too.'

'Thira, if you've solved the... thing,' said Krish, keeping his voice down, 'and getting out isn't an issue... then why are we still here?'

'We ain't leavin',' said Thira, ''til something's done about *them.*'

Thira nodded towards the stage. Ryker-Veere and Stroever stood together, preparing for their speech. Hush spread through the crowd in anticipation.

'My dear friends,' began Ryker-Veere, a more cautious opening than many had expected.

'I have been working hard these past few weeks on seeding the notion of dream legalisation in the press, thanks in no small part to many of my firm friends in this room. And despite your number dwindling – no, I shall not deny it! My theatrics at Kierbecker put many off!' He twiddled with his now-empty glass as a reminder of his stunt in the beer hall. 'Despite that, I am glad to say that Mr. Stroever and I have something phenomenal to announce to you, the chosen few. And, make no mistake, the City changes this very fade...'

And with that, Lord Ryker-Veere took a seat. The crowd awaited with a palpable eagerness. Stroever was already standing.

'Every twenty-first night, by tradition, Čevljarski Most is permitted to host the Dream-Pedlars' Parade,' began Stroever. 'To some it is an expression of humanity at its most idle, its most debauched. To others it is a celebration of our freedom and imagination. And NightTime is when our imagination runs wild. In the plain light of day, we see all things. In the darkness, we wander strange roads in our minds. And dreams, when safely administered, can be perfect catalysts for the escapism we crave in NightTime.

'But what if the parade did not have to end any time soon? What if it were to expand beyond Čevljarski Most? Dream-pedlars on every street corner or in shops attached to apothegaries belonging to many of the esteemed persons here tonight. Lord Ryker-Veere has spearheaded talk of legalisation, but if night were to end soon, we may lose momentum. Would the debate vanish with the night?

'So, imagine, if you will, a perpetual NightTime.'

A murmur of discontent spread amongst the crowd but withered as Stroever continued.

'Dreams would be big business in such a time, and should the sale of dreams be legalised, we would have a responsibility to provide safe dreams and set-up regulatory bodies to save the lives of those who choose to over-indulge. The business opportunities would be endless.

'And so I come to the canisters that have been handed out to you.'

The guests began toying with the petite, shining silver canisters.

'Please, turn the nozzles, just for a second, and have a guess at where the gas has been harvested from...'

Tiny hisses all around. The scent of gas seeped into the air.

'Krazlan?'

'Brackstone?'

'Oogondo?'

'Jiangsu?'

Stroever was now climbing the metal stairs to the gantry.

'Good guesses, but I regret to inform you, all wrong.'

'Rua da Batara?'

A great humming noise was emanating from somewhere unknown.

'Not Rua da Batara, no.'

Stroever turned to address his audience, staring down at them from the gantry. They looked up and beyond him at the glass ceiling of the factory. A great shape loomed across the sky. The incessant humming persisted.

'Watch... First a single pulse, then three, then another single burst, then five and finally a long pulse. Are you watching? One... three... one... five... and then a long burst...'

The shape was clear. They could make out the gas-star, dormant and lifeless, as were all stars in NightTime, though it was rare for them to be on the move at this time.

And then they saw the unbelieveable.

The star lit up. It blazed with light. Gasps from the crowd, blinded by light and blasted by heat. The light vanished and the warmth receded. A moment later, it flared up three more times. Another single burst followed, then five more in quick succession and finally a long blast of light.

The light, the gasps, the stifling warmth, breaking the spell of the long, cold night, bewitched and terrified the crowd.

Amongst the audience, Krish felt warm. His eyes lit up with hope that he'd see daylight on his own world again soon.

As the blinding light receded, revealing Isri Stroever standing defiant on the gantry, the crowd's chatter rose from an undercurrent to a tangible storm of noise.

'I have the technology!' cried Stroever from the gantry, silencing the crowd. 'Now, we can mine the stars! But I need your investment! Your contacts and experience! We can roll this out across the entire borough and perhaps farther still! An endless supply of gas!'

He began to descend the stairs, heading back to the stage. 'We shall bring Night Eternal! Set the stage for legalisation and an abundance of dreams! You fear the night? You want to see the light of the stars again? The stars are ours! And they will shine for a premium! We rose from the factories! We rebuilt the city in our own image! And tonight we take control of the stars themselves! Join us! And only those who sign on THAT piece of paper can be a part of this momentous endeavour!'

The clamour of the crowd rose again, and in seconds the first person stepped forward and signed their name on the paper. Then they came thick and fast, refusing to queue, fighting to be the next. Stroever watched from above, unmoved, unsurprised. He descended to be surrounded by admirers firing questions at him. Ryker-Veere stood to one side in the shadow of Stroever, desperately trying to conceal his dismay.

'I've seen it, mate,' said Thira. 'I know where this is going... Stroever has no plans to bring day back. Not 'ere, not anywhere. Not for no one. Do you get it?'

'What do you mean?' said Krish.

Before Thira could answer, the three of them spotted a man

running from the dreamers' room. He went directly to Ryker-Veere and whispered in his ear. Ryker-Veere looked at the man and asked a question eagerly. The man nodded with absolute certainty.

Ryker-Veere made his excuses, waded through the crowd, and departed, de Clercq hot on his heals. Stroever was watching.

'Thira!' said Krish. 'Ryker-Veere knows! We have to go! Now!'

'Mate, trust me, he—' began Thira.

Aemea seized them both by the arm.

'Krish, Thira, please! Listen to me! It's time! It's a second away now! All my futures are heading in one direction and now is the time! I can't avoid it!'

Madam Ckrystafis watched them with increasing intensity. She marched in their direction.

'I think this way would be best...' Aemea dragged the boys to one side.

Madam Ckrystafis picked up the pace. The guards rushed forward.

Thira yanked his right arm to the side and the staff unfurled itself, took shape, glowing gold, solid and sleek, humming with magic.

They backed into the woods, away from the stage and the guests. A guard sprinted out of the undergrowth and Thira lashed out, a wave of gold knocking the man to the ground, unconscious. Ckrystafis rounded on them. She pulled an instrument from her pocket and slashed in Krish's direction. She caught the edge of his finger and Krish felt a sting like a papercut. There was the tiniest cut on the tip of his little finger.

Thira threw Ckrystafis to one side with a blast of green. Aemea dragged the three of them towards another set of doors beyond the forest. Thira saw a padlock on the door and aimed his staff at it. Sparks flew and the padlock fell to the ground. He swished his staff and the door flew open.

§

Ryker-Veere had not run as fast as this at any time he recalled. De Clercq had to help him up the stairs. He was panting uncontrollably. He staggered along the corridor to his hotel room.

Inside he made it across the room and collapsed in front of the safe. The large chunk of metal had been placed to one side of the room. Ryker-Veere went to get up and found he did not have the energy. He paused for a moment, trying to get his breath back.

'H-h-h-help me, woman!' he managed.

As de Clercq stepped forward she looked at the pathetic heap of a man crumpled on the floor. Her sense of duty to him suddenly faded into obscurity. All those times she had obeyed him now felt like someone else's memories. Where she may once have felt pity for him, she now felt nothing.

'No.'

Ryker-Veere panted and panted.

'Wha-what?! Y-you've never... never said the word "'no'" in thirty years!'

De Clercq approached and looked down on him, toying with the picture slides on the side of the safe. All those moments privately resenting him, fantasizing about the worst, most horrendous thing to do to such a lazy, self-righteous, privileged, entirely dependent aristocrat. Only now did she realise what the best thing to do to someone like that was.

She turned and walked away without another word.

'D-d-de Clercq! De Clercq! What are you doing, woman?! De Clercq!'

She did not know what that sensation was swelling within her hollow form, but it was not regret. She left the hotel with nothing but a burgeoning smile.

He did not need her. Not now. He felt the strength returning to him. He took to his feet, steadying himself against the safe. He selected the three slides, pressed them into the lock in the exact order his dreamers had informed him, and turned the handle.

A low metalic clang. He opened the safe, dizzy as the oxygen flooded his brain, excitement coursing through him.

His face fell.

Within the safe there was a single slip of paper. He scanned the safe interior to make certain he was not mistaken.

He lifted it and read:

Devil claim you, thief.
I.S.

A corridor devoid of sentinellight

A tiptoeing girl who is ever so bright

Through the kitchen door, for the Woman she'd set

A trap of candle-wick-web, with which she'd met

Eva approaches the room, then slips inside

Her secret domain is the best place to hide

Within a doll's house big enough to climb in

Tiny chairs, beds, pots, pans and a rolling pin

A world of miniature but for one thing

A most special object her father did bring

52
GLASS

Krish, Thira and Aemea burst into a room of soft light, a warm, welcoming scent in the air. A machine whirred away. Most of the room was taken up by a large vat, mechanical stirrers turning round and round in the thick white liquid.

A guard threw the door open and hurtled straight towards Aemea. Krish grabbed hold of a large pole and struck hard against his legs. The man fell but just got hold of Aemea's foot. Aemea tripped and dropped to the ground, falling head first into the vat.

Thira aimed his golden staff at the guard. A flash of blue rendered him unconscious as Madam Ckrystafis burst into the room, the opening door knocking the staff clean out of Thira's hand. Aemea pulled her head out of the vat.

'Timetimetime! Happeningallatonce! It'shappeningnow! Everything'shappeningnow!' she shouted.

Krish hurled his full weight against the open door and Ckrystafis, still standing in the doorway, was thrown forward into the room and onto the ground. Thira dived after Ckrystafis and the two grappled on the floor, baring teeth. Krish launched the pole into Ckrystafis's side, throwing her off of Thira.

Krish threw the staff to Thira who caught it. Ckrystafis jumped to her feet. She seized Aemea by the neck and held her under the liquid.

That smell... warm... like milk... and something else.

Krish and Thira stopped in their tracks as Madam Ckrystafis held the squirming Aemea under. Thira aimed his staff at Ckrystafis.

'Let her go!' screamed Thira.

'You are not long for these streets, Thira!' said Madam Ckrystafis, murderous glee in her eyes.

'Let her go!'

'I would surrender now, young Thira. You will not harm me. Not if you want the antidote...'

'What?!' said Krish.

'LET-HER-GO!' Thira inched closer to the vat.

Krish saw the knife clutched in Ckrystafis's free hand behind her back. She flicked a switch on the hilt and a drop of black liquid appeared at the tip of the blade.

'Thira!' said Krish.

Thira went for Aemea as Ckrystafis grabbed hold of Thira and held the blade aloft. Red light shot from the staff, hitting Ckrystafis in the chest. In shock, she dropped the knife and it tore down her front, leaving a diagonal line of inky black in its wake. As Thira was thrown against the wall,

Ckrystafis fell to the floor, dead.

Krish sprinted forward towards Aemea.

'KRISH, NO!' cried Thira.

Krish pulled Aemea's head above the surface and she gasped desperately for breath. The scent of milk and liquorice overwhelmed him. The tiny wound on his finger stung like hell as the liquid mixed with his blood. A dizzying sensation, and

then the form, the colour, the sound, the feeling of the room
Krish was standing in changed entirely.

First the silence.

Then a sound like distant rain.

Glass slowly smashing somewhere just out of sight.

A fizzing, tingling noise, like butter frying in the pan,
popping candy in the month.

The room was still there, but it was darkened with pools
of dim light emanating from unseen sources. All was blurry.
As Krish moved his head, objects and people in his line of
vision became distorted. It was like seeing through rounded
glass.

He saw figures. Aemea by his side, frozen in the moment of
being retrieved from the vat, Thira in mid-shout. They were
partially obscured by shadow, or unfocussed, like they were
moving. Moving so fast that it appeared as if they were not
moving at all.

Here and there, through the glass-like air of this world,
both vivid and fuzzy, he saw beams of rainbow light, reaching
out from the darkened edges of the room and fanning out like
sunlight through a prism.

Then he heard the voice.

He could determine no age or gender, but it was gentle and
patient. It had all the time in the worlds.

As the seconds, the hours,
The years, the ages march on,
Neglect not the dust at Its feet,
Myrthali! The Sands of Time!
Take It! They say,
And reclaim that which is lost.

As the seconds, the hours,
The years, the ages march on,
Neglect not the dust at Its feet,
Myrthali! The Sands of Time!
Take It! They say,
And reclaim that which is lost.

As the seconds, the hours,
The years, the ages march on,
Neglect not the dust at Its feet,
Myrthali! The Sands of Time!
Take It! They say,
And reclaim that which is lost.

As the seconds, the hours,
The years, the ages march on,
Neglect not the dust at Its feet,
Myrthali! The Sands of Time!
Take It! They say,
And reclaim that which is lost.

Yes... That which one has frittered away, now to reclaim and expand. Time will not enslave us, will it, young Krishna?

'Er... Hello?'

You will not have to conceal the clock from your kitchen in the garden once time — as the second hand and her squandering companions see it — loses much of its meaning for you.

'How... do you know about the clock in the garden? I didn't think anyone had noticed.'

Oh, it is still there now. In your own time, that is. Leaves and vines embracing it, tiny insects sheltering within its mechanisms.

'But... how...?'

Why, because you told me, young Krishna. It is your description. You WILL tell me, ARE telling me, HAVE told me. You will tell me many things. You will tell me that which I must know above all else.

'Er, right.'

You see, I am beyond time as you know it. All moments are now. Life, death, time, stories. Yes, stories. I know your hatred of them and, as you saw, are seeing, shall see, your instincts are right, even if your reasons are not.

'Right. No, sorry, hang on... What?!'

All in good time...

'Oh. Right. Look, I'm not best with all this explainy stuff at the best of times – would a straight answer be too much to ask for?'

I am simply stating that your dislike of stories is something you can harness, use to your advantage. Remember this.

'Er... okay.'

Excellent! In this moment beyond moments, you are bending the rules, but you cannot know yet all that you will know.

'Think my head's going to explode.'

Your instinct about her was right.

'What...? Oh... The devil?'

If that is the title you have chosen for her. Although it may soon be passed to another.

'Erm...'

All in good time...

''Course. Quick question – what the hell's going on?'

You can't guess?

'It was Myrthali. I smelt milk and liquorice.'

Yes. The scent of Myrthali being mixed to extend a life. But Myrthali has other properties. It can have odd side effects if it enters the bloodstream or if you take vast quantities all at once.

'Aemea! She's swallowed loads! Is that why she can always feel the future? Why it was getting closer?'

Indeed. It is not meant to be consumed so fast. Time is a most curious thing. It spread out from her present, into her past, and all the way into her future. That is why she has such an unusual power. There is another property to Myrthali. One that is possibly unique to you.

'I... I touched it, so I'm on my way home?'

No. You are not.

'Oh.'

You will only be transported home once you touch raw Myrthali. There is none in this room. It is safely locked away. This you told, are telling me, will tell me. Raw Myrthali was brought here once, long ago, under very strict security. The Myrthali has mixed with your blood from the cut Madam Ckrystafis gave you. That has brought you here, to a place in between. As for the Myrthali concoction in that room, the one you call devil cast a spell on you to bring back the Myrthali to your own world. The spell will confuse it. The Myrthali will not stay in this world or return to yours, but instead will be banished to some realm unknown. A forgotten corner of a lifeless universe.

'But the rest, the raw Myrthali, that's still there? I mean, in KnockThrice? The City?'

Oh, yes.

'Right. So how much longer will I be here?'

You are not here.

'Riiight.'

You are still in the room. We are beyond time here. But from your perspective, to keep things simple, I would say soon.

'Right. I mean seriously, I am well confused.'

You aren't even going to ask my name?

'Will I get a straight answer?'

No, but that is your fault for not asking the right questions.

'Okay. Look, my friends are dying, possibly, so I might just get going, if that's alright with you?

As you wish. Just remember – as I know you will, are, have remembered – trust your instincts on stories. And your instincts regarding the one you call devil also.

'Noted. Anything a little less mysterious that actually makes sense?'

All in—

'In good time. Yeah, got it.'

Excellent! We shall meet in time, Krishna. When there is no time left to be spent. And when we do, then you shall tell me that which I must know.

53
THE ANSWER & THE ANTIDOTE

Krish gasped. It was as if he'd broken the surface of a body of water. He fell backwards onto the ground.

The room was clearer yet less vivid than it had been seconds ago. Air rushed in and out of him. For a moment he'd forgotten about breathing, the beat of his heart, all those normal things you did as time passed.

Thira was by the wall, Ckrystafis dead on the ground and Aemea sat up in the vat. She was completely dry and the Myrthali mixture was nowhere to be seen.

'What happened?' he said.

'You... just kinda flickered, went all hazy and then... well, then nothing,' said Thira.

Krish and Thira turned to Aemea.

'That... that was Myrthali?' said Aemea, catching her breath.

Krish nodded.

'Where is it now?' asked Thira.

'Gone,' said Krish. 'Somewhere none of us can get it. It's the raw Myrthali we need though. That's in the safe.'

He noticed everyone was eyeing him with bewilderment.

'There was a voice,' he explained. 'It was odd. Time froze. I heard someone I'll meet in the future. Or that's what it said. Said it's only the raw Myrthali that's any good to us, and that's still in the safe.'

'Someone from the future?!' Thira was puzzled. 'Blimey. Things get weirder and weirder with you, mate!'

'Tell me about it,' said Krish. 'Aemea, are you okay?'

'I... You know what? I don't think I've ever been better.' She looked around like a newborn taking in the world for the first time. 'I can feel... now. Just now! And that's it! How wonderful!' She jumped out of the vat.

There were voices outside.

'We'd better get a shift on!' said Thira, staff at the ready. 'Hang on!' He ran over to Ckrystafis's body and searched her comprehensively.

'What? What is it?' said Krish.

Thira stopped, closed his eyes and sighed. He muttered to himself. 'Never keeps any on 'er. Makes sense.'

'What?'

'Nothin'! Let's get the 'ell outta here.'

Moments later they were sprinting through the forest, away from the sound of the guards, branches and prickly gorse catching their clothes as they ran. Voices came from ahead and they ducked down behind a holly bush. They spoke in whispers, catching their breath.

'Where did that Myrthali come from?' said Krish. 'Ryker-Veere must have only just opened the safe.'

'It ain't Ryker-Veere. It's Stroever.'

'Stroever?!' said Aemea.

'Yep. 'E's been playin' Ryker-Veere all along. 'E's got plans for the City and we've gotta stop 'im!'

'Thira... what was Ckrystafis saying?' said Krish. 'She said something about an antidote.'

'Yeah. She poisoned me. Something called Shrilwood's Knee. Think I got a fade left, at most. But I know somethin' she don't. The tower in Stroever's gaff – that's where 'e keeps a supply of antidotes.'

'To all her poisons?' said Aemea.

'Yep,' said Thira. 'Well, most of 'em, I guess. Was tryin' to get 'im to give me more details.'

'How did you get information out of him?' said Krish.

'Bit of ad lib, bit of magic, bit of luck,' said Thira. 'That's when I found out about the decoy safe that Ryker-Veere 'ad taken. Wouldn't tell me the combination to the safe, though. Like 'e' trained 'imself never to reveal it. But I know where to find the real safe.'

'And how exactly are we meant to stop Stroever's plan?' said Aemea. 'Whatever it might be.'

''E'll drain the world of light. 'E 'as this ship, the Selkirk, and a device that can spear stars.'

'Spear stars?!' said Aemea.

'Yep! 'E can get aboard 'em and drain 'em of gas. Turn out the stars. So, 'e'll make night last forever, 'ave dreams legalised, get people addicted, then Ckrystafis 'as created all these poisoned dreams that eat away at yer. In time it makes you all depressed. Bloody 'orrible!'

A great black cloud was slowly spreading through Krish's mind. He thought of how much he was craving light, how the endless dark with no relief gnawed away at his mental health and smothered all hope.

'He'll trigger suicides,' Krish said. 'It could affect anyone. Everybody! It'll spread and spread and, depending on how strong he makes those poisoned dreams, he could clear the whole world.'

'Is that what he wants?' said Aemea. 'To empty the City of people?'

'Yep,' said Thira. 'And in time I reckon 'e'll achieve it.'

They could see movement in the overgrowth heading their way.

'We need to get to old Ckrystafis's poison kitchen,' said Thira.

They followed Thira through the forest, crouching as they went. He led them to a mound in a clearing covered in moss. Set into the mound was a wooden door. Thira turned the handle and led them in.

Krish and Aemea followed Thira into the room and took in all the neatly arranged plants and herbs around the room. Thira immediately began to search manically. He yanked open drawers and threw open cupboards but only found more ingredients. He swore under his breath.

'She don't keep 'em 'ere,' he said. 'Mixes antidotes when she needs 'em and takes 'em with 'er.' He swore again.

'I'll keep looking,' said Krish, starting to search. 'What did you say it was called?'

'Shrilwood's Knee,' said Thira.

They tore the room apart but had no luck.

'I can't find anything,' said Aemea.

''Course ya can't,' said Thira solemnly. 'She left me on my own 'ere loads. She obviously didn't keep any antidotes or books on the stuff 'ere. The tower at Stroever's gaff is our only 'ope.'

'And talking of Stroever,' said Aemea, 'we're missing the most obvious question – why? Why do all of this?'

'Got a rough idea,' said Thira. 'From stuff Stroever said and thanks to a dream Ckrystafis showed me of Jane Stroever.'

'Who?' asked Krish

'Isairis Stroever's wife. And speakin' of Isairis, there's

something else Ryker-Veere don't know about Stroever. Somethin' 'e should 'ave realised long ago. But the point is, Stroever
started boastin' about 'is innovations. All 'is plans to mine the
stars for their gas. Keeps the plans for 'is star-piercing equipment somewhere very bloody safe!'

'Where?' said Krish.

Thira pointed upwards.

'I take it you don't mean in the ceiling?' said Aemea.

'A star,' said Thira. 'That one 'e controlled for 'is little show.
It's still speared by the Selkirk. There's a box on the wall inside
the star. 'E described it to me.'

'Another Ujhelyi lock?' said Aemea. 'Like the safe?'

'Nah, no pretty pictures this time.'

'Then I can pick the lock.'

A silent conference between the three of them.

'If we find the plans, what do we do with them?' said Krish

'Destroy 'em! said Thira.

'No!' said Aemea. 'He may have copies. But if we made the
plans public knowledge... Well, it won't stop the technology
existing for people to copy, but there will be outrage once the
public knows. And at least it won't be solely in Stroever's
hands.'

'Fine, but 'ow the 'ell yer gonna get up to that star then?'
said Thira.

Aemea thought for a moment. 'Well, I suppose if Shad,
Stavast and I can storm Stroever's ship, we could find the plans
on the speared star.'

'Oh, yeah! Sounds well easy!' said Thira.

'The odds are against us, I admit,' said Aemea, 'but we
must try, and fast. The only other issue around getting the
message out there is that Ryker-Veere controls much of the
press.'

'What about a dream?' said Thira, having a brainwave.

'Yeah! Memory's the easiest one to make! Those gas-stars spew gas, right? M'magic's a bit rusty but there's this exponential growth spell that's surprisingly simple. I create a memory dream with the plans in it, make a few globes up, enchant 'em to grow and the dream spews out onto the streets of the City. Everyone will see the plans in their dreams!'

ShadowThief pointed enthusiastically at the sky. *Don't you realise what you're saying? You'd restart a star!*

'Yes!' said Aemea. 'I'm not sure if that will be enough to trigger day again, what with the economy being as it is, but—'

'Actually...' said Thira. 'Not saying I'm an expert, money and all that works pretty differently where I'm from, but Ckystafis did say things were improvin'. The war's all but over and Stroever's biggest worry 'as been NightTime endin' before 'e can carry out 'is plan. So...'

Night could end, said ShadowThief.

They all breathed in the possibilities for a moment.

'That's all very nice, but how are the plans going to make their way into the dream?' said Aemea.

'All ya need to do is add a small bit of the plans, could just be a corner. Don't even 'ave to 'ave anything written on it as long as it's part of the paper it's printed on,' said Thira.

Thira searched the room. He found five dreamglobes and got to work filling them with oil and various other ingredients.

'You figured it out?' said Krish. 'How she escapes? The woman in the final dream.'

A dark look from Thira. 'Yeah. I worked it out.'

Krish was furious at Thira for holding back.

'Well, how, for god's sake?' Krish screamed. 'Does she climb? Dig? Poison? Parachute her way out? How?'

Thira looked at Krish long and hard. 'You wouldn't like it.'

'How?'

Thira scanned the kitchen. He found what he was looking for. He seized a bowl and dropped it loudly on the bench in front of Krish. A collection of shiny dark red fruit stared back up at him.

'The cherries?' said Krish.

'They're poisonous?' said Aemea.

'Knew it as soon as I saw 'em,' said Thira.

'So, she poisons the guards?' said Krish.

'Mate, when I say ya won't like it, just take my word for it!' said Thira. 'The cherries will open the safe.'

'Why?' said Krish. 'Look, if she kills a few guards, I get it, but how does she get out of the prison?'

'There's cyanide in cherry stones,' said Thira. 'Not enough to kill ya, and if ya swallowed a cherry stone most likely it'll just pass through ya just fine. Bloody stupid to put it to the test, though. Point is, ya'd need a few stones and ya'd 'ave to crack 'em open. The shoes and the needle could help get it out, but even without 'em ya could find a way.'

'But how many cherries would she need to poison all the gu—?'

'Krish, mate, ya're not listenin' to the story. She escapes, but she don't leave the cell.' Krish began to fill with gloom. 'Dhriti knows she can't get away. She don't wanna be tortured. Don't want to give away information that could cost the lives of 'er friends.' Krish was going red with fury. 'So she kills herself.'

'No.'

'That's what the cherries are for.'

'No!'

'It's just a dream!'

'What if it was based on a memory? What if it actually happened?'

'Well, maybe it did. Not all stories end well, Krish. I'm sorry but that's the answer...'

'No. Suicide's never the answer.'

'Krish, I know what you mean.' Thira spoke slowly. 'Jane Stroever knew it weren't the answer. She knew that nothing was worse than nothing, but she was concerned that without someone to help, that she'd act before she could think clearly. Stroever should have listened to her. But Dhriti was gonna die, so she did it on her own terms. It's not the same.'

Krish watched as Thira continued mixing the dream. He suddenly felt grief for Dhriti. He thought of all the people who had died during his journey through KnockThrice. And all those he might still lose. And was it his imagination, or was Thira slowing down?

Thira finished his work and pushed the five dreamglobes towards Aemea.

'Soak a scrap o' paper from the plans in each for two minutes and then drop 'em into the 'eart of the star,' said Thira.

'Thira,' said Krish, 'You're talking like... like you're not going to make it that far.'

'No,' said Thira. 'I'm stickin' with you. We gotta get to Stroever's and take the Myrthali off 'im. All these ideas to plunge the City into darkness, to use the poisoned dreams Ckrystafis created, that's what 'e needs the Myrthali for. Without it, 'e can't finish 'is work to transform the City. Will take 'im years! Decades!'

'So Ryker-Veere's not part of this?' said Krish.

'Oh, Ryker-Veere's part of the plan. Just not in the way 'e expects.'

'I just don't understand the barbarism of the man!' said Aemea. 'To create a whole lonely world just for himself.'

Thira looked at Aemea side-on. 'Oh, 'e will not be alone.'

'Helena?' said Aemea. 'I had heard his sister was still around.'

Thira's upper lip curled up. 'Sister? You lot really 'aven't been payin' attention, 'ave yer? And 'e don't give two 'oots about 'Elena.'

'Who then?' said Krish.

'Take it no one's mentioned the name Eva?'

Footsteps approach, Eva has been discovered!

The Woman bursts in, her refuge uncovered!

Behind father's object is the place to hide

The strange little safe, pretty slides on the side

'I hated you from the fade you stole my sleigh!'

'I hate you too, mum-dumb, now please go away!'

A sour smile, of love the Woman bereft

And then she drew close, spoke these words and then left:

'Don't call me "mum", child,' she said and then kissed her

'You know full well I am your little sister'

54
THE BULLET & THE BLADE

'You knew, didn't you? You've always known!'

Isri Stroever turned slowly on the bottom step of the metal staircase in the factory to face the man shouting at him. Lord Ryker-Veere shoved his way past the guards attempting to hold him back. He was redder than usual, his hair a mess and his clothing ruffled.

'You've been playing games with me, Isri!' screamed Ryker-Veere. 'Toying with me when all along— Unhand me, man!' Ryker-Veere threw off the guards attempting to hinder him.

Stroever peered down across the empty stage, the reception area where all the guests had been milling about not half an hour ago. He looked past Ryker-Veere to the guard next to him.

'Did he have anything on him?' said Stroever.

'No, sir,' said the guard.

'Devil curse you, man!' cried Ryker-Veere. 'These are my men!'

Stroever smiled to himself, a brief, self-satisfied joke.

'His name is David,' said Stroever.

'What?! Who?!' spat out Ryker-Veere.

'The guard standing next to you. The one who has been in your employ for over twelve years. His name is David.'

'I don't give a blue jaunt, damn you! Now tell me – where is it?'

The smile hung on the corners of Stroever's lips. 'Why don't you step into my office, Anders...?'

Ryker-Veere took one last look at the guards who stood back, then followed Stroever up the staircase.

'Thank you for your service tofade, gentlemen,' said Stroever to the guards. 'Sleep well.'

The guards nodded their approval to Stroever and left.

A fire smouldered in the grate. Deep orange light shimmered in the shining dark wood of the coffee table and in the leather of the armchairs by the fire. Stroever closed the door behind Ryker-Veere, entombing them in the cosy, darkened room.

'Where is it?' said Ryker-Veere.

'The Myrthali?' said Stroever.

'You know damn well I'm talking about the Myrthali!'

'Safe. Very safe.'

'You knew! You've always known! Your father was a fool to pass on his great empire to you!'

'He was a fool. For his misguided trust and grating flamboyance. Yes, he was. I am glad more than anything that that man is dead.'

'You were there! That night when Helena told me where your father was! When he was hiding at the Beggar's Lantern, the ignoramus! For years I thought it was my imagination, my paranoia, but you were there! Behind those doors! I saw you!'

Stroever sank into his armchair, folding his gloved hands in his lap. A smile festered on his lips with quiet satisfaction as the fire crackled away.

'Anders... I can tell you with absolute certainly that that fade I was nowhere near the house.'

Ryker-Veere was genuinely taken aback.

'You're lying! I saw you!'

'Why do you want to keep on living, Anders?' Stroever's casual tone chilled Ryker-Veere to the bone. 'You really want to be this pompous, self-righteous, overgrown infant for decades more to come? For centuries?'

Ryker-Veere lowered his voice. For a while he was flustered. 'Now-now-now, stop that!'

'This is what you want?'

'Stop that!'

'Just to keep on living like—?'

'I don't want to die! Is that...is that really a surprise to you? To anyone? I-I-I see my birthdays grow in number and all I see beyond a certain point in my future is darkness! Worse than darkness!'

'No.'

'No?! What do you mean, 'no'? Damn you!'

'You cannot outrun the inevitable, Anders. You know this. So, tell me – why?'

Ryker-Veere spent a moment catching his breath, ignoring the inviting chair next to Stroever's by the fire. 'My work. It is unfinished.'

'And there we go... You are a man who fantasises about his own funeral, Anders.'

'*Lord* Ryker-Veere, damn you!'

'Your vanity is endemic within yourself. You wish to conquer death, to enjoy seeing your own legacy unfold, merely to appease your own sense of self-love. You want to live long enough to witness the entire City unanimously declare you its saviour. And let me tell you now, no amount of Myrthali will allow you to live long enough to sample such a delusion.'

'*My* Myrthali, you little runt!'

Stroever let out a sudden sharp, high laugh, a disturbingly uncharacteristic guttural noise from deep inside which silenced Ryker-Veere.

'When you took the safe,' said Stroever, 'the duplicate safe you believed contained the Myrthali, you truly thought it now belonged to you, didn't you?'

'I saw you!' said Ryker-Veere.

'You did not.'

'I saw a child run from that spot! I looked into your eyes! I spoke to you as a boy – do not tell me you do not remember! You were there!'

'The child you saw was not me. You saw my daughter, Eva.'

'Your... your daughter?'

'Eva. Helena's older sibling.'

Ryker-Veere stood there, completely lost, staring at the man slouched in the chair in front of the fire.

Stroever continued. 'So curious that the moment you became deaf in one ear, you failed to notice that you had also gone blind in both eyes.'

'What in blue blazes are you blathering about? The safe was left to me, in the agreement Isairis and I—'

Stroever leapt from his chair, a hellish fury in his eyes. 'DO NOT SAY THAT NAME IN MY PRESENCE AGAIN! ISAIRIS STROEVER IS DEAD!'

For a moment, Ryker-Veere gazed opened-mouthed at the man in front of him, utterly bewildered by the redundant statement he'd just made.

And then he saw...

Isairis Stroever had always dressed older to impress his peers. He had a long beard and a round belly and gave the impression of an experienced old warhorse. But his jollity, incurable optimism and naivety at business revealed a younger man.

Isri's slim figure and upright stature gave him a sense of youth, but the receding hairline, crow's feet and furrowed brow belonged to a man who had been worn down by time.

Isri Stroever looked just like the man Isairis would have become if he had survived his own death.

But now Ryker-Veere saw that the man before him was not Isri Stroever, son of Isairis, because Isri Stroever had never existed.

'My old friend...' said Ryker-Veere. His anger melted down into something between awe and fear. 'It is as if a single fade had not passed...'

Isairis Stroever stared back at him.

One by one, he peeled off the gloves and dropped them to the floor.

'I thought I had passed all the theatrical traits of my former, *wretched* self on to you, Anders,' said Stroever. 'But one remained.' Stroever held up his hand and flexed his fingers in front of his face. 'Incredible how a pair of gloves and a reluctance to shake hands can convince people you are someone else.' He was mesmerised by the fire flickering across his fingers. 'Myrthali is most curious. To live each fade seeing the same face in the mirror, unchanged by time. You desire to take it for yourself, Anders, but believe me, a life unchanged becomes dull. A numb existence. No... I have lived as long as I have lived for another...'

'But the child I saw was most definitely a boy!'

'You saw what you expected to see. When my beloved Jane and I had our first child, Eva, I felt cursed. The child was sick. We gave Eva every comfort, every luxury, but were prepared for her inevitable death. And being female, she could not be my heir.

'My expectations were high for our next child, but she too was female. Helena was healthy and inquisitive, and I pondered if there was a way to change the law, to stop my empire passing to some obscure male cousin. But Jane doted on the unwell Eva who reminding her of herself. As a child, Jane suffered an injury to the head which left her paralysed down her left side.'

'Preposterous, old boy! Jane was no invalid!'

'She hid it well, though it had a profound effect on her when she first sought work as a youth. She wanted to make certain that Eva would not face similar challenges, that we should lobby for changes in government, but I would not listen.'

'But I never once heard the name Eva spoken in your household!'

'We cut Eva's hair, kept her in hiding, told Helena to call her Isri. We had even registered her as "Isri" at birth in case there was a chance to pass my empire on to a fictitious male heir. This would turn out to be a fortuitous decision.'

'And the Myrthali? When did this enter into your plans?'

'We discovered quite by accident that the forest had healing powers for Eva's condition, so we spent much time there. That's when we found her. The ancient creature from another world hiding in our forest. When she told me of the Myrthali, I realised I could halt the disease in its tracks. Not cure it, but pause it.

'The ancient creature did not approve of this usage of the Myrthali so I locked it in a safe. She cracked the combination, but I stopped her in time from stealing much of the Myrthali.'

'You said you'd never opened that damn safe!'

'Of course that's what I said. I did not want you to suspect that I was already giving Eva Myrthali by then to save her. So, following the ancient creature's attempted raid on my safe, she disappeared with a flask of Madam Ckrystafis's versiriam. I never understood why she took the versiriam until I realised you were chasing dreams, Anders. Ckrystafis often spoke of how those wishing to hide a secret would place clues in dreams and then use the versiriam to wipe their minds of said secret. In this case, the combination to the safe. Just so no one could extract it from her by torture.'

Ryker-Veere's head was dizzy with revelations now. 'And after your dealings with Hanch, the name Isri was there waiting for you?'

Stroever inhaled deeply through his nose. 'I was a fool not to negotiate with Hanch. After I refused a meeting, he issued his threat. Like a coward, I ran, though I stayed close by at the Beggar's Lantern, as I didn't feel he was entirely serious. I did hatch a plan with Madam Ckrystafis to have him poisoned, but thanks to Helena and yourself, I never got to put this into operation.

'Hanch's ruffians made their way to the Beggar's Lantern and roughed up a gentleman in a suit similar to mine, I am led to believe. Perhaps he was a banker drinking away his financial woes in NightTime, perhaps he had high blood pressure, who knows; but whatever was the case, when he was struck, he did not get up again.

'I felt certain that if I waited a few more fades, Hanch would relent after realising his terrible mistake, but his accomplices informed him that they'd killed Isairis Stroever. I hesitated to return home, my mind becoming excited with the possibilities that could proceed my "death", so I sent Madam Ckrystafis to "identify" the body. But, paranoid that a telegram to my own address would be intercepted, there was one person I did not inform of my intentions.'

'Jane...'

Stroever's voice quivered as he spoke her name. 'Jane. I

thought it would be difficult, but I believed she was strong and would pull through for Eva and Helena. Instead, she telegrammed her sister to come and help. The darkness got her before her sister arrived.

'I hid away on the factory floor. I knew I was unlikely to be found there. I scratched and tore and destroyed the vile man who was Isairis Stroever. He killed Jane! And I will never forgive him. Helena had already been taken into care by Jane's sister, but Eva ran away to join me on the floor of the factory. She always felt safest amongst the trees. The two of us knew that place better than any of the workers. Of course, she found me without much searching. My beloved Helena had betrayed me but now I saw the perfect child in Eva, every inch her late mother's daughter.

'We both took Myrthali. Me, so I could re-emerge in time as Isri, my non-existent son; Eva, to freeze the sickness within her. We brewed the Myrthali in small quantities in secret in the factory only when we required it. We then locked the raw Myrthali away in the safe. I took heggarum santai, a variation of versiriam perfected by Madam Ckrystafis, whom I met when we were searching for a cure for Eva. The heggarum santai means I know the combination as I open the safe, though at no other time. I cannot say the three slides out loud, and I cannot be forced to open it under duress.'

'And when did you make your damn duplicate safe?'

Stroever smiled. 'Oh, long ago. Just in case.'

'I should have seen that the man who emerged from the factory was the same as the one who'd gone missing all those years previously, but I did not believe. Isri's resemblance to Isairis was surely only skin deep. You were not the same!'

'It was so peaceful, Anders. So tranquil in that forest. And that is the future I shall bring to the City.'

Ryker-Veere was beginning to understand. 'Those dreams of yours – they are poisonous!'

'Madam Ckrystafis has perfected the art of the slow-release poison. It can be years before it triggers. Slowly, one by one, the City will empty...'

'It's barbaric! You really think Jane would have wanted this?'

And now Stroever exploded. 'The City spat out Jane! It rejected her! I will rebuild it! Eva is healed by greenery, and so I shall recreate the City in the image of the forest... Great towers shall become mighty trees! I shall tear down bricks and iron and steel and let birds fly and beasts prowl! I shall heel the City of the pestilence of humanity and create a pure world for my Eva...'

'Isairis, my old friend, this is insanity!'

'Do not call me by that name! We are both responsible for the death of Isairis Stroever, and I am glad at last to return the favour.'

Ryker-Veere loosened his collar, feeling himself perspiring. 'So, I was right. You were poisoning me.'

'Your instincts aboard the Selkirk were indeed correct. You made me sample your food and drink, though I had indeed poisoned both. One helpful side effect of heggarum santai is that it makes you impervious to most poisons.'

A cold shiver passed through Ryker-Veere. 'How long have I got, old chum?'

Stroever's smile broadened. 'As long as I choose. I knew that your vanity would be enough to keep you alive until I had your contacts and investment to create my fleet of star-spearers.

'And although I despise the name I was born with, perhaps, for official purposes proceeding your funeral, I shall let the authorities know who I am and claim my inheritance.

Remember the contract we signed long ago, Anders? It all passes to the surviving party... Your punishment is to age and die as I take over your empire. Much the same punishment I gave to Helena – she ages while her younger sister remains unchanged.'

'You have become everything Jane would abhor! She would use such a power to better this world, not destroy it!'

'I shall turn the City into a sanctuary for our child. Jane shall live on through Eva.'

A cold, dizzy terror swirled through Ryker-Veere. He looked down and spoke simply. 'You see me only as a hollow egotist? That I care for no one other than myself? So, if I live only to pad my own ego, then, in my own mind at least, I'd better die a devil-damned hero.'

Stroever's eyes narrowed. 'You believe you can stop me?'

'For Jane's sake, I do.'

'Ha! You are nothing, Anders! Nothing! An idiot masquerading as a buffoon. A traitor!'

Ryker-Veere sidestepped, an armchair now between himself and Stroever. 'We're all traitors in our line of work. It's a cutthroat industry, old chap!'

Stroever caught a flash of light from a metal object in Ryker-Veere's hand. He suddenly recalled Ryker-Veere's slight-of-hand antics at Kierbeckerstraße and that the guard who had searched his old business partner usually carried a knife.

In the instant Stroever's hand dived into his jacket, Ryker-Veere kicked the chair in front of him, knocking Stroever off-balance. Ryker-Veere rushed forward and lunged at Stroever with the knife, piercing his chest just as his old friend pulled something from his pocket. A flash of light, cordite in the air, his throat ripped from him by the blast. Emese's pistol hit home.

Ryker-Veere's fine white shirt was soaking in warm

redness. Blood and pride poured from the fresh gash in his neck and into his lap. He crumpled onto the floor by the fire and died with the smell of iron in his nostrils.

Stroever clutched at his chest. He winced in soundless agony, blood dripping to the floor. He looked at the wound knowing that no amount of Myrthali would hold back death for long.

He was hunched over on his knees, his arm outstretched, one hand on the ground, holding himself steady.

He sucked in the pain and took to his feet, muttering a single word as he left the room.

'Eva...'

55
THE SPIT & THE SPRAY

They parted on the shingle beach, the beady eyes of sentinels passing overhead.

Krish and Aemea broke their embrace.

'In my experience,' said Aemea, 'it's always that one last job, that final adventure sailing off to streets new, that is fatal to the heroes of the story.'

Krish shrugged. 'I was never a big fan of stories.'

'They are good for escapism, but at some point, you must take their ideas and escape for yourself. I intend for Shad and I to come out of this one alive.'

'Seems like a good idea.'

'It does. And then we will go as far as we can go. Perhaps I shall retire before I am old enough to fall into the trap of working for a living.'

Krish laughed.

Thira stepped over to join them, fresh from an exchange with ShadowThief.

'Them visions back, Aems?' said Thira.

'Curiously, they are,' said Aemea. 'Though I'm not sure I approve of "Aems".'

'Fair dos. Back to an hour?'

'No. Just a few minutes. They're extending in time fast, though I'm paying them less attention now. I know there are many roads I can take, some feel better than others, but I am very happy in the now, just the same.'

'So, what ya feelin' a few minutes from now?'

'Emptiness and anticipation, but there's warmth too. And for that I am glad.'

Krish smiled and turned to ShadowThief. Her eyes glinted in the dark. A sentinel passed over and she shimmered with colour, every line of her tattooed skin dancing in ambers and aquamarines and scarlets and emeralds and indigoes. She took her knife and tore away the dark between them. She cupped a hand around each of Krish and Thira's faces. They returned the gesture and the three of them were lost in the worlds of each other's eyes for some time.

ShadowThief said many things without uttering a word. They nodded their understanding and the four of them embraced tightly. Then, in a moment that they all knew had come too soon, Krish and Thira went in one direction, and Aemea and ShadowThief in the other.

§

Below the deck of Captain Stavast's small but sturdy vessel, by the light of a single lantern hanging from the ceiling, amongst the rope and tinned supplies, a small group listened intently.

Aemea, Emese, Edris, Emna and Esna perched on a crate while Stavast hovered by a large chest. ShadowThief listened from up on deck through the open hatch. She was pre-occupied with cutting away the dark, tearing blankets of shadow from the night and adding them to a growing pile.

'The ship I has spied!' said Stavast. 'On the wide waters of Elstran's Pass, just nor'west o' Chronometer Dock. Pierced a star it has indeed. Decent-sized crew on deck. No idea if any lubber's keepin' watch aboard the star itself. The harbour-master says it's a private endeavour and for shipping to keep back. Feels like a good command to disobey...'

Stavast opened the crate and tossed aside the lengths of rope on top of the large object within. Everyone leaned forward to see what was inside.

'Something from my warring youth,' said Stavast. 'Terrible thing, but fadenigh is its time!'

The metal object was the size of a human torso and was painted dark blue, ridged in places like the dips and troughs of the waves.

ShadowThief banged her foot several times on the deck.

'She says that killing is to be a last resort,' translated Aemea.

'They'll be unwise to incur the wrath of this old seadog.' Stavast slapped his thigh excitedly. 'Aye, I feel the froth boiling within me! The spit and the spray rising in the waterways of my blood! If there's war this fadenigh, may we see starlight and calm waters on-the-morrow!'

§

The Selkirk was anchored some way from the harbour walls on the wide channel of Elstran's Pass. A thick line of wire led from the aft section to a spear which had pierced the low-lying gas-star. Six tugboats surrounded the Selkirk. All seven vessels had armed guards stood on deck, watching, waiting.

Traffic through the nearby shipping lane gave them a wide

berth. One vessel, a small dark-blue boat, a hobbyist's pet project no doubt, was drifting gradually in the direction of their port side. A young guard strolled forward, readying himself to holler across the waves at the old fool at the helm, but then the hobbyist's vessel turned, correcting its course.

'Steady, steady...' said Stavast on the bridge of his little boat.

Edris was below deck in the aft section, listening through the open hatch.

Emna and Esna stood on deck at the aft, right next to a large object under a tarpaulin.

Stavast turned to Aemea. 'What ye sensin'?'

Aemea closed her eyes and felt nothing. 'Wait...' A minute more and she felt dampness and exhilaration. 'Now!'

'NOW!'

Edris pulled the lever by the winch. The rope began to flow. He picked up the large wire-cutters.

From the stern trailed a rope, the metal device from the chest at its end. The ridged blue exterior blended in perfectly with the waves and passed unnoticed by the tugs.

'Bottleorum-bottleorum-bottleorum...' Stavast counted in time with the 'TAT!-TAT!-TAT!' of the winch as his boat passed parallel to the Selkirk's bow.

The device passed through the water, getting closer and closer to the tug nearest the midsection of the Selkirk's port side.

'Bottleorum-bottleorum-bottleorum-bottleorum-bottleo-rum-CUT-IT!'

Edris snapped the wire-cutters together. The rope was cut, and a moment later the device hit the tug and exploded. A thunderous roar over the water and fire shimmered across the waves. Men jumped overboard, and within seconds the two tugs either side turned and headed towards the flaming vessel to retrieve the men from the water. The tugs were now all gathered around the Selkirk's port side as Stavast drew level with the vessel's bow.

'NOW!' cried Stavast.

Emna and Esna threw the tarpaulin off the paddle wheel and lowered it over the stern. The wheel began to turn. Stavast steered hard-a-starboard and the tiny vessel picked up steam. Stavast's little boat's bow now faced the Selkirk. The boat darted forward along the great ship's exposed starboard side.

Bullets shot across the water from the tugs. Stavast shielded himself by steering from his knees, air rushing through the glassless windows of the bridge.

Aemea and ShadowThief hung off the port side of the boat, shawls of shadow draped over them. ShadowThief had three sealed dreamglobes on her back and Aemea had two.

Aemea and ShadowThief jumped into the water and swam furiously forward towards the Selkirk. Aemea heard bullets pattering against the water. She swallowed great mouthfuls of water as her head slipped beneath the surface, her eyes darting between herself and ShadowThief. The sealed dreamglobes were covered in cloth for protection, but one bullet would be enough to smash them to pieces.

Stavast cut the engine as his compact vessel screeched along the side of the Selkirk. Edris ran a rope from their boat's aft and through one of the Selkirk's fairleads. Emese ran a second rope from the boat's forward section into another of the fairleads. The ropes took the strain and Stavast's boat came to a halt alongside the mighty ship.

Below deck, Emese and Edris threw open a hatch in Stavast's boat, jumped into the water and began to swim under the ship.

Emna and Esna aimed their rifles at the middle deck, drawing the crew's eyes away from the water. Bullets ripped across the deck of Stavast's boat.

ShadowThief grabbed for the rails several times unsuccessfully as the Selkirk rocked. She seized the metal and hauled herself up. She looked back at Aemea, her hand outstretched and pulled her up, the dreamglobes clattering together on her back.

The tugs were now regrouping, churning the water as they sped round the Selkirk's starboard side to intercept Stavast.

Emese and Edris swam as fast as they could under the ship, their eyes begging for light, their lungs screaming for oxygen.

The crew of the Selkirk rushed towards the little boat now lashed to their side, rifles raised when Stavast cried out to them.

'Place yer weapons down, shipmates! Drop 'em, drown ye! Stroever and that bulbous barnacle Ryker-Veere are yer masters no more, Devil Spare 'Em!'

The crew saw the rusted nails set into their old captain's eyes. Stavast didn't know if they'd swallow his bluff, but he sensed their hesitation. Stavast grabbed hold of the railing and hauled himself up with the agility of a much younger man. His boldness was disarming. They kept their rifles aimed at Stavast.

Aemea and ShadowThief crept into the armoury and helped themselves to a couple of rifles.

Emese and Edris felt their gag reflexes twinging, moments from suffocation. Then a shaft of sentinellight cut through. They followed it, beating their legs against the freezing water. They broke the surface and gasped desperately for air. They hauled themselves up onto the ship's exposed port side, away from the tugs now gathering around Stavast's boat on the starboard side.

'Get back to yer ship, Stavast!' cried the deck officer along the barrel of his rifle. 'I'll give you five seconds, then I swear I'll put lead between those two iron nails of yours!'

'Deck Officer Colgan?' said Stavast. 'Offered yer half-digested lunch to the beasts of the deep on yer first fade, ye seasick lubber! Stood as immovable as the pillar of a pier by the fourth! All 'cause ye listened to yer captain. Aye, ye'll not shoot me, Ben Colgan.'

Deck Officer Colgan took a step forward and aimed pointedly at Stavast.

Emese and Edris climbed aboard on the opposite side of the ship. They crept along the deck in the direction of the armoury, keeping their heads down. Aemea and ShadowThief were waiting for them. They passed Emese and Edris rifles and the two pairs split up and headed towards the sailors surrounding Stavast.

The tugs drew closer to the Selkirk, guns pointing at Stavast in every direction.

'By the mermaid's particulars,' said Stavast playfully, 'I swears ye fears nothin' more than an unarmed man...'

Esna and Emna stood implacable on the deck of Stavast's boat, rifles at the ready.

From the left, Emese and Edris darted out and held their rifles to the heads of two of the men surrounding Stavast. From the right, Aemea and ShadowThief did the same. The men on the tugs hesitated and, in that moment, Esna and Emna jumped aboard and held their rifles up to the two remaining men.

Deck Officer Colgan glared back at Stavast, Emese holding a gun to the back of his head.

'Yer masters are dead, Ben,' said Stavast. 'Yer really want NightEternal? Tell 'em to stand down, drown ye!'

Colgan waited two seconds more then gave the command.

The Selkirk's crew placed their rifles on the deck and the men on the tugs lowered theirs.

'Excellent choice, life,' said Stavast with a smile. He turned roughly in the direction of ShadowThief and sensed the disturbance in the air that was her nod of approval.

'He's right!' came a voice from across the deck. The radio operator had emerged from below clutching a piece of paper. 'Ryker-Veere is dead! Stroever gone, leaving a trail of blood behind him!'

Stavast laughed heartily. 'Oh, merciful Majesty, Ye turns the tide as I turns the helm,' he muttered to himself. 'Toss yer weapons into the deep!' he cried and the men on the tugs obeyed. 'NOW, FLEE!'

The men on the Selkirk quickly ran to the water, jumped overboard and swam to the tugs which departed soon after.

Emese, Edris, Esna and Emna lowered their weapons.

'Stand easy, shipmates,' said Stavast.

'I abhor firearms!' said Aemea to ShadowThief. 'Did I look convincing?'

ShadowThief let out a soundless chuckle: *I guess!*

The quiet was broken as the winch by the harpoon gun clanged into action. With a loud *TAT-TAT-TAT!* the cage began to descend from the star, making its way to the deck.

ShadowThief knife was ready in her grip as the cage arrived. It was empty. Aemea and ShadowThief exchanged worrying glances but still climbed aboard.

'I can spare yer one deckhand if yer need,' said Stavast. 'Maybe two.'

Aemea looked up at the star and concentrated. 'No,' she said. ShadowThief scanned her to check she was sure. 'We'll be fine.'

Stavast nodded.

Aemea and ShadowThief began their ascent.

TAT-TAT-TAT-TAT-TAT!

The star loomed above them, stifling heat radiating from it. Closer and closer, the great shape filling their vision.

56

THE SHADOWS & THE SCREAMS

They came to a stop. The door was invitingly open.

A moment between them.

'Come on,' said Aemea. They opened the cage and climbed the stairs into the star.

The hiss of gas was all around, its scent clawing at their mouths and nostrils. Aemea and ShadowThief strode cautiously across the gantry, observing the billowing clouds of gas above and below them. Walkways cut this way and that through the clouds. The strange yellow light, a subdued glow, enveloped them, leaving no space anywhere for shadows. ShadowThief's blade sat comfortably in her grip, ready.

They approached the workstation described to them by Thira. Above the control panel was a further selection of switches and dials on the wall, and to one side was a small box. They untied the dreamglobes on their backs, placed them on the metal of the gantry and removed the protective outer layers of cloth. Within, a lump of wood and a number of herbs were soaked in oil. Aemea produced two hairpins and got to work trying to pick the lock of the box on the wall. Shadow-

Thief placed a hand on her shoulder. Aemea turned and her friend held up a single finger: *Back in one minute.*

Aemea nodded as her friend departed. She was feeling almost three minutes ahead now – nothing but calm and concentration. She could crack the lock in time. She carried on tinkering with the mechanism.

A shot of fear. An echo from a few minutes in the future.

'Shad – SHAD!'

Aemea looked around. She couldn't see ShadowThief anywhere. She returned to work, feeling the fury of the minutes to come fizzing within her.

And then—

A scream tore through the air, echoing in the great chamber. The woman's scream was high and shrill, carrying on and on with peaks and troughs as if her very life was being ripped out of her. At last, the scream became a low, protracted groan, then vanished, fading into the hiss of the gas.

The interior of the star was now too quiet. Aemea breathed irregularly. She knew she had to get back to work, shaking, scarcely able to hold the pins in the lock. *It's not real... It's not real... I know it's not real...* She knew what was coming and was ready to turn and see that terrible face at any moment.

She became aware of the clanging of feet on metal. The footsteps were too heavy for ShadowThief's. She kept working but the shaking was too much. She turned and faced him.

Those horrible, sleepless eyes. The tall, stick-thin frame and the long, frayed hairs coming down from under his top hat. He toyed with his simple, black-handled knife, examining Aemea with a vile, hungry smile, a clouded black glass marble in his free hand.

'G-good-good fade to you, MalJack Strode,' said Aemea. 'J-just got something I need to s-sort out. B-be with you in two ticks.'

Aemea turned slowly, her back tensing, expecting a knife to slice into her any second, but all she felt was heart-racing tension in the minutes to come.

The hoarse cry of a man. MalJack Strode replayed the dying scream over and over again. The footsteps drew closer. He was toying with two marbles at once now, letting the piercing screams of the poor souls shriek through the air.

Aemea sensed her body flooding with adrenaline in the minutes to come. *Don't turn. Don't strike out. Do as we agreed. Complete the task.*

Two more steps. Closer and closer. The creak of his old clothes as he leant in. He said not a word. Breath stale with rotting meat curled around the hairs of her neck and up to her nose. Her shaking hands guided the pins into place and the lock reacted.

Two feet crashed against the metal of the gantry as ShadowThief landed. MalJack turned, his knife ready, but darkness whipped across his vision and the amethyst blade pierced his shoulder. He lashed out and ShadowThief withdrew her blade to meet his. They parried back and forth as he pushed her back along the gantry, his own blood splattered across his clothes.

As he backed her into a corner, fighting with the fury of a wounded animal, she began to slash lower and lower, using his height against him. Flesh wounds across his upper legs, one right above the knee. He went to kick her away and missed. She plunged her knife into his thigh and he screamed soundlessly, bringing his blade down hard towards her neck.

ShadowThief rolled to the side, her head crashing into a post, losing her grip on the knife. MalJack ripped the amethyst blade from his thigh and chucked it in the direction of the clouds of gas. The blade clattered onto the gantry below.

Aemea turned the pins and opened the box. She seized the papers within, rifled through them, fearing she'd drop them as her hands shook uncontrollably. She'd found it! Four pages – one on the star-piercing harpoon gun and three on the controls of a gas-star.

ShadowThief scrabbled backwards as MalJack stabbed and stabbed at the floor of the gantry, trying to pin her down. His knife became jammed in the grate and ShadowThief kicked his hand away with all her might. He recoiled in agony and she brought her foot up to land between his legs. MalJack fell backwards, clutching himself with one hand, just able to keep hold of the railing with the other.

ShadowThief was on her feet. She struck out with her fists, her teeth bared, pummelling the ancient creature who had torn her voice from her. Her fists smashed into his face, into his jaw, across his nose, breaking it with a crack. He kicked her away, throwing himself forward, and, yanking his knife out of the grate, he dived at her again. She leapt forward, took hold of his shoulders and threw herself off the gantry, dragging the ageless nightmare with her.

Aemea, struggling to control her shaking hands, ripped the corners off the pages of the plans and placed one in each of the five dreamglobes. She kept scanning the gantries and billowing towers of gas for ShadowThief, just catching the view of the blur of limbs as her and MalJack plummeted through the air to the gantry below.

ShadowThief and MalJack crashed onto the lower walkway. MalJack's knife clattered to the floor next to them. ShadowThief kicked and scratched at the wretched man's face, cutting deep bloody grooves in his skin.

MalJack lashed out, his fist colliding with her cheek, smashing her lower lips against her teeth, allowing blood to flow thick and fast from her mouth. She struck back, her fist smashing into MalJack's face and he was knocked aside.

MalJack took to his feet and leered over ShadowThief just as she managed to stand upright.

GO! cried ShadowThief, mouthing the words soundlessly. *GO!*

MalJack laughed noiselessly as he bore down on her. She backed away, red streaming down her front. She pulled out strips of shadow strapped to her side and lashed MalJack with darkness. His blade still out of sight, he retaliated by hurling clouded black marbles at her. With every smash of a marble came another petrified scream, a chorus of the dying. The light came and went, screams ripped the air, their battle strobed and blood-curdling.

The glimpse of a blade. ShadowThief snatched at it, but MalJack seized his own knife from the walkway floor first. He slashed at ShadowThief, closer and closer, backing her into a corner.

GO! FLEE!

Another muted laugh and he kept slashing, closer and closer.

She took hold of the railing, jumped over the side and swung herself around the other side of MalJack.

She ran. The walkway veered off to the left. She followed the path but was faced with a dead end. She turned. That gleeful grin greeted her.

GO!

He shook his head. Those sleepless, delirious, bloodshot eyes glared at her. His smile broadened. She stepped backwards cautiously. ShadowThief's heart raced. MalJack was close enough to strike. She retreated another step and shadow enveloped her. She leapt backwards some distance, stumbling and falling onto her back on landing. Seeing his opportunity, he bounded after her but realised only too late that there should be no shadow in the heart of a star.

As he stepped into darkness, he found no footing.

MalJack screamed silently as he plummeted through the gap in the walkway, masked by shadow, straight into the trap she had set.

The spider-like body briefly reappeared on the other side of the dark as MalJack Strode was swallowed by the towers of gas within the star, a wide-open mouth ushering forth a silent scream as he vanished from sight forever.

ShadowThief, her legs still hanging over the gap she'd barely clearly when jumping backwards, breathed in deeply, exhilarated. She was so relieved that she almost choked on the gas. She took to her feet and yanked away the curtain of dark she'd hastily placed over the gap in the gantry,

'Shad! *Shad*!'

ShadowThief's smile vanished. She looked up to locate the voice of her friend as she ran. The amethyst blade was there on the ground near the stairs. She picked it up and hurtled up the stairs.

'Shad! Shad! Are you okay?'

ShadowThief ran up to Aemea, nodding enthusiastically. Aemea let out a deep sigh of relief.

'MalJack...?'

ShadowThief shook her head with finality: *Gone*.

Aemea closed her eyes for a moment, sucked in all her anxieties then breathed them all out.

'I said I would stay, complete the job no matter what, but I almost couldn't, Shad. I worried it would be the last I saw of you.'

ShadowThief leant forward, their foreheads met, their arms rested on each other's shoulders, and they breathed in relief.

Minutes later, they hurled the globes into the gas. There

was no sound of glass smashing but after a few seconds there was a noise like distant thunder.

They ran. As they headed across the gantry the way was filled with billowing towers of purple gas. Then blue, then orange, then the vision of the plans appeared before their eyes.

§

Aemea and ShadowThief climbed out of the cage and onto the deck of the Selkirk.

'Cast off!' cried Captain Stavast as Emese, Emna, Edris and Esna untied the ropes of his little old boat, allowing it to float away.

'What happened?' said Aemea as they marched onto the bridge.

'Harbourmaster,' said Stavast. 'Seems some landlubbin' officers of the law are keen to have a word in my shell-like.'

'Oh,' said Aemea. 'Are we running away then?'

'That would very much be to my pleasin'!' said Stavast.

Perfect! said ShadowThief. *Running is good.*

'Indeed,' said Aemea. 'For a moment there I thought we were going to have to endure the tedium of prison again.' Aemea peered over in the vague direction of Ha'penny Row. 'I hope they made it, Shad. Hope may not be worth much but...'

ShadowThief nodded, filling in the rest of the sentence.

Emese released the cable from the harpoon gun and they sped off into the distance.

As the ship sliced through the water, Aemea and Shadow-Thief looked over the side, back towards the dock and streets beyond. A line of warm amber was streaked through the waves, leading up to the gas-star they'd just departed from. The star glowed deep orange, fluffy white clouds from the dream it emitted gathered around, casting a warming glow all around.

'I've... I've never seen anything like this, Shad,' said Aemea. 'It's like day is breaking but just around one star and... Wait! Look!'

Other stars on the horizon were twinkling into life, breaking the spell of night. Light and colour and hope painted the cityscape. The dark had been vanquished at last and no more could fear crouch in the void, festering in the grim imaginings of the bitter night. Aemea and ShadowThief blinked then basked in the warmth of the long-overdue relief of dawn.

ShadowThief allowed a smile to spread slowly over her sore face. She put her arm around Aemea and her friend nestled her head on ShadowThief's shoulder.

'You know, Shad,' said Aemea, 'I like the dark. It sharpens everything, and I am all the more fond of day thanks to the night. I wish they'd come and go in quicker succession, though.' She looked up at ShadowThief. 'So, where now?'

And so her friend pointed out over the dazzling seas and told her.

57

UPON DEVIL'S JUDGEMENT

Some hours before dawn, Krish and Thira kept low along the shingle beach as they approached the Stroever residence. The silhouette of the rectangular tower capped with its pointed cupola was darker than the grey-brown of the night sky above.

'The thing with this time-thieving' malarkey is, ya just never have enough time,' said Thira.

Krish saw that he looked weak. He leant over and placed the back of his hand on his friend's forehead, something he'd seen Mum do.

'I can't tell if it's just the night but... I think you're getting colder,' said Krish.

Thira accepted this with a grave nod. 'When ya go...what 'appens to me...? Until the next time we rock up searchin' for Myrthali, I mean?'

'I... I don't really know, Thira.'

Thira chewed this over in his mind for a few seconds. 'You really didn't think this through. My parents... gone. I know I'm still there but... You really didn't bloody think this through!'

'I'm sorry.'

'Hmm. It's okay. Well, it's not but... I really wanted to be 'ere, but... Something 'ad to give, I guess.'

'Yeah. I guess.'

Thira nodded to himself. 'Next time... ya make time. *We* make time. Just to... ya know... I dunno, 'ang around or somethin'.'

'What do you mean, "hang around"?'

'I don't know, mate. But we should find time.'

Krish nodded and Thira mirrored this. They looked into each other. Not like they had done on the banks of the river near the remains of Sccifihr'ei. This was something quite different. It was all too rushed, too incomplete.

They continued on their way without another word. Thira's magic was weak but he managed to enchant a sodden rope they took from the wreck of a boat to raise up and loop round a weathervane. They climbed upwards and onto a ledge by a dark window.

'I like your new staff, by the way,' said Krish.

'Pretty 'andy, eh?' said Thira.

'Can't believe all that stuff Stroever told you in his sleep.'

'I know, mad, right? 'Im pretendin' to be 'is own son. 'Im and 'is kid Eva taking Myrthali and never agein'.'

'Why didn't Helena just take the Myrthali in secret?'

'Dunno. Perhaps she didn't want to. Or 'e threatened 'er or summink.'

'But if he'd just believed his wife—'

'Jane.'

'Yeah. If he'd just believed that she was really ill, perhaps this wouldn't have happened. He might have just gone back to being a nasty, old businessmen.'

'Yeah, maybe. Messed up guy.'

They peered over the rooftops and saw the front entrance.

'No guards,' said Krish.

'Yeah,' said Thira. 'Not on the outside.'

Thira tinkered with the lock on the window using his staff. He managed to prize it open and they climbed inside.

Darkness greeted them.

'Too easy?' said Thira.

Krish nodded.

They tiptoed forward.

'Thira, can we have some light?' whispered Krish.

'Less magic, more shuttin' the 'ell up,' said Thira. 'I don't want to give us away. And look...'

Orange light seeped in through a crack up ahead. They followed it and came to a curtain. They pulled it back to reveal a large drawing room with a fireplace, several armchairs and a dining table. A flight of stairs led to an upper level.

'There's no one here,' said Krish.

'Keep quiet...'

They crept up the stairs, every creak of the house deafeningly loud in the uneasy hush. Their eyes struggled to adjust in the dim light from the handful of gaslights on the walls of the landing.

Thira stepped on a floorboard which screeched disagreeably and the sound of footsteps scuttling across the floor above broke the quiet.

Krish and Thira froze. When the disturbance had ended, they found a row of doors in the corridor ahead. They explored an empty bedroom with a grand four poster bed. They could find nothing in the room aside from darkness, dust and cold bedsheets. The next room was very much the same.

'No one lives here, mate,' said Thira.

'Not on this floor,' said Krish.

Then they found a linen cupboard at the end of the corridor, though there was no linen on the shelves.

'Never trust an empty broom cupboard,' said Thira. 'Very suspish.' He turned his staff in circles in front of the cupboard, lights of dull blue and yellow washing over the small room. Then he huffed irritably and dropped the staff to his side.

'What is it?' said Krish.

'Feels like I'm tryin' to do something first thing in the mornin' – it just ain't 'appenin' right now. Plus, I don't really get all the technology of this world. It's easier to uncover trap-spells waitin' to be triggered, but hidden locks...'

Thira picked up his staff and tried again. One of the shelves responded to his spell, twinging as if it was loose.

'A-ha!' Thira pushed the shelf downwards.

The click of a lock. Thira pushed the wall and it swung open. The scent of mould and damp reached their noses. In the gloom ahead of them, they saw a fireplace with what looked like knives fanned out in a display above it.

Thira raised his staff defensively. They exchanged apprehensive looks and ventured cautiously into the dark.

'An 'ouse within an 'ouse,' said Thira.

'But still no guards...' said Krish.

The smell of rotting flesh grew stronger. Just visible through the murk they saw thousands of tiny creatures scuttling all around them. The odour of decay was strongest here. Amongst the swirling sea of insects were a couple of long objects laid out on the floor. The boys realized it was two corpses, ransacked of most of their flesh, with great craters in their stomachs as if something had burst out of them.

Suddenly, his friend stopped moving forward. He was shaking.

Get it out...

What?!

GET IT OUT!

His friend ripped open his shirt revealing the pale flesh of his chest.

GET IT OUT! GET IT OUT!

Lines raised from his friend's flesh, five flexing fingers wriggling to life on his pale skin...

Something wasn't right. His friend... his friend... what was his friend's name...?

Get it out, damn you!

This wasn't right but he had to save him!

The gnarled fingers lifted out of his friend's chest, a hand reaching from his friend's heart as if an intruder in his torso was about to rush forth and rip him apart.

CUT IT OUT! CUT IT OUT!

Krish ran forward, seized one of the knives from the display of weaponry on the wall then ran at his friend, not looking up at his face. The scent of foul flesh whipped into his nostrils. He stopped. Pale flesh... No. This was not Thira.

DEVIL SPARE YOU, CUT IT OUT!

Krish followed his nose, turning and bringing his foot down on the glass globe.

The dream squirmed soundlessly and died. The smoke cleared and he turned to see Thira standing in the room, the floor bare, only the fireplace, the fan of knives and the blade in his hand were real. Thira also held a knife.

'I knew it weren't right,' said Thira. 'All yer words were wrong. Didn't sound like you.'

'Yeah,' said Krish. 'Same. Didn't look like you either. You were just some nameless friend the dream tried to trick me into thinking I knew.'

'Should have realised Stroever's defences would be dreams. Come on. And any strong smells... don't trust 'em...'

Thira looked towards the staircase now visible through the doorway next to the fireplace. They ascended the darkened stairs, keeping their noses peeled. Thira tried to conjure up a gust-of-wind spell to waft any odours away but he seemed weak.

Up and up they went. No pictures on the walls, no windows.

Another trepidatious step and the scent of straw met Krish's nostrils.

'Krish!' cried Thira.

But the dream had enveloped them.

Krish was running now, pelting the stone ground scattered with straw, flaming lanterns all around. A snarling beast was on his tail. He saw a large window ahead. He sprinted, climbed onto the windowpane and opened the window wide, looking down at the flowing river just a few metres below. He turned back, the bloody beast spiked with swords and spears and sceptres, but still living. It hurtled forward, its jaws wide open. He looked once more at the flowing river and tried to discern where that scent was emanating from...

He turned to the great, sharp teeth of the muscular beast, covered in wounds and weapons, patched with black bloody fur, and raced towards it and that foul scent...

Those fearsome eyes rushed towards him and—

A crunch of glass and the beast vanished to be replaced with the panting Thira, a crushed globe under his foot.

They caught their breaths then went over to inspect the very real window. There was no river below, just a great drop to the stone of the streets. The distance from here to the ground did not look survivable.

'Nasty trick!' said Thira.

'We must be near the top,' said Krish. 'Can't be much more of this tower left.'

Thira nodded. His energy was dwindling, his eyes blinking slowly from time to time as if he was about to drop off.

'We'll find the antidote,' said Krish.

'Talk to me,' said Thira. 'Just keep talkin'.'

Up and up and up they went. The way became darker. Thira tried to light the stairwell with his staff, but he was struggling. They sniffed the air but detected nothing. Even the scents of dust and gas had faded.

Then, instinctively, Krish and Thira reached for each other's hands. They clasped to one another, their hands joining comfortably, reassuringly together.

'Talk to me,' said Thira again as the light dwindled.

The darkness was all-consuming now.

'You remember when we got to Čevljarski Most...?' said Krish.

I HEAR YOU.

' 'Course I remember,' said Thira. 'Seems like a long time ago, but it weren't.'

LATE AT NIGHT, I HEAR YOU.

'Was great. Last time I can remember actually 'avin' fun.'

I AM EVERY LITTLE FEAR AND APPREHENSION, SIMMERING AWAY IN THE BACKGROUND OF YOUR MIND NOW COME TO THE FORE.

'It was amazing. Running around, messing about. Just like back on Ilir, when you showed me that card game.'

THERE IS NO WAY FORWARD. NO WAY BACK. YOU ARE STUCK HERE WITH THESE THOUGHTS AND YOU WILL GO NO FURTHER.

'Many-ruled splat? Ha! Good game. Good times.'

EVEN IF YOU WAKE, YOU WILL SEE NOTHING. YOU WILL NOT MOVE.

'And that's when I thought, this is bloody good.'

YOU ARE MAROONED HERE.

'I could do this forever.'

EYES OPEN, UNBLINKING, STUCK FOREVER IN THESE THOUGHTS.

If it's just me and Thira doing stuff like this from now on, I'm okay with that.'

ALL THESE FEARS, ANXIETIES, PARANOIAS - YOUR ONLY COMPANIONS FOR THE REST OF TIME!

'I'm okay with that.'

STILL YOUR OWN HEART! IT CAN BE DONE! IT SHALL BE DONE! STILL!

STILL! STI–

A little crunch and the dream wheezed, withered and slithered off into a corner to die. They could smell the dust and the gaslights again now.

'Cor, that was a bit full on, weren't it?' said Thira. He looked over to Krish. 'Soppy bastard!'

Krish smiled. 'I meant it though.'

'I know. Thanks, mate.'

They looked down at the crushed dreamglobe. 'Was that you or me?' said Krish.

'Dunno,' said Thira. 'So obvs must 'ave been me.'

They laughed.

'Pretty smart, huh?' said Thira. 'A scentless dream.'

They climbed another staircase and entered a long corridor lined with doors.

'Must be almost there,' said Krish. He marched along the corridor and tried several doors only to find empty rooms. Thira staggered forward and Krish became aware of just how pale he was looking now.

Somewhere up ahead a beam of golden light was streaming into the corridor.

Krish went to investigate the light while Thira tried a few more doors.

The golden light became brighter. There was a spiral staircase at the end of the corridor leading to a hatch which was propped open, but it was the source of the light which caught his eye.

'Er, Krish...' came Thira's voice.

'Thira!' said Krish, a smile blossoming on his face. 'Look at this!'

The source of the light was a small window. Through the glass he saw the spreading light of dawn. The rooftops glistened in warm light, the amber and gold of the gas-stars drifting overhead, the bone-white sentinels had retreated to a place unseen. In the distance, fluffy clouds of purple and pink drifted across the shimmering sea, the gargantuan bolted wall that was the edge of this world just visible through the haze. Krish lit up inside and felt lighter.

'It's amazing! Thira!'

'Krish, I, er, think I've found the room.'

'The clouds! Your dream, Thira! It's working!'

Krish turned and saw Thira standing in the corridor by an open door. Next to Thira stood a slim girl, her skin as pale as milk. She clutched a large red object to her front protectively.

Krish walked up to the girl.

'Er...hi...' said Krish.

The girl said nothing back. Krish was unnerved by those still eyes. He went to pass her, to head through the doorway, but Thira's eyes ushered a warning.

'You're Eva, aren't you?' said Krish.

'That's my name, yes,' said the child. 'But its persistent use causes wear and tear, so my father will send you a bill if you overuse it. Do you understand?'

'Er...sure. Your father's Mr. Stroever, isn't he, Eva?'

'Did you hear what I said?'

'Yeah. He is your dad, isn't he, Eva?'

'He is. And stop using my name! It's meant to be a secret! You're not here to make me take my medicine, are you?'

'No.'

'Good! Mummy-Helena doesn't know, but I don't want to take it anymore! I threw it down the sink! She's not actually my mummy anyway.'

'Why did you stop taking it, Eva?'

'It doesn't help! I'm not getting better! I'm just the same and nothing changes, and I don't want it! It's a trap! Staying the same is a trap and I don't want it!'

'I see. Eva, is there anyone in that room?'

'Daddy's not here and Mummy-Helena went to the roof to see the view.' She glanced in the direction of the spiral staircase. 'She has the key to the stairs but I'm not allowed up there.'

'Okay... Well, the hatch is open now, Eva. Why don't you go and see the view? It's a beautiful morning.'

'What's morning?'

'What's mor... Erm, well, it's what's going on out there right now.'

'What is it?'

'Go and see. But tell me, is there anyone in that room?'

The girl glared at Krish. 'I'll tell you if you'll play a game with me.'

Krish glanced over at Thira. He was slouched against the wall, looking paler than ever.

'Sure,' said Krish to Eva. 'But once you're back from the roof. There's no one in that room, is there, Eva?'

'I want to play the game with the mice. The one where you trap them.'

'Yeah, I know that game, Eva. You try to catch other mice in a trap, don't you? Like a little cage?'

'No! No! The mice stay where they are! That's what Daddy says! If you play it properly you don't need a cage! The mice get fat and lazy and full of dreams, and they get sad, and you don't need a cage! You trap them wherever they are, in their own heads, and you kill them just like that, and you don't need a cage! I'm very good at it.'

Krish saw Thira sliding down the wall, fading fast.

'Sounds great, Eva,' said Krish. 'I want to play that game the moment you get back from the roof!'

'Okay!' said Eva. Krish suddenly noticed that the girl, still clutching the large wooden object to her front, looked weak, tired almost. She smiled then went to run off in the direction of the staircase, but Krish stopped her.

'Oh, and tell me, Eva,' said Krish. 'Who did you say was in that room?'

'No one, stupid!' said Eva. 'It's my room! My special room and everything in it is mine!'

And with that, Eva ran off towards the stairs, carrying the red object with her.

Krish helped Thira into the small room. There was a little skylight above. Ornate dolls, wooden figurines, toy gas-stars and model steamer boats were scattered all over the floor. There were shelves full of storybooks and a cabinet set into the wall. In the centre of the room was a gigantic doll's house, a great toy mansion which was taller than either of them.

They began to search manically. Thira found a medicine cabinet on the wall. He waved his staff, the glass smashed and he searched the vials within. He had to place one hand against the wall to steady himself, allowing the staff to clatter to the floor.

'Let me help,' said Krish stepping in.

'I know what I'm bloody lookin' for!' spat out Thira. 'Find the safe.'

Thira kept searching but it was easier for Krish to locate what he was after.

The side of the large doll's house swung open with ease, revealing tiny figures sat at the dinner table, neat little bedrooms, servants in the kitchen and miniscule games spread out across the drawing room floor, though this was all on the lefthand side of the house. On the right, the house was just a hollow shell containing a large safe with metal pictorial slides on the side. It looked identical to Ryker-Veere's.

He slowly searched through them and found the three he was after:

MEDICINE – WOLF'S HEAD – CHERRIES

'Can't believe we travelled across the whole City and Stroever had the answer all along,' said Krish.

'We only travelled across one corner of one borough, mate,' said Thira, still examining the vials. 'City's massive! And you would never 'ave got it outta Stroever. 'E took that heggarum santai stuff to make sure no one could. Oh, and remember – the Győri dream was the first one, second one Julija mixed, and prison one was last.'

Krish nodded and swapped the order of the first two slides:

WOLF'S HEAD – MEDICINE – CHERRIES

He checked the piece of paper he'd jotted the slides on once more and saw ShadowThief's handwriting on the back:

To heal, first you must name your disease.

He turned back to Thira. He ran over to him. He tried to hold him up. Thira was bent over, breathing heavily. All the warmth had gone from his body. Krish looked into those haunted eyes. His friend looked back and shook his head.

'It's not 'ere,' said Thira. 'You... you found 'em?'

Krish nodded. Thira staggered over to the safe. Then all the strength went from him and he fell onto the floor. Krish flooded with terror. He couldn't lose him. This couldn't be it.

'Maybe... maybe... I don't know...' said Krish.

'Actually bloody say sum'ink, ya twonk!' muttered Thira.

'If I go... touch the Myrthali and go... maybe I can find a way... think something up,' said Krish. 'Time will move for me, but not for you. I can come back with a solution.'

'And what if no one even knows what Shrilwood's Knee is in your world?'

'I dunno... But... if we wait it might be too late... Or if I could use some Myrthali!'

'Thought that devil whatsit took it off you last time?'

Krish pulled the plastic sandwich bag from his pocket. He looked at the safe.

He placed the three slides in place. His heart beat fast as he pressed in the slides. A deep metallic thud. A great sinking feeling before he tried the handle. He pulled. The heavy door opened slowly. Inside were several large bowls full of sand. Dull in colour, but familiar. There was much more than King Obsendei had had. This was it – Stroever's Myrthali.

'Any in there that's already brewed?' said Thira.

Krish shook his head. He passed Thira the plastic sandwich bag.

'Can you fill this?' said Krish. 'I want to make sure I've definitely got some in there before I touch the Myrthali. I've got an idea...'

Thira nodded. He extended his arm from his spot on the

floor and scooped up a healthy quantity of the Sands of Time. He offered it to Krish. Krish looked down. Could he do it? Could he leave now? Would he see Thira's eyes again?

Krish extended a finger towards one of the bowls of Myrthali.

'Please!'

Krish and Thira's eyes shot across the room. One hand was raised, pleading, surrendering, the other clutched at a wound on his chest, his shirt dripping with redness. The blood pitter-pattered playfully onto the carpet.

'Please...' Isairis Stroever staggered into the room. 'Please... Krishna, Thira... please... I have a child... my Eva... without the Myrthali... she'll die... Do you hear me...? She'll die...'

'That girl,' said Krish, barely taking his eyes off the terrible sight of Thira at his feet.

'You saw her?' said Stroever, pleadingly, his free hand lowered, cupped, begging for whatever would be offered. 'My Eva... Where has she gone?'

'She'll really die?'

Stroever's eyes became glassy. The tears hit the ground faster than the blood.

'Yes. Without the Myrthali the sickness will take her... Please, Krishna!'

Krish had Stroever in his peripheral vision as he looked down at Thira. He sucked in his fear and confusion and spoke firmly. 'How long has she lived?'

'Krishna! Please! She will die!'

'Is she a child anymore? Really?!'

'Her body, her mind, they are a child's. Please!'

'Stroever, tell me – if you died, right now, if you died and she lived... what would happen?'

'Please, Krishna, please! Thira, please! Tell him to stop, Thira!'

Waves of guilt and hatred and fury and guilt once more surged through Krish's mind. He sensed the determination in Thira's eyes, the teeth gritted under locked lips. He thought of the poison flowing through Thira's veins, injected by Stroever's servant, Madam Ckrystafis. And he thought of the child. Those unreadable eyes.

'What have you taught her, Stroever? If you died and she lives, what would she do?'

'Thira, please! Thira, tell him! My Eva!'

Then Thira spoke, his voice hoarse and tired. 'When's the last time you saw Jane's dream, Isairis?'

For a second Stroever was taken aback but then he continued. 'The City spat out Jane as it spat me out!'

'Yeah, your world spat 'er out, but she didn't want to burn it, she wanted to better it,' said Thira, a fierce, quavering determination in his voice. 'Ya're always there, Stroever. Calm, quiet, actin' like ya're the better man. Like all that stuff about fairness yer wife was bangin' on about 'as sunk in. But it ain't. Yer wanna think it was another guy with another name that didn't listen when 'is wife said she was ill... But it was you. Now ya wanna take the thing that killed 'er, turn it around, fire it back on the City and rip it all down until it's just you and yer kid left. And ya've convinced yerself ya're doin' it all in 'er name. In the name of the kid you 'ad together. But Jane didn't want nuffin' like this! She wanted something better! She just wanted people to bloody listen! To understand! So I 'ope ya've seen the light of the stars outside yer window, mate, 'cause it's Jane's world that's comin', not yours!'

Stroever looked away from Thira to Krish again, pleading.

'For my Eva... please...'

Thira looked into Krish, his eyes resolute. Thira placed a cold hand in Krish's and they held each other firm.

'You brought Eva up to be just like you, didn't you?' said

Krish, not looking away from Thira. 'I think you're a sick man, Stroever. Perhaps it would have been easier to heal yourself rather than destroy the City. But just like with Jane... you weren't listening.'

'Please! Please! I beg of you!' Stroever brought himself to his knees, one hand still on the fatal wound, the other raised in surrender. 'I am at your mercy, Krishna! Thira! See, I lower myself to my knees and, Upon Devil's Judgement, I may never rise from them again. Please... do not let my Eva die...'

Krish felt the plastic bag of Myrthali in his grip between his and Thira's hands. They stared into one another, eyes firm, the decision made. Krish and Thira's hands came apart as he lifted the bag to his lips, his free hand close to a bowl of Myrthali in the safe.

Krish's eyes met Stroever's.

'I'm sorry...'

A mighty scream, tearing into his ears, ripping through his consciousness, the guttural, animalistic cry of a dying creature. Stroever leapt to his feet, his bloody hand unsheathing the blade Ryker-Veere had stabbed into him, blood splattering across the carpet as the dying man raced across the room, his eyes ablaze, the knife held high. Krish bypassed terror in an instant, threw the plastic bag under his tongue, plunged his hand into the cool sands of the Myrthali as his eyes searched for Thira's and—

On the roof Eva joined her sister for dawn

To dispel untruths as if pulling a thorn

'I recall back when I wasn't filled with scorn

I remember Mum and the day you were born

Placed a bow in my hair to make me your gift

Now the curse over my life will at last lift

You will no longer need to look after me

You can do as you please, have fun and be free'

So the sisters embraced by the light of day

As one's eyes shut, she passed the other a sleigh

58

THE DEVIL & HIS APPRENTICE

—then Krish found himself standing in his own bedroom.

The sound of the video he'd left playing on his laptop made him jump. He'd forgotten that he'd left it on while he slipped out. That had been weeks ago, but maybe less than an hour had passed in his world. Dad was still downstairs watching a documentary on the Nazis. Joshi was probably pottering on the internet in her room.

He removed the bag from his mouth. It was still there, the Myrthali. Nothing exciting about its colour, but he'd done it – he'd outwitted the devil.

Krish looked down at the floor to his left. That's where Thira had been moments ago. He was gone. How could he be gone? Was his life really on hold until he entered the next world? Could he find out what Shrilwood's Knee was and how to cure it? He picked up his phone from his bedside and searched the internet several times, but found nothing.

Krish's heart was still racing. He hid the Myrthali at the back of his sock drawer and headed downstairs.

§

He snuck out the back of the house; his father, with the TV up loud, heard nothing. He made his way across the garden, passing the swing as he headed for the gate.

'Ya made quick work of that one, boy.'

Krish spun around. The foul creature was there, toying absent-mindedly with the swing.

'How do you know?' said Krish.

'Ya hardly aged this time,' said the devil.

She was right. It had been nonstop since he'd arrived in KnockThrice. He must have been there just a few weeks, whereas he'd been in Ilir for months.

'He'll be there?' blurted out Krish. 'As soon as I arrive in the next world? He'll be there? No time will have passed?'

The devil gave him a disagreeable stare. 'Thought it was a she ya was after?'

'ANSWER THE QUESTION!'

The devil was genuinely taken aback, her eyes darting to the house for a moment. 'Whoever ya took will be there, unchanged.'

Krish sighed deeply and buried his hands in his face, exhaling the relief.

'What happened to ya there, Krish?'

'Don't you call me that! You never call me by my name! Why now?'

'Hush, boy, hush! Daddy'll hear!'

'I... I need to spend time finding a cure for a poison. Shril-wood's Knee. Do you know it?'

'Do I know...? No. Can't say as I do.'

'What about the Myrthali? You have it? Is it safe?'

The devil had stopped playing with the swing. She looked

at him untrustingly, her head turned away slightly as her eyes remained on him.

'Whas ya hidin', boy?'

Krish tried to think of anything other than the plastic bag in his sock drawer. He concentrated on Stroever and Eva.

'I think I condemned a child to death. I mean... I didn't have time! I had to decide! I had to stop this terrible, terrible scheme to kill millions. Maybe billions! And she'd lived a long time, decades. She was still a kid but... I didn't want to make the decision... I was rushed!'

'Ya said.'

'I know! I didn't want anyone to die but... I let it happen. To save others I let it happen and... Oh, God! Did I do the right thing?! It doesn't matter. It's done.'

'Am I invited along to this conversation, child?'

'Shut up! You made me do this! I think I may have changed a world. Maybe even made it a better place but... I didn't want anyone to die!'

'But ya liked it all the same, didn't ya?' said the devil, her sly smile making a return. 'Oh, I can see ya gorging on the power! What is it ya thinkin'? I sees a dying, desperate man. Horrible sight, horrible! But somethin' deep down in ya liked it...'

'Shut up!'

'Ya did, didn't ya?'

'Shut up!'

King Obsendei had got down on his knees when he handed him the Myrthali. Isairis Stroever had begged him on his knees he'd begged him to save his child's life. Two great monsters and he'd had the power to bring them both to their knees.

'Ya're full of fear and fury, boy, but ya're enjoying it too! The adventure! The power!'

'The friends. The friends too. I-it's not just about—'

'What happened to the girl ya wanted to see again?'

Krish inhaled deeply. 'His name is Thira.' He glared at the devil.

'Oh, I apologises for my mistake, child! Glad yer found 'im. Ya look at me like I is judgin' you and I ain't. I's not like them types in your world. I 'as seen strange things in many worlds, child, unnatural things, but love is never one of them.'

Krish's heart soared and swooped as he tried to process his feelings for Thira.

'He wasn't just similar. He had the same memories and he even started gaining the same powers. He relearned magic.'

The devil's eyes widened. 'How has ya done this? Should have been little more than a shadow in colour with a few words at the ready... What has ya done, boy?'

'What is he? Is he real?'

'Truly I don't know, young 'un. This is not what I had expected, no. An impression is what I thought ya'd get, nothin' more. But if this boy, this Thira, has memories... Never in all my travels....'

'I... I just didn't expect...'

'This is darkest magic, boy. You cannot create life out of nothin' and life cannot just go away again once it has come into bein'. Ya've created someone who cannot reach their full potential. To save one life ya've cursed another to a half-life. A quarter-life. A ghost of flesh and bone. A spectre not of one who was, but of one who has not yet lived!'

'But he *is* alive!'

'And ya've selfishly tethered him to this meagre existence. And you call me devil! You has committed a great evil, boy! How does it feel?'

'Shut up.'

'Hungerin' for cruelty now, eh?'

'Shut up!'

'See how selfishness drives yer!'

'Shut up!'

'What will yer create next, boy? Which will ya destroy? Ah! Ya see now! I 'as shown ya what power is and now ya'll be Master of Worlds! King Eternal brandishing ya crown of Myrthali! Ya'll usurp the throne of God, toss She to the wolves and become the Creator and Destroyer of Life! You is a devil now and I is bowin' down to ya and beggin' to be ya lowly apprentice!'

'I can create life but not save my Mum?'

'That is why I calls ya Destroyer also! Ya brings Thira into existence, but he is a flicker only. He will be gone soon as ya return from the fourth and final world.'

Krish felt the tears coming.

'Spell only works when ya travels to the worlds of the Myrthali, not the other way round,' continued the devil. 'Gettin' into a demon chamber is rare, and demon knows now. Will 'ave sealed itself off forever. And I told ya...if the original dies, then so does the copy. Imitation can't last long... trust me...'

Krish, physically and emotionally exhausted, collapsed onto the seat of the swing. He rocked slowly backwards and forwards, a child weighed down by adult's thoughts.

'I'm going to bed,' he announced to the ground.

The devil came over and patted him on the knee affectionately. For once, Krish found the creature's presence comforting.

'Ya did well, Krish,' said the devil. 'Little devil better go and rest now.'

'Why won't you give me any?'

'Rest now. Two more worlds and we is done.'

Krish's mind was racing through the last few weeks and suddenly he remembered the ancient woman in the cell. She'd spoken her name just before she died and Krish had recognised it, but only now did he recall where from.

'Kalrika Mavalrh – it was her,' said Krish. 'I remember! I remember her from the story of the harvest of time! She was the oldest of the magicians and all that! She knew about the herb, she found it and she dropped it into the potion! And the Empress Benhu'in kept her alive, forced her to stay alive to create more Myrthali... You knew it was her?'

'I did.'

'But you said that Myrthali was a word meaning "time".'

'"The Sands of Time" in old Bahrtakri.'

'That's not what Kalrika Mavalrh said! She said it was after her daughter who died!'

'Stories, boy. They simplify things.'

'Did you know Kalrika? And the Empress? You say you're her heir, but did you even know her?'

'I am heir and the Myrthali is mine by rights. Thas all ya needs to know, little devil. Go home and sleep now. Maybe ya sees Mumsy in the mornin'.'

'What aren't you telling me?'

'Sleep now. The rain is comin'. Sleep...'

§

'What's the next world like?'

'Hush, little devil! Sleep...'

The conversation continued as Krish lay in bed, waiting for sleep to claim him.

'Tell me.'

'Wild. Unchartered. Nameless world. New world. Fresh out the box. Snows they fall. Fall and fall and fall and fall! Underneath, a whole frozen world waitin' for the thaw. And day and night unlike anything ya ever seen, boy.'

'Can't be weirder than in KnockThrice.'

'Yer don't know the half of it...'

§

Morning came and it was sweeter than any morning Krish had ever remembered. He emerged from bed much later than he'd anticipated and looked out of his bedroom window with wonder. A blazing sun had risen to join a deep blue sky.

He picked up his phone and found the article Joshi had sent him. He suddenly felt guilty for shouting at her. Perhaps, in her own stupid big sister way, she'd been right. He opened the article in his browser and bookmarked it for later.

Krish went downstairs and out onto the patio overlooking that peaceful, familiar patch of life. It had always been dull, his parents' domain, their passion project, and now he saw what they loved about it. Light glistened in the droplets of water hanging from all the greenery in the shelter of their little garden. There had been nowhere like this in KnockThrice, where nightmares hid around every corner and dreams of horror scented the very air. He breathed in the sweet tranquillity of this place.

The warmth of his local star was healing his creaking body after all the physical pain of sleeping on trains and on the floors of derelict buildings. He'd recover. He could fix things. He had time. There must be a cure to Shrilwood's Knee out there somewhere.

An overwhelming sense of peace swept over him, and he wanted to make amends for every tiny wrong he'd done. And he'd start with the clock in the garden.

He strolled barefoot across the patio and the lawn, enjoying the sensation of the damp grass underfoot. For a moment he ignored his family, who'd braved breakfast outside for the first time this year, despite the breeze undoing the work of the warm sun above.

Krish retrieved the clock, knocking out the dirt and creepy-crawlies from the inner rim.

'Oh, so that's what happened to that bloody clock of yours, Ash!'

Krish smiled instinctively but it took him a few seconds to register the voice. He turned and saw his father sitting there with Joshi and—

'Mum?!'

'Well, who else were you expecting?' Mum replied with a chuckle.

'But... Why are you here?'

'Discharged herself late last night!' said Dad, looking absolutely knackered.

'But what about the operation?' said Krish.

Mum banged her mug of coffee pointedly against the surface of the table. 'Decided that even your father's cooking is better than hospital breakfasts. Still got a big decision to make about that operation. Will it help or just make me a bloody living ghost, shuffling about all over the place, eh? Anyway, whatever I decide, however much time I've got left, I'd rather be home.'

BEFORE YOU GO

Well, I really hope you enjoyed reading *The Dream Pedlars' Parade*, but I have a very quick favour to ask. If you can, I'd love you to go online quickly and write a review. It can take less than a minute, and one line is fine. This will help persuade readers to give my book a shot and make those hours and hours of work worth it. Thank you so much!

Mark Bowsher

ACKNOWLEDGEMENTS

I'm so grateful to Stephanie Bretherton and Breakthrough Books for taking on the Myrthali series. They're books which mean a heck of a lot to me. Thanks for the support throughout.

Amelia Kyazze for her unflinching developmental edit which helped get the book in the best possible place it could be. Patrick Kincaid for his highly detailed proofread and ongoing support. Ivy Ngeow for her wonderful work on typesetting – the final version of the book looks stunning.

Lyall McCarthy for his wonderful cover art and incredible map of KnockThrice – his work always blows me away.

Emma Brand and Jay Besemer for giving me initial feedback and ongoing support.

Now, one of the main reasons I write fantasy is that it doesn't necessarily involve a lot of research, but I did rely heavily on one book when it came to Madam Ckrystafis's kitchen – The Poison Garden, a guide produced by the Alnwick Garden. Great book, great garden, please don't eat anything.

All the friends and fellow authors that were there during both writing and crowdfunding.

Jacqui Knighton for doing a final proofread.

And finally, Zsuzsanna Ujhelyi and our Layla. Zsuzsi proofread, translated some sections into Hungarian and helped every step of the way. I really couldn't have done this without you.

SUPPORTERS

Thank you so much to everyone who helped these books come into existence!

Jack Bowsher
Neil Bowsher
Hannah Brackstone-Brown
Sam Bradley
Lucy Rowena Bradshaw
Jenny Braham
Emma Brand
Stephanie Bretherton
Jake Burke-Martin
Christopher and Jessica Burns
Nat C
Clem Cairns
Jonathon Carley
Jamie Chipperfield
Chris
Sue Clark
Gary Clarke
Rik Clarke
Jason Cobley
Jude Cook
Ben Coombs
Heather Coombs
Alexandra Corrsin
Jon Dalgaard
Gemma Dand
Carl Davidson
Ava and Finn Davy
Ben Debnam
Luke Deckard
Chris Douch
Kevin Duffy
Wallis Eates
Kirsty Fox

Rebecca Franks
John Fricker
Annie A Gibbs
Vincent H
Ellie Harris
Maximilian Hawker
Dan Hitch
Kerry Hood
Mary Horlock
Stephen Hunt
Jacinta Hunter & William Ingham
Iqbal Hussain
Jenny
ILM Frieda Jones
Julie Jones
Kecske
G. M. Ker
Patrick Kincaid
PhantomOfTheKnight
Jacqui Knighton
Ferenc 'Feri Bácsi' Kovács
Sophie Large
Andrei Lionachescu
Shakeela Looker
Amy Lord
Katy Lynam
Dr. Lynda Lynch-Gibbs
Caroline Mabey
Julian McCarthy
Lyall McCarthy
Alicia McClendon
Fox McKay
Aidan McQuade

Sam Melling

Charlotte Murray and Florence Murray-Kohter

Adam Nemo

Ayaka Oba

Irenosen Okojie

Zoltán Orbán

Lev Parikian

Joel Parrott

Rachael Parsons

Hazel Pinner

Joshua Prentice

David Puckridge

Imogen Quick

Rea Rhine

Laura Richmond

Noo Saro-Wiwa

Rachael Scotson

James Silvester

Carla Sinclair

Rashmi Sirdeshpande

Michael Smith

Louie Stowell

Lucy Sullivan

Wendy Sweet

Pawel & Aleksandra Szumlas

Lauren & Ben Tansey

John Tarrow

Anita Thomas

Julie Thompson

Vivienne Tucker-Earl

Gábor Ujhelyi and Éva Ujhelyiné Kovács

Zsuzsanna Ujhelyi

Robert Valentine

Mark Vent
Marie Vickers
A. Vogel
Emma Walker
Mike Wilson
Frances Winfield
Wyngarde

www.ingramcontent.com/pod-product-compliance
Lightning Source LLC
Chambersburg PA
CBHW071956110726
47910CB00005B/1556